RICHILENE TRUNK

by Virginia Blakeney

*To my adorable friend —
Barb!
All the best,
Virginia Blakeney*

Copyright © 2020 by Virginia Blakeney
All Rights Reserved
ISBN: 9798485652166

This book is a work of fiction. Names, characters, businesses, organizations, places, events and incidents are either the product of the author's imagination or used fictitiously.

Cover art by Virginia Blakeney
Author photo by Ron Rand Photography
Jacket design by Virginia Ray and Liza Powers
Original song "New Orleans Has You" by Virginia Blakeney Briner
Rays of Sunshine Publishing

DEDICATION

To the people of Lafayette County and Oxford, Mississippi, thank you for encouragement in my creative endeavors, and to the City of San Antonio, Texas, the San Antonio Writers Guild and numerous women's clubs during my writing process. You made this happen.

ACKNOWLEDGMENTS

To my friends Ilene and Richard Pacun, owners of Richilene Industries, Ltd., who graciously allowed me to fictionalize their glamorous corporation.

For initial research assistance provided by Pamela D. Arceneaux, Senior Librarian/Rare Books Curator at The Historic New Orleans Collection. She started me on the path. I am grateful.

To Virginia Ray, without whose vision and hand-feeding through the process this book would never have been.

Unbridled thanks to my family, especially to Shavonne, Ray and Smackie.

Chapter 1

LeFleur Plantation, Louisiana, 1796

In the sweltering heat, perspiration glistened on the ebony faces assembled at the steps of the Greek Revival mansion.

"You're all set free. Free to leave here or remain on the plantation and be paid a wage."

Their eyes widened in disbelief. Some cried, some smiled broadly. Some hugged one another and prayed. Gasps of "Thank you, Jesus!" and "Praise the Lord!" filtered through the crowd. Gilbert LeFleur's words echo even today.

The kindness they'd shown Gilbert during his bereavement caused him to free all his slaves. The fever of 1796 had not been the worst New Orleans and the surrounding area had ever suffered, nor would it be the last. His family's plantation, LeFleur, lost fifteen souls. In all the years not one resident had left the plantation except to purchase land of their own. When he finished burying his parents and all the legal matters, he returned to Switzerland to school.

He felt abandoned by the world and embraced his studies with fervor, so much so that weeks passed before this sad eighteen-year-old noticed the gorgeous brunette with the beautiful smile. She attended a nearby girls' school and had reason to visit his school often as the late-born daughter of his widower headmaster.

An outstanding academic record and his need for a father figure brought Gilbert and the headmaster closer. They shared many confidences, including the older man's heart condition report. "My daughter Katté worries about me constantly," he said.

Her fears proved well-founded. In a short time Gilbert helped with a third funeral. Katté needed Gilbert as much as he needed her. Their mutual pain clouded real emotion and desperation replaced it.

The Swiss mountain atmosphere combined with desolation hurtled the young students to a false state of euphoria, spiraling into an impetuous marriage. They went directly to LeFleur Plantation. Her almost immediate pregnancy caused devastating emotion to surface. Once happy, care-free Katté had suddenly been transplanted from jewel-like mountains, vitreous lakes and verdant pastoral meadows to what seemed to be a savage morass. Undulating, smothering vines plagued with grating sounds of unnamed insects, flies, mosquitoes, crickets and frogs completed the alligator-infested, brackish Louisiana bayous.

"Gilbert, often when I see magnolia trees at a distance, I think of the flowering elder trees at home-- so creamy and white."

"They do look similar, darling, they sure do."

Their baby, Jean Paul, called J.P., was six weeks old when she wrapped him inside her dressing gown. Waters whirled about her and the infant. Thoughts of *I'm freeing myself. I'm floating. I'll take my baby with me,* filled her being. Then sudden shouting, the baby being pulled from her arms. *Don't take my baby!* much confusion and lying on a huge tester bed with insect netting hanging in cloud-like drapes.

In a languid voice Katté often questioned, "Will we ever go back home? Will I ever see the mountains again?"

"Yes, my love. As soon as you are able to travel. We will, we will," he said, stroking her hands.

She lay listless for days before drifting into an irreversible insensibility from which she never recovered. Her face embraced a peaceful, almost frozen smile. Words from quivering lips never formed.

Months later back in Switzerland her world became black and white marble squares on the sunlit floor of the mountain-view room in a private sanatorium. She knew no one. The stunning hot house floral fantasy surrounding her eluded her also.

Daily she clenched her thumbs into tiny fists and set her rocking chair into perpetual motion. Once glorious dark curls, now prematurely gray, radiated like dandelion puffs. For months, Gilbert came every day. Katté remained as oblivious to him as to her majestic mountain view. Finally, he and J.P. returned to Louisiana.

On a rare day when Gilbert went to New Orleans without his three-year-old, the sight of an elfin young woman left him dumbstruck. *I have no right to look at her this way. She's beautiful. She's coming toward me.* She waltzed by, leaving Gilbert in her wake. She gave not a single direct glance, but the tall man in the black cape did not go unnoticed. She felt her heart flutter from peripheral peeks.

He raced after her, "Mademoiselle, I am looking for the Banque de la Nouvelle Orleans. Could you help me?"

"Certainly. It's on the next square. I'm going that way," she answered, pointing as she went.

"I've been in Switzerland for quite a while and I still get confused. Oh, my manners...I'm Gilbert LeFleur," he said, bowing deeply.

"I'm Larissa...oh, there's my father. Goodbye," she said, darting across the street.

Gilbert motioned for his driver.

"Follow them and report back to me at the hotel," he said, pointing toward the Hotel St. Louis. Years later he would wait for her ship in this same hotel.

"She's the Russian's daughter, Mr. LeFleur," reported his driver. "They live in Bosolét Parish, not too far from the Bellemonde Plantation ruins. She and her mother provide embellishments for the ladies' emporiums. My wife has bought some."

Gilbert's second ruse, pretending to search for the Bellemonde ruins, gained him a proper introduction to Larissa's family. He told her almost immediately about Katté. After that, stolen moments in a friend's New Orleans courtyard and the Bellemonde ruins provided all-too-brief trysts. Larissa begged him not to, but Gilbert could bear the situation no longer and approached her father with his plan of divorce and remarriage to Larissa.

"Vot if she become sick, vil you leef her, too?"

So taken aback, Gilbert did not answer immediately. "Sir, the law in Louisiana is difficult. It would be so much easier in Switzerland and..."

"...Leef my land! Neffa set foot here agin. Neffa botha my dotta agin!"

Into this scene came their neighbor, Marcel, bringing a gift of wild grapes. Marcel's initial reaction to the disquieting scene was that Larissa's parents owed a debt to the dashing young man in the black carriage, the dashing young man in the scarlet-lined cape reaching almost to his ankles. *He looks like a wealthy landowner.*

Larissa's Kievan parents had honeymooned in Germany where a misinformed cousin told them of a golden land in Louisiana. They returned to Kiev, sold everything and went to America. No one had told them of the oppressive heat, mosquitoes, swamps or alligators. The horrible misrepresentation of Louisiana by Scotsman John Law cursed the lives of countless emigrants.

Many settlers went farther up the Mississippi River. Larissa's parents decided to stay— not a wise decision. Within a few days of Marcel's wandering to their home unannounced and seeing Gilbert and the LeFleur carriage—with its distinctive crest—both her parents died of yellow fever.

Larissa found herself isolated except for contact with Marcel and trips into New Orleans to take her beautiful embellishments. She had been taught at home by her mother who had German and French tutors herself, so had no friends from those days. She longed for friendships as young girls do. Bustling New Orleans intimidated a young woman of such protected upbringing. She glimpsed a carriage she thought to be Gilbert's—a sudden ache in the pit of her stomach—but when it passed, she saw no crest. *Life is so cruel to have taken Gilbert out of my world.*

Marcel, kind Marcel...Marcel, so handsome. He is beautiful. He'd even hired someone to manage Larissa's farm and allowed the man to live on his. *He's so handsome and kind... Gilbert LeFleur is so different from Marcel—he's mischievous, with a beguiling smile...courtly manners. He's not especially handsome, but walks with a regal air.* And he had, which she could never forget, proposed.

When her father had stormed into the house, Marcel busied himself by following her mother into the kitchen with the grapes. Larissa pulled a ring from her pocket and tried to give it to Gilbert. "It was bought for you and I would never give it—or any other ring—to anyone else."

She looked at the emerald and diamond ring he had given her in secret in the New Orleans courtyard and knew it must always remain a secret. *Where is he? Why did he not come to my parents' funeral?*

Through the glade, Marcel appeared, and dread overcame her. *He is too kind. I don't deserve his kindness.* She put down her sewing, tucked the ring in her apron pocket and rose to greet him.

"He is a good man. Marcel must never know about Gilbert LeFleur" almost became Larissa's mantra. After many long walks in the woods, teaching her to fish and endless cups of kefir, a milky Russian drink he'd developed a taste for, Marcel asked her to marry him and she accepted.

They exchanged vows in a beautiful chapel in the old town attended by her farm overseer, newly married himself, and two of her older clients who presented her with a lovely wedding gown. A simple gold ring sealed their troth.

Marcel soon dismissed thoughts of indebtedness by Larissa's parents. He discovered that not only did she own a homestead free and clear, but also had finances in excellent order. Her father's trapping had provided a tidy sum in her bank account, added with income from the beautiful handwork she and her mother had taken to the dressmakers in New Orleans for all those years. The black carriage with the coat of arms haunted him, but he dared not ask.

A son, Luther, born prematurely with hair as dark and straight as Larissa's, loved life -- a happy baby and a happy little boy. Two years later a baby girl died at birth. The doctor said there would be no more.

The farm overseer took his wife's dowry to purchase the Arceneaux farm from Marcel, thus relieving many of his responsibilities. His pride kept him from using Larissa's money. She continued to furnish embellishment for clothing in New Orleans and her reputation and wealth grew.

Chapter 2
Turning Point

A trip into the city for supplies and to deliver Larissa's work provided a pivotal happening for the Arceneaux family. Marcel and Luther waited for repairs at the blacksmith. Larissa ran errands and made deliveries. She finished and returned to their unhitched wagon. A tall man in a dark serge suit approached the wagon and bowed deeply.

"Good afternoon, Larissa."

"Gilbert, is it really you? It's been almost five years."

She blushed, perspiring. Her insides twisted. She thought of the ring hidden in her jewelry box.

"My son J.P. and I were in Switzerland for a while, but we recently returned to Louisiana. We will not be going back. Katté is the same; nothing has changed, nothing will ever change. I heard you are a mother now... A son, I believe?"

He was dying inside but kept a brave smile.

"Yes, his name is Luther. He's four," she said, longing to touch his hand. He was so near.

"That must be him I see coming. He looks like you. I need to be going."

He tipped his hat, climbed into his carriage, closed his eyes tightly and cupped his mouth. *Why did I have to see that child? He's mine. I know he's mine.* He signaled his driver with a tap of his cane and they sped off.

Luther charged toward the wagon with Marcel leading the team of horses. Larissa patted her upper lip and brow with her handkerchief.

"Marcel, that was Gilbert LeFleur. He was here so many years ago visiting my home. He has been living in Switzerland."

Marcel's eyes trailed after the carriage, but he managed to smile.

"Yes, I remember."

His serene manner at that moment proved at odds with his thoughts. *I want Larissa to ride in a carriage like that. I want her to have a fine house. I want her to have fine clothes. I want...I want...She will have.*

From that day on, their lives began to change. He spent less and less time with the farm and devoted almost every waking hour to his traps. His pelts— always clean, lustrous, almost devoid of snags or nicks and reputed to be the best in Bosolét Parish—drew premium prices. Larissa's father had taught him well and she admired him. But she would never be able to give him her heart.

Without telling Larissa, he began paying on a tract of land near the river and Bayou Conét. Two days before her birthday, he came home early.

"Please prepare enough food for a two-day trip, clothes and bedding for the three of us. On Saturday we will go to a special place...a surprise," said Marcel, turning pale and sitting.

"Are you feeling ill?"

Larissa rushed to his side. His shirt fluttered from his own rapid heartbeat.

"I'm fine; I'm ready for supper. How about you, Luther?"

"Yes, Father. Is the surprise big or small? I like surprises."

"It's very big, but I won't tell you anymore."

Clear weather greeted the Arceneaux and the family soon bumped along toward Bayou Conét. Young Luther played with a jumping-jack Larissa's father had made for her when she was a child. Marcel gave serious attention to the road, which at best was not good. He looked tired. A turn in the bayou lane and looming to their left was the LeFleur plantation—the name "Ruvasha" arced over the distinctive familiar crest. *What a strange name for a Creole's home.*

Larissa had never seen Gilbert's home nor did she previously know LeFleur Plantation had been dubbed a name for a private joke the two had shared. She was speechless.

How odd, Marcel thought, that he had not remembered seeing the LeFleur crest when he'd first visited the land at the bayou road's end. Probably he had been too excited at the prospect of purchasing it or perhaps a subconscious effort to put Larissa closer to the source of life he wanted for her had clouded his thoughts.

Their wagon stopped at an unbelievable botanical wonderland. They rested in a clearing flanked by Bayou Conét's showcase of cypress knees, pastel orchids, palmetto palms and wading birds. Delicate water lilies punctuated the panorama with color. Spanish moss provided the scene with a mysterious, silvery burnish. On the other side, oak trees canopied a grassy knoll gently tumbling to the sparkling river dividing Tachérie and Drapeau parishes. Even more spectacular, nature had rived into the knoll creating a bluff.

Larissa spoke first.

"This is breathtaking."

"Not only is it breathtaking, it's our land. We'll add more acreage as we're able. It just may be—someday—the finest holding in Tachérie Parish."

"Father, is it really our land?"

"It sure is, Luther. Look, Larissa, your house will be there," Marcel said, pointing, "overlooking the river."

Tanned bare feet ran staccato over wood violets and velvety moss blanketing the inviting water's edge. Lacy fern brushed Luther's face where only a few days earlier dogwood had rendered the swamp aswirl with mini-floral snowstorms. A sudden splashing sent him scurrying back to his parents.

"It's just swamp deer, Luther," Marcel assured him. "They're not even as big as the ones we have at home."

Luther drew more than an afternoon of chasing cranes and frogs from this experience. After only deer, rabbits and birds as playmates, he now had a private menagerie complete with a lush, green carpet. In sharp contrast, a crude log cabin stood in an area later to be part of the slave quarters of magnificent Vermillion Hall Plantation.

True to Marcel's dreams, their lives would soon change.

An isolated happening involving slavers in New Orleans would influence the lives at Vermillion Hall in ways never to be imagined. A child, as yet unborn, a byproduct of this incident, would bring comfort to generations of Arceneaux.

Chapter 3
The Slave Block

Phillippe stood chained and coffled to other frightened unfortunates, about to enter a slave block in New Orleans. His grandfather, a member of the elite South Carolina Wolf Clan, had been captured by warring tribes and sold to Caribbean slavers. Now a twist of fate had brought his grandson to these shores. They removed his bonds to better exhibit his physical perfection—and he simply fled.

Maybe this island is not large and there will be boats on the other side.

Palmetto palms cut him as he zig-zagged through his treacherous bayou escape route. With quicksand at every step, then dense woods, his legs ached. Two pursuers straggled nearer. Screams from an Indian child chased by a wild boar infused him with energy.

He pushed the child behind a fallen tree, swooped at the hog, threw brush to distract it and lanced a limb into its face, catching it in one eye—and still it charged. Philippe continued his thrusts, but the raging pig knocked him off balance and he lost his footing. The pig came in for the kill, blood clouding its vision. Phillippe seized the boar from behind and gripped its head in his powerful arms. The animal thrashed to free itself. His hold tightened and a horrible squeal emitted, scattering birds in every direction. The hog's eyes rolled and its corpulent neck snapped. It grunted a low, rumbling snort, then silence. In the wrestling, a tusk pierced Phillippe's arm. Seeing his own blood, he fainted.

Through the forest duff his pursuers advanced to recapture their prize. A tomahawk whizzed by one slaver's head and lodged in a tree. A dozen or more whooping Indians descended on the threesome. The slavers fled in a rain of arrows and barely stopped until they reached the safety of New Orleans.

Philippe awoke on a makeshift litter being carried into a peaceful Chickasaw Indian village where wisps of Spanish moss traced over waddle and daub housetops and a lazy river gurgled and looped. It was a simple village, in harmony with the hamlet of Watermark for as long as both the elders could remember. Dogs playfully nosed at snapping turtles and children mined the riverbanks for berries and crawfish. Fires crackled.

White buckskin caught Phillippe's bleary eyes as he regained consciousness. A goddess-like figure emerged from a lodge to welcome him. She spoke in perfect French and asked if he understood her. He answered affirmatively in perfect French. A medicine-man began to remove a brave's temporary leaf poultice to tend Phillippe's wound and scratches.

"I am Princess Loquetoula. Little Howling Bear ran to tell me of your courage," she said, pointing toward the pole-trussed trophy carried by two braves who had already gutted the animal. "We were once as many as the raindrops, but now our numbers are few. You would honor us by becoming a member of our tribe."

Although part black, Phillippe maintained much of his Indian heritage and answered quickly. The lure of two deer roasting in pits sealed his decision. His nostrils flared and he thought of the islands, knowing his former home was a life away in this strange new world. He had to be concerned with now.

Not every tribe member proved pleased with the new addition. Four pairs of eyes watched Phillippe's every move for different reasons. Princess Loquetoula's coy young daughter, Shining Moon, evidenced love while Little Howling Bear longed to emulate him. Little Howling Bear's mother, Sun Ray, feared for his safety. Little Howling Bear's father, Yahoc, detested his being there. Yahoc had once sat at the right hand of Princess Loquetoula in council. Now Phillippe occupied that seat.

In time, Shining Moon became Phillippe's wife, Little Howling Bear his shadow, and Sun Ray walked a dangerous line trying to quell Yahoc's contemptuous anger. Sun Ray's cries often pierced the night and Phillippe could bear her misery no more. He rushed from their lodge and entered Yahoc's without permission. Sun Ray's bruised and swollen face told a sad story.

"You must beat your woman no more! Enough!"

Phillippe grabbed Yahoc's arm as he swung at Sun Ray again but Yahoc broke free and slipped a knife from a sling in the dwelling's central post. Little Howling Bear scooted out to get Princess Loquetoula.

The two men jousted, Phillippe using only an arrow he grabbed from the floor. Princess Loquetoula entered to find Yahoc holding his knife to Phillippe's neck. She stared him down and he dropped the weapon.

Princess Loquetoula lifted the house's entry flap and pointed outside. "You are banished from our tribe forever. Leave now."

Yahoc left without saying a word, taking only his horse and weapons.

In the ensuing years, Sun Ray chose another husband from a neighboring tribe. Little Howling Bear became a young brave and took a wife from his mother's new tribe. Phillippe and Shining Moon became parents of a beautiful green-eyed child they named Besa Loque.

To the amazement of everyone, the little girl could shoot an arrow with great accuracy at age four. She relished the stories her father told of the woods and islands so far away and proved to be a skilled hunting companion. Her most prized possession, a flute he had carved and taught her to use for mimicking bird calls, rested on her blanket every night. Besa Loque exhibited interest in everything, often to Shining Moon's dismay.

"Mother, why am I dark and you and grandmother are not as dark? My father is dark."

"We will talk to your grandmother," Shining Moon said.

"The child wants to know about her skin. You have lived in the white man's world. I have not. Perhaps you can explain better than I am able to."

Princess Loquetoula's rich voice began in a slow cadence. She chose simple words from a distant memory.

"My mother was an Indian princess also, just as you are, but my father was a Scots-Irishman, a white man, so your skin took the color of my father, my mother, myself, my Indian husband, your mother and your father."

The child looked confused and she continued to stare at her grandmother.

"It's like mixing many paints together to get many different colors," said Princess Loquetoula. "You know, like we use to paint the stories on the walls of our houses."

"Where are your mother and father? I know your, uh, husband was killed. Where are the others?" Besa Loque asked. "Why are my eyes green?"

"My father was Shanahan Laird, a wealthy, green-eyed plantation owner in another part of this country. He married my mother and sold his plantation. They moved to a city called Boston. I was born there and went to a school for girls. We lived in a big house and my father decided he would like to be head of the town, like a chief or princess for a woman. They call this job 'mayor.' Most of the people in Boston voted for him and he was elected mayor, but the other man, Hegarty O'Brien, who also wanted to be mayor, shot and killed him."

Princess Loquetoula stopped talking for a while and Besa Loque tugged at her sleeve.

"What is a school and what happened then, Grandmother?"

She wondered what a plantation was, too, but didn't ask.

"A school is a place where you go to learn many things about this big world that we live in."

The Princess smiled, knowing this answer would not be enough.

"My mother and I returned here to her people who owned most of this land as far as you can see from the tallest hill. It would take several days by horseback to cover all of it."

"Where is your mother?" Besa Loque asked.

"She fell ill and never recovered. She died."

"Died is like when the bird falls or the deer stops running?" Besa Loque turned to Shining Moon. "...or when something is killed?"

"Yes, that's right."

"I'm so sad I will never see her or my grandfather," Besa Loque pouted.

"I'm sad, too, but I have you, your mother and your father. I hope to never lose any of you."

Chapter 4
The Canoe

A soft rain fell when Phillippe and Besa Loque left before dawn to fish three miles downstream where a waterfall created a small lake.

"We need to be there when the fish wake up," he told his daughter.

They fished until noon. An unmanned canoe came crashing over the falls and Phillippe waded out to bring it to shore. Its blood-spattered insides made him release it to float downstream so Besa Loque would not see it. He freed their catch.

"We must return to the village. There's trouble."

Minutes dragged even though they rode a swift Indian pony. About a mile from the village a cloud of fetid smoke overwhelmed them. They arrived to sun filtering away clouds, shining on skeletons of houses and indescribable carnage. The charred earth told a horrible story of attempted escape and capture with even the dogs slaughtered.

Unknown to them that rain-shrouded morning, at first light white settlers had attacked the village in retaliation for a night raid resulting in the rape and murder of a woman and her two daughters. The renegade Yahoc caught with her horse two hours later, failed to tell them he was no longer a member of the tribe before they hanged him.

Fearing for their lives, Phillippe and seven-year-old Besa Loque fled south on their horse. This would not be the last village to be burned. Many tribes afforded them refuge for even as a small child the granddaughter of

Princess Loquetoula commanded respect. Her life from seven to twelve proved to be without incident, then Phillippe died from a hunting accident.

The bird stick flute and her knowledge of mimicking bird calls were all that remained of Phillippe. His tales of wondrous sights beyond the forest spurred her to see them for herself. Against the tribal elders' advice, she wanted to experience life on her own. Her dark complexion presented an open invitation to greedy slavers as she set out on her journey.

Ready to leave New Orleans after her errands, Larissa stood horrified at the sight of a beautiful child chained in the back of a wagon.

"What are you doing with that child? Turn her loose."

"We gonna sell her."

"Look at those green eyes. She's not a slave."

Larissa pulled a small derringer from her purse and leveled it at the men.

"Turn her loose or I'll have you charged with kidnapping."

The disreputable men complied and hurried to get away.

Details of the child's white deerskin clothing appeared perfect, fringed and beaded. Black hair cascaded below her waist. Her green eyes were piercing. She looked like a painting.

"Do you speak English? Do you have a home?"

"Yes, I speak English, French and Chickasaw. I have no home."

"Will you come with me? You will be safe."

She placed her fringed leather sack in the carriage where Larissa motioned.

Now the great-granddaughter of a Chickasaw princess who'd owned most of the land in Northern Louisiana and the granddaughter of a Boston-schooled Indian princess resided just outside New Orleans on Vermillion Hall Plantation. Everyone loved and admired Besa Loque, especially Larissa. She doted on her so much that Marcel often remarked, "I guess she makes up for the little girl we lost. I hope so."

Larissa gave Besa Loque a sunny bedroom on the second floor, but the young girl's love of the kitchen caused her to spend every minute she could there.

"Besa Loque, you are not a servant. You are like our child."

"I know, Miss Larissa. I've always worked, and I love to cook."

Besa Loque's bird stick performances enchanted the plantation denizens and her royal carriage convinced all that they were in the presence of someone special. Exotic beauty added to her mystique. In spite of the admiration, Besa Loque worked with enthusiasm and the surly-dispositioned head of the kitchen, Vedette, chose her as her only confidante.

"Besa Loque's too long to say. I'm just gonna call you Besa," she announced.

Winter swept in a bit early during Besa's second year at Vermillion Hall. Dried peaches plumped to near-fresh juiciness in a bubbling cobbler. Onions, carrots and potatoes swirled around lumps of beef stewing in a rich gravy. Huge corn pones rose in the oven and two containers of fresh milk had been lowered into the well to cool.

Vedette answered a faint knock at the kitchen door and stood horror-stricken. In front of her, having difficulty standing, an emaciated Indian pointed to his open mouth and rubbed his stomach.

"Go away!" she screamed, grabbing a broom.

Besa rushed to help but saw beyond the man to a frail squaw harnessed to a travois with a half-starved little girl lying on it.

"Quila, it's me, Besa Loque," she said to the man in Chickasaw.

In three years, Besa had grown almost to womanhood, so at first Quila failed to recognize her. Then his glazed eyes flickered with recognition, focused and softened.

"Princess Besa Loque," he replied in English, too weak to show emotion but nodding his head slowly to allow the information to sink in. "You lived in our village."

"They need food, Vedette. I'll go get Miss Larissa. I know she'll approve."

"You never tol' us you was a princess."

Besa bit her bottom lip, rolled her eyes and rushed to Larissa, who did approve, and the visitors were fed, clothed and given temporary housing in a storeroom emptied for that purpose.

Carpenters built a new cabin for them in record time and Quila and his family became an integral part of the plantation. His squaw, Deenah, boiled Spanish moss to rid it of insects, dried it and stuffed it in mattresses on the floor because they refused to sleep in traditional beds. She taught Vedette to make hominy. Her trips to the woods and swamp produced roots and herbs for poultices and other cures. Larissa taught her to sew white-man style.

Hunting and fishing occupied Quila's time. He transformed deer antlers into spears and rakes, fish bones into fishhooks and taught Vedette to smoke-dry fish. Quila's tiny daughter, dwarfed by malnutrition at their arrival, thrived and began to weave silk-finish baskets from pine needles for Hatch Washington, the supervisor slave, to take to New Orleans when they were still allowed Sunday afternoon outings to barter, sell and socialize in Congo Square.

"I go with you," Quila announced to Hatch and the other servants loading into a wagon one Sunday afternoon, as he hopped in with a bulging feed sack and settled into a corner.

Once in New Orleans, he left the group and headed to the waterfront.

"Be back before sunset, Quila," Hatch called after him.

This scenario was repeated for many months as Quila went to town with them, his filled feed sack in tow, then left them, returning before sundown with an empty sack to ride back to Vermillion Hall, where he was always greeted by suspicious looks from Vedette.

"Besa, that Injun is stealing something. I know he is."

"Vedette, he's an honest man. He wouldn't do that."

The next Sunday Quila returned, came to the kitchen and asked Besa to "get Miss Larissa." When she came, Quila took a mixture of paper money and coins from a large scrap of cloth and offered the money to her.

"I can't take this, Quila."

"You must. This is to pay you for our food, our shelter. When our village was burned, we came here because dogs chased us when we stopped at other houses, but your dogs did not so we know you would not harm us."

"Where did you get all this money?"

"When I make spears from horns of deer, I have circles left. I take these and make rings. When the great ships are in, I put a ring in each of my daughter's small baskets and the sailors and other people give me money for my rings."

Larissa took the money and thanked him.

"You and your family may live at Vermillion Hall as long as you wish."

He smiled the first smile anyone had ever seen on his face. Besa overheard and held her head a little higher. She entered the hall in back of Larissa to finish laying the table for supper.

Larissa spilled the contents from the cloth onto the library desk astounded to see close to eight hundred dollars. *How many rings? How many baskets? How many Sunday afternoons?* She told Marcel about the money.

"I know you'll find some way to help them. They do so much for us here, we should be paying them. Quila fells trees in half the time it takes us."

She tucked the money-filled cloth in a desk drawer and vowed to see it put to good use.

The famous House of Richilene sparkled. Bullion silken cords held swags of pink taffeta and sheers against three main salon walls. A white marble staircase curving to the balustrade-edged second floor led to Ilana and Erik Richilene's offices and living quarters. Gilded Louis XIV velvet upholstered chairs in darker pink were set in orderly rows two deep on one side of the room, reflected in gold-leaf mirrors.

The youthful ladies' emporium owner rose from her desk. Ilana greeted Larissa and praised the new embellishments she spread on an elongated table.

"I have a helper now, an Indian woman named Deenah. Half of these are her work."

Ilana bought everything.

Age and height separated the two women, but their Russian backgrounds would ultimately forge a long personal and professional relationship.

Larissa took Quila's money to the Banque de la Nouvelle Orleans, unfolded the square of cloth in J. Leenard Ragland's office and tried to open an account for Quila and Deenah.

"But Larissa, they have no last name," J. Leenard said.

"Well, just put Quila and Deenah Vermillion."

"As you wish."

When Larissa returned to Vermillion Hall, Hatch waved in a frantic attempt to stop her from pulling into the carriage house. He raced toward her. "Miss Larissa, it's Mr. Marcel!"

Besa took Larissa's arm to help her down. Hatch's Uncle Sib led the team back to the stables.

"Have you sent for Dr. Cornevise?"

"Mr. Marcel, he's gone, Miss Larissa. It was too late."

"Where is he?"

"His body is already back in the ballroom. Vedette and Minerva cleaned him up proper. He's gone."

She hurried toward the great hall.

"What happened, Hatch?"

"You know he's been lookin' poorly. The debarker down at the mill jammed and he went to free it up. He looked dizzy...and he staggered into the headsaw..."

"Oh, that's horrible. I tried to get him to go to the doctor, but he wouldn't."

By now Larissa surveyed the linen-draped table holding Marcel's body, handsome even in death, even with grotesque, blood-laced scars leading from neck to mid-torso.

Besa held to Larissa but said nothing.

"Miss Larissa," said Vedette. "We didn't know if you'd want his black or gray suit on so we just spread that sheet over him."

"That's fine, Vedette. We'll use the black one and...has anyone sent for Luther?"

"Yes, ma'am," Minerva answered. "Hatch told his daddy to get him and Uncle Lamb has already left for St. Aloysius to get Mr. Luther."

Her "thank you" barely audible, Larissa felt faint. Besa's tear-stained face reminded her this was the second father the young girl had lost. She did not allow herself to cry, but cradled Besa and it gave her strength.

Gilbert and J.P. LeFleur summered in Europe and neither knew of Marcel's death until early fall. When they did come to call, their visit was filled with awkward silences and incomplete sentences. Gilbert never mentioned Katté and Larissa never asked. Her bond with Gilbert had been severed years ago and could not be reconnected. As before, all he could offer now was sympathy.

Besa sensed Larissa's angst and interrupted.

"They need you in the kitchen, Miss Larissa."

She did not want to relive Marcel's death and she knew Larissa didn't either.

"Goodbye, Gilbert, J.P. Thank you for coming. Please, see the gentlemen to the door."

Besa almost laughed but covered with a cough and showed the visitors out.

"You're a Godsend, Besa. Thank you," Larissa said, fanning herself.

Chapter 5
Echo Trading Post

"Yes, the doll in the pale blue dress with the black hair. Please put a big blue bow on the box."

Larissa paid the toy shop owner and took the package to her carriage. *One more stop.*

"Do you have a blue dress smaller than this one?" she asked, lifting the hem of a larger dress. "And a hair ribbon to match?"

Purchases made, she thanked the dress shop clerk and prepared to leave.

"Shoes, she needs shoes," she said aloud, almost to herself, but the lady in the shop heard.

"What size, Mrs. Arceneaux?"

"Oh, I don't know. Her feet are so small."

The clerk took a pair of fine blue kid shoes from beneath the counter—uppers of satin, ribbon rosettes, lace-trimmed—and placed them in front of Larissa.

"She'll need stockings, too."

With Luther in school at St. Aloysius, Larissa had time to fill her empty nest by concentrating on Quila's little daughter, Echo. She thought of her long-dead infant she could never buy dresses for.

Down the tree-lined streets, past Bayou St. John, past Lake Pontchartrain, along the white shell river road to Vermillion Hall. *This trip has never seemed this long. Home, at last.*

"Besa, will you go get Deenah for me?"

"She's in the strawberry patch, Miss Larissa. She'll be dirty."

"Just ask her to come to the back door, then. I actually want to see her little girl."

"You should see what she's done. We were losing a lot of strawberries to the heat, so she covered them in Spanish moss and stuck cane strips in the ground to help us know where each plant is. We'll have a big crop this year."

"Besa, her daughter is so shy."

"Yes, she is."

"Why was she named Echo?"

"She was born in a cave on a riverbank. With her first cries they heard an echo."

Deenah came to the door and Larissa had her call Echo. Head tilted, the dark-eyed child with waist-length black hair took the packages and sat on the herringbone walk, legs stretched out like picket fence slats. Larissa thought she looked much younger than her seven years.

"Open the packages, Echo. I bought them for you."

Echo slowly slid the blue bow from the package, cupping it like a flower.

"Look inside the box," Besa urged.

Tissue paper pushed aside, Echo dug out a doll with dark eyes and straight black hair dressed in the same color as the ribbon. With eager hands and fingers, she hugged her close.

"She has black hair. Is she like me?"

These were the first words Echo had ever spoken to Larissa.

Deenah pushed the other packages closer to the child.

"These, too."

Echo placed the doll back in its tissue paper and opened the brown paper holding the dress.

"I have a dress like my papoose," she said, carefully picking up the ribbon. "And the flower from the box is the same color, too."

The other packages left her giddy. She had never had real shoes, shoes the same color as the flower. Echo tore at the ties fastening her deerskin dress, dropped it and stood as she came into this world.

"I want to wear! I want to wear!"

"You must have a bath, Echo," her mother said.

Vedette handed Besa a huge towel from the kitchen to wrap around Echo and Larissa invited them to the second floor.

"I can't, Miss Larissa. I've been in the strawberries. I'll get your house dirty."

"Nonsense, all of you come in."

They traipsed up the stairs to Larissa's bedroom. A sun-heated reservoir on the roof to catch rainwater refreshed Echo, who splashed in a huge tub and didn't want to get out. Larissa dressed Echo in her new clothes with a handsewn petticoat and other underwear she'd made only the day before. She led the child to a cheval mirror.

"Is that really me?"

She'd never seen herself in such a large mirror. Echo hit at her hair ribbon to watch it bounce and smiled an embarrassed grin.

"What is that?" She pointed to a huge bed draped in blue.

"That's a bed," Besa answered.

The gifts and attention had infused the usually timid child with courage.

"I want one," she said, running to bounce in the middle of the bed.

"If your mother says you may, you shall have one," Larissa said.

Vedette shook her head and laughed.

One week later Uncle Lamb crafted a miniature bed from sturdy cypress. Larissa fastened a hook in the ceiling of Quila's and Deenah's cabin and swathed the bed in lace the same hue as the bedcover.

Gifts empowered the once quiet Echo, whose energy now proved boundless. Larissa gave her fabric scraps and she made butterflies, birds and flowers that Deenah sewed to large baskets. Soon the baskets became sought-after items with Quila's waterfront trade. His wharf-treks continued, and he began to buy colorful bolts of cloth, thread and assorted trinkets. One day he asked if he could buy a horse and keep it at Vermillion Hall.

"Certainly, we have plenty of room and hay in abundance," said Larissa, refusing to take his money.

Quila traded goodness-knows-what for a small wagon and soon covered the back roads of Tachérie Parish and Bayou Conét as a traveling store. He visited plantations fearlessly now for Luther had given him a formidable looking hound—actually very gentle— that stayed at his side. The dog's reddish color inspired him to name it Sunset.

Quila and Sunset waited at the water's edge where bayou dwellers plied the streams to reach his wondrous array of needles, pins, wire, nails and cloth. Also welcomed were vegetables from Deenah's garden. Baskets made by Echo's tiny fingers continued to sell well.

The setting sun blazed behind Quila as Larissa watched him return from one of his forays and the perfect solution came to her. She went to greet him.

"I brought a basket of fresh shrimps for your table, Miss Larissa."

"Thank you, Quila," she said, deciding to wait to tell him her new strategy and taking the shrimp to Vedette before she went to make her decision reality.

Noonday activity filled the Vieux Carré. Larissa marched into her banker's office to buy an undeveloped strip of property lying between Ruvasha and Vermillion Hall plantations.

"It opens to Bayou Conét."

"But doesn't it flood, Larissa?"

"No, there's a huge oak there. Marcel carved Luther's initials in it when we first bought our property. We've made a visit to that tree periodically and there's never been any high water in that area. I want the property for Quila and Deenah."

"Larissa, I can't do that."

"Why not?"

"There's a restriction in the original deed that prohibits selling it to anyone with Indian blood."

"That's ridiculous. Change the restriction."

"I can't, but maybe we can get around it."

"How?"

"We'll draw up a deed and put the land in trust for them. It doesn't say we can't put it in a trust situation. When they die, it will automatically pass to Echo."

"J. Leenard, you're brilliant. Thank you."

"Larissa, do you realize how much their account has grown?"

"No, I really haven't been keeping up with it."

"You asked me to invest part of it in the Cotton Exchange. They've had a prosperous year," he said, showing her the figures.

"That's wonderful. These people are very deserving. Both are industrious. Even their young daughter makes baskets for her father to sell."

"Consider the deal done. I'll have the papers drawn up immediately."

Larissa engaged two carpenters. Her own sawmill had already cut the cypress. She headed toward the newly in trust property with their wagon following her carriage. On stacks of waiting lumber beneath the giant oak bearing Marcel's carving *"LA,"* she unrolled her plans for a trading post "with one great room and four smaller ones." The crew looked pleased.

She returned to Vermillion Hall, leaving the carpenters her drawings and building supplies and decided to wait before telling Quila and Deenah. On the fourteenth day, Larissa asked Quila, Deenah, Besa and Echo to join her for a short trip. At her direction, workers had cleared a much wider path than had previously led to the newly in trust land. A large room with shelves and tables faced the bayou. A broad deck ran the length of the large building. Steps led to the water and a large, floating pier complete with iron circles for pirogues—those Cajun boats made from large, hollowed-out logs— to dock. Four smaller rooms adjoined the dogtrot structure. Built of enduring cypress, it stood as a monument to benevolent planning and hard work.

"This is for all of you. You worked for this. You earned it. Hatch can make Echo's bed longer as she grows taller," Larissa said.

"Will Princess Besa Loque come and live with us?" Deenah asked.

"If she wants to," Larissa replied.

"No, I want to stay with you, Miss Larissa. I would never want to leave Vermillion Hall," Besa quickly answered.

She would soon regret this decision.

Chapter 6
The Richilene Trunk

At Vermillion Hall Plantation, nineteen-year old Luther invested every waking moment in thoughts of his flaxen-haired twenty-five-year old fiancée, Camille Crumpton. The little-girl voice of this English-born, porcelain-complexioned woman enchanted him. It mattered not to him that she spoke no French, but it bothered her no end. She tossed her hair in a schoolgirl gesture at her failed attempts and donned a brave face. Camille visited Vermillion Hall often and catered to Besa.

"Why, it seems you're the most intelligent person here," she told the girl. After Camille's aunt and uncle in New Orleans announced the betrothal, Larissa leased a maisonette in town to have wedding clothes made and never returned to Vermillion Hall to live.

This proved to be opportune for both the House of Richilene and Larissa whose long-standing professional relationship with Ilana and Countess Aviva Bogoff, the head designer, took a deeper and more personal turn. Ilana asked Larissa to join the staff of the soon-to-be-established Paris House of Richilene. The Countess could manage the New Orleans salon.

The simple but elegant wedding freed Larissa from responsibilities of the plantation. She could now seek other horizons.

"Besa, I'll be moving to Paris soon. I'd like you to go with me."

"No, Miss Larissa. I love Vermillion Hall. I could never leave here."

"Well, if you ever change your mind, just let me know."

"I have almost the same life with Miss Camille only we don't sew together like you and I did. She's trying to learn French, but she's having a hard time."

Despite the social differences between her parents, Larissa knew they had experienced a loving marriage; she saw the adoration Luther had for his gentle-born wife and prayed the reserve she saw in Camille to be the same sophistication her own aristocratic mother had possessed.

"The Countess is comfortable with our daily routine. She is our other creative genius," Ilana said. "We've done everything but pick up your Richilene trunk from Harris Lloyd & Son."

Ilana stopped for a moment to tick off items mentally, then resumed.

"I've had your trunk plaque engraved. The trunk is my gift to you," she said, turning to her servant. "Walter, please pick up Miss Larissa's trunk on Royal Street."

"Larissa, we sail for Europe soon. Erik writes that the building renovations in Paris are almost complete. We'll stop there briefly then go on to Russia to gain inspiration and search for relatives."

"Their winters are frightening," she said, looking sad. "We must not get snowbound."

"Russian winters do not frighten me as much as Paris in any season."

"That's an odd thing to say. Why should you fear Paris?"

"What if they do not like my creations?"

"Nonsense! They will be enthralled when you work your magic, my dear."

"If you have that much faith in me, how can I fail? When do we leave?"

"Speaking of traveling, have you seen your trunk?"

"No, I forgot Walter had gone for it."

The Countess overheard their conversation from behind the portiere, swung the drape aside and said, "Look, is it not fantastic? It is crimson."

Sadness crossed the Countess's face.

"I wish I had had such a trunk when my late husband and I did so much traveling for the Russian-American Company. The Count was such a kind man and I will never be able to see Paris with him again."

"Oh, I'm sorry," she said, blushing. "I should not be dreary. We had three wonderful years."

"I understand completely," Larissa stammered. *Red was Marcel's favorite color.*

The vibrant color made it appear larger than the Richilene trunks she had seen before.

"It's, uh, huge. How large is it? I think I remember that red in Russian means 'beautiful.'"

"It's the same as the others, thirty-two by forty-four by sixty inches," said Ilana. "It's the only civilized way to pack gowns for traveling. The Countess and I came up with the idea."

"Dresses hung by the waists never wrinkle. They're held by wooden clamps over strong cypress racks," said the Countess, demonstrating.

Larissa opened three rows of velvet-lined double drawers that completed the lower half of the trunk, amazed at the workmanship.

"Look at the inside plaque with *Harris Lloyd & Son* on it." Ilana said. "When the screws are removed, a secret compartment for valuables is revealed."

She handed Larissa two delicate keys with the Richilene crest on them.

"It takes both of these keys to reach the hidden compartment."

"Two plaques—one outside with my initials and one to hide secrets. I like this."

Larissa smiled and thought of Gilbert and the LeFleur coat-of-arms. *I don't want to leave his world, but there is nothing for me here.* She thanked Ilana.

"Letters to your cousins have been returned, Ilana. How will you begin your search?"

Chapter 7
The General

Larissa and Ilana disembarked in Paris to a happy Erik. After signing many papers, they at last left for Kiev. At Brest, they found their carriage change to a coach-and-four smelly and deplorable. Their drivers made several insulting comments about the lazy frogs in Russian only to learn in the same language that the ladies were Ruskies.

They traveled past endless dross hovels, vast farmlands and forests before reaching the center of Kiev. *Mother Russia.* The wood-domed buildings resembled whipped cream swirls. Exotic minarets, some gilded, some painted storybook colors, stood proudly. The mystical blend of Oriental-Slavic architecture provided a visual feast.

Decorative signs in French and Russian swung from countless structures and enabled blended commerce. Where wooden sidewalks stopped, staggered planks allowed relief from mud. The architectural splendor left them dizzy.

The driver's boots squelched in the mire as trunks and belongings were lowered. Hotel staff attempted to help, but they assured them: "This is our job," and insisted taking the luggage of Ilana and Larissa to rooms, which they declared, "Unsuitable," and demanded that management, "Find something nicer for these Russian ladies."

The new suite had last been occupied by a member of Tsar Nicholas I's family.

General Stefan Menonovitch filled the room when he entered the hotel. He was lean and broad-shouldered and all eyes were anxious to see him, all ears waited to hear what he had to say. From his glistening boots to his military braid-adorned hat, everything about him was in perfect order.

The hotel manager introduced him to Ilana and Larissa. He removed his cap and bowed deeply. When he straightened, his eyes devoured Larissa.

He handed Ilana a list of possible leads.

"Tomorrow we shall visit the Office of Ministry. I will call for you after breakfast. The Ministry of Births is one street from there."

Ilana thanked him. Larissa nodded, but did not speak. As a rule, she did not care for uniforms—they made her uncomfortable—but when she met the General, she put aside her misgivings. Resplendent in blue jacket with red trim, sashed and campaign-beribboned, he towered above her. The roles of delicate sparrow and adroit falcon had never been more perfectly cast.

General Menonovitch called for them in a droshky. The lightweight carriage presented a sharp contrast to rickety carts and clumsy wagons plying the timber trackway streets.

His impressive bearing jolted the Ministry of Births personnel to attention, but Ilana and Larissa examined endless records and came up empty-handed. Next, they went to the Ministry of Marriages, where the next-to-last heavy volume remained unopened. Larissa ran her fingers over the cover's alphabetized list of names and found a near-faded reference to her Great-Aunt Rosinya's marriage.

"She was my grandfather's youngest sister. He was the oldest of sixteen children."

Ilana shared her happiness. The General suggested they investigate immediately by going to the Registry of Land Records. Ilana stayed to research the last book.

"I'll stop by the post and send a driver back for you, Mrs. Richilene."

Ilana and the General were in luck at the Registry of Records and soon found Aunt Rosinya's home, nestled in a stand of white birches. It was larger than most in the area with unique, leaf-patterned shingles. The house proved as welcoming as the Aunt herself. The elderly widow's son was on a foreign mission, she explained as she served kefir, borscht and cheese dumplings. Rosinya sent her servant off in an oxcart and surprised her grand-niece when the woman brought back carts and carriages full of cousins.

Over cinnamon-flavored bobkas, Larissa smiled and thought, *I'm home.* Later, with reluctance and tears, she promised to return and left.

They made their way to the Podal Harbor market. Almost before the driver stopped the carriage, Larissa leaped into the milling, gawking crowd of happy-faced shoppers. She quelled their curious stares saying, "good afternoon," in perfect Russian. They delighted her by returning the greeting. Fresh caviar and unfurled bolts of silk amazed her and she bought both.

A babushka, a glacier-white apron covering her ample bosom, sold them kalachi. Her brown laced boots bore scuff marks from the cobblestones. When Larissa bit into the delectable treat, warm cheese oozed down her arm. The babushka cupped her apron hem to whisk away the cheesy mess. The General paid for, but refused to take, a second pie and the old woman clapped her hands, her broad smile revealing several missing teeth. A tiny child, in a woven basket at her elbow, had cheese from his mouth to ears.

They tried to visit every vendor's stall. Finally weary, they returned to the hotel.

"I will call for you before dawn tomorrow. Have them awaken you early, by four, and bring plenty of paper, your chalks and ink. We've been to Podol Harbor market. Tomorrow is something different. After that, we will have two more sections of our town, Old Kiev and Perchersk."

When Larissa returned to their suite, she spread her sketches for Ilana's admiring eyes.

"While we were gone, were you able to locate any relatives?"

"No, the bloodbath pogroms killed or scattered them all over the world. Many changed their names to avoid persecution."

Then her sadness vanished, and she smiled.

"What about you, did you find your aunt?"

"Yes, and cousins of both my parents. They thought I looked like my mother."

"I'm glad for you. Maybe next time for me," Ilana said, shifting her attention. "These details you've drawn are wonderful. All the white designs on the dresses make them look so crisp and fresh."

"Most of these are very old. My cousins told me how they keep the linen work so white. They rub soap into the fabric, lay it on grass to dry in the sun, and it bleaches in the process. They wash the soap out then starch and iron it."

Ilana nodded.

"These designs will be lovely to incorporate into our clothing. You really had a full day. Thank you for all your hard work," said Alana, brushing her hair and slipping into bed.

"Tomorrow is another adventure. The General won't tell me what or where."

Ilana sensed Larissa's excitement.

"Goodnight, Larissa."

The four o'clock knock came too soon. Larissa dressed, put black bread and cheese in a large, woven bag, tip-toed out and waited in the lobby, wanting to return to the warm covers.

The General called for her in a partially enclosed carriage. Cool morning air refreshed and kept her alert as they entered a clearing protected by a dense grove of trees. Even before dawn, groups of brightly costumed peasants mingled in a carnivalesque atmosphere. Carefree Ukrainian couples leaped through bonfires, their red, gold, white and black costumes swirling.

Enthused by the light-hearted activity, Larissa sketched for two hours.

"This tradition is not unlike ancient Druid practices," the General said with a grin. "But tomorrow is something new."

"I look forward to tomorrow," said Larissa, her dark eyes twinkling. "You're not a pagan are you?"

"Do you think so? Some say I am. Tomorrow you will see another side of me—and Russia. I will call for you after breakfast."

Chapter 8

The Longmeadow

Luther had installed his bride Camille as mistress of Vermillion Hall before Besa's sixteenth birthday. Besa's life changed when she became personal attendant to the new Mrs. Arceneaux. Camille struggled to emulate Besa's French, but her linguistic abilities would always be lacking.

Soon Camille hated her now-pregnant body—and pretty much everything else. She insisted the once free-roaming hunting dogs be penned in a dog yard, she criticized the cooking and refused to go into the red ballroom, saying, "the color nauseates me." She stopped the servants' Sunday excursions to Congo Square saying, "Luther, I've heard the slaves are planning a revolt. We must not let them get together to plot."

Besa longed for the serenity of Vermillion Hall when Larissa had made the decisions, taught her to read and sew and made her feel loved. If she had known what life would be like with Camille, she would have gone to Paris and shared Larissa's life, but Besa would be the only source of maternal love for the child to be born from the marriage of Camille Crumpton and Luther Arceneaux.

Although Luther failed to see it, his wife made everyone around her miserable. He was trapped by Camille in an iron web of icy beauty, by a little-girl voice of underlying venom and the woman about to bring forth his child.

With no complications, Camille gave birth to a son.

"We'll call him York, since I'm descended from the House of York."

Luther agreed, as he did with almost every suggestion she made.

Besa loved the child instantly. Camille turned him over to her and a wet nurse and returned to horseback riding within days. By taking York with her to the kitchen, Besa could spend time with Vedette, but the kitchen that held such warmth now would one day hold horror to haunt York for the rest of his adult life.

On Camille's usual morning ride in the longmeadow, her horse shied from a snake, causing her to land on her spine on a flat stone property marker. She took a nasty spill, but her recovery was complete although she remained in bed. *If I never walk again, I won't have to perform wifely duties for The Peasant.*

And she didn't.

York flourished in Besa's care. On rare occasions, Camille allowed her to take a carriage to visit Echo Trading Post. A virtual beehive of people and pirogues greeted them as they neared. Little Echo smiled broadly, head tilted. She displayed a wardrobe she had made for her doll, Flower, to Besa with great pride and led her into the store.

Bayou women admiring Deenah's dress creations stopped to greet Besa and York in French. Deenah nodded to her visitors and pointed to a plate of mandelbrot. Larissa had taught her to make the hard, almond treat like Italian biscotti from a Russian-Jewish recipe. York took one in each hand.

Furs towered in mounds on the deck where Quila chaffered with two men. He waved, his once-gaunt body now fleshed and youthful. He jiggled a baby alligator skin at York and watched Echo's delight. These trips to Echo Trading Post stood out as highlights of Besa's life and she liked to pretend York was her child.

At Vermillion Hall Plantation the only laughter inside the great house came from York, Luther or Besa, who soothed York's feelings, hushed his fears, doctored his toddler bumps and scrapes, fed and rocked him to sleep.

With tenderness, she would care for him and his next generation.

Chapter 9

A Special Place

The General greeted her without his military splendor dressed in a blue, side-fastening peasant shirt, Cossack trousers and bulky boots. A shock of brown hair grazed his brow.

"Today I take you to a special place for me. It will help you understand why your mother and father might have left and gone to America."

The three-steed troika tore through the countryside and jolted to a stop at a humble cottage protected on one side by a stand of slick-barked white birch, the symbol of Russia. Harsh wind swept the desolate landscape, rearranging tufts of dried grass. Neither bird nor animal disturbed the wind's melody in the vast grassland steppe beyond. This immense area gave birth to *burans*, but the white birch stand protected the Menonovitch home somewhat from the violent steppe dust storms. Even in late summer, stirrings of winter abounded. Larissa tried to imagine the scene covered in the monumental snow of her mother's stories, but having never seen snow, it was difficult to picture.

From some faraway chimney, a faint smoke scent brought her back to Stefan Menonovitch's words, "This is what my father left. We would have starved here...a family of seven...even our cow...eaten by wolves. No milk for the children."

He skimmed a handful of dirt and freed it to soar with the wind.

"This podzol soil would grow nothing," he said, brushing his huge hands together. "Not even the turnips matured. We lived on cabbage. Cabbage is hearty, like Russians. It survives."

He chuckled.

She resisted the urge to tell him a broomstick planted in Louisiana soil will sprout. It seemed flippant and the American humor would probably be lost on him. She thought of twenty-odd years ago when Marcel had taken her to a special place. What a contrast was lush Louisiana to barren Ukraine.

"It must have been horrible for all of you," she said. "I've never known hunger."

"My father entered the military and served faithfully. The French defeated us the summer of 1807 at Friedland, where he was killed by Napoleon's Prince of Moscow, Duke d'Elchingen, General Michael Ney. I followed his career. He was shot by his own men some years later. It was justice."

Stefan helped Larissa from the carriage. He kicked a dirt drift against the cottage door, then pushed it open. Three field-mice scurried into a massive fireplace oven with an enormous roof-like shelf.

"All the family slept there to keep warm."

The crude ladder, missing a rung, still leaned against the wall.

Larissa took everything in but said nothing, fearing to intrude on his painful memories. *This must be difficult for him.*

"To survive, we left. I joined the army, too. My fate was better than Father's. My grandparents asked me to leave the military. At that point, I just wanted to destroy."

He motioned for her to leave.

"Do you still feel that way, General Menonovitch?"

He ignored her question, saying, "Please, call me Stefan."

"If you like. And you must call me Larissa."

Outside, she raised her face to the sun, happy to breathe fresh air. They stood in front of the time-eroded, rough-hewn walls that testified to the once-sturdy cottage where the Menonovitch family planted dreams never destined to become reality. She studied his weather-etched face.

He looks so vulnerable.

"We signed the treaty of Tilsit, Tsar Alexander said we were friends with France, but the alliance could not bring back my father. It should have been cathartic, should have removed the bitterness to tell this to someone. It wasn't. It didn't. Always...war...war...war. I hope to not live to see another."

He stroked the weathered door as if caressing a child.

Soon they returned to their troika and made their dusty way back to Kiev and dined on black bread, cheese and kvas, a Russian fermented drink like sour beer (although she preferred kefir).

"Is good. Is hearty like Russians," said Stefan, his intense gaze into her black-brown eyes absorbing her every syllable. "I have heard of your Southern plantations. They must be very beautiful."

Embarrassed, Larissa tried to shift the conversation back to Russia.

"The Dnepr reminds me of our river near Vermillion Hall, the name of our home. My mother described it from her youth here. She had many happy memories of her life in Kiev...but life was not always easy in my country in the early years."

He looked concerned.

"I'm sorry she immigrated to America, she might not have died so young, but then, we'll never know."

"My mother died young also, but she remained in Russia all her life."

"It must have been especially difficult for your father after her death."

"Yes, it was. He remained in the military to keep his sanity. What of your father?"

"He and my mother died within days of one another of yellow fever."

"Do you have brothers or sisters living?"

"No, they are all gone. I have a son in Paris with the French Embassy, probably spying on us and our troop movements," he said with a laugh. "He has a Ruskie name, but he is French, just as his ballerina mother, who died when he was born."

"How long were you married?"

"We never were. She did not want to leave Paris, nor I, Russia."

"My husband is dead, too. I have a son, Luther, who lives at Vermillion Hall."

They conquered Old Kiev and Pechersk next. She was inspired by churches, buildings and even peasant carts. Everywhere exotic influences expanded her imagination. The General covered Kiev as in a militaristic campaign. She drank in every religious shrine, fair or festival for a fifty-mile radius.

Stefan's daily regimen also included a calculated campaign to conquer Larissa Arceneaux. His fingers traced lightly on her arm when he seated her, helped her from a carriage, opened a door — anything that brought them near one another.

Soon their trip to Russia drew to a close and goodbyes needed to be said. A message sent to Aunt Rosinya assembled another cousin's get-together. Stefan seemed to enjoy himself more than anyone.

Ilana pored over records in a nearby village and did not join them. The Russian spoken in Ilana's Paris home as a child served her well in trying to locate relatives. Since the wars and pogroms, she was one generation removed, so her search proved futile. Other cities had to be saved for another day. It was time to go back to Paris.

Their coach arrived at the hotel. For the first time, Stefan made a clumsy reach for Larissa, felt her relax, then held her with the gentleness of comforting a baby bird. Not sure as to what he should do, he blurted out, "Is time we kiss."

They did.

"I am a soldier, I have no time for marriage, but I visit Paris. Often I am at the Russian Embassy. My son lives in Paris, as you know. I come to see you there."

His previous self-assuredness had dissolved into short, jerky sentences.

Confused, she boarded the coach. Ilana was puzzled, too.

A smile played on Larissa's lips and remained there for most of the trip. *I come to see you* kept tumbling through her thoughts. Would he?

Larissa captured the kinetic fairs on paper, savored them in her memory and Paris ladies wore Kievan-Ukrainian influenced designs for decades to come. The reconnection with her heritage would take her on an unexpected twenty-year adventure.

Back in Paris, Larissa's thoughts returned to colorful ribbon streamers affixed to flower crowns. Happy dancing people flooded her thoughts and she re-lived every second of each thrilling moment of her Russian excursion.

I come to see you.

Chapter 10
They Intrude, Monsieur

Renovations on the building to be the home of the Paris House of Richilene took longer than planned. A new completion date was announced, and Erik reverted to his first love, painting. His comely model Allegra viewed Ilana and Larissa's return with disdain.

"The turpentine smell is horrible, darling," Ilana said, almost as an apology, before she and Larissa left.

"They intrude, Monsieur. Can they not see how important to you is the art?"

"Sure, they understand, Allegra, but we have a business to run and this is only a diversion for me," he said, cleaning his brushes.

"Tomorrow may not see me here," she pouted, going to change.

"I have a show in a few weeks, but if you choose not to return, I'll get another model," he said calmly.

She threw the dress she had been posing in over the changing screen and said, "tomorrow I may; tomorrow I may not," and slammed the door.

Erik draped a cover over the painting and added it to the thirty-some already locked in an adjacent room.

Renovations continued and Erik's art was put on hold as workers needed him at the building. Ilana and Larissa were able to return to the apartment to work.

"He's become obsessed with sketching me. One would think him a lovesick swain. I remind him that we are already wed," Ilana said with a laugh. "I'm glad he's with the workers today and not with me."

"Perhaps we were too long in Russia and he just missed you."

"He won't let anyone, not even Allegra, see his paintings. He keeps them under lock and key," she said, motioning toward the tiny room and returning to sort dress designs. "His art seems to be his life."

The door to the Richilene apartment swung open and Erik greeted them saying, "It is good and it is bad."

"What is bad? You've run out of paper and pastels and can no longer sketch me?"

"No, the Countess is ill and I must return to New Orleans. The good is that our building will be ready in two weeks and we have many orders to fill."

"Erik, you can't go, you have your gallery opening," said Ilana. "You and Larissa can remain in Paris. It will take at least two months to get the salon stocked and ready for business. I'll go."

"I've booked passage on the *Triton*," he said. "It sails at five o'clock."

Larissa helped her pack. En route to the dock, they dropped Larissa at her apartment, where a message awaited her from the General.

A slight knock awakened Erik the next morning. Dressing robe flying, he answered to find Allegra with downcast eyes.

"I come back. I bring croissants. You like croissants? I know how important to you is the art."

Her eyes savored his muscular perfection.

"You'll have to wait. I'm not dressed."

She peeked into the bedroom when he put the pastries in the kitchen.

"Where is Madame?"

"She had to return to New Orleans. I'll start some coffee."

Allegra smiled, stroked her neck to mid-bosom and began to change into the seventeenth-century gown.

Chapter 11
The Gold Band

It's been two weeks. He'll be here tomorrow.

Larissa read and re-read his message. With Ilana gone, her workspace became her own apartment and the centerpiece was her note from Stefan resting in a crystal bowl in the middle of her dining table.

They'd be moving everything into the Richilene building tomorrow, so she would not be needed, but she would have to take her designs to the sewing room ladies the day after.

Stefan arrived on schedule. He did not wear his military regalia but strode into her apartment in a perfectly tailored navy suit and held her for a full two minutes before uttering a word. His massive hands feather-stroked her face and raised it to meet his rangy height. One tender kiss, followed by, "You are my little sparrow." He reached inside his coat pocket and produced a small, wrapped package.

Larissa's eager hands tore at the golden ribbon, removed the burgundy silk wrapping and lifted a stunning sapphire and diamond brooch from a velvet bed.

"I've never seen anything so lovely."

"I'm glad you like it. The jeweler is working on a complete parure. The matching earrings and necklace were not ready."

"You kept your word. You said you would come to Paris. So much has happened in the weeks since we were in Kiev."

She pinned the brooch on her shoulder. Her ecru gown gave it the perfect setting.

"Ilana had to return to New Orleans. Her husband Erik went back to his first love, painting, while the remodeling took place...and they are turning the building over to him today."

"Does he associate with the Left Bank famous and infamous?"

"Oh, yes, they lived in Paris before coming to America. His friends have arranged a gallery showing for him. He paints all day and works at the House of Richilene most of the night. I don't know when he sleeps."

Stefan checked his pocket watch.

"Is time we eat. Let us go."

Larissa decided her new brooch would get more attention on her hat. His eyes followed her fingers as she pinned it there, then she took his burly arm.

"Ah, always the designer," he smiled.

At the Cafe Gloire', Stefan ordered in flawless French.

"Why didn't you tell me you spoke French?"

"You never asked. Give you two more days and you will know all my secrets."

"Can you tell me where you are staying or is that a secret, too?"

"I'm at the Russian Embassy. This trip is not entirely for pleasure."

"Oh, are you on a mission?"

"Are you a spy?"

"If I am, I would be an American spy, not French."

"Situations are still a bit tense between Russia and France. I'm just here to make sure there is no misunderstanding."

He squeezed her hand.

"Is good I am here—for mission or pleasure."

Back in the carriage she asked, "Would you like to drive by the House of Richilene and meet Erik?"

"No, I want you all to myself today. Tomorrow I will visit you there. I want you to be my guest at the Russian Embassy's New Year's Ball this weekend. My son Vladimir will be a guest also. You two must meet. See, the week is gone. No time to visit Erik today."

They headed to the flower market.

Stefan introduced her to the Paris only locals saw. He knew the town as Larissa did not. *Bucolic or suave, he is the perfect man.* With the carriage wheels clicking on cobblestones, she snuggled closer and for the first time in years, felt relaxed.

Back at Erik's studio, Allegra had many emotions, but she did not feel relaxed. *The business is an interference to the art. I understand Monsieur; Madame does not. I hope she stays in New Orleans.*

She looked around the apartment and began to load painting supplies onto a large tray. Erik had loaned her his keys, which she had taken the liberty of copying—without telling him. She put the supplies down and wandered into the bedroom, touching Ilana's clothes, pretending they belonged to her.

She threw a fur wrap on one shoulder, stepped to the vanity and sprayed herself with Ilana's most expensive perfume. *Why would anyone need a steamer trunk that large? She didn't take it with her. I guess she will come back.* She grimaced, then tried a key on the locked room. It didn't work.

Several trips later, Allegra had moved all the supplies to the studio apartment one flight up. The broad expanse of windows provided better lighting. *Madame will not have to smell the turpentine horreur and I will not have to smell Madame.*

With a jaunty red rose boutonniere accented against his pearl-gray vested suit, Stefan arrived at the House of Richilene. Excitement engulfed the sewing room ladies as they took in his height, his self-assured movement, the way he gazed into someone's eyes when being introduced—all contributing to the aura he created. He and Erik had the immediate bond of two straightforward men.

"Your establishment is impressive, Erik. Is the one in New Orleans as grand?"

"It is about the same size. The color scheme there is pink, white and gold instead of emerald green, white and gold, as here. Ilana favors pink. I like green."

Dressed in her favorite pale-blue gown, Larissa fussed with her hair and pinned the brooch on her shoulder. She surveyed her surroundings, remembering how her mother had taught her to dance in their humble home...their humble home...such a huge contrast to her lavish apartment. *If my mother could only see me now.*

A knock startled her daydreams.

Stefan repeated what would become a ritual. When she greeted him, he held her a long time without speaking, kissing her tenderly, and producing a velvet box.

"A courier delivered this earlier today, my little sparrow," he said, straightening his dress-military uniform and thrusting out his chest.

From inside the black velvet box he handed her, gleamed the promised blue sapphire and diamond necklace and earrings. She removed the brooch from her moiré gown and nestled it in her hair. Stefan fastened the necklace and handed her the earrings.

"You are perfection, Larissa."

"I've never had such extravagant gifts. You make me feel like a princess...and pale blue is my favorite color."

"You are my princess, little sparrow. It is time we go, and you make me the envy of every man at the embassy. Or I may decide not to go at all and just stay here."

He placed an ermine cape Ilana had given her around her shoulders.

"Vladimir, this is Larissa Arceneaux; Larissa, my son."

The tall blond man with blue eyes like his father's took her hand and kissed it.

"You are exquisite," he said, leaning closer and whispering. "No wonder my father loves you."

Larissa blushed through every introduction the entire evening. A plethora of turbans, saris, tiaras, lavish gowns and ambassadorial sashes swirled to waltzes and fast-tempo burreés culminating in a feverish Cossack dance.

Stefan did not sit when they returned to Larissa's apartment.

"I cannot ask you to live in Russia. Your work is here," he said, beginning to extinguish and lower the lamps. "And you cannot ask me to live in Paris... but you are mine."

He continued to pace, then suddenly positioned himself beside Larissa on the settee. He kissed her fingertips, then her neck...

By the next morning, what she had once mistaken for shyness had proven to be nothing but respectful restraint. His departure for Russia two days later filled her with bittersweetness, bitter that he had gone and sweet that she knew he would return.

With Marcel it had never been love; loneliness and need, yes. When she dropped the gold band he had given her into the Seine, Larissa felt a weight lifted, pacifying her last remaining guilt. *I was a good wife.* She stood and watched lovers stroll near the river

I'm alive!

Chapter 12
The House of Richilene Opens

Stefan left two suits and much of his wardrobe with Larissa. The gray skies of January did not dampen her spirits. This was fortunate, for Erik now painted almost eighteen hours a day preparing for his show, placing responsibilities on Larissa she had never thought herself capable of handling.

Amid champagne, canapés and much fanfare, Larissa opened the House of Richilene two weeks early. Erik and Ilana's friends ordered with a frenzy, as did half of Paris. Erik made an obligatory appearance.

Vladimir Menonovitch brought three friends from the diplomatic corps and their wives. They stayed until closing and insisted Larissa join them for a late supper and much conversation.

"You are from mysterious New Orleans. Does everyone there really speak French?" one wife asked.

"And you eat the alligator, oui?" her husband asked.

"Oui," she said, and they all laughed.

"We must not tire our guest with so many questions," Vladimir said. "It is time I see her home. She's had a long day."

At Larissa's door, Vladimir's mood became serious.

"Thank you for humoring my friends."

"It is I who thank you for a lovely evening."

He turned to go, then retraced his steps.

"My father explained the importance of your work. After tonight I understand completely...and his military obligations.

So please understand me..."

He wiped perspiration from his brow.

"I don't want to intrude in your life, but I would be honored... I mean...since I never had one...if you would be my mother."

Larissa began to cry.

"Oh, I'm sorry. I didn't mean to offend you."

"Vladimir, you haven't. That is probably the sweetest thing anyone has ever said to me."

She raised on tip-toe to kiss him on the cheek.

"Yes, yes," she said. He patted her shoulders, and left with tears in his eyes.

Opening night of Erik's show at Galerie Éclat created an artistic buzz in Paris. Allegra arrived with her entourage from art school, bursting into the salon and screaming, "That is not my face! That is not Allegra! That is the face of *Madame!*"

Erik rushed to her side.

"Allegra, I told you I needed a model for costumes. You were never promised to be in my paintings."

She ran from him and went from painting to painting, saying loudly, "See? It is not the Allegra! See? It is not the Allegra!" until the gallery owner had her escorted out.

Shaken, Erik tried to regain his composure. The crowd closed around him and heaped accolades. *Paris Review* art headlines would proclaim him a genius.

Paris, France
3 February 1830
My Darling Ilana,

My show at the Galerie Éclat was all I had hoped for. Carot, Inges, Lethiere and Remond have been most supportive. They and I frequent the sidewalk cafes and hinterlands in search of inspiration, but it is not living to be without you. As I wrote earlier, Larissa managed the House of Richilene beautifully and allowed me to paint, as she still does.

How my heart yearns for the sight of your lovely face, which I have sketched and painted hundreds of times. I know it was irritating to you to be captured so many times in pastel, but I needed your poses, for my entire show glorified you. Your likeness is the rage of the Paris art world and my heart. All of the paintings sold.

My fervent hope is that the Countess will return to good health. I need you.

Your loving husband,
Erik

Although scarlet fever is usually associated with children, Countess Aviva Bogoff's malady finally waned. Ilana read Erik's letter and arranged passage from New Orleans to Paris immediately.

Deenah Vermillion had been lured from the Echo Trading Post three days a week to help at the House of Richilene and J.P. LeFleur volunteered to handle the accounting duties, so Ilana knew the Countess could manage without her. Never could she have imagined the revulsion that awaited her in Paris.

Chapter 13
The Will

Hannah Delchamp's family's sugar cane fortune shone like a beacon for free-wheeling Robard Christian R.C. Zedohr, fresh out of law school and hopelessly in gambling debt. He proposed marriage to Hannah and she refused; he bristled when she married another wealthy Creole's son, Russell Toustee', and bristled again when she had twin sons within a year. He recovered enough to find another fat-dowried socialite shortly after.

Robard Christian could still hear his father's caustic words.

"I've given your five sisters substantial dowries and they've made wise investments. You've spent every cent I've given you," he said, stroking his massive beard. "You're going to have to work to prove yourself."

The following year Xavier K. Zedohr and his son had another pivotal conversation.

"With your mother gone, I don't need this big house anymore. I'll buy a maisonette. That will be big enough for my needs. I'll give you and your fiancée Mary Elizabeth this house for a wedding present, provided she converts to Catholicism."

"Father, I've talked with her, but I just don't know at this point."

I mustn't push too much and lose her big dowry.

"You realize how important it is to me to have a grandson to bear the Zedohr name, don't you? You have only sisters, so it is up to you...and he must be born into a Catholic family."

"Yes, sir. I've always known how important a grandson is to you. I think I can persuade her to convert."

"I don't want you to think. I want you to do it. Your work at the bank has been first-rate. Now let us see you apply some of that persistence to your personal life. Your diligence got you promoted to vice-president, so promote your religion."

After two years, Robard Christian and his Catholicized wife, neé Mary Elizabeth Chavannes, remained childless and would for another decade or so, but one burden lifted when old man Zedohr died and R.C. became president of Creole State Bank. His anticipation of the reading of his father's will matched only his disappointment when it was actually read.

J. Leenard Ragland's clear voice began: "I, Xavier Kleine Zedohr, being of sound mind and a bonafide resident of the state of Louisiana, city of New Orleans, Orleans Parish, declare this to be my last will and testament. To my five daughters— Florine Zedohr Farrar, Delphime Zedohr Mara, Lillianne Zedohr Bois, Viola Zedohr Barrios and Adele Zedohr Thames— I leave five pieces each of jewelry of their choice from my deceased wife Isabella's collection, having previously given them sizable dowries.

"My Creole State Bank investments have been transferred to Banque de la Nouvelle Orléans. To my grandchildren born of my daughters' marriages and their future children born within ten years from the date of this will, I leave five-thousand dollars each from the aforesaid Banque de la Nouvelle Orléans. To my sons-in-law Gary B. Farrar, Jeffery M Mara, Dumas H. Bois, Louis L. Barrios and Wellington "Wells" J. Thames, III, I leave one thousand shares each of stock in the New Orleans Cotton Exchange. To my daughter-in-law Mary Elizabeth Chavannes Zedohr I leave my collection of rare books, which she has always admired, and my late wife's diamond engagement ring."

R.C. did not have to wait to learn why a beautiful, plump woman in a widow's veil had attended the reading of the will.

"To my friend and companion of many years, Patrice Lenore..."

R.C. rose from his chair, but J. Leenard motioned for him to sit down.

"...a free woman of color, I leave my maisonette at #109 Rue Legendre, New Orleans, Louisiana; three horses and two carriages; all of the contents (except the aforementioned books); the sum of seventy-five thousand dollars and a lifetime income of ten-thousand dollars to be paid on January 2 of each year from my investments at Banque de la Nouvelle Orleans.

"Upon the death of Patrice Lenore, the Banque de la Nouvelle Orleans investments shall be given to my son, Robard Christian Zedohr's first male heir..."

Oh good, now he's getting to me.

"If Robard Christian Zedohr has produced no male to perpetuate the Zedohr line by age forty-five, the Banque de la Nouvelle Orleans investments shall go to the Orleans Parish Catholic Diocese, as will all of my possessions real and personal not mentioned in this will.

"To my son, Robard Christian Zedohr..." By now R.C.'s palms were a damp mess. "Whom I have already given employment, a home, and a generous education, I leave one dollar and my best wishes."

R.C. loosened his collar, tugged at his vest, and cursed under his breath. Mary Elizabeth stroked his arm, but he pushed her away.

J. Leenard continued...

"If my heirs feel compelled to challenge this will, it will be void except for the bequest to Patrice Lenore and the remaining proceeds will be used to fight their legal actions indefinitely. The remaining stock in the New Orleans Cotton Exchange will go to any female children Mary Elizabeth Chavannes Zedohr might have from her marriage to my son Robard Christian Zedohr. I appoint my good friend and business rival J. Leenard Ragland as executor to administer this will without bond, given this 17th day of October 1834. Witnessed by Russell Toustee' Barton M. DeWitt."

Patrice Lenore bustled from the room without speaking. R.C. hoped she was out of his life. *I never knew my father to like fat women, even those pleasing of face. I can't stand fat women...and a mulatto at that.*

The economic losses of 1837 failed to affect most of Louisiana's affluent. Ruvasha and Vermillion Hall plantations continued to flourish—at least financially—despite the downtrend.

Chapter 14
R.C. Zedohr

Unique in Tachérie Parish, or Louisiana, Quila and Deenah Vermillion's burgeoning venture provided the only one of its kind. Their success allowed them to hire a Cajun couple, Marie and Jules Pascal, to help. Quila built them a cabin on the property and the young pair became indispensable. The Pascals assumed almost complete responsibility for Echo Trading Post in just a few weeks.

While Deenah continued to assist the House of Richilene, Quila returned to his rolling store rounds and resumed his forays via pirogue to take goods into Bayou Conét to people too old or infirm to make the waterway trip. He charged them just a fraction of the price usually paid.

Echo, in school in New Orleans, could not always be around. After helping the House of Richilene during Countess Bogoff's illness, Deenah—Mrs. Quila Vermillion—held a place of importance in the New Orleans fashion world.

Quila, Deenah, Marie, and Jules scuttled around in synchronized harmony as Besa and York arrived. Sunset's rust-colored puppy descendants were spread outside the Echo Trading Post where he lazily raised one ear and repositioned himself on the sun-toasted cypress porch.

Four-year-old York jumped into the puppy mix as did a large calico cat that never had been told felines and canines are avowed enemies. Besa delighted in almost every childish move York made. She wished Miss Larissa could see him.

Deenah greeted her visitors and gave Besa a yellow dress she'd made for her. Quila's simple clothing—breeches and a shirt laced at the neck—contrasted with his go-to New Orleans attire of suit vest and top hat.

Besa enjoyed being able to speak Chickasaw with them and felt a familial connection. York loved these visits, but often had to be reined in to keep from hurting the animals.

"I'm going to the city today. You come with me?" Deenah asked Besa, who still held memories of New Orleans that frightened her.

"I'd better not. Miss Camille probably would not approve."

"You stay longer. I must get ready."

Deenah braided her flowing ebony hair and piled it high beneath a silk and feathered hat, changed her dress and left for the city with her handwork.

Mary Elizabeth Zedohr saw Deenah at the House of Richilene and admired her ornamentations. She remembered her plain dress that needed, "something to make it more à la mode".

Their conversation continued outside on the sidewalk where Mary Elizabeth's husband, Robard Christian, happened by.

"What do you mean...talking to a savage? Are you trying to ruin us socially? Go home this minute," he roared.

Mary Elizabeth glared at him, reddened, got into her waiting carriage and gave a defiant wave to Deenah, who did not speak.

He is not a brave man. He is a coward.

The fervor with which R.C. Zedohr had pursued Mary Elizabeth before marriage was now replaced with marathon criticism. His father used this technique to manage R.C.'s mother, so he knew firsthand the way to keep a woman in line.

"Don't let a woman get too uppity or she'll try to run your life," he'd often heard from the elder Zedohr.

The following day proved to be another example of R.C.'s scurrilous methods.

Vice-President of Creole State Bank Thaddeus DuPree, Sr. opened his boss's door, saying, "A Dr. John Gorrie to see you, Mr. Zedohr."

"Always glad to talk with a distinguished member of the medical profession. What does he want, Thaddy?" asked RC, envisioning new accounts.

"Something about a patent to make ice," the VP whispered. He knew not to waste R.C.'s time. "Shall I tell him you're busy?"

"No, he sounds insane, but send him in anyway. I need a good laugh."

R.C. lit a cigar and Dr. Gorrie entered. DuPree closed the door and strained to hear the conversation from the other side. After only a few minutes, the wooden floor creaked and Thaddeus DuPree jumped back.

R.C. bustled the good doctor from his office with an admonition the entire bank could hear.

"It's a hare-brained scheme and I'm not going to loan you any money," he said, drawing his head back and exposing his toad-throat double chin. "The very idea. Maybe in Apalachicola, Florida they don't know the only one who can make ice is the Good Lord, but we here in New Orleans do."

Dr. Gorrie swept through the bank lobby with dignity and tipped his hat. His invention, a precursor to air-conditioning, would still be around when lumps of dirt represented the naysayers.

R.C. congratulated himself. He'd used the same tone of voice to send that beggar running that his father had used with him. It felt good to hold so much power. It felt good to deny people their dreams. *It wasn't my fault that I wasn't born poor like my father and haven't had to scratch for everything.* The victory proved short-lived, however, as he thought back to the string of tests and humiliations heaped on him by his father.

He closed the brocade drapes, extinguished the ornate lamps and sat in complete darkness, chain-smoking black cigars. A timid knock came on R.C.'s private alley entrance to his office and he opened it to an apprehensive Hatch Washington.

"Mr. R.C., that land you sold me near Bayou Baquet has some mighty strange stuff on it," he said, pointing toward his wagon.

"What kind of strange stuff? What's in your wagon under those feed sacks? A gator?" sneered R.C.

Hatch stammered, "Oh, old boots, buckles, a kettle, tin cups, barrels, bottles, a heavy box...and bones, lots of 'em, but I don't know what this box is."

"Let's have a look."

He flipped the burlap sacks back to uncover a small metal chest and scraped dried mud off it to reveal the seal of the King of France.

"Hand me that hammer, Hatch," he said, breaking the seal.

Gold coins and jewels glistened in the afternoon sun on the chest that pirates had last handled.

"Is this stolen, Mr. R.C.? Am I in trouble?"

"I fear you might be, but I can get rid of it for you."

"I'd sure appreciate it; I don't want no trouble with the law."

"Tell you what, bring it in the back door here to my office."

For once R.C. did not care about dirt on his expensive carpet. He opened the heavy drapes.

"To make sure you don't have any trouble, I'm going to give you two hundred dollars in case something should come up. Now this must stay a secret between you and me. You didn't tell anybody, did you?"

"No, sir. I was scared to tell anybody. I knew I could trust you 'cause you work at a bank."

R.C. "Rat Cheese" Zedohr went to his personal office safe, removed two hundred dollars and gave it to Hatch.

Chapter 15
Fatal Miscalculation

Erik worked at a feverish pace to have everything perfect when Ilana returned from New Orleans. This had been their dream. Paris's terrible winter was enough to keep the carriage trade near cozy fires at home most days. One dismal day brought a blinding snowstorm before the noon hour.

Erik closed the salon early and sent his carriage driver to deliver Larissa to her nearby apartment on the Grand Boulevard. The concierge at Larissa's invited the driver into his quarters to get warm. When the storm became worse, he remained quite late, until the storm abated.

The snow fell more lightly and his driver returned and delivered Erik to his Left Bank apartment on the wide Boulevard du Montparnasse.

He entered his dark foyer and fell into something that knocked him down. He tried to right himself but stumbled over something else and cut his head. Dazed, he sat for a moment, ignoring the blood from his wound, then reached to light a lamp.

His eyes widened in horror. Snow had drifted in the open apartment windows. Allegra Arietta's lifeless body dangled from a chandelier in a near-frozen state. Ilana's Richilene trunk lay on its side. Allegra wore a flowing silvery velvet peignoir and a diamond necklace last worn by Madame. One dainty slipper lay on the floor.

He knocked on doors until someone answered and sent for the gendarmes. Later he could not even remember who had helped him.

The larger of the three policemen arrived, cutting Allegra's body down without saying a word. They talked among themselves, then the taller one asked, "Why all the blood, Monsieur? Did she struggle?"

"I don't know."

"But, Monsieur, your wound...did she hit you?"

"No! I mean, I didn't struggle with her. It was dark, you see. I just got home."

The officer did not reply.

"She was my model, but I haven't seen her in two weeks."

Erik compressed his wound with a kitchen towel.

"I must have hit the trunk when I fell. Her name is Allegra Arietta."

"Was, Monsieur," the shorter gendarme corrected.

"You say you just arrived, but since all the windows are open, it is impossible to know when she died."

"You could have killed her this morning," the other one added. "Where have you been all day?"

"At work... since about ten this morning."

"Where do you work?"

"The House of Richilene at #7 Rue Rabalais. I own it with my wife."

"Where is your wife, Monsieur?"

"She is in New Orleans with our other business. I needed a model, so I contacted the École des Beaux-Arts, where she is a model..."

"Was, Monsieur," interrupted the shorter man, who appeared to be in charge.

"They introduced her to me."

"Do not leave Paris, Monsieur. You will be hearing from us."

As they started to remove the body, Erik asked if he could have his wife's necklace.

"No, it is evidence. Goodnight, Monsieur."

The next morning, Erik tried to concentrate at work but his head throbbed. *Why did this have to happen?* He crumpled the *Morning Gazette* and dropped it in a basket.

Larissa went about her duties and tried to engage him in conversation, which proved impossible. She, the first to see the three police officers, hoped they had come to tell him his nightmare had ended.

"I arrest you for the murder of Allegra Arietta."

The three gendarmes took Erik away, denied him bail and taunted him, saying, *"The Cour d' Assizes* will deal with you, you monster."

Weeks later, Ilana finally returned to Paris amid emotional chaos. Larissa orchestrated practically everything connected with the business. Erik continued to proclaim his innocence and Vladimir had started his own investigation. A diary found in Allegra's room further implicated Erik: *"I am afraid. He has threatened me. I have been in his bedroom. He is so unreasonable. He talks of love. His wife is in New Orleans. Diary, I am so unhappy."*

The chief of police pressed the red leather book to his heart. *She refused his advances and he killed her.*

At the time, Erik did not know that the police chief was Allegra's father.

Chapter 16
The Contradiction

Vladimir canvassed his friends and learned that one, Charles Morel, had seen Sonata socially until she decided to go to school in Italy.

"She and her sister Allegra did not get on very well," Morel told him, "Sonata is a beautiful blonde and Allegra was jealous. Constantly she took her clothing to spite her."

"But Allegra's family is dark, Italian. Is Sonata adopted?"

"No, she looks just like Chief Arietta's mother from Corsica—blonde and blue-eyed. I met her when she visited."

"I see. What a shame she did not feel her darkness was beautiful, too."

"Sonata couldn't come home for Allegra's funeral, but she came in for the memorial this weekend. We're meeting at noontime tomorrow at Antoine's. Would you like to join us?"

"Sure. Could I bring Larissa Arceneaux along?"

Morel nodded. He later alerted Sonata that the meeting would be more than social.

Vladimir and Larissa waited at Antoine's and contemplated leaving, but Charles Morel and Sonata appeared at last.

Sonata viewed them through tear-reddened eyes. Quick introductions made, she spoke, "I don't know what I would have done without Charles... My parents left for Corsica before I got home. My grandmother is ill, so I didn't get a chance to talk with them...and Allegra's memorial is this weekend."

Her hands shook when she lifted her glass.

"You told Charles earlier that you didn't know Erik Richilene had been charged with murder. Why not?" Vladimir asked.

"Their message only stated that Allegra was dead."

Charles squeezed her hand. "I told them you would be extremely helpful. Just take your time."

"So you knew no details about her death until you returned to Paris yesterday?" Vladimir asked.

"That's correct, Monsieur Menonovitch. When I was home on holiday, she was happy one minute and distraught the next, but that was so typical of Allegra."

"What can you tell us that will help Monsieur Richilene?" Larissa asked.

Sonata lowered her eyes and took several deep breaths.

"She was obsessed with Monsieur Richilene."

"How do you know?" Larissa asked.

"I loved my sister, but she was not very truthful. My parents knew this also. It caused so many problems."

Tears fell freely and Charles put his arm around her shoulders.

"Tell us how things were untrue," said Larissa. "Or would you like to rest for a while?"

"No, thank you. Let me continue. When I was home last holiday, she talked with me. I could not abide her lurid prattle...I'm sorry to speak of the dead this way...but that is why I chose to go to school elsewhere two years ago."

"This doesn't explain the diary... just because you two didn't get along," Vladimir said.

"I'm sorry I'm rambling, but this is so hard. All of the diary is true but twisted. She was insane. She wrote she was afraid. She was afraid he would replace her with another model, if she didn't quit being so mélodramatique. That is the only thing he threatened. Allegra lived in a dream world."

She looked disgusted.

"Tell us about the bedroom," Larissa asked.

"She went into Madame's boudoir when she moved some painting supplies...she tried on Madame's clothes and pretended she was Madame. He was not even there."

"What about 'unreasonable' and 'love?' What did he say about those?" Vladimir asked.

"He was unreasonable in her eyes because he talked of loving his wife and did not say he loved Allegra. He hired Allegra to model clothing and nothing more. She even wrote me a letter contradicting what she'd told me earlier."

"Do you still have it?" Larissa asked.

She pulled a creased letter from her pocket and handed it to Larissa.

Dear Sonata,

Erik must have painted his wife's face on all of his paintings to try and please her. She is very demanding. I know he loves only me and Madame is still away—forever, I hope.

I can win him from her. I will go to his apartment and pretend to kill myself. The timing must be perfect. He comes home every day at noon. He will save me and then I will know he loves me.

I moved all of my things into your room because it has three windows. I know you won't mind. I wore your pink dress and spilled red wine on it. It looked prettier on me anyhow. Maman said so.

Your sister,
Allegra

Chapter 17
Absolution

Larissa and Vladimir hurried to the House of Richilene to share the letter and new information with Ilana.

"Let's wait to tell Erik. We don't know how soon the French legal system will consider the new evidence," she suggested.

With renewed hope, the women returned to Larissa's apartment, where Ilana had been staying since returning from New Orleans.

The Ariettas arrived from Corsica in time for the memorial. Sonata respected her sister's memory by waiting until the following day to tell them about the letter and Allegra's actions when she'd last been home.

Absolution proved as swift as indictment. At Erik's direction, Ilana closed their apartment and leased another, complete with upstairs studio, several miles away. She sold everything in the old apartment except their clothing, jewelry and painting supplies, including her Richilene trunk, and ordered another.

Two days after Erik was cleared and freed, Chief Arietta returned the diamond necklace in person. Ilana would soon sell it. When he came to the apartment, dark circles attested to the mental anguish he would carry for the rest of life.

"Allegra was always a difficult child. She thought she was inferior. Sonata, our beautiful blonde, was always noticed. Allegra craved attention," he said, wiping his deep brown eyes with the back of his hand. "We tried to make life equal for her, but she never had enough possessions or anything else, no matter how hard we tried."

"Chief, this is not necessary. I know it was all just a horrible mistake." Arietta regained his composure.

"But Monsieur, it was *my* horrible mistake. We often felt we neglected our other daughter, Sonata. I had to tell you this. Please accept my sincere apology for the entire situation, especially for the rudeness of my men. They've known Allegra since she was a tiny girl."

Erik should have been riding a crest of exhilaration. He was the toast of the Paris art scene, the House of Richilene provided clothing for half the crowned heads of Europe's families, and he had been declared a free man. However, prison confinement had damaged his creativity. He could no longer stay in a small room and only felt comfortable outdoors.

Mid-April Paris weather had not turned warm enough to be outside, but the biting cold did not deter Erik from tramping around the city like a phantom. He and Ilana began to live at the salon, where the ceilings were tall and the rooms spacious.

His dark good looks— a hint of gray at the temples making more than one Parisienne's heart flutter, hoping he might look her way—spawned countless tales of imagined escapades.

Late summer and the impending birth of his first child inspired Erik to again paint. He and Ilana now occupied their new apartment but gone was his desire to render neoclassical women. Now he painted serene landscapes and architecture in muted tones.

It would be many years before he attempted to paint the human form in his previous style. This served to escalate the price of his February 1830 pieces and collectors bid outrageous prices for them.

The birth of his son Issac signaled the emergence of Erik's new style. The Galerie Éclat, scene of his first coup in the Paris art world, accepted his current work with eagerness and the *Paris Review* repeated itself with unbridled praise.

Chapter 18
Thrown by His Horse

Gilbert Lefleur roamed the world searching for he knew-not-what. He checked on Katté in Switzerland, rode gondolas in Venice, toured castles in Ireland and marveled at Roman ruins. Until 1833 he had not trusted his heart or his emotions, but in late September, after visiting the Provence region, he made his first trip to Paris. He hoped to see Larissa, praying his searching would end.

Ilana and Erik greeted their former countryman and arranged a lavish dinner in his honor. This did not satisfy his real hunger.

"Larissa will be sorry she missed you. Her Aunt Rosinya in Kiev lost her son and sent for her," Erik said.

Gilbert kept a brave face while the other guests lingered. When they left, his mood changed.

"Ilana knows all this New Orleans news, but I'll just give you a recap of the happenings. My son J.P. married Tedelia Chavannes from Chambers Plantation in Baton Rouge and she bore him a son the next year—Jean-Paul, called Paul."

He seemed uncomfortable, but continued, "Luther Arceneaux and Camille Crumpton had a son just weeks before the birth of my grandson. His name is York. The boys aren't even four, but they do quarrel a lot."

He looked embarrassed while also wanting to say more.

"How do you think our business here compares to the New Orleans House of Richilene?"

"Ilana, I thought your New Orleans emporium to be the finest east of the Mississippi. Having seen this one, this is probably the finest in the world. I say this without prejudice, relying only on my keen powers of observation." They laughed and congratulated him on his astute perception.

"On a more serious note, we lost 5,000 people to yellow fever last year. Up to five hundred a day from the latter part of October until early November. The cool weather came, and the deaths stopped. Then cholera struck…but enough sadness. The Cotton Exchange had a bumper year and sugarcane is really flourishing. We're working on even better ways of extracting sugar."

Ilana served sweets and coffee.

"You folks have to work tomorrow," Gilbert said. "Thank you for a marvelous evening. I'm at LeGrande Hôtel. I'll drop by later in the week."

On the outskirts of Kiev, Stefan saw Larissa to Aunt Rosinya's where they waited several days for her son's ice-packed body, accompanied by a military honor guard. She had been notified, Rosinya told them.

"His horse threw him. I know little else."

Stefan heard government-suspected anarchy. If he knew, he could not say where Yuri had been serving at the time of the "accident."

Cousins flooded Rosinya's home again and she seemed to enjoy the warmth of family, but in her bedroom, she took Larissa aside.

"They had not been to see me in seven years before you came almost four years ago and they have not been back since. They have no time for a babushka and I now have no time for them."

The revelation shocked Larissa, who thought the feigned friendliness sincere.

"I'm so sorry. I had no idea."

"Look in this room. What do you see?"

Larissa saw a bed, a table, two chairs, a portrait of Yuri, a mirrored washstand and a clothing cabinet. "Why do you ask?"

"My relatives never asked if I needed anything. I could have starved for all they cared. They only came three years ago because they had never seen an American."

Rosinya shook but did not cry.

"Your Stefan brought packages from you in Paris, the only person who ever brought me gifts. My son sent me money, lots of money, but I have my pigs, my garden, my cows and my needs are simple. I never needed to spend much of it."

A smile filled her round face.

"I've left it all to you—this land and this house. Stefan took care of all the legal business for me."

Gilbert sailed for America a week before Larissa returned from Russia. Rosinya died of heart failure shortly thereafter while tilling her garden. She did not get to share in the startling events greeting Larissa on her return to Kiev.

Chapter 19

"Dear Mother"

Despite the House of Richilene keeping Larissa, Ilana and Erik busy, Erik found time to balance his salon duties and painting and his style reached the perfection for which he'd hoped. This gave Larissa another chance to visit Kiev as it was summer again and that was a slower time for the carriage trade and royalty of Europe.

Although in rough peasant clothing, Stefan greeted Larissa with decorum. Once inside Rosinya's home, he repeated his ritual of extended holding, kissing, and giving gifts.

Her new diamond bracelet sparkled in the sunlight when Larissa raised her wrist to admire it.

"I'm going to need a royal jewel chest to store all of my beautiful gifts."

"Then I'll scour the countryside for that, too. Anything for my little sparrow."

"You're not pillaging castles and bringing me their treasures, are you?"

"Something like that."

It would be years before she would learn he was in the Tsar's intimate circle and they shared the same jeweler.

Rosinya's caretaker came the next morning.

"I know you told my husband and me to use or sell all the vegetables and milk. Someone is stealing from the storehouse and often one of the cows is almost dry. We never stay in the house at night. There are no neighbors to keep watch, so we don't know what is happening."

"How long has this been going on?" Larissa asked.

"Several weeks now, ever since the weather turned warm. Nothing is ever locked except the house, but we latch everything, and it's always latched back, so we know it's not some animal. Small things are missing from the barn, too."

Lights burned a second night and they heard a faint knock. A strange woman in tattered clothing greeted them.

"Rosinya?" she asked, pointing over Stefan's shoulder to Larissa.

"No, I am her grandniece Larissa."

"Lay-ree-sha."

The woman looked confused and started walking backward, then bolted into the woods, her ragged clothing and disheveled hair flying.

"Should we go after her?" Stefan asked.

"No, she looked deranged. Leave the poor thing alone. Perhaps Rosinya had given her food or something."

Larissa prepared breakfast while Stefan milked the cows. She saw the milk at the back door, but no Stefan. She finished the food, went outside and found him on the path leading into the forest.

"I was worried about you," she said.

"Shhhh," he said, pointing deeper into the woods and taking her arm.

They moved to a brambled area where a ferocious dog of undetermined breed stretched the length of his rope. The animal lunged at them, teeth bared, but did not bark.

A small voice yelled, "Klah!" They did not know if "klah" meant "attack" or "stay."

The dog sat.

A tousled-haired three-year-old peeped from under a pile of rags in a dog cart. His jet-black hair contrasted against a nondescript sea of shredded cloth surrounding him along with buckets, an oil lamp and remnants of a well-tended campfire.

"Someone's living here," Larissa whispered.

"Where is your mother?" Stefan asked the boy.

He then realized the child held a gun, which he raised as the couple backed away.

At that moment, the strange woman crashed through the brush, her skirts full of berries spilling as she ran. She screamed something at the child in another language and he surrendered the gun, but she kept the weapon aimed at them and motioned for them to move away.

They obliged. Stefan tried to speak to her, and she seemed to understand some of what he asked in Russian. Larissa tried French but she looked puzzled. The woman pointed and said, "Lay-ree-sha," but kept the gun trained on them.

Larissa saw this to be a waste of time, touched her own mouth and gestured to the woman and child to follow them. They hesitated as she untied the dog to go with them. Rope and gun in hand, she said something to the child, and he shimmied down from the cart and they followed behind.

The woman washed the child's and her own face and hands at the washstand outside the kitchen door, placed the weapon on the table and ate.

Her manners are beautiful.

The guests finished eating and said, "thank you" in Russian. The mother put her hand back on the gun, nodded and said, "Chonya." Then she nodded toward the child. "Yuri."

Stefan identified himself and added, "Russian."

Larissa followed suit. "American."

Chonya said her own name again and added, "Krondistanian."

Stefan jumped up, quickly reseating himself when she reached for the gun.

"You speak Krondistani!"

She smiled and the wildness disappeared. "Krondistani, Krondistani," she said, patting herself on the chest.

"Yuri was Rosinya's son's name," Larissa said, almost to herself.

She gestured for Chonya to follow her to Rosinya's bedroom and showed her the portrait.

Chonya put the gun on the washstand and took the picture from the wall. She sat on the bed and held it, rocking back and forth.

"Stefan, we need a translator. This young woman is not here by accident. Go into town and find one."

"I can't leave you here to go into town. It's out of the question. We'll go together."

"No, I'll stay here. I'll be fine. Now, please go and try.'

An exuberant Stefan returned with a young Russian officer. Chonya saw his uniform and sprinted from the house with her son in her arms, clutching the gun again. The soldier called after her in Krondistani. She stopped and came back.

Major Anatol Nazarov introduced himself to Chonya and Larissa. He and Chonya talked for what seemed hours. Larissa listened, deciphering a word now and then. Chonya turned away and produced a letter sewn into her undergarments and addressed to Rosinya. She handed it to Nazarov. Little Yuri climbed into Larissa's lap and fell sound asleep.

Nazarov read the letter, then gave it to Larissa to read aloud.

Dear Mother,

If you are holding this letter, it probably means I am dead or imprisoned. This will serve to introduce my beloved Chonya Selnahr. Twice our wedding was interrupted. The first time, her professor father was taken away and executed. The next time, her mother. Her brother is a member of the Krondistanian secret police. We fear for our lives daily and pray that peace can return to Krondistan. If I am gone, the rebels will spirit her out of the city to safety.

I have given her a map to our home. Please honor her as my wife. I have told her much about you. I regret not having been able to share with you my work for the government, but the danger was too great.

Your loving son,
Yuri

Larissa passed the letter to Stefan and questions and translations began. They learned Yuri had served as a Russian spy in Krondistan and Chonya's own brother betrayed him, dying with Yuri in a blast he had set. The secret police tried to kill her, too.

She escaped and hid in the mountains, where she gave birth to their son. "He never knew I was with child; I didn't want to worry him," she said, her vacant eyes showing no emotion. "I cooked and made bullets for six rebel families who'd escaped from the cities and we lived in caves. Those women fought alongside their men. When I left, they gave me the dog and cart and the pistol."

Little Yuri had begun to perspire. Larissa put him to bed in his father's old room.

"How did you get past the checkpoints?" Stefan asked.

"Yuri stayed hidden in the cart and I acted crazy, so they always let me go."

"It's a miracle she made it here," Stefan said.

Chonya continued to talk as Nazarov translated.

"My Yuri spoke many languages. He was fluent in Krondistani, but I do not speak much of his Russian. I tried to get information at a house not far from here. When I said 'Rosinya' they threw rotten fruit at me and said, 'dead,

dead, dead, dead.' I did not know if they wanted me dead or if she were dead. Now I know."

She turned to Nazarov.

"How do you happen to speak Krondistani?"

"My mother fled Kronistan and came to Kiev. She met and married my father, a Russian physician."

Chonya looked relieved.

"This is your home from now on. Larissa wants you to stay, even though Rosinya is dead," Nazarov assured Chonya. "Has your dog had food? If not, let's feed him."

Little Yuri awoke and joined them. Chonya took the gun and rested it in her folded arms.

Larissa placed a pan of sausage and eggs outside the back door for the dog. She watched Anatol shoot a wistful glance at Chonya and Little Yuri caring for the dog.

Soon he was riding back to Kiev on the horse Stefan and Larissa had loaned him, happy he had promised to return the next day.

She's beautiful, even under all that dirt.

Stefan and Larissa hovered over Little Yuri splashing in a washtub. Thoughts of uninhibited Echo drifted back in her memories, then the grandson she had never seen and the life he would be enjoying at Vermillion Hall. She shuddered to think of what this child had endured. He and Chonya had stayed hidden and slept all day then traveled and foraged for food each night.

Larissa dried him with a Turkish towel and bundled him in one of Yuri's old shirts. His sleep-deprived body proved more than ready for bed.

He snuggled in Larissa's arms until Chonya emerged, bathed and looking so well-groomed in one of Rosinya's nightgowns that they hardly recognized her. Her formerly unkempt hair was neatly coiffed and tied with a pink ribbon.

All four slept well that night. Just after breakfast, Nazarov arrived in a carriage. He placed the borrowed horse trailing it in a stall and saluted an embarrassed Stefan, who was milking a cow and did not return his salute.

Then both heard Larissa scream.

Chapter 20

Chonya's Rags

Stefan and Anatol rushed to the backyard and found Larissa being chased by Chonya, who twisted like an animal when Anatol grabbed her. Little Yuri ran to protect his mother and fired her gun into the ground. Stefan wrested the weapon from the child.

"Please, get my clothes back," pleaded Chonya in Kronistani, translated by Anatol.

Larissa held the smelly garment she had attempted to burn in front of her and watched Chonya tear at it. After removing a sewn-in waxed packet, Chonya handed its contents to Anatol. Stunned, Larissa watched Chonya pitch the dress into the fire.

Anatol waved the paper in the air.

"This is a Krondistanian certificate of marriage."

"I thought Yuri wrote the wedding was interrupted twice," Stefan said.

"No, the wedding was completed the first time, the celebration was interrupted three times; that is when I escaped," Chonya said.

"That means she and Yuri were married, so little Yuri was legally born to a Russian citizen," Larissa said.

Rosinya's sparse wardrobe did not provide much worth sharing but Larissa's did. A grateful Chonya looked wonderful in her new clothing.

"We'll get cloth from Kiev and make little Yuri some clothes before I leave. I can remake some of his father's clothing for him immediately."

Larissa, Stefan, Chonya, Anatol and little Yuri went to Kiev three days later to the Military Records Bureau. They then visited the Ministry of Births, where they registered little Yuri as a Russian citizen born to a Russian diplomat serving in a foreign country. Chonya, as a political refugee married to a deceased member of the Russian Foreign Service, received citizenship, also.

Later they went to the Ministry of Land Records, where Larissa transferred Rosinya's property into the name of the daughter-in-law Rosinya had never met. Next, they stopped at the bank.

The last stop brought them to a sumptuous meal at the home of Dr. and Mrs. Otic Nazarov, Anatol's parents, where Krondistani became the official language with polite Russian translations thrown in from time to time.

After the meal, Stefan watched the Nazarovs amusing little Yuri and he asked Anatol, "Why have you never married? Does your career come first?"

"No, I could leave the military. I'm trained as a physician, also. I've been looking for a girl like my mother. I may have found one," he said with a wink.

Rosinya's caretakers continued to help and Anatol's mother became a temporary resident at the farm, "to help Chonya adjust." Truth be known, the older woman relished reliving her youth and hearing news from her homeland.

Larissa could have returned to Paris with her dignity intact had little Yuri not climbed in her lap and whispered, with a big kiss, "My Babushka."

She left her newest relatives with regret and broke into tears when Chonya, at Anatol's tutoring, was able to thank her in Russian, saying, "You leave me with a grateful heart."

Her thoughts raced to Vermillion Hall and her own grandson. York was about little Yuri's age and she had never seen him.

Chapter 21
Rolfo

The New Orleans House of Richilene had suffered somewhat from the economic problems of 1837 the previous year, but the Paris House of Richilene balanced things out by attracting wealthy clients. Larissa's able staff allowed her to visit Kiev often to check on Chonya. By now, Anatol and Chonya had married and been blessed with a daughter, Yesina.

Anatol left the military for medicine. Seven-year-old Yuri reveled in the love of his new grandparents and his new, patient Papa, who taught him the correct way to handle a firearm. Watching Yuri, Larissa longed to return to New Orleans to see her own grandson. Ghosts of long-ago lingered in her thoughts too often. Although they frightened her, they also beckoned.

Larissa, in Europe, proved not the only expatriate longing for her homeland. Back in New Orleans, Mother Superior Sister Claire, a former teacher at the Ursuline Convent, now found her calling with the Hilon Hospital and she, too, entertained thoughts of returning to her adopted Italian home.

God must have intended for me to help care for the yellow fever and cholera victims or He would not have led me here.

She prayed for the unification of her country, loved her adopted America and its lushness, but ached for the breathtaking, hilly terrain of Rome.

In a vineyard near Rome, in a countryside Sister Claire loved so much, a young boy close to the same age as York did not enjoy tutors and a life of privilege.

"Good little fishy," Rolfo said in a childish voice. "Jump on my hook and hold on. What a supper you'll make with your brothers and sisters in my basket."

This stream near an Italian vineyard provided a food source and escape for the young fisherman. Cypress trees, scrubby under normal, dry conditions, had reached unusual proportions and Rolfo fished at the water's edge of the now engorged, rushing mountain-fed stream. Lengthening shadows obscured the water's sun-flecked surface. Nestled in the stream's shallow mini-cove, seven meager trout flopped in a loosely woven creel someone long ago fashioned from osier tree switches.

"Sofia will cook you brown and tender and our stomachs will be full. She will be proud of me."

Maybe Ludii won't come home and we can eat supper without his fussing. He always fusses when he drinks wine.

Rolfo used a forked stick to disentangle the hook from the fish's mouth, rolled its barb in a wad of muddy clay and stuffed it in his pants pocket. Wisps of dark curls matted the eight-year-old's perspiring forehead. He swatted a bug and wiped his upper lip.

Trophies from the quest and fishing pole in tow, he cast a wistful look at the splendid rising moon. While fishing days before, he had spoken with one of the grape picker's children. He thought he had found a friend, but the only time he saw her again was when they were all working in the vineyard. Then the crop was in and her family was gone.

Moonlight splashed the clearing near the hovel. Everyone had gone except Ludii, who sniggered as he saw the boy approach. Rolfo was alone, alone with *him*. He shuddered. Rolfo felt relatively safe when the others were in the house, but now *it* would begin again. Bile rose in his throat, but he proceeded toward the house.

Ludii slopped water from the wooden buckets as he swung them in the back door. With a twisted, suggestive smirk, he patted Rolfo on the rump. The child darted from his reach, but Ludii grabbed and broke the fragile ribbon around the child's neck that held a small wooden cross with intricate carving. The creel crashed and fish scattered. Panic. This monster had taken his cross, all he had to remember when there had been warmth in his life...thoughts so distant he could not reconstruct them in his child's memory.

"Come here boy. I won't hurt you. Want your cross? Take it from me like a man."

The words were a silent scream in Ludii's mind, born of the hundreds of unmerciful beatings he had suffered at the hands of his teacher, his heavy-handed father. As much as he hated those words even after twenty years, he wielded them against Rolfo as they had been used against his own lost innocence.

Religion could not be beaten into a person. No crucifix had protected *him* from evil.

"Every time I call you and you don't come, I'll cut another piece off your precious cross. Come here, boy!"

He hypnotized the boy with the image of the broken cross. With clenched teeth, Rolfo pushed himself behind the shadow of the tattered curtain dividing the cooking area from where they slept.

Enraged, Ludii grabbed a boning knife from a shelf and cut a sliver from the cross. He dangled it before the child's eyes. Rolfo, witnessing the rape of his beloved icon, lowered his head and charged across the floor. He rammed Ludii's soft, overfed belly and knocked him off-balance, weakening his grip on the cross and allowing Rolfo to reclaim his treasure. He crammed it into his pocket and ran faster than ever before.

Stunned for a moment, Ludii struggled and, with great effort, scrambled to his feet, sheer bulk slowing his pace. Perspiration drenching his shirt, he returned to the silent hut and eased his bloated body onto a stool. He sat staring vacantly into the dusty fireplace, frustrated by his own impotence, until he could bear it no more.

He plunged the knife blade into the table—to its hilt.

Chapter 22
To Roma, 30 kms

It seemed Rolfo had walked for days. He did not know where he was going nor where he had been. The tree, loaded with tasty-looking fruit, lifted his spirits as he peeled the thin orange skin and plopped a fleshy chunk into his mouth. He spit, sputtered and threw it on the ground. It was a Bergamot and completely inedible. He tried to erase the bitter taste by eating some grass. The fish from the day before flashed in his thoughts. His stomach rumbled and he wondered where Sofia was.

Sofia, sweet Sofia.

While Sofia lived in the hut, she had taught him to read, so he recognized a "Roma 30 kms" sign. His feet blistered in the heat and his sandals afforded no protection from stones that bruised his toes, making his progress even more unbearable, but he bore it. After Ludii, he could bear anything. He kept walking...to Rome he would go.

A shrouding mist descended as mud oozed in his sandals with each soggy step. He began to hear the thudding of horse hooves. As it grew louder, he watched a brougham carriage slosh to a halt.

"Get in lad, you're drenched. Where are you going?"

"To Rome."

"Here, put this blanket around you."

The distinguished driver touched his own dark clothes and eyed the loose weave in the frail child's shirt and pants. Rolfo burrowed into the soft woolen blanket and fell into an exhausted sleep.

The driver stroked his gray beard.

Never had children of my own. Wouldn't have thrown one away if I had.

He let the boy sleep as long as he could.

"Boy, boy, wake up," he said, shaking him gently. "This is as far as I go."

"Are we in Rome?"

"I'm afraid not. Maybe we can get you a ride at the inn across the street. I went to school in England with the owner. One of his guests might be going to Rome. His family makes the finest cheese in this country. Now you stay here."

He tied the horses and walked to the inn.

Rolfo relieved himself behind the low building the gray-bearded man had entered. Graybeard returned with a burly man in lederhosen who spoke in booming guttural tones.

"This is my friend, Otto Brunner, boy."

"Gott in himmel, vot a scrawny little dunneskind."

Rolfo almost bolted before the blustery Tyrolean reached into a knapsack and handed him a ripe apple, but the fruit was too much to refuse.

"Dis iss my vife Helga und I am Otto. She's mute. Dare are times I am tankful ven I hear udder vimin dat she cannot speak."

"I'm Rolfo," he said.

Helga was a great beauty, probably half-Italian. Her striking black curls framed an oval face. She watched Rolfo devour the apple, handed him a lump of cheese, raised a cupped hand to her mouth and pointed toward the inn. Otto left immediately, returning with a tankard of milk. Rolfo clutched the pewter container with both hands and drained it.

"Keep the blanket, boy."

Graybeard was pleased with himself. Rolfo, who had never had a blanket, gave a quick smile. Helga climbed into the back of a leather-covered wagon and motioned for Rolfo to join her. Inside, cheese swung from hooks and a leather wine pouch with spigot hung within Otto's reach. He thought Helga's white blouse, tightly laced bodice and black skirt the most wonderful clothing he had ever seen.

A blue woven scarf exactly the shade of her eyes and tied from neck to waist contrasted against her black hair. Shiny shoes and black stockings covered feet scarcely larger than his own. Her hands were occupied with a dainty gold chain she attempted to unknot.

Rolfo stretched his open hands toward her and she gave him the chain. He had untangled fishing line many times; this was easy for him. He returned the jewelry to her and she nodded.

"What is she trying to say, Otto?"

"She iss tanking you vor repairing her chain."

"What's *tanking?*"

"Ven you do someting vor somevun, dey say 'tank you' und you say, 'you're velcome.'"

"Always?"

"Ya, alvays."

"I didn't know that."

The cart stopping cut short Rolfo's near-doze.

"Ve have to stop vor de night; too dark to travel."

Rolfo cringed. He hated nighttime.

"I must go on to Rome," he said urgently.

"If you must, yust stay on dis road."

Otto made a tight roll of the blanket, fastened it with rope and secured it between Rolfo's narrow shoulders with a knot. Rolfo bobbed his head.

"Tank you."

"You're velcome."

He waved to Helga.

Lombardy poplars cast long shadows on the sun-dried road. An almost obscured moon peered from behind a cloud and lighted a "Roma 6 kms" sign. His bedroll had become heavy, but Rolfo remembered his goal. A threatening storm never materialized, then a lightning bolt startled and scattered a small pack of wolves from their advantageous view of the tiny, bedraggled soldier trudging along the road where Caesar's triumphant legions had once returned home.

For Rolfo, many battles remained.

Everywhere he looked crosses created looming shadows in the Eternal City. Women wearing heavily starched white and flowing black clothing scurried about, usually in twos. For emotional warmth and security on his first nights he patted the pocket that held his own damaged cross.

In this city he scavenged scraps from refuse and found a new home beneath a bridge.

Chapter 23
Our Daily Bread

Five days later, torrential rain continued for almost a week, paralyzing the city. Raw sewage trickled near a half loaf of discarded bread eyed by two boys advancing from different directions.

"Get back, that's mine," shouted the smaller boy. "I haven't eaten any food for two days." He scooped up the bread.

"They haven't eaten all day, and they're little ones," the taller boy said, motioning to a motley, rain-soaked group cowering behind him. "I told you they haven't eaten today."

He grabbed the front of Rolfo's shirt, but Rolfo wrested free, gave him a violent shove, took a defiant bite from the bread and glanced at the smaller children.

"They do look hungry. Here, you," he said, relinquishing the bread.

Still on guard, the taller boy relaxed a bit and smiled in disbelief.

"Where are you from?"

"I don't know."

"What do you mean, you don't know?" He tore the bread into several pieces and gave it to the children.

"I'm stronger than you, so it really doesn't matter, does it?"

"Where do you live?"

"Over there," Rolfo said, gesturing toward a small bridge near an encroaching stream.

"You can't stay there."

"Why not?" he asked through clenched teeth.

"Because it's starting to rain, and it floods. Do you have anything over there?"

"Yes, my blanket."

"Quick, get it and come with us."

Rolfo dashed under the bridge where rivulets from above deposited mud and pebbles onto his temporary home. He snatched the blanket and joined the others, his heart in his throat.

Half-clothed little bodies ran helter-skelter through blinding sheets of rain still chewing their morsels of bread. Rolfo's heart pumped double-time. The destination did not disappoint. On higher ground, they welcomed him to a much larger bridge with a cozy area like a small house. Scavenged treasures abounded. Remnants of rugs, fabric and discards from once-grand buildings covered rock and dirt walls.

"I'm Gian Prudore," said the taller boy, sorting and arranging the children by height. "This is Carmine, who eats more than all of us, but stays skinny. This blond-haired curly top is Angelo. This smiling face is Davide, who is happiest chasing bugs, and this plump little one is Mario. Where do you come from?"

"I'm Rolfo and I really don't know where I come from. A vineyard somewhere."

"You really don't know where you come from? Don't you have a mama or a papa?"

"What's a mama and a papa?"

"They're where you come from."

"But I don't know where I come from."

"Oh, well, it doesn't matter. You'll sleep here," he said, motioning to a snug corner where Rolfo pitched his blanket.

The little ones walked to the dripping edge of the entrance and relieved themselves in unison then clambered into their crude beds. Rolfo unrolled his blanket and a weary Gian dropped onto his own.

Sunrise flashed under the bridge as Rolfo bounded out of bed. Gian looked at Rolfo's feet, which he tried to hide under his blanket.

"People in Rome throw away shoes better than those sandals."

He immediately saw hurt on Rolfo's face.

"Maybe not much better than those, but a little better. Pick out a pair from that pile in the corner."

The nuns had tried many times to give the bridge children food, but they refused their offers and ran away. This puzzled the women because their bundles of used clothing were always gone when left out in the open.

"Don't take anything to eat from those women. They may try to poison us."

This bewildered Rolfo because the women seemed to have the kindness he had hoped to find in the city. Gian, who had told him he was eleven and self-appointed protector of the band, continued.

"They look sweet, but I followed them into their church one day and you wouldn't believe what I saw. They had a man nailed to a cross and blood was running out of his hands, feet side and head."

"Maybe they didn't know he was in there."

"Oh, they go in there all the time. They knew he was there. Sometimes they sing, too, like they're happy about being there. When I saw him bleeding, I ran all the way to the fruit sellers and hid under a basket 'til dark. I still hear them singing when I go to fish coins from the fountain, but I always run away when they come out."

That fountain with the peaceful statues became their primary source of income.

"Men don't beg," Protector Gian decreed to his small group of "men," who ranged in age from about four to eleven. Gian was the oldest; tall, proud and alone, his mother dead and his father in prison.

Gian washed on Thursday, that being the only day he was allowed to visit his father, but he made the four younger boys bathe every day.

Even the smallest hands kept busy with jobs he scrounged for all of them—jobs they largely worked in exchange for food. He always saw that the younger ones ate first but little could be done to improve their living quarters. He worried constantly about their coughs.

One Thursday, Gian returned to the bridge in a hostile mood. Rolfo had never seen him like this except for their first meeting. After much prodding, he confided in Rolfo.

"Two of those women who bring us clothes were at the jail today. I told my papa not to talk to them because of what they did to that man. He laughed at me— me, his own son! He *laughed* at me. Even told me we used to go to church before he was sent away. I told him I didn't remember it. I'm confused."

"He wouldn't tell you a lie, would he?"

"No, my papa never lies."

"Did he say why they have that man on a cross?"

"He tried to explain it, but our visiting time was over and they made me leave."

"Can you go back before next Thursday?"

"No, he told me to go to the church and one of the men who wears black—he called them priests—would explain it to me. Rolfo, I'm not scared of anything, but I'm scared to go back to that church."

"I'll go with you, Gian," said Rolfo, placing a less-than-confident hand on the older boy's shoulder.

Chapter 24
Father Bocchetti

Rolfo endured fitful sleep anticipating the visit to the priest. He dreamed of Ludii wearing a black robe and a wicked priest living in the vineyard. He dreamed of knives and crosses. Each time he awoke in a cold sweat with his blanket serpentined around him.

The dreaded day arrived.

"Today we go to the church," Gian said.

Sunshine blessed Rome and their workday lasted well into the afternoon. Gian arranged bread in the center of their stone slab table and told the boys to
bathe in the fountain and add their fare to the meal.

"Rolfo and I have business to take care of."

As they made their way to the church, Gian chattered in an unnatural voice. Rolfo said little but took many long, deep breaths. They approached the church with bravado.

The two ill-kempt boys resembled tiny, foraging animals as they cautiously entered the imposing cathedral. With trepidation, Rolfo eyed the Christ figure on the cross and his eyes widened with each heart hammer.

Against the altar aglow with votives was silhouetted a lone priest preparing vespers. Since their bare feet had not announced entry, they were within touching distance of the priest when Gian spoke.

"My papa told me to come to church and you could answer some questions for me."

The startled priest dropped a glass holder that shattered like a Roman candle against the stone floor, then brushed the broken glass aside with his shoe and glared at the boys.

"Sit here on the pew and we'll talk."

The priest eyed the boys suspiciously. They should know better than to interrupt him in his priestly duties and they would not be the first street urchins to attempt to steal from the poor box.

"My papa said you are called a priest and that man on the cross is not really a man, but he once lived and you work for him. I don't understand, but I can see now that he is carved out of wood. He looked so real the first time I ever came in here."

"Who is your papa?"

"Lorenzo Prudore."

"I don't know him. Does he come to this church? Where does he live?"

"No, he doesn't come to this church. He lives at a jail because the son of a man he worked for stole money from his own father and blamed my papa. He said we used to go to church before mama died."

"I see."

The priest's face softened and he smiled, but that was the wrong thing to do in front of this bewildered young man.

"You're laughing at me like my papa," said Gian, standing to leave. Rolfo shot up also, but the gentleness of the priest's face caused them to sit again.

"My sons, it is not an easy story to believe, for it sounds like a fairy tale, but it is as real today as it was nearly two thousand years ago," the priest said, starting the story. .

Rolfo fingered the broken cross in his pocket and pondered how it fit into this strange story. The priest had told Gian to call him "father" but he couldn't bring himself to do that. "We have to go now."

"Come again soon, my sons."

"I could have listened to him talk forever, Rolfo, but the young ones do not know where we are and I heard the clock strike seven."

They returned to the bridge in silence, each trying to sort out this new information. They wanted to know more about the Holy Mother and how a young boy of twelve could teach grown men. Ultimately, knowledge that started this day would guide both of them, especially Rolfo, through many dark times.

On their second visit, they ate early. With Carmine, Angelo, Davide and Mario in tow, they sprinted to the fountain.

"Bathe yourselves, dress in these clothes and sit here in the shadows near the church until we come out."

Gian told the priest his name.

"And your name, my son?"

"Rolfo Roma," he said, his smile widening because he liked the sound of the last name he had just given himself. He lived in the beautiful city of Rome, so why not?

"I am Father Bocchetti and please call me 'Father.'"

By the third visit, it had become easy for the two to call him "Father." All of them now ate the food left by nuns, although they remained careful to keep the younger ones hidden, fearing the authorities might send them away.

Why couldn't Ludii have been more like Father Bocchetti?

The priest's robe spilled over the pew like a serene, rolling landscape. Rolfo stroked its rich fabric and stared, enthralled, as a dying burst of sunset gave life to the stained-glass window figures. Father Bocchetti spent many hours in prayer on Gian's and Rolfo's behalf. Never in all his years had he prayed so diligently for two individuals as he now did for these boys. The depth of their quest thrilled and amazed him. Their sincerity and intelligence seemed beyond their years.

Father Bocchetti held his chin in deep thought. At last he spoke.

"My brother Fabrizio is an attorney, Gian. Give me all the information you have concerning your papa and I will pass it on to him. I can't promise anything will be changed. We shall see."

Chapter 25
Bayou Conét

Halfway around the world near New Orleans, Louisiana, two boys, both age nine, the same age as Rolfo, skipped rocks across Bayou Conét as it rushed toward the road like an angry intruder.

York Arceneaux and Paul LeFleur knew to watch out for swamp panthers and quicksand. The brackish water also teemed with alligators, snapping turtles and water moccasins.

"Camille said for me not to go into Bahkonay," said York, curly-haired and the sturdier built of the two. "But we could get a *little* closer."

"I know not to go into Bahkonay, but I don't know why you call your mother by her first name. Why do you?"

His straight black hair shone in the late-afternoon sun.

"I don't know. She must not mind. I've always called her Camille."

"Well then, why don't you call your daddy Luther?"

"Camille calls him something else, but I can't call him that to his face, so I call him Daddy."

"What does she call him?"

"Promise not to tell. Cross your heart and hope to die."

"Cross my heart and hope to die and stick a needle in my eye."

"She calls him 'The Peasant' but doesn't let him hear her say it."

"Why does she call him that?"

"She says he'll never be anything but a farmer. My grandfather, Colonel Crumpton, was a great soldier in India. I'll be a great soldier someday."

"If he was such a great soldier, why did he quit fighting?"

"Honestly, don't you know anything? England didn't have any more wars to fight, you simpleton."

"Is he gonna come over here and start one?"

"He's dead. He died in Memphis."

A wave of sadness crossed Paul's face.

"I'll share my grandfather with you. I didn't know you didn't have one."

"I don't want your mean old grandfather. He drove your grandmother crazy."

Paul pounced on York in one powerful leap, rolling and tumbling closer to the murky waters of Bayou Conét. "Take it back. He did not."

"Yes, he did."

Two partially submerged alligators scrimmaged to the bayou bank. One snapped at York's loose shirt. The boys stopped fighting and tumbled away in horror toward Paul's mansion, Ruvasha. With adrenaline pumping, several yards later they realized York was injured. Blood streamed from a nick in his side.

"You're bleeding, York."

"I'm wounded!" (Young soldiers are never injured, but wounded...)

Ruvasha awaited behind beautiful iron gates bearing the LeFleur crest. First to greet them was Abraham, a curly-haired foundling of four.

"Bud, bud," he said wide-eyed, waving his little finger at York.

"It's not *bud*, it's blood. Hush!"

J.P. LeFleur, Paul's father, examined the gash while York protested.

"I want Aunt Besa."

Soon Tedelia hurried out with a pillow slip and wrapped it around York. J.P. lifted him into their carriage and the three sped to Vermillion Hall to be met by Hatch Washington and Aunt Besa.

"Sweet Jesus, Massa York's bleedin,'" Hatch said.

"Go get Mister Luther and Miss Camille. Quick, Hatch," said Besa. "And bring that baby back to the kitchen where there's water."

She ran beside the carriage

"Mister Luther, what happened?"

York's groans became louder when he heard Besa's voice. J.P. explained the situation.

Luther appeared at the great hall back door, lifted York from the carriage and placed him on the long kitchen table. Camille, in her wheelchair, watched from the cavernous hall facing the kitchen. She appeared to almost rise but repositioned herself and remained seated. A sudden surge of new-found energy or just a devoted mother's concern? Whatever reason, Hatch reported the wound-cleansing process in a running narrative, so she contented herself as an observer, almost detached, but visibly perturbed.

I must be in control.

At this moment, she was not.

The Peasant is directing everything. I will have to talk to him when we are alone. He has not even consulted me. My mother was never in control. My father controlled everything, and look what a mess he made of everything

Drummed out of the British army for cowardice, then escaping his shame by coming to America, he'd taken all her mother's inheritance to give them a fresh start in Memphis—and squandered it on drinking and womanizing. It finally killed him, but not before her mother had taken her own life with poison.

She remembered the pain of returning home with friends from a trip and being assaulted by a jungle of buggies and wagons—and an auction in progress. Creditors and bargain hunters ravaged her beloved Alba Rosa Plantation eager to get their share. She fought her way through the crowd to see her beautiful mahogany tester bed being loaded onto a wagon by two sweaty workmen. Watching the gavel fall on the sale of her mother's portrait, she rushed to the Colonel.

"Father, how could you?"

He hung his head and mumbled something, taking the remaining sip from a silver pocket flask and dropping in on the lawn.

Her friends hurried her away. Two days later, she requested to be taken to the Memphis Normal Institute for Dames, where she accepted a job teaching elocution and lived in the connecting teachers' home.

Colonel Crumpton died five months later. The de la Caine relatives insisted Camille go to New Orleans and live with them.

"My sister would have wanted you to be with us. It's not proper for a gentlewoman to live alone," her aunt said.

"Father was working on a big investment, but his health had not been good and he wasn't able to properly manage his finances anymore."

Her Aunt smiled and nodded.

"I accept your kind offer. You are absolutely right. Alone in a city is no place for a young woman."

Camille had already faced humiliation on two continents.

Memories of India, England and embarrassment encased her. Her temples throbbed.

My father was a great man until alcohol drowned him. I don't care what people say. They didn't know how brave he was.

"Mrs. Arceneaux, your son is going to be fine. The wound is superficial."

"Well, now, Mr. LeFleur, are you a doctor? What happened? Who did this to him? What makes you think..."

York walked toward her and interrupted.

"Camille, Paul and I were fighting near Bahkonay and..."

"I knew it. I knew it. That boy is as crazy as his grandmother Katté. You are never to play with him again."

She whirled her wheelchair around and rolled toward the lift to go to the second floor without a word of sympathy or comfort to her only child.

Besa gathered the bewildered, bandaged boy into her arms and sat in a massive rocking chair in the side gallery.

"We'll go out in the dog yard tomorrow and you'll get to hold one of the new puppies, little Master York."

"Aunt Besa," York said in a drowsy voice, "don't call me little, please."

"Yes, sir, Master York," she said, continuing to rock him and sing a haunting field chant. "Oooo, oooo, oooo, oooo, oooo..."

Someone from the slave quarters behind Vermillion Hall picked it up and relayed it over the plantation and it sounded like the swell of a symphony, surging and ending as quickly as it had begun. All was then quiet, except chirping crickets, low frog voices and the muffled, embarrassed conversation Luther was having at the mansion's front with Tedelia and J.P. LeFleur.

"Thank you for bringing my son home."

"Luther, Paul didn't do anything to York. An alligator nipped him when they got too close to the bayou. We've warned them so many times...York told us on the way over here."

"I apologize for Camille. She just hasn't been herself since her accident. Remember how pretty and sweet she was when she first came to Vermillion Hall as a bride? She was so gentle, even scared of my hunting dogs. We still have to keep them penned up, even the puppies. It must be awful to sit in that wheelchair and have to be lifted out. Please, say you'll forgive her."

Tedelia caught both of Luther's hands in her own.

"We know she was upset. We all get upset when something happens to our children. We are just glad it wasn't a serious injury."

"York is always welcome in our home, Luther," J.P. added. "Don't forbid him to come there, promise?"

"I promise."

Chapter 26

A Sudden Wedding

Emotions drained, Tedelia and J.P. climbed into their carriage to return home.

"Luther is a sincere man, but he is so blind. You know I went to school with Camille's cousin, Marole de la Caine. I've never told you this before, but Camille caused Larissa to move to Paris...caused her to leave Luther, her only child."

"How? She loves working for the House of Richilene."

He slowed the horses.

"You must be mistaken."

"Marole went to Vermillion Hall with Camille on her first visit to meet Larissa. When they were leaving, Larissa rushed out to give her a handmade pillow, but Camille was saying horrible things about her and Larissa went back inside."

"And Marole de la Caine or Larissa told you this?"

"Marole told me. Larissa apparently never said anything to anyone. She moved from Vermillion Hall as soon as Luther's and Camille's engagement was announced two weeks later."

"I always thought that marriage took place a little quick."

"Well, there's more. Camille took her grand tour—Europe and India—but she was penniless when she came to New Orleans to live with the de la Caines. You'd have thought she was a princess. They were ready to ask her to leave when she met Luther."

"That's heartless, Tedelia, so soon after the death of her father. Would they really have asked her to leave?"

"There's still more. Camille pitched black pepper in a de la Caine kitchen servant's eyes because she scorched a dress. The poor woman almost lost her sight."

"This is too much. I never knew you to be such a gossip, Tedelia."

He cracked the whip to speed their return to Ruvasha. Tedelia rolled her eyes.

"Yes, but as you mentioned earlier, this sounds like gossip, so I won't tell you anymore."

"Don't do me like that. I'm sorry...what else?"

He slowed the horses to a halt and patted her hand.

"Lies, many lies. 'It's a shame Marole doesn't like your singing, Aunt Etta. Why, I think you have a beautiful voice,' or 'your mother doesn't like the way you have your hair dressed, but she hates to tell you for fear she'll hurt your feelings.' She caused constant dissension."

"They were happy to have a speedy wedding. I can see why now."

"Oh, and Luther drops by to see the de la Caines when he's in New Orleans. Except for the wedding and York's christening, they've had nothing to do with Camille."

"I apologize. I judged you hastily...and you've stayed silent all these years..."

"There just never was a reason to discuss it before. I feel sorry for her having to be in a wheelchair all the time."

"So do I. It will be hard to keep the boys apart."

"Maybe she'll soften with time, J.P."

"I hope so," he said, giving the team full rein.

When they entered the semicircular drive to Ruvasha, Abraham rushed toward the carriage as it crunched to a stop. Tedelia stepped down and lifted the child into her arms. He melted into the crook of "my Te's" neck snuggled, then raised his double-row lashes and gave her a quick peck on the cheek.

"My Te, bud, bud on York?"

"No, Abraham, no more blood on York. He's going to be all well."

He wiggled down and went skipping up the fifteen marble steps of the Ionic-columned Greek Revival mansion, counting them as he went. Paul smiled at his baby brother, chased after him, and both disappeared into the back hall.

Only four years ago as a newborn someone had left him on Tedelia's doorstep in a straw basket with a card written in a clear hand that read simply: *I was born March 7, 1835. My name is Abraham.*

Practically every household in New Orleans had such a basket, identical to the many sold on Congo Square where, on Sunday afternoons, slaves and freemen peddled their wares, made music, danced and forgot their troubles—if only for an afternoon. The olio throng—Creoles, foreign sailors, low-born and rich—haggled over nuts, vegetables, fruits, colorful prints and handcrafted items.

All inquiries to find the child's birth family proved futile. This adorable, precocious child who called Tedelia "my Te" was hers to keep. Years later the city of New Orleans would owe him a debt of gratitude.

Chapter 27

Fire is Such a Permanent Solution

Back at Ruvasha in the massive library Paul sat at Gilbert LeFleur's feet.

"And that's why Grandmother Katté lives in Switzerland?"

"That's right, son. She is too ill to live here in Louisiana with us."

"Then why did York say you drove her crazy, Grandfather?"

"Some people talk when they should be listening. Your grandmother was a beautiful girl when I met her in Switzerland. She loved life and everybody loved her. Moving so far away from her homeland must have made her wither inside like a rose left out in the sunshine too long. I didn't know how sick she was until it was too late."

"Will I ever get to see her, Grandfather?"

"I don't know son; I just don't know."

Gilbert gazed intently out the window toward Bayou Conét, the watery playground he'd loved as a boy and still loved and thought of Katté's revulsion toward anything connected with it.

Paul hugged Gilbert from behind.

"I love you, Grandfather."

"I love you, too. Now run along and play."

Gauzy floor-length curtains beside French doors wafted in the room like graceful dancers. The gallery gave a magnificent view from the third floor of the river as it splashed by Vermillion Hall. Camille sat reading.

"Camille, I've wonderful news. Mother is coming to visit, according to this letter."

He waved as he walked toward his wife.

"She'll be here in three weeks. "

"That is good news, Luther. I do hope she's gotten rid of some of her hostility toward me. She used to be so cruel when just the two of us talked. I can't imagine why she disliked me so much. I can only think it is because you are so wonderful, and I would be taking you away from her."

"I'm sure she didn't mean to be cruel. I read the letter she wrote you when York was born and when you had your accident and she couldn't have been nicer."

"That's just it my dear, dear Luther. She knew you would see both those letters. I'll be very kind to her while she is here and pretend not to notice her rudeness," she said, stroking his hand. "And Luther, please help *me* be a nice person when our York chooses a bride."

"She intends to stay in town in the Richilene maisonette, so she won't be any bother to us."

"See, my darling? She's trying to make me look bad. I'm so hurt."

She blinked her eyes furiously, placed her hands over them, and whimpered until the desired tears fell.

Luther wiped her tears away and in doing so, dropped the letter.

"I'll get Besa to make you some hot tea and bring it up here myself," he said, heading down the stairs.

Camille bent very low from her wheelchair, plucked the letter from the floor, twisted it into a spear, lifted a candle from the table, rolled her chair closer to the fireplace, ignited the paper and aimed it into its new home. Flames licked it to ashes. *Fire is such a permanent solution for so many problems.*

She pinched her face to make her eyes appear swollen and waited as night descended on Vermillion Hall.

She heard Luther's footsteps on the stairs and his voice from the doorway, saying, "Is something burning? I smell smoke."

"Yes, I think the servants are burning brush."

He put the tea tray onto the marble-topped table and caressed his wife's shoulders.

I wish she could hold me like she did when we first married, but she is so fragile...

He took an almost painful deep breath then sighed.

"I'll send Besa up in fifteen minutes to help you get ready for bed. Goodnight, Camille."

After alerting Besa, he retired to his rooms, closed his eyes and tried to remember how it had felt to hold his wife in his arms.

Camille took tiny sips of tea, glanced at the fireplace and curled her thin lips in a self-satisfied smile.

Chapter 28
Suzette Valois

Sunlight peeped through gaping slits in the heavy draperies of the mansion's windows where white furniture covers gave a ghostly appearance to the sitting room. The handsome man looked in the library and ballroom but did not go to inspect the kitchen. He climbed the stairs leading to the bedrooms of his deceased twin brother's house.

What are you doing here?" he asked the startled young woman packing clothes in the largest bedroom.

She sat, feeling faint. "You shocked me. I didn't know you would look so much like Pierre."

"Are you all right? Why are you here?"

"I'm his wife...his widow."

"I never knew he was married."

"No one did," her eyes welling with tears. "I'm Suzette Valois Faine."

"I'm Antoine Faine. Our family vineyards kept us busy traveling so often we would not see one another for months, but he never mentioned you."

"He couldn't. No one knew. Someone in France notified me when he died. They didn't know I was his wife."

She wiped her tears.

"I lived here with my maid Margaritte. I had to move with her into her small cottage as I have little money and now she has died."

"I don't understand. Why would Pierre keep you a secret? If you don't mind my saying, Mademoiselle, you're beautiful. My family in France will be so proud of you."

She struggled for words.

"Could we go downstairs and talk?"

"Certainly."

Antoine carried her basket of clothes downstairs, opened the drapes and removed covers from a settee.

"Pierre planned to be in France just for a short while. He never knew I gave birth to his son."

"I have a nephew?" Antoine's excitement matched Suzette's distress.

"I gave him away."

"What do you mean, you gave him away? What kind of woman are you?"

Hysterical, she cried unashamedly.

"I'm an octoroon. I'm a woman without my child because I could not afford to give him a decent life. My husband could never admit to being married to me because he would have gone to prison. I have worked to support myself selling fruit in the Vieux Carré and ached for my son every day. That's the kind of woman I am."

Without thinking, he reached to her with tenderness and held her.

"I'm so sorry. I didn't mean to hurt you," he said, trying to soothe her and stroking her hair.

Oh, no, Pierre used to do that.

"I would have come to New Orleans sooner had I known. My parents are older, and they needed me after Pierre died. We sold the vineyards."

Her tears lessened.

"Please tell me everything."

"My son is beautiful; almost five. Margaritte took him to the LeFleur Plantation, Ruvasha. She sent word to the family as she was dying and told them his mother had died when he was born. That was the first contact she'd had with them since his birth. As you can see, I'm as white as you and my son is, too. I see him when they bring him and their other son into the city, but at a distance. He looks just like Pierre. Just like you."

"What can I do?"

"Nothing. I wouldn't upset his life now."

"We will get this house put in your name."

"You're too kind. I can't afford to keep it and I have a house. Margaritte was an octoroon, too. Everyone thought I was her daughter. Her house is mine. I just come here every once in a while, to get some of my belongings. Pierre and I were only married a year."

"You can't continue to live like this."

Suzette gathered her clothing and Antoine insisted on taking her home.

One week later, Antoine called on Suzette unannounced. His large frame filled the doorway of the tiny whitewashed cottage she had shared with her former servant.

"I want you to be my wife," he announced. "Don't answer, just listen first. We will travel separately to Illinois to meet in three days and be married."

He dropped to one knee and placed a beautiful ring on her hand.

"I've loved you from the moment I first saw you."

She began to cry, then smiled.

"You will return to New Orleans with a new identity and a marriage license from another state. Oh, and another thing, you are going to Pass en Blanc; no one needs to know your heritage in New Orleans."

The steamboat *La Belle Creole* took her safely to Illinois, where she met Antoine. They returned to New Orleans as Mr. and Mr. Antoine Faine. She, née Santé L'angchaux, lately of Chicago. He sold the old house and bought another in the Garden District. They divide their time between Paris and New Orleans.

Margaritte's house is now a candy store.

Chapter 29

Nine Months Later, the Janus Gate

Scrubbing and cleaning the walkway had been a long and tiring task, but the owner of the villa would reward the young man amply. Rolfo, squinting at the duel faces of Janus peering at him, also repaired the wrought-iron gate, the gate that had sagged and creaked when he first opened it. He had not told cook what he was doing, but she followed him when he asked for a spoonful of tallow to grease the gate. She smiled and padded with bare feet to investigate his actions, clapped her hands and started swinging the gate back and forth.

"Oh, it has been broken since this old white dog here was a fuzzy puppy," she said, motioning to a sleeping Bolognese mass of canine fur. "Master will be so pleased."

And he was.

It was a long walk back to the heart of the city. The clock in the Palazzo di Montecitori struck eight. Rolfo had never been this late. All was quiet—too quiet.

Where are they?

"Are you hiding from me because I am late? I've been working. Look at the money I earned."

He threw the handful of coins on the stones and heard nothing but a vacant clinking echo from beneath the bridge.

"Gian, Carmine, Davide, Angelo, Mario...where are you?"

Silence.

He sped to the church, tripping several times as he went. Candles glowed like sunrise and he felt good for a moment. His tongue seemed to stick to the inside of his mouth when a strange priest approached him. His voice came out in a high-pitched squeak, "Where is Father Bocchetti?"

"He had legal business today, something about getting some boys in a home. He'll be back tomorrow."

Rolfo's worst fears were confirmed. The church had put his little bridge family in a home. *Would they be harmed as Luddi had harmed me? Would I ever get to see them again?* He decided to return to the bridge but stay hidden when they came back to get him and secretly follow them and set the boys free. Yes, he would set the boys free.

Rolfo spent an anxious night jumping at every slight sound near the river. Finally, he fell asleep a little before seven the next morning. So well-hidden was Rolfo in the doorway of a nearby building, Gian did not even discover his hiding place. When he returned to the bridge shortly after, his calling, "Rolfo, where are you?" went unheard and he left.

The day before, everything had happened so quickly. Father Bocchetti's brother had been able to prove Gian's father innocent of all charges and he was released from prison and received something called restitution. Lorenzo Prudore had gone to the bridge with Father Bocchetti and taken his son and his small band to a new home. The children gathered their bundles of clothing, slung them over their shoulders and walked to the waiting cart like a string of hand-joined, cut-out paper-dolls. They glanced back and forth at one another; fearful someone would be left behind. No smiles crossed those solemn little faces so unsure of what was happening.

The children had never ridden in a horse-drawn cart. Would their new bridge home be as cold as their old one? Would they have a fountain to bathe in? Where is Rolfo? Gian tried to reassure them as they climbed into the cart and snuggled like a basket of frightened puppies. Gian's father cracked the whip and the old cart began to bump along. A terrible sense of emptiness clouded Gian. His friend, his brother. *Where is he?*

With the bridge in the distance, Lorenzo Prudore turned to his son, "Gian, I always wanted more bambini. Now I have my big family. We will return for your friend Rolfo later."

Gian smiled. *My Papa never lies.*

Sounds of barking dogs and much commotion awakened Rolfo. An especially cold night had left his chest aching. Brightly painted carts and wagons rolled past him in a slow procession followed by a string of high-spirited ponies. Never had he seen such a sight. What was happening? Briefly, he was lost in the moment and forgot he ached and that his family was gone.

"What is this?" he asked a man also watching the parade.

"Zingari."

"What are Zingari?"

"They are people who travel from country to country. They have no homes but the wagons they travel in."

"Tank you," Rolfo said, remembering a poem Sofia had quoted:

"*Hark, hark, the dogs do bark. The beggars are coming to town,*
        Some in rags and some in tags, And some in velvet gowns."

Are these the people she had been describing, he wondered.

The parade was wondrous to watch. The people seemed so happy. A grassy area near the river provided the perfect campsite for the gypsies. Rolfo wanted to learn more, but for now he had to get back to the church.

Where could they be, his family? In his frenzy, he stumbled as before. Father Bocchetti was still not at the church. Rolfo just knew something terrible had happened. He did not know Father Bocchetti was at that very moment searching for him at the bridge. Nor did he know that the day before he had helped Lorenzo Prudore and his growing family settle into their new home, a home Rolfo should have been part of. He rechecked the fountains and all the markets for his family to no avail.

Later, a surly new jailer said, "No one here named Prudore. Maybe they hung him."

A baker by trade, Lorenzo had taken his restitution money and purchased the same bakery where he had once worked. A gate on the cobbled street next to the bakery opened to a common piazza shared with two other families. Clothes bounced on lines stretched from windows to interior balconies and the aroma of garlic and tomatoes filled the air. Limestone stairs led to a two-story apartment over the bakery on which Prudore had made a modest down payment. This would be their home.

Mario waddled to the third floor with Carmine following closely behind just in time to stop him from tumbling out one of the open windows facing the street. *We'll have to keep those shutters closed.* Angelo and Davide stopped on the second level, lingering on a small wrought-iron balcony where a yellow butterfly hovered near a pot of red geraniums. Davide watched contentedly until it flew away. Angelo breathed deeply. The breeze from this lofty view, so unlike the stagnant air beneath the bridge, would be etched in his memory for the rest of his life. The spires, the domes, the crosses—all seen from a glorious new perspective. Never had he been so aware of rooftops nor had they looked so wonderful. He wanted to touch them and some day he would.

Gian, although extremely appreciative, felt terrible guilt for leaving Rolfo. They had promised to always be there for one another but now he felt helpless. *Is he injured somewhere? Has Ludii taken him?*

Chapter 30
We Mog at Ten Tonight

Rolfo left the church and returned to the excitement of watching the encampment with labored steps. The merriment of the music, dancing and campfires temporarily soothed his bruised feelings. The Zingari saw him watching, recognized him as a kindred soul, fed him, talked with him and invited him to travel with them when they broke camp. He accepted. Rome did not hold much promise for him. His family vanished; he did not know where to look.

"...And your name is Rolfo Roma. You even have a name that sounds like you belong. You are one of us, no?" said their leader, Prince Swar, a tall, cocoa-complexioned man, narrow shouldered and wearing an open-to-the-waist voluminous white shirt. It was topped by a gray tabard over fawn-colored breeches. Rolfo admired the man's finely tooled shiny black boots and belt.

Rolfo nodded and gave a slight smile.

"I'll get my blanket from the bridge."

He returned to the blazing campfire. Only once had he felt he really belonged: when Gian had taken him in. He tried not to think of Gian or the boys—Angelo, with blue eyes and blond curls framing his angelic face; Carmine, painfully slight, but the heartiest eater of all with ebony eyes blinking from a thin face; Davide, a perfect child with swarthy complexion and a penchant for chasing bugs; and last, but certainly not least, rotund little Mario, who greeted each day with abundant enthusiasm. He hoped they were not being mistreated. *Why did they leave me? It must really be for some horrible reason.* He pulled the blanket around his shoulders and watched the glowing embers.

"We will mog at 10 o'clock tonight," Prince Swar said in a low voice as he leaned into the campfire circle. LaLa, Prince Swar's wife, made a place in the back of her wagon for Rolfo. He wondered why she had her own wagon.

The caravan rumbled north in the shroud of night. He thought he was beyond crying, but tears stained his face. He could only hope what life had in store for him now...only hope.

Meanwhile, Gian stood on the balcony and wondered where in this big city Rolfo could be. They had vowed to be there for one another. *Rolfo had been there for me when Papa was in prison. Why could I not be here for Rolfo now? Did Ludii come and find him? We have food and beds. What if he is somewhere hurt?* His throat tightened.

By the time Father Bocchetti arrived at the bridge again, the Zingari and Rolfo were making camp near a mountain-protected waterfall with an inviting cave. He said a prayer for Rolfo and returned to his church.

Rolfo's candle flickered wildly as he probed deeper into the cavern behind the falls. Something skittered by him; a tiny Italian cave salamander. *What a prize this would be for Davide.* He thought of his bridge family and wiped tears before returning to the encampment.

Prince Swar appeared in the clearing as Rolfo approached.

"Good morning, my little friend. Did you sleep well?"

Rolfo remembered nothing of his exhaustion-induced sleep in the back of LaLa's wagon while they traveled, but he nodded.

"Rolfo, the ponies need water. Are you strong enough to carry the buckets or would you like to lead them two at a time to the waterfall?"

The boy's face mirrored apprehension, but he said, "I am strong enough to carry buckets."

The brimming buckets stretched his knotty biceps until they ached, but the ponies were soon watered. His fear of horses would eventually disappear.

Delicious smells emanated from the bubbling cauldrons. Gypsy women served Rolfo seconds of thick stew full of wild onions and field mushrooms he had helped gather. He dipped black bread in the stew and washed it down with goat's milk coffee sweetened with honey.

"I can help clean up," Rolfo said.

"No," LaLa answered. "This is women's work. You may bring us two buckets of water from the falls in the morning. That will be a help."

She placed a hand on her hip and appraised Rolfo from head to toe. He felt uncomfortable.

"Be sure to catch it dropping from the falls above and not in the pool below where you water the horses and we wash. There it is *marhime*, unclean."

He explored the cave and waterfall again, watched birds and rabbits with rapt attention and became drowsy from the soft murmur of the wind-caressed trees. Prince Swar roused him from a grassy knoll.

"You will sleep in my wagon, Rolfo. Here is a nice bed for you."

Rolfo shuddered, thoughts of past sleeping arrangements haunting him.

"It is a very nice bed, Prince Swar, but could I sleep under the wagon so that I might watch stars?"

"Sure, I like to watch stars myself and the heavens smile on us tonight."

Rolfo watched through the wagon wheels as the agile man spread a thick quilt on the grass then smoothed a lighter eiderdown coverlet with multi-colored yarn ties on top of that.

Is he going to lie down with me? Rolfo felt sick and blanched.

"Here is your bed," said Prince Swar. "I sleep in my wife's wagon, so mine is yours anytime you'd rather sleep there. When we mog, she has to drive."

Rolfo watched him disappear into LaLa's wagon.

"Tank you," he called and ducked under the covers. Prince Swar returned and placed his hand on Rolfo's shoulder, who sat bolt upright and threw back the cover. "Here is your blanket my little friend. Good night, sleep well."

Rolfo's heart still pounded when LaLa neared silently. He jerked away when she looped a red scarf around his neck.

"What are you doing?" he cried, throwing the scarf off.

"Tie that in a knot," she said, unfazed. "We're closer to the mountains. It will keep the cold away." She handed him something black. "And put this on. It belonged to my brother before he joined the Spanish Army."

She looked at his scruffy shoes but said nothing.

"Tank you."

She did not answer. He smiled and slipped into the much-too-large military-style coat with gold braid on the cuffs. It reminded him of the ones he had seen policemen in Rome wear.

"I will shorten it for you tomorrow," she said.

Arms crossed, he rubbed both sleeves, smiled again, then darted beneath the wagon and his snug covers. Violin music lulled him into the most restful sleep he had ever known.

The plaintive cooing of mourning doves roused him before dawn. He scurried past the string of ponies, startled them and raced to the falls to fill the wooden buckets.

Awakened by the ponies' neighing, Prince Swar walked the perimeter of the camp. Rolfo returned with LaLa's water. She took the water without speaking, handed Rolfo bread with crisply cooked meat on top and a cup of dark, sweetened coffee. Did he finally have a family, something to make him feel like he belonged? He had lost Sofia, Gian, Davide, Mario, Carmine and Angelo. Who or what would be next?

The gypsy children had begun to talk to him and it pleased him, but he felt like a grown man and their games seemed foolish. He must help provide food, not waste time.

Rolfo discarded his remnants of shoes in favor of perfectly tooled Moroccan leather boots Prince Swar gave him before they mogged. He rubbed them and looked at the distorted reflection staring back from their shiny black surface.

Camp broke and they headed toward France. Sitting proudly on the wagon seat next to Prince Swar, Rolfo pulled his coat tighter against the morning chill. *I don't want LaLa to make it smaller. I like it big.*

Prince Swar purposely chose the Ligurian Sea route, where excited travelers snapped up their wares and services, but ominous clouds lurked behind mountains and dogged their progress.

Chapter 31

The Coastal Route Near Piombino, Later that Day

A chevron of sheldrakes winged overhead, storm petrels wave-dipped and chattered. Herons, egrets and bitterns busied themselves feeding. Rolfo observed in minute detail these wonderful sights, listened to their discordant orchestration and felt glad to be alive.

A booming, "Prince Swar!" ended his reverie.

The powerfully built owner of the voice grabbed the lead horses' bridles and brought them to a sudden halt. His vivid red shirt, billowing gray trousers, black mustache and flowered sash made him look evil to Rolfo. He did not like this man. *He is the same size as Ludii.*

"Ah, Malik, who but you has a voice that can frighten leaves from the trees? What can I do for you?"

"No, it is what I can do for you, my friend. I will take those pathetic horses from you. Are they all dead with old age and blind, or just these two?" he said, motioning toward the string of ponies and standing in front of a phalanx of men who unified their ranks into a wedge.

"They were sired by King Ferdinand of Spain's prized stallion, *Westwind*, and they are already promised."

"I do you a favor," Malik said. "They will not live to make it to the promised land."

"The ponies are not for sale. Turn loose of my team, old friend."

"As you wish," said Malik, releasing his grip and running his fingers through his thick, black, shoulder-length hair, throwing his head at a haughty tilt as a final insult. He patted a side dagger and stepped away. The caravan left an angry Malik and his cohorts standing in the rut-deepened road. Rolfo took a long deep breath and exhaled when the road snaked and the disgruntled band faded from sight.

Noontime came fast, and Prince Swar halted and signaled for the seven other wagons to stop near a stream. The sun mottled shadows on the weary entourage through the canopy of trees. A brisk wind quelled the first two efforts at fire-making by LaLa and the other women.

Prince Swar motioned to Rolfo.

"Come, I show you how to water horses. Here, take this rope. He won't hurt you. See how gentle these big beasts are?"

Rolfo's heartbeat quickened. *Stay calm.* Each led a single pony to be watered until only two of the eleven remained.

"Now, you take both of these by their reins. I'm here with you...easy... that's good. You did well."

Rolfo beamed. He had done well. No one had ever told him that except Sofia when she taught him to read. He and his bridge family struggled to get enough food to fill their grumbling innards for one more day. There was never time for *you did well,* only d*o we have enough to go around?* More often than not, they didn't, so he and Gian went without.

"*Patshiv!* It is time for *Patshiv!*"

The call announced celebrations held between tribes to ensure friendship. Malik's voice thundered into the quiet encampment. Bear trainers with their chained lumbering beasts, musicians, women bearing kettles of food on poles, disheveled children and the remainder of his degenerate posse swarmed the campsite.

Before long, with the meal well underway, a smiling Malik and others of his tribe mingled with Prince Swar's band.

"This gold necklace would please your woman, Prince Swar, and look at this net. You could weave strips of cloth through it to block the boiling sun when you are camped. Both of these prizes for a cask of oil."

LaLa immediately pulled her husband behind her sister Tanya's wagon. "Do not trade with them, my husband. He is bi-lacio, no good. You know he is a thief."

"I know, but he saved my life when we were young. Maybe they *do* need olive oil."

"We are in Italy. Why do they not trade with someone else? You know the necklace and net are worth more than the oil. He is up to something."

"I know, but he tried to get the ponies and I refused. I have to trade with him now or he will lose face with his people."

LaLa's skirts swished with her sudden turn and she rejoined the kitchen-under-the-skies workers, but side-glanced to see Prince Swar completing the trade. She muttered something about Malik's people "being cruel and keeping bears to earn money instead of working for it."

Rum-soused Malik loitered all afternoon, taking advantage of the forced hospitality and amusing the children with his concertina, oblivious to nasty looks from LaLa. His music soon ceased and his clan, not noticing him asleep under a wagon, drifted away in small groups, cask suspended from a pole.

"Prince Swar, we will stay here for the night?"

"No, Rolfo, we mog as soon as the women are finished."

"But Malik is still here. His friends left him sleeping."

"Well, wake him up," said Prince Swar, returning to his wagon.

Rolfo sidled toward a groggy Malik and poked him in the back with a stick.

"Malik."

He groaned, but did not rise. Rolfo poked again. Same groan.

"Malik."

No response. He nearly heaved from the alcohol stench. Rolfo returned to Prince Swar. "I can't wake him."

"Kalahn, Yesef, put him in the last wagon with the net. We cannot leave him here alone. He will be jailed. We will take him to his people."

"Why will he be jailed? I saw drunk men in Rome all the time and they were not jailed."

"Rolfo, different rules apply to Roms. We are not like other people. It is sad, but it is true."

Wagons in line, Prince Swar driving in lead gave the signal to mog. Two sudden cracks before they had gone fifty yards and his wagon tilted precariously to the right side. Prince Swar scooped his sinewy arm around Rolfo, steadied the team with his other and braced his boots securely against the inside front of the wagon. Drivers from the other wagons leaped down to right the crippled one. LaLa ran from her wagon and stared at her husband through tearful eyes

"There is no worry. I am fine." He lowered Rolfo and swung himself down. "And so is Rolfo, right?" he said, roughing Rolfo's dark curls and tipping LaLa's nose with his index finger.

"This wheel was replaced in Rome," Prince Swar said. "See the sawdust on the hub?"

The men exchanged knowing glances.

"Are you sure?"

"Yes, I do it myself, Kalahn."

"Look, it has been sawed in two," Yesef added.

"Both of these wheels have been weakened by a saw."

"That is why Malik played his concertina so loud, to drown out the sawing noise," Yesef said.

"Your woman was right. We should never trade with him. She always say that."

Repairs made, two hours later they head toward Piombino. As they approach town, two riders with a local official meet them.

"There's the Zingari who stole our fishing net," said one.

"My son saw him," said the other

"You're all under arrest until we can learn what happened," said the brow-mopping official. More townspeople joined the fray in progress. Rolfo's heart sank. Would he be jailed as Gian's father was? His stomach knotted as he imagined himself isolated from other humans, or worse, locked away with Luddi. He felt faint, then had a prolonged coughing attack. A woman gave him a cup of water.

"Tank you."

"There is the man who stole my father's net," a young villager said, pointing to the sleepy Malik, who was climbing from the last wagon to see what was happening

The crowd cried, "Hang him!"

Two townspeople pounced on Malik and pinned his arms back. He jerked an arm free and grabbed for his knife. The crackle of Prince Swar's horse whip stopped and his whip-welted hand dropped the knife. He tried to run, but the whip cracked again, wrapping around both ankles and bringing him to the ground. The crowd forced him down and sat on him.

"This man and his people have caused us much trouble. Your net is in the wagon at the end. See if it is not in good repair," Prince Swar said.

The fishermen slowly examined the net and nodded that it was. Prince Swar stood over Malik, produced the gold necklace from the pouch and handed it to the perspiring official.

"We have taken far too much of your valuable time. Perhaps your wife will forgive our intrusion on the Sabbath with this presentation of a small gift."

Prince Swar used his out-in-the-world language, not his Gypsy patois, and hoped that the official actually had a wife.

"But, but...what about this man...and what he did?" The official asked.

Prince Swar behaved as the prince he truly was. He looked him squarely in the eyes and said, "We will mete out punishment befitting the crime. He is not one of us, but we feel responsible for his actions. We are simply pilgrims on our way to Mont Saint Michel to worship."

He lied. They'd never go near the ancient abbey.

The townspeople nodded in agreement, not necessarily because they were a genial bunch, but because the stolen item had been returned and they were not anxious to have the gypsies remain in town.

Malik protested loudly against being manacled to the wagon as they headed north toward France. Prince Swar ignored him.

"I am a leader of men. This is how you treat me? Me, who saved your life?!"

Rolfo's tender ears should never have heard Malik's ranting. Prince Swar said nothing, but when the caravan finally stopped, he explained Malik's punishment.

Chapter 32
The Cross

The maritime route proved advantageous with the influx of visitors during this golden time of year, but fog choked the coastal way, forcing the caravan to make camp. The wagons settled in a copse of birch trees tinged with yellow about one hundred yards from the road

Prince Swar ordered Malik to help with the meal.

"I will not. That is the work of women. I will not help them."

"Yes, you will, or you will not eat. You had no respect for our safety, so we have no respect for your position. Now get out of that wagon and start a fire."

Malik scrambled from the wagon, chains dangling and clanking.

"But I save your life once...and this is how you thank me?"

"I saved you from being hanged when we go into Piombino. We are even."

"You are a *Beng*, Prince Swar, a Beng."

"I may be a Satan. Now get busy."

Sullen Malik's effort was half-hearted until Prince Swar's horse whip cracked near his backside, increasing his lackluster effort to double cadence. They prepared the thick breakfast pancake, bokoli, with chunks of meat in record time.

Miles away from the forest, news of the bakery in Rome reopening soon had the neighborhood abuzz. It had been closed since the former owner learned of his son's skullduggery.

"Hoist it higher on the left, good...no down a little...there...perfect," said proud owner Lorenzo Prudore. A large, white sign with black letters read: *Panifio Prudore e Figli,* Bakery of Prudore & Sons.

Lorenzo moved back a few steps into the street, admiring his shop and wiping unseen tears away with a giant knuckle. He reached down to hug his boys, then screamed. "Look out!" as a carriage bore down on him, stopping inches away.

Black taffeta billowed and an embarrassed matron rushed to the children.

"Oh! I'm so sorry, my liveryman said this horse was too high-spirited for me. Are you injured?"

She brushed graying hair from her temples and held her cheeks with both hands.

Lorenzo inventoried the children and said, "We are in fine health. My sons—my sons —and I are in fine health."

He repeated to emphasize "sons" and the fact that all was right in his world more than to allay the women's fears.

He dismissed his neighbors' help with a handshake. The children jumbled into the piazza, giggling and chattering, oblivious to the danger they had just avoided.

"You are coming to my humble bakery? I am honored, Signora."

She stepped inside.

"Where are your wares, Signore?"

"I have bread baked only for my family, as we are not yet open. We will have bread in two days."

"My servant Artur once worked with you here. He tells me your bread recipe is the best in all of Rome."

"Artur was a good man. I cannot take credit for the recipe. It was my grandmother's," said Lorenzo, adding, "Do you have a big family?"

"No, my family is either with or serving the Lord. I am alone, but I often entertain. I am Signora Catarina Rolfolini and I will return in two days, Signore Prudore, with a less eager horse."

Lorenzo mulled over "with or serving the Lord" and considered himself fortunate, indeed.

In the woods, the gypsies took advantage of an isolating fog to produce goods for eager sojourners still crowding the road. Prince Swar positioned a mandrel in a vise with care, looped shiny metal over it and began to fashion a gold ring. Rolfo watched in quiet, wide-eyed amazement. He had seen him shape horseshoes on his anvil, but never witnessed any task as delicate as this.

"Would you like to try one?"

"Could I?"

"Certainly. Here," the Prince said, handing him a metal loop.

Rolfo eagerly placed the annular gold over the mandrel and began to create a simple ring— the first step of a journey that would ultimately take him halfway around the world.

Prince Swar put his tools away, then noticed Rolfo fumbling with a cross.

"Where did you get that? May I see it?"

Rolfo pushed it into his pocket and backed away. He didn't want to show it to anyone because they would ask him where he got it and he didn't know.

"I'll return it to you. I only want to look at it. It seems to be broken."

Reluctantly, Rolfo handed his cherished cross to Prince Swar nodding.

Much later Prince Swar returned the cross. He'd replaced the original, soiled ribbon with a handsome gold chain and anchored Rolfo's treasure in a tiny, filigree frame.

The young man was thrilled with the refurbished cross.

"You put my name on the back! Tank you."

"No, I didn't put your name on it. When I cleaned it, the letters were already there."

Did Ludii give this to me? Puzzled, Rolfo wondered if Ludii had cut other words off.

They camped another day in the same area and before nightfall the fog lifted. Their next stop in Roman ruins resembled a small village overrun by vines near a boscage and rushing stream. Malik's clanging pots announced the morning. Seagulls chattered, screeched and swooped, begging scraps.

With labored breath, Rolfo scurried to get water for LaLa, a task he always performed unless Prince Swar needed him. On returning, he said to no one in particular, "France is beautiful."

LaLa continued her work but her sister Tanya smiled, and Malik overheard. He turned the roasting spit of goat and jeered.

"Beautiful...ha! What are we now? Tyrols, Italians, Frenchmen? It does not matter where we are. Beautiful, indeed. We will always have a life that is hard. We are Roms. We are free to roam so we can decide where we want our lives to be hard."

He forced a laugh.

"Just do not let us stray into Romania," he said, wagging a finger. When they hung our Anton last year, he left a woman and three babies."

Hot grease dripped from the meat and sizzled on the embers below.

"What did you do?" asked a captivated Rolfo.

"We left," Malik shrugged. "But I sneaked back and poisoned a flock of their sheep. Let them think it was the evil eye."

"I do not believe in the evil eye," Tanya said through clenched teeth. "Quit filling his head with nonsense."

Malik ignored her and directed his next comment to Prince Swar.

"You keep me shackled to your wagon like a dog. When I get loose, I may bite somebody."

He strained and stretched his chain closer to them and gave a low growl.

"You will be freed as soon as we can find your people. Someone might kill you if we left you to fend for yourself."

Malik moved the roasted goat to an enormous pan and stashed a large slice of meat in a heavy canvas bag under his shirt.

Ominous clouds and turbulence turned an arid day to black turmoil, hurtling firewood and cooking utensils airborne. Poppy petals created a red snowstorm.

"A *mistral* is upon us!" Tanya shouted.

"Get in the wagon, Malik. Look at that cloud," Prince Swar yelled.

"LaTusche! LaTusche!" the children screamed in gypsy patois for "dark" as they sought safety under an almost sand-cached bridge that had survived since Rome ruled the world.

Dust-laden wind grated in the Gypsies throats; oppressive, choking wind, dancing in eddies along the rocky shore. It tugged at the children's faces like a potter working clay. The sudden squall clawed at their clothes as if to undress them.

Rolfo watched the men lash down the tents and frap the wagons to trees. He tried to help.

"Join the other children. Go quickly, Rolfo."

"But the horses and goats..."

"We're taking care of them. Go."

He fought his way to the protected bridge area where the other children had taken refuge from the gnashing gusts. Then the wind stopped, and a soft rain fell for hours, cleansing some of the grit. One baby goat died. One wagon was damaged. Then all was calm, and all were safe. No horses were lost. They peered out and joined in salvaging the drenched and disarrayed encampment.

Malik escaped. He sat wet and bedraggled, hidden in a rock crevasse until night, gnawing on the huge slice of roasted goat like an angry rodent. After the caravan mogged, he beat the remaining ankle restraint with a rock until it broke.

"Signore Prudore, I have neither children nor grandchildren," Signora Rolfolini began, placing a hand on his arm to get his undivided attention. "So I would not dare to dictate how you raise your sons."

Lorenzo stopped arranging bread, gestured for her to sit and eased himself to a long bench near the bakery's front door. Gian assisted the steady stream of customers. *What am I doing wrong?* Lorenzo thought and dusted flour from his hands.

"Your sons need education. My plan would take away your little assistants, but I am prepared to loan you Artur. I will continue to pay his salary, and he already knows the business. The boy's schooling I will also pay for."

"It's too much to think about. I cannot allow you to spend your money." Lorenzo rose to return to work. She stood and stared at him.

"But I am an old woman. Should I die tomorrow, what good is my wealth, if I have not used it to benefit anyone but myself?"

He thought of his own lack of education and said, after a long pause, "but I know I will be able to pay Artur very soon myself. Do you want to ask my sons?"

"If you like." She smiled and tossed her fringed, black shawl around her shoulders.

"I would like for you to do so. Please ask them. They are in the cortile."

Lorenzo motioned for Gian to join Signora Rolfolini and the other children.

"...and your papa says that you may go to school," said the Signora with a smile. "Would you like that?"

Her words were greeted with a mixture of bewilderment and more smiles.

Gian thought of snobbish, slick-haired sissies he has seen in black suits, wearing stupid looking hats and shiny shoes. Angelo wondered if he could learn to build buildings. Carmine blinked but looked pleased. Davide didn't understand what school is, but tried to look pleased. Mario didn't understand either but gave a loud "si!" to her question and did an impromptu dance—just because he is always happy.

The Prudore sons began school the next week. Gian excelled in math and soon made trips to the bank for his papa wearing a black suit with his hair slicked down. Angelo, about seven, still looked after Davide, made good grades and drew countless buildings. Davide, about six, amazed his teachers with his knowledge of nature and absorbed all learning. Mario, about five, proved to be the school favorite with both students and teachers in spite of having a bit of the truant in him. Carmine, about eight, continued to watch over Mario, proving to be a good student in all areas. His nervous blinking all but disappeared.

"It has been three months now, Signora Rolfolini," Lorenzo told his smiling patroness one beautiful spring day. "I can at last pay Artur myself, and today I am hiring another assistant."

Gian waved from the back.

"Your help has been greatly appreciated by me and my sons."

Signora Rolfolini smiled, giving Lorenzo a large order and admonishing him, saying, "Don't you get so busy that I can no longer buy all the bread and pastries I want. I've told all my friends this is the best bakery in Rome. That may have been my undoing."

Lorenzo assured her that would never be the case and she watched Gian place baked goods in her baskets and remembered the face and dark eyes of her own two-year-old grandson, Vittorio, those years ago. *Would he have been as tall as Gian?"*

Chapter 33
Larissa's Confession

Prince Swar's *Kumpania*, that traveling group, ventured to many countries. He and LaLa took pride in the quickness with which Rolfo grasped languages where they visited. His infectious smile increased their revenue by putting clients at ease. He grew quite tall but remained slim. More than one anxious father admonished his daughter for eyes lingering too long on "that gypsy boy."

Far away at Ruvasha Plantation, J.P.. greeted Tedelia, saying, "I almost forgot to tell you about seeing Luther in town yesterday. He told me Larissa is due this afternoon on the *China Rose.*"

Beyond the parlor, Gilbert LeFleur pretended to have not overheard this information, went upstairs, dressed with care and returned smiling.

"It's close to the noon hour, but don't set a place for me. I have business in New Orleans. And don't wait supper for me. Do you need anything from town?'

"No, Papa."

"No, Papa Gilbert."

"Thank you for asking. Cook's making cherry pie. I'll save you a piece."

"You do that, Tedelia, you do that," he said, wagging his finger at her like a metronome, smiling and sprinting to his carriage like a man thirty years younger.

He had been thirty years younger when he first saw Larissa, but he'd married Katté at eighteen and become a father before his nineteenth birthday.

Alone with a three-year-old when their paths first crossed, Larissa had enchanted him; a beautiful, doe-eyed creature who parted her dark hair in the middle and looked like a child. *Heck, she was a child; sixteen years old.* By the time he reached New Orleans, Gilbert had remembered every detail of their long-ago love affair.

A sudden squall sent the *China Rose* off course and delayed its arrival by several hours.

Luther waited until nightfall and planned to send Hatch home with the carriage when he spotted Gilbert LeFleur in a sidewalk cafe.

"Mister LeFleur, how fortunate to see you. I was about to send Hatch home and spend the night in the city. My mother was due on the *China Rose,* but it has not arrived. Would you be so kind as to tell Camille I won't be coming home, so that my servant and I both might remain here?"

"My boy, I'd be happy to, but my business has not been concluded and I'll be forced to stay the night here myself."

"Well, I'll just send Hatch on with the message to Camille."

"I think I have a plan that will work for both of us. You take a message back to Ruvasha that I'm delayed and I'll stay and bring your mother home when her ship arrives."

"That's very kind of you. Camille has never been alone at night since her accident. I hate to be away."

"I understand, my boy. Happy to do it. You go home. When you see my children, tell Tedelia to give you that piece of cherry pie she was saving for me."

The crew repaired sails as the *China Rose* bobbed and creaked. At last the sea returned to normal. On deck, Larissa found the Big Dipper right where she had left it the night before. Suffering from a bit of seasickness, Ilana Richilene remained in their cabin below.

Father Prejean, a fellow passenger, joined Larissa. He had many questions about this country where his new assignment was taking him.

"Look, Father, a shooting star. Does it really mean that someone just died?"

"My dear Mrs. Arceneaux...may I call you Larissa?" he began in his heavy Irish brogue. "If we are to be superstitious, is it not as easy to think someone just became an angel or that a baby was born? Perhaps a soul did enter the Great Beyond, but I don't think the master plan includes celestial fireworks for the just departed."

"You're right, Father," she said with a laugh. "It is just as easy to think of happy things."

"I could be sad at leaving Paris."

He was.

"It was my second home. I am going to a new home, a new parish, but many of my former Irish countrymen will be in New Orleans, so I will not be sad."

He thought of County Limerick, the view from St. Basil's of Castle Blakeney, green meadows, stone fences, thatched roofs, shepherd's pie...especially shepherd's pie.

"It saddened me to leave Louisiana ten years ago, but I found a wonderful life in Paris." Larissa's words intruded.

He came back to the conversation.

"Why did you leave New Orleans?"

"Will this be treated as confidentially as confession?"

"If that is what you wish, Larissa."

"My son fell in love with a beautiful...fairytale princess. A fair-haired girl from Memphis, Tennessee, originally from England. Soon after they announced their engagement, I moved into town to have wedding clothes made and became fast friends with Erik and Ilana Richilene. They liked my clothing suggestions, so they asked me to go to Paris to work for them."

"This surely is not confessional information."

"Oh, but this may be," she said. "When the new queen comes in, the old queen needs to leave the hive."

"Ah, that is more confessional material," he said, smiling. Sensing Larissa's pensiveness required solitude, he decided against more questions. "Goodnight, Larissa."

"Goodnight, Father."

Although sea spray rendered her face sticky, she licked her salty lips, knew she couldn't sleep, and stayed on deck in deep thought.

What had Marcel Arceneaux thought when he had seen Gilbert at her wilderness home, her father's neck veins bulging and her crying? She had so many unanswered questions from years ago. Marcel had died without revealing his thoughts. She knew about his family, but very little about the man she'd been married to when she gave birth to two children and helped found a plantation.

Arriving in 1785 with the second wave of Acadians banished from Nova Scotia, the Arceneaux had wisely chosen not to build in New Orleans proper, for in 1788 raging fire devoured the sturdy buildings in the city like acid-drizzled silk, sparing nothing but the brick and tile Ursuline Convent. Perhaps this was the Almighty's way of cleansing the mosquito-infested city of those pests that showed no mercy in killing low- or high-born alike.

Bosolét Parish appeared to be a safe haven and the Arceneaux family prospered, some trapping, but mostly farming. Wild fruits and berries contributed to their well-being. Then both parents and Marcel's brother died of cholera. Marcel managed quite well, but longed for human contact. Larissa's father spoke French and Russian. Marcel spoke French and English and they communicated as good neighbors and assisted one another with repairs and crops. She knew of Marcel's inventiveness and her father was a man of the soil. He understood the earth and what it had to offer, but Marcel would rise from farmer to plantation owner by exploiting the earth and its resources to the fullest extent.

Why am I thinking of my so-long-ago life? Marcel is dead and gone. There is no way I can ever know what he thought about Gilbert LeFleur back then. I have Stefan now. Nothing else matters, not really. Below deck, Larissa placed a damp cloth on her cabin mate's forehead, but knew little else could be done to make Ilana comfortable.

She rested against pillows in her stateroom and continued an attempt to dissect her thoughts. *How will I feel about New Orleans? I'm sure to see Gilbert. I wish I wouldn't.*

Chapter 34

The China Rose Is Dockin'

In New Orleans' Vieux Carré, Gilbert LeFleur anxiously called to a young child running errands who stopped and smiled.

"Yessir?"

"Boy, you wait on the docks and tell me when the *China Rose* makes port."

The child gleefully clutched the coins he'd just been given and headed for the waterfront. Gilbert re-entered the Hotel St. Louis at Royal and St. Louis streets, removed his silk hat—beaver had gone out of vogue—and settled onto a tapestry chair, nervously tapped his black lacquered cane on the marble floor and fingered the handle's gold crest.

His apprehensive thoughts returned to those of many years ago when he had delayed being candid with Larissa's parents for fear of losing her. It would probably have made little difference, if their love for one another had been out in the open sooner, but how could he explain a wife in an asylum, a three-year-old son, and convince them his intentions toward their daughter were completely honorable? He wanted to marry Larissa and the laws in other countries would allow him to do so, but Louisiana's laws prohibited such actions.

He had agonized over the proper way to present this in the most favorable light.

"I'll go back to Switzerland, divorce Katté on grounds of insanity, but see that she is cared for and then return for Larissa..."

He was rejected...and Marcel Arceneaux wandered up with a basket of wild grapes. Marcel, the final victor.

Oh, to live life over. I'd have kidnapped Larissa and eloped to Europe. Her father rejected me; now I have only memories.

"Mister LeFleur," the young messenger called in a sing-song. "The *China Rose* is dockin'."

Gilbert watched sweat trickle down the freckled face of the young boy at the hotel's door, thanked him and bounded to his carriage for the short ride. Man-made cotton bale mountains waited for transport to exotic ports. Smells of coffee, baked goods, fish and rain-freshened flowers overwhelmed his senses.

Larissa's first view of the Vieux Carré from the ship's deck was a wisteria-framed vignette resembling a decorated cake. Carefree Paris seemed drab by comparison. The vitality of New Orleans continued to fascinate her, this polyglot of nationalities held tightly together by lacy wrought-iron balconies (*galleries* to Orleanians), indescribable food, determination, and lush bougainvillea draping courtyards and spilling onto sidewalks, or banquettes, as the Creoles called them.

Gilbert's pounding heart throbbed his temples. Larissa's eyes shone like faceted jet. *She looks so tiny.* Sedate, composed, yet when she smiled at him, his insides crumbled as sandcastles in an encroaching tide. He rushed to the gangplank and grasped her valise. *Stay calm.*

"Hello, Larissa. Luther asked me to bring you home to Vermillion Hall."

"Hello, Gilbert. You're looking well."

She, too, had a pang of long ago, but recovered enough to fumble with introductions. She felt so strange to introduce him as her friend to Father Prejean. *Friend. What an odd name to have to call him, but what else is he? Nothing.*

"You are the first person I have met in my new country. I shall always remember you."

"I'm honored, Father. Please call on me at the LeFleur Plantation, Ruvasha, if I might assist you in your work."

"I am the one who is honored, Oh, I see my little welcoming party."

He waved to a gaggle of nuns and priests only a few yards away.

"Goodbye, ladies, sir."

An entourage of Richilene employees met Ilana with three carriages, waiting for her French creations eager patrons anticipated with bated breath.

"Hello, Gilbert, goodbye Gilbert. Come to dinner soon. Goodbye, Father, Larissa. Lovely crossing."

She made a horrible face alluding to her unfortunate sea sickness.

They were alone. The carriage ride brief, too brief. Now silence begged for conversation. Two maisonette house servants greeted them at the door, took her luggage and invited them in.

Delicious strawberry tarts and coffee soon filled a marble-topped table to overflowing. Gilbert seated himself and Larissa vanished into another room to return shortly. Gilbert ignored the refreshments, helped himself to a stiff drink, and tried to stay calm.

He stood and took both her hands in his.

"It's been so long. I've never stopped loving you."

He swooped her into a sudden embrace and hungrily sought her mouth. She recoiled as if burned.

"Miss Larissa, your trunk's here."

The startled pair regained their composure.

"Thank you. Tilly, please, have them take it to my room."

Again, the coffee and tarts left untouched. Gilbert poured himself a second large glass of whiskey, gulped it down, stood and used one of the dainty, white napkins to mop his usually dry brow.

"Would you like some more coffee before we leave?" she pretended.

"No, thank you. I think not."

He dropped the crumpled napkin onto the table.

Standing as a soldier at attention, he helped Larissa into the open carriage, fearful of making another awkward move. They headed for Vermillion Hall.

At the Arceneaux Plantation, Camille strained to maneuver her wheelchair from the caged brass lift, a prototype of the elevator that Luther had devised.

"Besa, help me!" she screeched, snatching the elaborate comb from her flowing blonde hair and throwing it across the room.

Besa raced from the dining room to assist. More than once servants and Besa had hurried to whisk away evidence of broken vases, hand mirrors and other Camille projectiles. She calculated for Luther never to be around when these outbursts occurred.

Most plantation owners allowed Sunday afternoon outings to Congo Square where freedmen and slaves, all people of color, met to play music, dance, barter their wares and exchange gossip. Camille did not allow these outings. Her servants longed for the days when Larissa had been mistress of Vermillion Hall. Camille held the plantation in a vise as cold and unfeeling as the metal on the wheelchair confining her.

This day was no different. Camille dreaded seeing Larissa. She loathed her, loathed her as only a woman can hate another who holds the key to her innermost secrets.

Why did the peasant have a mother who is so in control of her own life? Why didn't my mother have control? My life would have been so different.

We'd not had to have left England. I could have married someone my equal, someone with a title, and enjoyed things in life that mean nothing to these Barbarians of the Bayous. I, I, who am descended from the House of York.

Chapter 35
The Ring

Summer had not yet assaulted New Orleans. The broad boulevard and gentle breeze reminded Larissa of Paris...and Stefan...dependable Stefan...constant Stefan.

"What is my grandson like, Gilbert?"

"He's my grandson's best friend. They're together all the time," he said, not adding, *when Camille has not forbidden it.* "He spends a lot of time with his dogs." *Camille hates dogs.* "Calls his mother by her first name, the little dickens." *She doesn't deserve to be called mother.*

"Does he look like Luther?"

"Can't say that he does. I've always thought Luther looked like you. No, he doesn't look like Luther."

They sped along the white shell road. A corridor of arched magnolia trees formed an inviting entrance to Ruvasha. Her eyes lingered.

"Your trees have certainly grown taller since I was home."

"Yes, we don't cut them back much because Paul and York like to play soldier in their exposed roots."

York insists that Paul play soldier. There's so much I'd like to say to her.

At a curve, they passed the LeFleur pier across the road from Ruvasha, where a large pale blue boat docked.

"Oh, you have a beautiful boat with 'L' on it for LeFleur."

"Glad you like it. Everyone thinks the 'L' stands for LeFleur, but you and I both know it doesn't. We both know why it's pale blue, too, don't we?"

Larissa turned her gaze from Gilbert and the river and did not answer.

He changed the subject.

"Construction has started on this property," he said, pointing to a new pier. "A Roussel family from Natchez purchased the land. We haven't met them yet. General Roussel is in textiles and I understand he's a former teacher at West Point."

Clouds marbled the azure sky behind Vermillion Hall. Luther, York, Besa, Hatch and other servants crowded the path to greet "Ol' Miss."

"So this is my grandson. What a fine young man you are."

At nine, York was almost as tall as Larissa. He hugged her with enthusiasm.

Uncle Sib, Hatch's uncle, came forward, his battered brown hat in hand. Larissa took his hat and placed two packages of pipe tobacco in it. He took it back and held the brim with both swarthy, work-worn hands like a prospector panning for gold. Overcome with emotion, he said, "sometimes I loses my voice, Miss Larissa. Things ain't like they used to be. Thank ya'."

Larissa patted his shoulder and turned to Besa, hugging her.

"I have gifts in town for all of you, and hard candy for the children. I just didn't want to take time to unpack."

Gilbert cleared his throat.

"I'll be getting back home then. Goodbye, all."

A hoped-for invitation to stay a while didn't come.

"Thank you for bringing my mother from town, Mr. LeFleur."

"Glad to do it, glad to do it."

"Thank you, Gilbert. It was very kind of you to wait for me."

"Anytime, Larissa, anytime."

They watched the carriage until it disappeared from the curve of the long driveway.

"He's a fine man, Mother. It's sad his life took such an unfortunate turn."

"It sure is."

They mounted the marble stairs arm-in-arm to where Camille skulked just inside the door.

"Mother Arceneaux." *She had never called her that.* "We're so sorry the *China Rose* was delayed. This Louisiana heat must be unbearable after living in Paris."

"Oh, I lived here over forty years, Camille."

She bent to kiss Camille lightly on the cheek, which the younger woman received on her raised chin, but did not return.

"So it's not really bad."

Camille muttered inaudibly and Larissa nodded and gave a slight smile. *Better not to pursue this conversation.*

Larissa surveyed the rose garden Marcel had loved where the roses were now white instead of Marcel's favorite color, red. When the ballroom was under construction, she had favored pale blue for the wall covering, but Marcel had again wanted red and that is how Vermillion Hall Plantation got its name.

"Camille changed those years ago, Mother, something about the House of Lancaster using red roses as their symbol and warring with the equally royal Yorks. It was very important to her."

He said nothing about his wife's attempt to have the ballroom redecorated in white silk. That was the only conflict where he had failed to bow to Camille's wishes but remained adamant and her silk purveyor hurried back to New Orleans.

"It really doesn't matter anymore, Luther. Your father has been dead sixteen years now. I had originally wanted the ballroom in pale blue, but red was his favorite color..."

"Red is your son's favorite color, too," Camille said.

"I'm embarrassed; I didn't know. Speaking of your father, he and I planned to free our slaves, then he died and I was flooded with responsibilities and I'm ashamed to admit this, but it became secondary with me having to run the plantation alone. You and I had mentioned it, too."

"Camille and I have tried to discuss this many times, but it always ends in a deadlock."

"That's unfortunate. It's not a necessary institution. There must be a better way to live."

"Camille reminds me she is helpless and needs our servants."

"I see," said Larissa, her conscience aching. *The LeFleurs have employed freed slaves for years. Why can't the Arceneaux?*

Luther gazed toward the long meadow where Camille had her accident nine years ago. took a deep breath and released it with resignation.

"Miss Larissa, Mr. Luther, supper is ready," Besa called from the ballroom doors.

Larissa surveyed the dining table.

"Besa we always ate as a family at mealtime. Where is *your* plate?"

"Vedette needs me in the kitchen, Miss Larissa."

A splendidly appointed table awaited the diners. Luther eased Camille from her wheelchair onto a chair to his right and Hatch seated Larissa to Luther's left. York requested to be moved from his mother's right to sit next to his grandmother. Camille nodded approval with tightened lips. *I had to say yes. Everyone was looking at me. They're always looking at me.*

Besa switched York's place setting.

"May I serve now, Miss Camille?"

"Yes."

First Besa positioned Larissa's plate in front of her, then did the same with York's and Luther's, then served a finger-drumming Camille. *Will that Indian ever get anything right?*

Besa thought, *Camille eats like a bird, picking at her food. She has even begun to look like a bird.*

After supper Larissa removed a diamond and emerald ring from her bejeweled purse and gave it to an astonished York.

"I want you to have this. Some day you can give it to your wife. Put it in a safe place."

She looked at Luther, saying, "Your father gave it to me."

This ring was not on her hand on the ride to Vermillion Hall. She had never worn it since Gilbert gave it to her thirty years ago.

York thanked his grandmother and raced up the stairs to place his treasure in a polished mahogany musical jewelry box she had sent him from Paris two years earlier at Christmas. It played bits of Mozart's opera, "The Magic Flute."

"Mother Arceneaux, isn't he a bit young to have such a valuable item?" Camille purred.

"You may be right, but he seems very responsible. I hope you don't mind him having it this soon."

"No, not really. I just always assumed you would pass something that valuable on to your only son's wife," she said, wiping make-believe tears from her eyes.

Luther clenched his teeth but said nothing.

"Camille, Luther gave you such a lovely ring when you married. I never dreamed you wanted my ring. I did not intend to slight you."

"Luther, push me to the lift. I have a terrible headache. Goodnight," said Camille, pursing her lips and lowering her head to one side without making eye contact with Larissa.

"I'll be back shortly, Mother," Luther said.

I don't remember ever seeing my mother wear that ring.

Upstairs, York surveyed his growing trove: a gold collar button, a small silver pocket knife, a British military medal with an attached blue ribbon once belonging to his Grandfather Crumpton, two red bird feathers, an alligator tooth, and now this gift from his Grandmother Arceneaux. *Why would I ever want to give this ring to a girl? Maybe...if she was as nice as Aunt Besa.* He fell asleep on his bed amid his treasures. The music box gently wound down.

"Miss Larissa, would you like some more coffee?" Besa had heard everything from the doorway.

She brightened and sprang from her chair.

"No, but I would like to walk in the yard some before it gets completely dark. Walk with me?"

"Let me put this tray down when we pass the kitchen. Vedette said she'd finish up for me. She knew I wanted to visit with you."

"What's this business of your not eating with the family?"

"Oh, I'd rather serve good food to people than sit with bad company."

They both laughed, but Larissa was not amused.

Out the back entrance of the great hall and along the herringbone brick walkway toward the slave quarters they meandered.

"Besa, be sure to give the rest of that cake, when morning comes, to the children. It looks as if they are already in for the night."

Past the dog yard, toward the long meadow on the white shell path, the two women strolled.

"Besa, come back to Paris with me when I return to France at the end of the month."

"I can't, much as I would like to. Master York needs me." *I must protect and comfort him.*

"I understand. Besa, what in the world is that? What's out there in the cemetery?" she said, indicating the stone figures looming in the distance.

"That's more of Miss Camille's doing. Italian statues."

Each of twelve vaults was topped with a four-foot angel.

"It looks so strange. It was pretty and simple before."

"Those crypt angels remind me of vultures waiting for the dead." *Vultures with greedy claws and beaks like Camille's.* Besa heaved a heavy sigh.

"I don't want to see any more. Let's go back to the house. I need to return to New Orleans." *I really need to return to Paris. It was a mistake to come here.* Revulsion engulfed Larissa. The desire to see her son and grandson had pushed reason aside, but the reality of Camille became larger than ever. She feared she would never see Luther or York again.

Luther was waiting downstairs when Larissa entered the parlor. His smile lacked enthusiasm.

"Entertaining probably tired Camille more than we realized. I can drive myself back to town. You can stay with her."

When he protested, Larissa said, "I won't have it any other way. That's final."

"Mother, Camille's mother had nothing to leave her when she killed herself. I think your ring was more of a symbol to her than something she really wanted. I'm sorry for her actions. You did the right thing."

York stumbled sleepily from his bedroom to peer through the spindles of the double winding staircase banister.

"Goodnight, Grandmother, thank you again for the ring. Will you come again tomorrow?"

"I don't think I can. There's business in town, and I need to visit Echo Trading Post, also. Goodnight, York. Supper was excellent. Besa, tell Vedette too. Goodnight, Luther. See you in two or three days." She left.

"Master York, wash your feet before you get in that clean bed," Besa called up to him.

"I'll see that he does," said Luther as he climbed the stairs.

"Daddy, Camille said Grandmother owns Echo Trading Post and not Quila. Is that true?"

"Not really, son. It's a complicated business arrangement."

He pulled York's shirt over his head.

"What does complicated mean?" York knew. He was pushing.

"It means, in this case, that your Grandmother and Quila have an arrangement that is not actually on paper, but both parties—that means Grandmother and Quila—have agreed on certain terms. Like a deal that they have shaken hands on."

"I don't understand. Camille says we should be getting money from Quila because people on Bahkonay trade furs and things with him and he's getting rich from Arceneaux property."

"York, it's not Arceneaux property. Quila just can't have a legal deed to it even though it belongs to him, and he worked for it. Now get those feet washed."

Echo Trading Post remained in York's thoughts for many years. The situation would continue to fester. York splashed his feet in the washbowl Luther placed on the floor. His eyes narrowed. *Quila getting Arceneaux money. It's not right. It's not right.*

"Thank you, Daddy."

Larissa had turned her carriage onto the River Road when someone waving caught her attention and she stopped.

"Miss Larissa, I was down at the sawmill when you got here. I wanted to see you."

"How are you, Uncle Lamb?"

"Oh, passable. You ever wondered how I got my name?"

"Would you like to tell me?" Larissa knew something was amiss. He never made small talk.

"My mammy said I was so dark and had so much hair 'til I looked like a soft little lamb, so that's what she named me."

A big smile played over Larissa's face.

"You know. Mammy worked for Miss Tededia's mama at Chambers Plantation up Baton Rouge way. That Miss Dorothy was a fine lady. She died and we moved to Ruvasha when Miss Tedelia married Mr. J.P.."

He pursed his lips over a huge set of whiskers and started shaking his head.

"At's afore she started all that Cat'lic biness. She was Babtis when she was a girl."

"You're right, she's a Catholic now."

"We shoulda stayed there, Miss Larissa.. The LeFleurs set everybody free. Life here at The Hall ain't like it was, no sir, ain't like it was afore you left."

He almost whispered and cast a furtive glance toward the mansion.

"We never has figured out what religion Miss Camille is," he said with a laugh.

"Uncle Lamb, why *did* you and Hatch come to Vermillion Hall? You were free at Ruvasha."

"My boy Hatch, he wanted to buy a piece of land. Mr. R.C. Zedohr at the bank said he'd loan him half of the money to buy it. The only way we could get the rest was to sell ourselves to you. My brother Sib already lived here. He said you was nice folks."

Larissa wasn't smiling anymore, although she tried to look pleasant. She'd talk with Luther about what conditions were like now.

"I'll be back in two or three days. Thank you for coming to speak to me, Uncle Lamb. Goodnight."

The overwhelming fragrance of magnolia, the welcoming breeze blowing from Lake Pontchartrain, and the hordes of twinkling fireflies surrounding Larissa on her drive back to town reaffirmed why she had made this voyage home. Intoxicating New Orleans would always be just that: intoxicating. *I've been so selfish and blind as to what was happening at Vermillion Hall.*

Chapter 36
Manumitting

Three days later, after an extended visit with the Vermillion namesakes at Echo Trading Post, Larissa made a second trip to Vermillion Hall.

"I'm setting Uncle Lamb free, Luther. Take his papers from our safe and give them to him. He's an old man. He doesn't need to be working at the sawmill anymore."

"Will he stay on here, Mother?"

"No, Quila and Deenah want him to live with them at Echo Trading Post. He can help them; just light duties."

"I've freed Hatch and his Uncle Sib. Hatch wants to stay on to help manage things and Uncle Sib won't leave without Hatch, so they're both going to live here and I'll pay them."

"All the servants are to be allowed trips to Congo Square again. Hatch made a down payment on a piece of land before Camille stopped them from going to sell and barter. He's had no income and stood to lose it with no outlet for his beautiful animal wood carvings. I'd like for you to go to R.C. Zedohr at Creole State Bank and pay it off. We owe it to him."

"I agree, Mother."

"Luther, this is such a small step. We need to do a lot more. What about Vedette?"

"She's free, but she won't leave Besa and Besa has no reason to leave. She's my little sister."

By now they had opened the library safe. Camille wheeled in from her secreted position.

"So this is how you undermine my authority," she said, nostrils flaring.

"This needed to be, Camille. Mother and I talked of it years ago. It's deplorable we waited for so long."

"But, Luther..."

"I don't want to hear any more about it. We'll free ten servants a month until we have gotten to everyone and they may continue to live here if they like. We'll pay them, too, for any labor."

Camille blanched. She'd never seen him this angry. Her wheelchair caught in the library rug. She bumped over it, fuming, and pushed herself to the lift. *They're scheming against me. Tedelia has already asked me to let the boys take their lessons together again at Ruvasha. What are they going to do against me next?*

With this issue settled, Larissa could at last enjoy her return to the lush surroundings she loved, the wondrous bayous. Camille loved nothing; hated her mother-in-law for loving this barbaric wilderness, hated her for knowing Camille's evil heart and hated her for giving birth to the stupid peasant. *She'll be here for a while, then back to Paris. I should be going to Paris, not her. The parties...the music...*

Once a genial community, Vermillion Hall had become a monarchy ruled by a haughty queen on a wheelchair throne.

"I need Besa to care for York," Camille whined. "But Vedette and Minerva don't know the proper way to set a table. Luther."

She continued her diatribes in the little-girl-voice that previously had melted her husband. Once he had been a proud romantic. Now he was almost relegated to lord-in-waiting, but his backbone was not completely gone.

"Besa is not a servant. She is a member of this family. She cares for York because she loves him, the same reason she cooks. She *loves* to cook. It's your job to train Vedette and Minerva the proper way to set a table and quit complaining about it."

Nine-year-old York often seemed detached from reality. Cause and effect proved beyond his comprehension unless it involved some personal acquisition.

A year ago, York had discovered Ruvasha was four feet taller than Vermillion Hall and told Camille. She launched a relentless, wheedling campaign to add another story to their mansion and Vermillion Hall soon had a third floor.

"But it will be so much cooler that high over the river."

Paul LeFleur, York's best—and only—friend, knew and tried to overlook York's shortcomings.

"He didn't mean to push me into that swing, Grandfather. He just doesn't think sometimes," he said, nursing a bruised forehead.

Gilbert LeFleur held his tongue when his grandson came home with injuries, but he knew the situation could not continue. *I'll ask Tedelia to have the boys' tutor come to Ruvasha instead of Vermillion Hall. York likes to play soldier around our magnolia trees, so he'll be happy. Now to convince Camille.*

"Miss Camille isn't able to be up and around whereas I can keep an eye on them," he said reasonably, and Tedelia agreed, despite thinking, *I asked her three weeks ago myself and still don't have an answer.*

Chapter 37

The Vermillion's Daughter

Larissa's invitation to Ilana's dinner party tomorrow night distressed her. She read it and re-read it, dreading the thought of seeing Gilbert again. *Gilbert...kind Gilbert...encumbered Gilbert.* A rap at the maisonette door jarred her back to reality. The young woman standing outside, so polished, so poised, looked familiar, but her silks, satins and sophistication confused Larissa, who just did not recognize her.

"I am Echo, Miss Larissa." Mischief flashed in her eyes.

"This can't be. You're all grown up. How old are you?"

"Almost twenty," said Echo, adjusting her hat veil.

"Oh, Echo, come in, have a seat. I'm shocked. Tilly, please bring us some coffee."

A smiling Larissa continued to shake her head in amazement.

"Mr. Luther stopped by the trading post and told my parents you were here. By then you'd already been to see them."

She eased herself into a chair and removed her hat.

"You look wonderful, just as Deenah and Quila did."

"Yes, they are so well-known in New Orleans I no longer have a name. I am simply 'the Vermillion's daughter.' Did you like the second story they added?"

"Oh, yes." *I forgot to even mention anything to Luther about the third story added to Vermillion Hall.* "Now what have you been doing these last ten years besides becoming beautiful?"

"I attended the Ursuline Convent School and I now work in the Hilon Hospital for Mother Superior, Sister Claire. She came after you left New Orleans. She's from Rome."

"That is wonderful. I'm speechless."

"I must hurry, but I just had to see you. I still have my doll Flower. She sits on my bed, and the bed is a lot longer now. Goodbye, I hope to see you again before you return to Paris."

She hesitated at the door.

"I've heard it is a beautiful place. Maybe someday I shall get to go there."

Larissa curbed the impulse to hug this young woman who stood so erect.

"You just might. Goodbye, my dear. Thank you for coming."

Echo's faint perfume lingered in the room as Larissa watched Echo disappear into the bustle of early morning French Quarter carriage and foot traffic and nodded to her neighbors washing down their banquettes.

Paris...maybe someday I shall get to go there.

Echo's words stayed in Larissa's thoughts. She had never dreamed of seeing Paris, much less Russia, when Ilana had persuaded her to help open the Paris House of Richilene ten years ago, when she had tried to wipe away all memories by leaving New Orleans—all memories of Gilbert LeFleur. Being near Gilbert would always be the deep ravine she must not allow herself to get too close to, ever again.

Chapter 38
Love Is in the Air

Inside the cloistered walls of St Aloysius, Father Patrick Joseph Prejean implored:

"Dear Lord, please open the hearts of these hospitable Orleanians in my new home here and let them see the great need our boys' school has for additional funds. Bless widows and orphans everywhere, the poor, the afflicted, souls in bondage...and protect me, your humble servant, Patrick Prejean, from the sin of gluttony as I go to this feast in the Paris of America. Amen."

Earlier that day at the New Orleans House of Richilene, preparations had wound down for the Sunday evening dinner party tonight. A knock on the door and the servant Mary opened one of the double doors and looked embarrassed. She kept her eyes lowered.

Ilana heard and came to the front as Mary backed away. She smiled and opened the doors wider.

"Well, hello Hatch. We haven't seen you in quite a while."

Hatch's eyes darted after Mary, then finally he said, "Yes ma'am, Miss Ilana. It's me, Hatch Washington comin' with a message from Mr. Luther."

"What's the message?"

"Miss Camille, she don't feel too good. I guess it's the vapors. They won't be comin' to your party, and for me to thank you just the same."

"Well, thank *you* very much for making the trip to tell us. Speaking of health, how is Uncle Lamb doing?"

"Oh, my pappy, he's tolerable."

Ilana nodded.

"Mary, please bring a basket of sweetbreads for Hatch and Uncle Lamb."

Mary returned smiling and handed him a cloth-covered basket. *Hatch Washington is the most perfect young man in Orleans or Tachérie Parish.* He thanked her, smiled, but avoided her gaze and left.

Mary leaned against the closed doors and sighed.

"Miss Ilana, I'll remove two place settings. Miss Camille isn't feeling well...again."

"Pity. I understand Luther rarely gets out anymore."

"Let me take those plates for you. Why don't you lie down for a while before your guests arrive? You look pale. Can I get you anything?"

"No, I guess this is to be expected. I'm just somewhat tired from the trip. Probably too soon to give a dinner party. Don't let me rest more than thirty minutes."

Later that evening at Vermillion Hall, Camille reclined with one of her headaches.

"You're such an angel, Luther," she purred. "I don't know what I'd do without you. I must truly be the luckiest woman in the world. Could you get me another cool cloth for my forehead?'

She closed her eyes for emphasis and touched her brow with her palm.

"You really should have gone to the Richilene's without me."

"I don't ever feel I should leave you alone at night. I'll go downstairs and get your cloth and soak it in well water. It will be nice and cool."

From the kitchen, Luther could hear the dogs, the dogs he loved so much. He remembered watching them weave around Camille when she first visited Vermillion Hall and her saying, "Get those filthy beasts away from me."

He also thought of the many times he'd seen York being cruel to the puppies.

Later, when first penned, their baying was intolerable. They had roamed free for years. Now their playful dispositions soured and fights were commonplace. They bristled when Camille came near, as if they knew she had caused their confinement. He climbed the stairs with false energy, bringing with him a large bowl of cool water and a cloth. Vermillion Hall had once been a happy place...

Larissa now stayed at the Richilene maisonette in town, not at Vermillion Hall, which she loved so much. *What am I doing? It was so easy to think only of Stefan until I actually got here. Now seeing Gilbert, lonely and still so caring, breaks my heart. I don't want to encourage him, but I feel like a girl when I'm in his presence, so giddy, so foolish, so confused.*

"Why can't I get this bracelet fastened?" she blurted.

"Do you need help, Miss Larissa?" Tilly appeared in the doorway.

"Yes," she answered truthfully. "Please." *If Tilly only knew.* She offered her wrist to the servant.

Leaving Vermillion Hall and New Orleans had been so painful, almost equal to the pain of leaving Gilbert, even though she had not been in his embrace now for years. The only thing she really longed for was the smell of Stefan Menonovitch's hair and the soft musk scent she would never ask the origin of, even as she allowed his pillowslip to go unwashed between his visits to Paris. By doing so, she maintained the comfort of his nearness for all those years, whether he was soldiering from Sweden to Sevastopol or serving in Russian embassies. She again regretted making the trip back to New Orleans.

Larissa mentally relived every thrilling moment of exploring the Russian countryside with her dashing general. Gilbert paled by comparison. She had loved Gilbert when she was sixteen, but it took seeing him again to know where her heart really belonged. Love must be nurtured, as Stefan had nurtured their love. *Could one love two men?* Poor Gilbert, shackled with responsibilities that would cripple him forever. The same word kept coming to her thoughts: constant. Stefan Menonovitch was a constant in her life.

Gilbert fussed with his clothes like a bridegroom. *Larissa would have made me a wonderful wife. I shouldn't have grabbed her. I know she thinks I'm foolish, but I haven't kissed anyone but her since after Katté gave birth to J.P. And her terrible sickness. I am so lonely and Katté is still alive in Switzerland, but she is in a trance.* After changing shirts three times, he finished his last button and went downstairs to wait for J.P. and Tedelia.

"I think I heard Papa go downstairs. Tedelia, are you ready?"

"Yes, I'm trying to get my smile-no-matter-what-Camille-says-face adjusted. I dread that woman. Her tirades about the Bible justifying slavery really upset me."

"Maybe she'll get a sore throat and be unable to talk. You never know how lucky we might get. She always has some malady."

"I believe it was you, Mr. LeFleur, who once called *me* a gossip in reference to Camille?"

"Your job is to look beautiful, woman. Mine is to make observations. Now let's go, beautiful Mrs. LeFleur. Isn't that right, Papa?"

Papa smiled but remained silent.

She kissed cheerful Paul and Abraham on their brows and hurried to the waiting carriage.

Chapter 39
Jezebel Painted Herself

In the homes of other invited guests, animated discussions also erupted.

"Josephine, I don't know why I ever let you talk me into going to the Richilene's dinner party. You know I can't stand to be in the same room with *'Rat Cheese'* Zedohr."

J. Leenard Ragland struggled with his tie, finally lifting his chin toward his wife and motioning for her to finish the job.

"Quit calling him Rat Cheese, J. Leenard. His name is Robard Christian. Mary Elizabeth is lovely, Larissa is the guest of honor, your cousin D'Eljoie and her husband Barton will be there...I can think of at least a dozen reasons why you allowed yourself to be talked into going."

She knotted his tie and stepped away to inspect her effort.

"I'm too much of a gentleman to tell you of his business tactics and his activities with women of the evening. He makes my blood boil. He's one scoundrel who's never let his education get in the way of his ignorance. And him a member of the bar...I wouldn't even speak to him if he weren't married to your niece."

"Calm down, J. Leenard. We've accepted. We're going. I don't relish the thought of seeing Camille Arceneaux myself. She's a cold woman."

J. Leenard kept information about R.C. Zedohr's disguises and lurid shenanigans to himself. Not a man given to gossip, he nonetheless did possess strong opinions.

D'Eljoie Dewitt, J. Leenard's cousin, and her husband Barton settled into their carriage.

"I hope J. Leenard and R.C. don't get into it again. They stopped just short of a duel at a town meeting last week."

"What was that all about, Barton?"

"It goes way back. They have considerable history."

"Well, tell me about it."

"Xavier Zedohr, R.C.'s dad, put a lot of his money in J Leenard's bank and R.C. can't touch it unless he has a son by age forty-five. He's been married a while now, and no children."

"But he has a good position at Creole State Bank as president. I'm sure he makes a lot of money."

"Not as much as wants and he wouldn't have had a job if Daddy hadn't owned the bank."

"Why did old man Zedohr put money in his competitor's bank?"

"Banque de la Nouvelle Orléans was not really his competitor. He and J. Leenard had helped one another out for years. That move guaranteed R.C. couldn't touch the money by one of his Rat Cheese business moves."

"Sounds confusing to me."

"There'll be more tension tonight. Mayor Toustee' and his wife Hannah will be there. They are expecting their third child. When R.C. got out of law school, he had heavy gambling debts. He proposed to Hannah Delchamps and she turned him down. She promptly accepted Russell Toustee''s offer of marriage and they had twin boys their first year of marriage."

"I never knew R.C. was interested in Hannah Delchamps."

"He wasn't. He saw her daddy's sugar cane millions and tried to become his son-in-law."

"Maybe we *should* have stayed home."

"No, no, I need to be there to promote my boss for his second term as mayor."

At the Zedohr Mansion, R.C. and his wife were also having words.

"You can't forbid me to talk to Mr. Ragland. I don't care what differences you have with him. Your daddy must have had good reason to make him executor of his will. Our families were friends before I even met you, R.C., and he's married to my Aunt Josephine. Did you forget that?"

"One would think a wife would support her husband's wishes, Mary Elizabeth."

"I changed my religion for you, Robard Christian, not my very soul."

She started down the staircase, pulled on her second white evening glove, then lifted her midnight-blue gown to avoid tripping. A mirror reflected an exquisite three-strand pearl choker clasped with diamonds completing her ensemble.

"I wish you would let me know if I ever do anything to please you. Even our childlessness you blame on me."

"Now, Mary Elizabeth, you..."

"There are more important things in life than producing a male heir to continue the Zedohr line. It's not my fault you only had sisters."

She continued down the stairway, R.C. dogging her steps.

"You are being emotional again, Mary Elizabeth, but then, your former religion encouraged those kinds of outbursts, didn't it? I simply commented earlier that your choice of gowns was somewhat old-maidish; not a bit like the fashionable ladies of New Orleans will be wearing to the House of Richilene."

Fashionable ladies, indeed. She seethed and glared at the white marble pedestal-perched Venus de Milo that epitomized R.C.'s view of women: helpless, victims, ineffectual. She jerked an umbrella from the hall stand, poked the handle toward the armless lady and knocked the goddess to the floor in a dozen pieces at the feet of her astonished husband, then pitched the umbrella on the rubble and marched triumphantly to the waiting carriage. *I always hated that statue.*

He followed in silence, thoughts zooming like frenzied minnows at feeding time. *What's gotten into her? She never stood up to me before. She is pretty when she is angry. Her dress is beautiful, but I can't let her know I like it. You have to keep women on their toes. She still has not given me a son. I'll make her life miserable until she does. That statue will be replaced Monday morning, too.*

R.C. replaced the statue several times in the ensuing years. Each time she decimated it.

The badgering continued. She did not have a child until years later when she gave birth to a perfect little girl named Angelique with shimmering blonde curls from R.C.'s German family and exquisite beauty from the Chavannes' French heritage. This allowed R.C. Zedohr's hoped-for-funds to accumulate thousands in interest before finally being dispersed, but not to Robard Christian Zedohr, instead to the New Orleans Diocese. By then he was forty-five.

At the mansion of New Orleans' mayor, a sweeter conversation ensued.

"Hannah, have the twins gone to sleep? Maybe we can slip out," he whispered.

She nodded to Russell Toustee"s question and reached for her evening bag.

"Finally," she said with a smile, waving to the twins' nursemaid.

"Darling, remember to keep the conversation away from my mayoral race. I'd always heard rumors about R.C. Zedohr. I really didn't believe them until I saw a campaign check he gave Schweigleman. J. Leenard brought it over to my office. I don't think Schweigleman is stupid. He knows J. Leenard and I are friends. Do you think he just made an error and ran it through the Banque de la Nouvelle Orléans by mistake?"

"Not likely. Maybe Mr Schweigleman just wanted to get you riled. If he did, it worked didn't it?"

Her husband gave a sheepish grin.

"I guess you're right. He knows how to do it. Perhaps I'm the one who should watch my tongue."

"With Barton DeWitt there, you know he's going to talk politics. You'll have battles on two fronts to watch out for. Lead on, commander."

In her maisonette, Countess Aviva Bogoff, widowed at twenty-one by the death of the Count, who had been an original participant in the Russian-American Company, had her own thoughts about the invited guests.

"The woman I dread most in Louisiana is Camille Arceneaux. She is so demanding. Always we must take the House of Richilene to Vermillion Hall. She never comes to us. I realize she's in a wheelchair, but she goes everywhere else."

"She's quit letting her folks go to Congo Square, too, Countess. Did you know that?"

"No, I didn't. Why would she do that, Dulcette?"

"She never said. Just stopped their good times. Now, how does your hair look?"

"Perfect, Dulcette. Thank you."

"I didn't do much to your curls. They're always perfect, morning or night. I think you sleep with your head off the bed."

"Dulcette, you're such a tease."

"You're gonna' get you a husband for sure looking as pretty as you do tonight."

"I don't want a husband. It would take a special man to replace the Count. I haven't seen anyone who even comes close. I love working at Richilene. My work is my husband."

"Uh-huh, Countess. You get yourself on to your party so they can start making your wedding dress tonight."

She walked away giggling.

At the quaint home of the Chavannes sisters, Doris swirled tea into her sisters' cups with a flourish and whispered, "You know most people call Robard Christian *'Rat Cheese'* instead of R.C. I sure wouldn't bank with him at Creole State Bank. I'm glad I have all my money over at Banque de la Nouvelle Orléans where J. Leenard can look after it. He's such a nice boy our Josephine married...and a Baptist, you know."

Myrtle and Nell nodded to indulge her. This proved to be the seven hundred-ninety-ninth time Doris had imparted this information to them in the last year.

"And our precious niece Mary Elizabeth, married to Robard Christian Zedohr, such a shame." She made three syllables out of "such."

The three sisters would soon perform for the Richilene dinner party. They did not approve of alcohol. It gave them a pious feeling to take money from non-believers and channel it directly to the Canal Street Baptist Church. The Lord would be pleased for them to use money for His work from such a wicked source.

Later fearing disdainful looks, their sisters Josephine and Tedelia and their niece Mary Elizabeth would abstain from toasts until the Chavannes sisters finished their musical offerings and left.

Entertainers usually arrive via the side door, but since the sisters were on a divine mission, they always made their entrance through the front to provide piano music and vocals for social events, accepting no direct fees but rather "a donation to the Canal Street Baptist Church will do quite nicely, thank you." Doris mused. *Oh, the Devil is going to be unhappy tonight.*

Each day the sisters coordinated their colors—actually, matched them—from their stylish chapeaux to their obviously not puritanical shoes.

"A bit of glitter on one's toes makes feet move faster doing the work of the Almighty. Don't you think so, sisters?" Doris said, motioning to the footwear lined up like soldiers.

The color du jour for Ilana's party was burgundy and the hats were replaced by dainty, "not too showy," according to Doris, "tiaras."

Doris slipped a white linen napkin under Nell's saucer and stared at her lips.

"Sister Nell, is that paint on your mouth? You know Jezebel painted herself."

"Sister Doris, it's berry juice from the tarts. Now drink your own tea and calm down."

Sister Myrtle twisted her mouth, repressing amusement.

"Finish your tea, sisters. It's time to get ready," Doris said. "We must get there before any of the guests arrive."

Chapter 40

The Dinner Party

At eight in the evening, the House of Richilene salon converted into a fantasy dining room with a huge banquet table. Garlands of greenery, magnolia and wisteria looped from drape-hidden hooks. The magic of candle glow bewitched the room.

The first guest to arrive, Countess Aviva Bogoff, was greeted by Mary's brother Walter.

"Good evening, Countess. Miss Ilana is in the drawing room."

Father Prejean came next, then Deputy Mayor Barton DeWitt and his wife D'Eljoie, J.P. LeFleur and wife Tedelia and the patriarch of the LeFleur family, Gilbert LeFleur. Then president of Banque de la Nouvelle Orléans, J. Leenard Ragland, and his wife Josephine, followed by Mayor Russell Toustee' and his wife Hannah, then Larissa and last, president of Creole State Bank, Robard Christian "R.C." Zedohr and his wife Mary Elizabeth.

Ilana greeted Mary Elizabeth, saying, "You look stunning. Thank you for wearing the gown we brought for you from Paris. It is an exact copy of one made for the emperor of Austria's niece Maria-Teresse."

Mary Elizabeth thanked her again for bringing the gown and watched R.C.'s smile change to a sneer. *Old maid, indeed,* Mary Elizabeth thought.

The other ladies gushed over Mary Elizabeth. R.C. used this as an excuse to make a quick exit toward Father Prejean.

"Well, Father, this promises to be a lively evening. How have you been?" he asked, not waiting for an answer.

Walter appeared in the doorway.

"Ladies, gentlemen, dinner is served."

Father Prejean escorted Ilana in and guided Larissa to her seat. Gilbert gallantly led the Countess into the salon. *I can't believe I'm not getting to sit next to Larissa.*

"Father, will you return thanks?" Ilana asked.

This mixed religious group encouraged brevity.

"Dear Lord, make us thankful for that which we are about to receive."

Guests dined on watercress salad, gumbo, sugared yams, wild rice, asparagus, broiled quail in cream sauce and flaky miniature rolls, enhanced with several wines. Father Prejean gasped at each item placed before him and under his breath said, "The saints preserve us."

Ilana rose.

"Ladies, gentlemen, I'd like to propose a toast to our guest of honor, whom we're fortunate to be able to call an associate in the House of Richilene, Larissa Arceneaux."

Larissa nodded graciously.

"Speech! speech!"

"Please, I'm no good at this. Ilana, where are you when I need you?"

"You are rescued. Almost ten years ago, we persuaded Larissa to join the Paris House of Richilene, but both of us wanted to make a side trip to Russia to reclaim some of our heritage. At Brest where we entered Russia, our comfortable carriage was replaced by one that was drafty, ill-equipped, had weathered at least fifty winters, and smelled of a thousand cigars. The drivers spoke about the 'lazy, pretentious French' and called us 'frogs.'"

She giggled.

"Larissa was more vocal then. She dredged up her parents' long-dormant mother tongue and gave them a stiff upbraiding in perfect Russian. We were treated as royalty for the remainder of the trip. But we are so fortunate to be back in Louisiana with our friends. Thank you for coming. Other special friends here tonight are expecting their third child in early fall. Congratulations, Russell and Hannah."

R.C. glared at pregnant Hannah. *I'm still without an heir and she already has twin sons.*

"While Mary and Walter serve pink marzipan roses, a selection of sweet breads, butter pound cake with chocolate sauce and blackberries, coffee and toasted pecans, we will be entertained by three charming ladies who ate their dinner early and are now waiting behind the drapes. The Chavannes... Misses Myrtle, Nell and Doris."

Walter lifted the curtains.

The Chavannes sisters' melodic voices resounded against the interior marble walls of the festive room. Even R.C.'s mood lightened for a while. Between numbers and numerous glasses of wine he asked, "Father, don't you ever worry about sins of the flesh?" The happy little priest patted his full stomach and smiled.

"Oh, dear Mr. Zedohr, my sins are not of the flesh, but rather of the fleshiness. I pray every day that my girth does not exceed my holiness."

Blurry-eyed R.C. stared straight ahead and did not reply. His disheveled clothing, which bore evidence of pre-dinner party imbibing, grew progressively worse.

The music ended and the Chavannes sisters left via the front door.

"Come, Larissa tell us of some of your adventures in Russia that summer," coaxed Russell Toustee'.

"There is far too much to tell at one dinner party, Mr. Mayor. There were many fairs to attend, costumes to gain inspiration from, and learning more about my parents and what their lives must have been like. I found relatives and my Great-Aunt Rosinya. She was wonderful—my grandmother's baby sister on my father's side. Now you add to this, Ilana."

"I, too, searched, although unsuccessfully, for relatives, but they had all been purged during the bloodbath pogroms. Larissa was able to locate her relatives with the help of a dashing Russian general who was once in the same regiment as my late cousin Micolai."

"Oh, what was his name?" Countess Bogoff asked.

Larissa reddened and Gilbert saw her embarrassment immediately.

"General Stefan Monovitch."

She did not add that he had been her frequent visitor in Paris for the last ten years.

"He was my late husband's cousin. Their mothers were sisters," said the Countess. "How delightful."

Delightful, indeed. Gilbert mashed a marzipan rose with repeated vigor until his fork threatened to bend. He imagined a wild country engendering even wilder passion between two people with responsibility to themselves alone. The pit of his stomach trembled.

"Please, tell Cousin Stefan I send my warmest regards, if you see him again."

"I'll do that, Aviva."

Larissa hoped the questions would stop. Although in the warmth of Stefan's company for all these years, she still could not bear to hurt Gilbert. Ilana sensed Larissa's uneasiness.

"Let's adjourn to the drawing room for cognac and sherry."

Ilana stood and directed the guests from the dining area.

J.P. and Tedelia pledged their support to Russell Toustee' and Ilana mentioned with pride that she had unearthed information about her French-Jewish grandfather who had gone to Kiev as a tutor to Polish nobility before the pogroms. Gilbert feigned disinterest in her Russian comments and gave Father Prejean a nice contribution for his boys' school just as "His Rotundness" took another slice of cake. Barton DeWitt launched into an explanation of Mayor Toustee''s platform and J. Leenard and Josephine joined the political discussion.

"You'll beat Sweigleman by a mile," J. Leenard assured him.

Two months later, he did so in the biggest mayoral landslide in Louisiana history.

R.C. gathered a resentful Mary Elizabeth, gave a curt nod to their host and left. The party mood improved by major proportion.

Old memories confounded Larissa when she returned to the maisonette. Her thoughts also returned to Echo's words. "Maybe someday I shall get to go there." *Will there be a way?*

Chapter 41
If She Had Only Known

If only Catarina Rolfolini could have been able to see and help care for her dark-eyed grandson, Rolfo/ Vittorio, who burned with fever before the Gypsies reached Marseilles, where vineyard owner Henri Entremont allowed them to camp on his chateau grounds.

"We are but pilgrims on our way to Mont-St.-Michel. You will be blessed for allowing us to stop here," Prince Swar said.

Later, Entremont told his wife Dominique, "I almost did not permit them to stay, but one of their children is quite ill. I heard his hacking cough and didn't have the heart to refuse them."

Dominique and her son Celestin took huge pots of soup, grapes, bread and apples to the gypsies that same night.

"What have you done for the sick child?" She asked LaLa.

"Boiled dried lungwort to contain his croup and tried to keep him warm."

"Please, give him some of this soup, if he is able to eat."

Gypsies do not usually eat food prepared by others, but LaLa made an exception.

When dawn broke, LaLa and Tonya returned the pots to the Entremont kitchen empty and shinier than when they were first forged.

In later years, Chateau Entremont would become a regular stopping place for Prince Swar's little caravan but Rolfo would create a life for himself elsewhere and would not reconnect with the Entremonts for several years.

Before Rolfo regained enough strength to venture from Tanya's wagon, they moved to another location where Prince Swar waved the wagons to halt near a gurgling stream. Exhausted, the child fingered his cross, his touchstone, and wondered why his chest continued to ache.

Multi-layered skirts ballooned and flowered as Tanya and other women slid from their wagon seats to the grassy knoll nearby. LaLa motioned Rolfo to remain where she had spread a coverlet on the grass for him and to "not help" with the water chores.

Rolfo's fever broke and for a few days his health seemed to return. His fear of horses heightened when Prince Swar placed him on the back of the smallest of the string.

"Naji means 'brave', Rolfo."

The frightened child protested, but Prince Swar insisted. A surcingle bound only a blanket to the horse—there was no saddle. Rolfo knew the commands. He arched his legs into Naji's sides, and the horse responded. They were both naturals.

His riding ability instilled confidence in the young horse and the horse instilled confidence in Rolfo. It was mutual love from the first time he felt the wind surge through his hair. He'd never felt such freedom. They were inseparable.

Apple baskets sat only a hand away from Naji with Rolfo around. If someone else attempted to water him, he pawed the ground and waited for Rolfo. What would the horse do when they delivered him to his new owner? Rolfo tried not to think about it.

Spring threw exciting colors on all the trees where the caravan snaked onto the grounds of a gypsy-friendly chateau near Saint Raphael. Their whistle lookout did not have time to alert them because the stable master rode up before the wagons ceased to creak.

"My master is anxious to receive his ponies," he said with a smile. "Are they as grand as the one I am riding now?"

"Even better. They are from royal stock sired by King Ferdinand of Spain's own *Westwind,*" Prince Swar replied. "I can bring them to his stables, then you may observe how your other horses compare to the new ones."

"Very good. We will expect you before noon tomorrow."

Rolfo knew this would happen, but he never thought it to be so soon. Sofia, Gian, Mario, Angelo, Carmine, Davide...and now Naji—all losses.

He did not eat his evening meal and felt nauseated with dreaded thoughts of tomorrow. Denizens soon overran the well-worn path leading from the chateau. They clamored for tinker services, exotic fabrics, jewelry... and for the first time Rolfo understood why LaLa had her own wagon. Hordes from nearby Saint Raphael joined the chateau's inhabitants and crowded to have their fortunes told. She foretold exciting events for them with her crystal ball and tarot cards. Those waiting and mingling watched, mouths agape, at the uninhibited dancing.

Colorful triangular flags flew from lines and poles, their soft, almost musical flapping blending unnoticed amid intensified kinetic patterns screaming of the gypsy passion for life, of their persecution, of their angst and their flight to survive; their camp a glorious circus.

Yesef applied resin to his bow and tightened the strings to his liking. Rolfo's fingers gripped and released in longing anticipation as he sat on an overturned bucket.

Yesef noticed.

"It's very easy," he said, handing the large instrument to the stunned lad, adjusting it under his chin and placing the bow in his small hand. "Keep your touch light. Now don't move your bow beyond this area of the violin's neck," he said, pointing to the center of the violin.

At first try, Rolfo's bow caressed a beautiful sound from the strings, but the next notes sounded like a suffering cat. He stopped and handed Yesef the violin and bow without a word.

"It takes a while, Rolfo."

The boy did not touch the instrument for days but would eventually regain his courage with pleasing results.

Activity at last ceased at LaLa's wagon. The shimmering ball sinking into the Golfe du Lion signaled the twilight preceding the soulful violin songs, unlike the lively music three hours earlier. Now the heart of the gypsy was exposed.

Campfires sputtered and popped, silhouetting LaLa against the fading light, beckoning Rolfo. She climbed the four steps. He did likewise and found himself in the womb of her wagon. She pointed to a small stool near a tiny black velvet-covered table. Countless candles illuminated her crystal ball and golden earrings.

"I see you learning many new things..." she said with a grimace. "I see ...I see...nothing more."

She covered the crystal ball and waved Rolfo from her with two quick hand motions. *I see disaster, death. I cannot tell him.*

The confused child scurried toward the smoldering campfires. LaLa's pupils contracted as if in pain. *He is so smart, so handsome, but he will not live to be a man. I must not allow myself to become attached to this child.*

Rolfo dreamed of horses running untethered through a vineyard and plunging over a cliff into the ocean; the water and air cold, the horses drowning; Sofia calling Gian and the rest of the bridge family, then Rolfo to the campfire to eat the fish she had cooked, then Ludii. Suddenly, the others gone...cold again. He ran from Ludii and fell into the ocean.

He awoke coughing to see LaLa under the wagon, pulling back the covers he had kicked off. She watched him feign sleep. He dug deeper under the covers. She arranged the red scarf and much-too-big black coat around his ears. He snuggled for a moment, then remembered the horses.

He slipped on his boots and scudded to the pony string carrying water. Naji nudged Rolfo's back and he gave him the apple from his coat pocket. Rays of first light flooded the scene. Early morning breath condensed in the air from animal and human alike. He looked at the ocean and relived his horrible nightmare. *Today is the day,* he thought, biting his nails.

Hours and minutes flew. The sun raced to an overhead position.

"Rolfo, would you like to go with Yesef, Kalahn and me to deliver the horses?"

His heart thought "no," but his pride thought "yes." He managed a feeble, "Yes."

Rolfo led Naji and felt he was taking him to execution. The estate owner beamed at the lively horses, their coats shining in the noonday sun. Sparrows twittered from open rafters in the chateau stables, strutting peacocks gave an occasional screech and a tiny black and white kitten peered from atop multi-stacked hay bales. Individual stalls afforded unobstructed meadow views. Fresh-scythed grass-smell permeated the air. Stately swans skimmed the surface of a weeping willow-fringed lake. *Stables neat and swept will make a nice home for Naji, far better than the trees and stars he sleeps under every night,* Rolfo rationalized.

Prince Swar accepted a bag of coins and concluded his business. The four started back to camp. Rolfo heard Naji whinny and looked back over his shoulder to see him pawing the ground. He took a deep breath to keep tears at bay and held it for a long time.

The following brisk morning, apple in pocket, Rolfo headed toward the camp horses. After a few steps he remembered, and let the apple fall onto the soggy ground.

A fevered Rolfo brought water to LaLa as she prepared their morning meal. She banished him to the back of Tanya's wagon, brought succulent broth and forced some down through his chattering teeth. With cool cloths on his forehead and warm ones on his chest she tried to comfort him. By nightfall his fever had broken, but horrendous coughing spells from the depths of his lungs punctured the air.

They stopped only to prepare food and tend the horses.

In Rome, Prudore's Bakery continued to flourish. Lorenzo eventually hired a cook named Dorcena. The children loved her. Each child had bakery duties except little Mario, who loved everything connected with baking and always tried to help. His one bad habit? Sneaking home from school at midday. Dorcena would secretly return him.

"Signore Prudore, I'm going to market," she often yelled to her boss far more times than she needed fresh food.

With enough forced returns, Mario at last accepted school and became his teacher's favorite. He started calling Dorcena "Mama" and before long Lorenzo made her Signora Dorcena Prudore.

Chapter 42
The Bohemians

"The Bohemians are here!" Sister Theresa squealed from her seat in the kitchen overlooking the countryside.

Kalahn, Yesef and Prince Swar approached the ancient convent, sounded the huge wooden door's knocker and waited for the nuns to assign them jobs. They received fresh food for tinkering, mending, et cetera—a fair exchange.

Inside the great cloistered area, they conducted most of their tedious work in two long-abandoned rooms added to the convent's outside walls. A large common fireplace divided the rooms once used by travelers seeking safely from roving bands of marauders. The men could do little for the eroding stone walls or the deteriorating roof, but they tried.

Raging waters from the flooding Saone in 1839 claimed lives and property but little evidence remained of excessive moisture where multi-hued gypsy wagons camped near an almost-dry river bed for about two weeks when they came through every three years or so. Their campfires usually created exciting shadows, dancing in merriment. This year no dancing, no singing. One might never know they had camped there except for the bright glow of *las fogatas*, campfires, as Sister Theresa called them. The usual sensual, vivacious violin melodies now resembled Russian dirges.

Prince Swar approached Mother Superior Albertine when they finished their last task.

"Sister, we are not religious folk, but we found an orphan on the streets of Rome three years ago. Although in rags, he was wearing a cross carved from wood. Probably a Christian. He has consumption. We fear he will not last the winter. A chill shakes the leaves and we cannot care for him properly in his last days."

Prince Swar's eyes filled with tears.

"We have gold, but no hospital would let us bring him in. Will you keep him?"

It became harder for him to speak, "and give him a proper burial? We will leave money."

"Yes, my son. We will care for him, but we do not want your money."

At dusk, Tanya's blue wagon jostled into the outer convent yard. With Sister Albertine directing, two men lifted a stretcher from the vehicle. She hoisted a candle to better see the frail, dark-haired, litter-bound boy, then slowed her pace so as to not extinguish the flame. She led them to a darkened room and motioned to a cot.

"Place him here, easy...there now."

Rolfo's weary eyes reflected the flickering candle.

"This is Sister Albertine, Rolfo. She will take care of you. Sister, this is Rolfo."

With that, they were gone. Tears falling freely belied the stone faces of the men trudging wordlessly from the cloistered area. Prince Swar wanted to race back and get him. *We are leaving him to die.* But he knew comfort to be the most important thing now. LaLa, weeping, had stayed in her wagon.

All the colorful wagons had gone when Sister Theresa went to milk the goats at daybreak. A wistful smile crossed her lips. She thought of their visits in happier times.

Light streaked Rolfo's sickroom. Sister Albertine, who'd sat with him all night, discovered that with his neat bundle of clothes the gypsies had also left a large bag of gold coins.

The frail young man lingered near death for days and on the seventeenth day he spoke, "Sister, I talked to a bright being last night. It told me we must beware. There is danger here. It was like a warm glowing light wrapping around me."

He must be near death. It's the fever. He's delirious, but I must instruct him.

"That's sacrilege, my son. We'll hear no more of that."

Three days later, his coughing lessened, and he asked for solid food instead of limited broths.

"Rolfo, when you were quite ill, you said you talked with a bright being who told you we should leave here."

"No, Sister, it said there was danger here. It did not say we should leave the convent. I'm still hungry."

Their conversation had delayed the evening meal by only minutes. As she led the procession to the fraiter, a decaying ceiling beam collapsed on the table where the entire small cloistered population would have been sitting for their evening meal. The sturdy table splintered under the beam's weight.

Sister Albertine looked at Rolfo, crossed herself and said a silent prayer. *He was sent to us.* It also became clear why the sparrows had not built a nest there this year. God's wild creatures seem to know, too.

The two rooms previously used by wayfarers and gypsies became the new home for Rolfo and, after six months, no evidence of his cough remained.

Sister Theresa's shoes scrubbed softly on the stone floor. She lighted a fire and gave a low whistle.

"Whee. Whee."

Rolfo's curly head bobbed up. He smiled, then ducked back under his blanket and she left.

He gave a feline stretch, jumped up, blanket over his shoulders, did a bouncy jig from the cold floor, dipped water from a bucket into a pan and managed to splash his face although the blanket remained glued to him by his elbows. He dressed in an equally hopping motion.

Opening the shutters, he startled a shivering, feather-puffed, mourning dove from its tree perch where tiny buds pushed their heads out on the convent's environed south side anxious to be part of the coming spring. Rolfo thought of the breathtaking wild poppies and looked forward to their reappearance.

Trying to get everything in the crumbling convent workable proved an endless task. Two passing wanderers temporarily repaired the ceiling. To be on the safe side, the new dining table and benches were placed in another part of the fraiter.

A weekly trip to town two years later earned Rolfo a nice income by caring for the citizens of Lyon as a tinker. Sisters Albertine, Theresa and others watched him mature. They altered his clothes and knew from the Bishop's edict that Rolfo's days with them were numbered. He was almost a man. The black jacket now fit and his boots had been replaced several times.

"Rolfo, we shall take the cart into town together when you go next Tuesday. I have business with a Monsieur Levron."

"I will enjoy the company, Sister," Rolfo said, an impish grin growing. "You're not going to make me take extra Latin lessons along the way, are you?"

"No, no studies for you on Tuesday."

Six days later in burgeoning Lyon Rolfo finished his rounds and met Sister Albertine at a beautiful old churchyard. A strained conversation followed.

"No, Sister, I'm not living with anyone. I'll run away," the young man said, his eyes reflecting terror.

"Rolfo, he is a kind man who would like to apprentice you to his jewelry trade. He has seen your work around town. He contacted me."

"But, Sister..."

"You know we cannot allow you to remain at the convent much longer. The bishop has already given us a deadline. You need a home."

"A home...a home can be a terrible place. This isn't a home."

Tears welled, and he began to bite his nails.

"Calm down, my child. At least go back to his shop with me and talk with him. If you don't like him, I'll write my sister in Paris and perhaps you can go there."

Reluctantly, Rolfo nodded.

Sister Albertine had hidden Rolfo's clothes in the cart to bring out later. They entered Yigal Levron's shop greeted by violin music. A small man, about sixty, wiry hair, wearing a torn brown sweater welcomed them. *Monsieur Levron has the same gentle voice as Father Bocchetti.* The boy's eyes played over the simple but beautiful furnishings as the three approached the large living quarters above the shop.

Levron caught him looking at the sweater and he said, "Oh, I have a nicer one, son. My late wife Hediah made it for me and I can't bear to throw it away."

"This would be your room, young man," said Levron, opening a door to the sunniest sleeping quarters Rolfo had ever seen. A book-lined window seat caught Rolfo's immediate attention, then a desk and marble fireplace. An ankle-deep Persian rug cushioned his feet as he walked near the bed and armoire.

"What is that piece of furniture, Sister?" he whispered.

"That's to put your clothes in, an armoire."

He thought of the simple pegs his clothing hung on at the convent's outer rooms and in the gypsy wagons and smiled.

"I'd like to stay, Monsieur Levron."

"Good, good my boy," Levron answered. He held up the violin. "Do you play?"

"I do...some...but I haven't played for a while."

Levron would learn Rolfo was modest about everything he did.

"Get that large bundle from the cart," said Sister Albertine, looking relieved but sheepish. "It's your clothes."

"Before you go, young man," Levron extended his hand. "Welcome to your home." He stuck an unlighted pipe in his mouth.

Rolfo dashed to the cart, bit his nails again and struggled several times to get a deep breath. *I can always run away.*

"Come to see us when you do not have duties for Monsieur Levron," Sister Albertine reminded him.

They watched her cart fade to a speck.

"My man Caleb makes supper for us," Levron said, motioning toward the kitchen. "And tonight we celebrate with two kinds of cake. Come meet Caleb."

⚜ ⚜ ⚜

After three weeks, Levron took Rolfo to the stables.

"You need a horse of your own. Which of these two would you like, this brown bay or coppery sorrel?"

"This one. Could I call him Naji II?" Rolfo said, motioning toward the beautiful bay with glistening black mane.

Getting Naji II made the convent-to-city transition easier, but reminded him of the gypsies with sadness. At least he still got to see the sisters. When jewelry instruction ended for the day, Rolfo either rode or groomed Naji II until dusk.

Other instruction began about six weeks later. It did not please Rolfo.

Chapter 43

Pass en Blanc

"My Te, York said somebody left me on our porch in a basket," Abraham said, having ridden back to Ruvasha in haste, neglecting to tie his horse.

"Abraham, come upstairs to my bedroom."

Tedelia's knees almost failed climbing the stairs. Prematurely gray hair framed her sad face. *I never wanted him to know he was abandoned.*

"It's not true is it? He said Miss Camille told him."

Tedelia had dreaded this day, knowing it would come. They reached the top of the stairs.

"Ten years ago, when you were five, an old woman named Margaritte summoned me on her deathbed by messenger to her cottage on Rampart Street. She claimed she placed you on our doorstep after your beautiful mother Suzette Valois died."

He tried to remain calm.

"Did you learn anything else?"

"Remember the straw basket we kept the kittens in when you were a little boy?" He nodded.

"Well, that is how God sent you to us."

She went to a chest and removed a red velvet box.

"With this."

She handed an age-yellowed card to Abraham. In a clear hand it read, *My name is Abraham. I was born February 1, 1833.*

"Then...I'm not...a LeFleur," he said, his voice jerky, his breath spitting out in near sobs.

He thrust the card back. Tedelia replaced it in its soft velvet bed.

"Yes, you are. Your birth certificate says *Abraham Valois LeFleur*. We'd never applied for one until Margaritte gave us that information. You will always be our child."

She held him in a silent embrace until his breathing returned to normal. "My Te, where was my..." he could not bring himself to say *Mother*. "...that woman's family from?"

"We don't know. Your father and I had attorneys check in New Orleans, Baton Rouge and several surrounding towns, but they could find no other Valois relatives."

"Did she live in New Orleans?"

"Yes. The census the year you were born listed a Suzette Valois at that Rampart address, but nothing after that. No death notice, absolutely nothing."

Abraham hugged her again and headed downstairs with confused thoughts. Halfway down, he turned and shot back up.

"My Te, Rampart Street is where colored people, freedmen...live. Am I black?"

"You are a LeFleur, but Suzette Valois was an octoroon. You are more white than black. You will always be our son."

The next day Abraham brought his Yale application to Tedelia for help. "What would happen if I put a different name on this?" he asked, eyes lowered.

"What name, Abraham?"

"Since I'm going so far away, I thought maybe I should have my new identity."

"What is your new identity?"

"My Te, I am a freed man. Shouldn't that be my last name?"

"Is that what you want?"

"I think so." *Being a LeFleur is so comfortable. Will I enjoy being something else? I have to find out.* "Will you let me do it?"

"If that's what you really want."

Although heartbroken, she smiled. *I'd best wait a while to tell J.P.*

He hurried to finish the paperwork before he changed his mind. His usually controlled hand was a bit messy. Having three first names was quite fashionable. *Abraham Valois LeFleur Freedman.* He liked the sound, but he liked being a LeFleur, too. This new challenge excited him.

When the registrar at Yale read an ink spot as an "i" instead of an "e," absent-mindedly he changed it and Abraham became Jewish on paper. In his innocent attempt to embrace this new-found ethnicity, he later would be accused of *pass en blanc,* passing for white.

At Yale, Abraham and Paul roomed together with "Mister Freidman" and finished in two-and-a-half years. Law called him back to New Orleans and *The Yale Literary Magazine* staff hated losing their most stellar editor.

He returned to New Orleans to first read law for a year, then clerk for a federal judge. Later he joined the firm of Winborn, D'or and Hough, but his proudest accomplishment would be his work in the postbellum period with the Freedman's Bureau. This would also prove to be his greatest challenge.

Chapter 44
Shooting Stars

Echo Vermillion's dream that "maybe someday I shall get to go there" became a reality when she joined the Paris House of Richilene. Erik had long ago turned almost every facet of the business over to the ladies. Their first born, Issac, was now away at University and their daughter Rebecca, two years younger, had taken a great interest in art, so she and Ilana made many painting excursions with him.

Larissa enjoyed working with her new staff, although she was in failing health. She did find time to visit Chonya, Anatol, Yesina and Yuri, now in medical school, who was no longer "Little Yuri." They had made one visit to see her in Paris, where astonished Yuri could not believe, "how well the dogs are treated here, Babushka...almost like children."

Stefan arrived at the apartment he and Larissa had shared for almost two decades. The gift-giving had stopped at her request.

Her skin was pallid. He'd never noticed the faint lines etched in her beautiful face.

"Is there anything I might get for you while I'm out?"

"No, unless you might bring me some extra strength."

Larissa had survived two revolutions in France, but the one in 1848 had been especially strenuous. Vladimir's warning to his *mother* had been, "stay away from crowds, go to the market only when necessary and come to see me at the Embassy as often as possible."

The latter he really urged her to do.

February in Paris proved cold and oppressive, but warm in contentment. Stefan placed small cakes on a tray and an oil heated porcelain veilleuse warmer, with a fresh pot of tea atop, next to her bed. He took a glass of wine before going out in the blustery, winter afternoon.

Returning with Vladimir, Ilana and Erik, he told Larissa, "We are being married at the Notre Dame Cathedral. Shush...don't say anything. Let me finish. We'll live wherever you like—Paris, Kiev or New Orleans. Papers for my military termination were filed before I left Russia. I've visited the Bureau des Mariages and everything is ready."

"Oh, Stefan, what can I say?"

"Just one word: yes."

She nodded with a sweet smile.

"What will I wear?"

"You'll be a beautiful bride in the white gown you wore on New Year's to the Russian Embassy ball. Ilana is laying your clothes out and she will help you dress."

Stefan lifted featherlight Larissa and placed her in the waiting carriage. Vladimir's driver navigated effortlessly through frigid, slick streets toward the cathedral. Ice-laden tree limbs snapped and tumbled. Not a bird was aloft where pigeons congressed under eaves in protected bundles. Horses snorted heavy winter breath and pawed the snow as huge flakes continued to swirl about their party. Echo joined them as well as other Richilene staff and members of both Russian and French embassies.

Stefan watched Vladimir and his friend Morel form a human-sedan to sprint Larissa inside to the altar. He thought of the irony. *A Russian general marrying in the same basilica where that thorn-in-the-side Napoleon had crowned himself emperor.*

An inundation of votive candle-glow reflected on Larissa's bead-encrusted velvet gown and hooded cape lined in Russian white fox. The cape spread over the golden altar where she resembled a glistening snowflake tsarina.

The priest motioned Ilana and Vladimir to join the kneeling couple at the altar. After an abbreviated ceremony, he pronounced them husband and wife. Larissa and Stefan bowed in prayer. The diminutive hand he reached for at prayer's end did not respond.

In denial, he stared horror stricken at the rose widow, drew in a trembling breath and placed his cumbrous arms around her. He turned to Vladimir with a faint smile, kissed Larissa on the forehead, and died of a massive stroke. Gusting snow ceased.

The frosty night reddened the noses of two young men stopping their snowball fight near one of Notre Dame's flying buttresses. The sky cleared.

"Look, Andre," said one, pointing heavenward. "A shooting star."

"Look, Pierre, another one."

Chapter 45
The Irish Channel

In the Irish Channel District of New Orleans, a familial scene lacking any tenderness would soon play out. Abby's father, Price Hodggers, reeked of alcohol, urine, sweat and occupational fish smells. His elbows and knees held the grime of forty-five Louisiana summers. Where baldness now peeked through, a mass of red curls had once bounced. He had been handsome but now the square jaw ladies had loved sagged and grew scruffy whiskers and the clear green eyes disguised themselves behind bloodshot veils.

He'd been a dandy once, he had, but now...*I don't even own me own boat. Oh, the girls would smile and wave as The Black Hawk chugged toward the Gulf. Then that hurricane broke her to bits. The next year, me Fiona died giving birth to Clive, and he ain't too bright.* Liquor amplified his self-pity.

He sloshed another tin cupful of rot-gut and without rising bumped his straight chair nearer the window. At four o'clock on Saturday afternoon the marathon drinking had already begun.

Me Fiona was made for working, but not for having children. Me Monique was made for child-bearing, but lame and too Frenchy to be any use at work.

Price Hodggers surveyed the dismal hovel, wiped his mouth with the palm of his hand and dragged it down to his stubble-covered chin, leaving his mouth in a twisted, disapproving "O."

"Where is that girl?" he said aloud.

Just then, the door swung open.

"Where have you been? It's almost suppertime. What have you been up to?"

Abby strained to get two baskets of clothes inside.

"Pa, I've been getting the clothes. We don't have enough clothesline to dry all of them, so Mrs. Wallace lets me use her line."

"That shouldn't take all day."

"She helped me iron them 'cause I took care of her children while she went to the market."

"Did she give you any milk? "

"No, Pa. I told you the only money they have is from *selling* that milk. Mr. Wallace is dying. He can't work."

She put the baskets in the small room, not bigger than a pantry, that she used as a bedroom, a pallet her bed.

"I asked you about supper, Abby. Are you deaf, girl?"

"There's a stew on the stove and Clive said he'd bring some bread."

Potatoes, onions and one piece of shredded chicken comprised the stew. Even though her hands bled from wringing clothes that morning, she wrapped rags around them and set the table.

"Speak of the devil. Here's your brother now."

Price hung himself half-out the window. Joey Pauratore's fish wagon stopped outside amid much yelling as Abby opened the door and Mrs. Wallace waved. She knew this Saturday night would be no different from the others.

"Mr. Hodggers, Clive and I finished our rounds at noon. I paid him and he bought some bread. Thirty minutes ago, I went to put my team up and there he was, sprawled out in our stables. I thought I'd better bring him home...evening, Miss Abby," he said, blushing. "Come on, Clive, get out of the wagon. My Dad expects me back home soon."

"No! Where's my bread?"

"You didn't have it when I found you. Come on, get out."

"Get out of that wagon or I'll beat..." Price attempted to rise but fell back down.

"Let me do this, Pa." Abby rushed outside. "Come on Clive, get down... supper is almost ready. It's gonna be fine. We don't need the bread."

"We don't need the bread? I'll come in then."

His bloodshot eyes looked ready to rupture. He misstepped climbing down and plopped where free-range pigs snorted and grunted in the mud surrounding the entire shrub-less neighborhood.

Price bumped his chair back to the table, Clive opposite him.

"Lose my bread, will you?"

Clive looked down as his father sucker-punched him, the table tipped, and Clive grabbed the serving bowl and threw it at him. It shattered, food flying.

Abby fled to Mrs. Wallace's to spend another night on her kitchen floor. The squalor of the Irish Channel hut she shared with her Pa and Clive would have horrified her deceased mother. At fifteen, her last three years had been weekends of endless drunken brawls. She knew how things played out. Her half-brother alternated between crying and rage, accusing his Pa of murdering his mother and throwing the food Abby prepared. Father, son, or both would pass out and sleep it off until cathedral bells from the nearby church signaled Sunday morning mass.

Clive splashed water in his face, combed his hair, and rushed to confession. Clive's stirrings roused his father. Abby tried to slip in unnoticed, but Price awakened and found his daughter wiping up the spilled food.

"Well, hello, little daughter. You look more like your pretty mother every day. Come to your old pa, girl."

She backed away. He tried his despicable advances toward her and groped to steady himself. She skirted out of reach. He reeled, then slipped and knocked himself out on a piece of broken pottery on the floor. *I should have swept that up after Clive threw it.* Painful regret and sympathy were reflected in Abby's face, but fright overwhelmed her. She lifted the latch and escaped with no plan, just the need to flee.

Abby fled Gravier Street, raced two squares north on Magazine, dodged carriages to cross Canal where Magazine changes to Levee, ran another square, and leaned on a wrought-iron fence to catch her breath. She next proceeded toward Jackson Square and the French Market.

Whiffs of rain freshened the heavy morning air, leaving her red curls in even tighter ringlets. She thrust her face skyward and took a deep breath. *I won't ever go back. Dear Lord, don't let him find me. Let me be happy.*

Chapter 46
"Can You Iron Linen?"

The old town, the Vieux Carré, bloomed into a promenading flower garden of parasols, hoop skirts and bonnets. Dark-skinned women in white blouses and colorful skirts hoisted fruit and other delicacies in baskets to balance them on their scarf-covered tignon heads.

Smells wafting from sidewalk cafes and bakeries made her dizzy. She tried to remember when she had last eaten. *Saturday morning? No noon meal and certainly nothing Saturday night.*

Croissants piled like logs waiting to be loaded on river barges in a window caught her eye. She patted her pocket. It jingled with coins from her labor of milking Mrs. Wallace's cow while she was away to be with her sick sister.

She selected a croissant through the open serving street window and held the two-cent asking price in her other hand so the young shop boy would know she had money. He looked at the red curls, smiled a shy grin and slipped two pastries into a tunnel of cone-rolled, brown butcher-paper.

Abby remembered. *My neighbor Bridey works in the kitchen at Rodin's.* She'd not had coffee in a long time and had never been in a restaurant—at least not through the front door—and she wasn't going to start now.

She sneaked a few bites of croissant and darted down two streets and up an alley. Bridey, peeling potatoes at the back door, squealed when she saw her.

"Abby, girl! Come sit here by me."

"... and I have money, and I'll stand right here by the back door and drink it, so they won't be thinking I'll be stealing their cup."

Bridey whispered to a waiter who had been watching with amusement and nodded to Abby. He returned shortly with a large, covered, silver tray and placed it on a platform used weekdays for draining vegetables. He motioned for her to take a seat on a lower platform. With a flourish, he placed a pristine white napkin on her lap and uncovered the tray. Her eyes widened. The tray held a miniature pot of steaming coffee, a sugar bowl, a pitcher of thick cream, a bowl of succulent strawberries, two slices of bacon, a scrambled egg and a fluffy, buttered biscuit.

She emptied the cream pitcher, sugar bowl, coffee pot and all the other dishes until not a clue remained that the tray had once held food. The butcher-paper cone she emptied, too.

She fished the remaining coins from her pocket and held them up to the waiter in two open hands. He selected one half-dime and two pennies, bowed and asked, "Will there be anything else for Mademoiselle?"

Abby thanked him in flawless French, shook her head and swallowed hard.

"It is I who thank you."

He responded in French.

Mademoiselle Janine DuBonnet exited Rodin's by the side door to her waiting carriage. She saw Abby and paused, remembering a young girl years ago in Paris, begging precious morsels they'd have thrown away. That girl also had red hair. Mademoiselle DeBonnet still had red hair.

The DuBonnet driver summoned Abby to the carriage, asking, "Can you iron linen?" Abby nodded.

"Good. I am Mademoiselle Janine DuBonnet and I need someone to work for me."

Abby looked puzzled.

"I will provide food, clothing and a place for you to live in exchange for your willingness to work. As you master more tasks, you will be given wages. Will you come with me now?"

"Yes, ma'am."

"What is your name?"

"Abby...er...Abigail Anne Hodggers."

Her blue eyes gleamed with excitement. She waved to Bridey and entered the carriage.

They rode along magnolia-lined boulevards cooled by refreshing breezes. Abby had never ridden in a carriage and fidgeted in an attempt to arrange the folds of her threadbare dress on the rich leather seat, then smiled faintly, apprehensive that this ride might only be in her imagination.

The driver drove to the back entrance of the mansion, under the porte-cochère, where they slipped unnoticed into Mlle. DuBonnet's personal quarters. She was tutored privately, introduced as Mlle. DuBonnet's niece and never asked to iron linen. Her hands would not bleed again.

Aunt Janine never asked Abby any questions. Her own past in Paris—too painful to recount—reminded her that some things are better left unknown.

Mademoiselle DuBonnet's School for Young Dames reverberated with excitement anticipating the upcoming Christmas Ball. Abby came to the school in early April and had seen the Azalea and Harvest balls, but the Christmas Ball promised to be the most beautiful gala ever held in antebellum New Orleans.

The finishing school ball was the talk of Orleans, Drapeau and Tachérie parishes. Society leaders in Baton Rouge, Mobile, Memphis and Natchez plotted to get their sons, nephews and grandsons on the guest list.

Camille Arceneaux was no exception. She continued to rule Vermillion Hall from her steel and wooden throne and gave no quarter to anyone standing in her way.

"Luther, be sure to mention the ball to Mr. Ragland when you do your banking. His wife is on the school's board of trustees," she purred.

Chapter 47

Marie LaVeau de la Voodoo Queen

With a cheetah skin over one shoulder and black lace draped in elegant folds, the beautiful mulatto's bare arms resembled bark-stripped crepe myrtle trees, strong and taut. She brushed past Mlle. DuBonnet and Abby and entered a tiny shop, then emerged almost immediately. Abby strained to see the black candles clutched in her long finger-nailed hands.

"Abby, it's impolite to stare."

"But, Aunt Janine, did you see her? Did you see her clothing?"

"Yes, ma chère, I saw her clothing, but we must hurry. We have business at the House of Richilene. Please hold some of these roses."

"Aunt Janine, who was that woman?"

"Marie LaVeau, the Voodoo Queen," she whispered. "Quit looking back, child."

"What does that mean? Queen of what?"

"She is a priestess of a religion that worships with snakes. Many people in New Orleans believe in her Black Magic."

"That sounds frightening. Do the snakes hurt them?"

"I've never seen one of their services, ma chérie. I wouldn't know. Come along now."

"Someone would have to be crazy to handle snakes, much less to have a religious service with them."

"Our maid, Perinne, went to her for a gris-gris. In her case, the anti-charm was a tiny bundle of sticks and a chicken bone to put a hex on her former lover's new love."

Mlle. DuBonnet smiled in disbelief that she'd even repeat this gossip.

"Perinne put the gris-gris on the other woman's doorstep. Marie said an incantation—a curse—and Perinne is still with him five years later."

Abby enchanted everyone, especially the Countess, who insisted on personally attending Mlle. DuBonnet's niece.

"Miss Abby has her own Richilene trunk, yes?"

"Miss Abby has her own Richilene trunk, no, but she will soon," she said, turning to Abby. "What color would you like?"

"Oh! Pale blue. Thank you, Aunt Janine."

"Miss Abby's hair is beautiful," said Countess.

The girl managed a shy "thank you."

"It must run in the family. It's the same color as Mademoiselle's."

Aunt Janine looked extremely pleased.

Abby stepped into the crisp November morning to await Mademoiselle DuBonnet's finalizing her business at the House of Richilene, secure that no one would recognize her with her new polished image. She loved the admiring glances from passersby.

A wind gust pushed a two-week-old *Picayune* to her feet. The headlines caught her attention: *"Local Fisherman's Body Found."*

"Three weeks after being reported missing, the body of Price Hodggers, aged 45, washed ashore at Point Blue. He was identified by his son, Clive Hodggers, of 711 Gravier Street. Funeral arrangements are pending."

Abby scooped up the dirty newspaper and crammed it in her beaded, silk draw-string purse and hoped no one had noticed. Nausea swept over her. *I never got to see him again. Why did Mamere have to die? Things would have been so different.* She leaned against the building to steady herself.

Mademoiselle DuBonnet came outside.

"Abby, ladies don't lean on buildings. Oh, I'm sorry ma chérie. You're ill aren't you? Let's go back inside so you can sit."

"I'd rather go home. I think I drank too much coffee."

"Here's our carriage. The Countess has ordered your trunk from Harris Lloyd and Son. I'll get the plaque engraved later."

Abby read and re-read the crumpled newspaper before burning it in the garden several days later. *Did Aunt Janine see it?*

Soon plans for the Christmas Ball occupied everyone's thoughts. Aunt Janine took Abby again to the House of Richilene, where she selected the palest of blue silks and instructed it be garnished with seed pearls over Alencon lace of the same color.

"My niece's ball gown must be perfect."

Janine DuBonnet beamed with pride at the attention Abby always attracted. When they left the House of Richilene, Abby's eyes found the spot where she'd seen the newspaper. *What if someone finds out?*

York Arceneaux's invitation arrived just before he returned from Yale University, where he had made a less-than-remarkable academic record for himself. His friend Paul LeFleur distinguished himself in all areas. Abraham Friedman had been elected freshman president and excelled in the classroom as well.

Camille ran her cadaverous fingers over the raised print. *York will meet someone his equal, not a swamp barbarian.*

Harris Lloyd and Sons delivered Abby's trunk and it occupied a place of honor. She polished the brass plaque with "A. A. H." on it until her fingers hurt.

"Stop polishing that plaque or you'll rub a hole in it," said her aunt. "It's time for another dance lesson. You must know all the latest dances, ma chérie."

Abby smiled and followed her to the ballroom, where a gaggle of girls awaited instruction from two male teachers. *Dear God, please, don't let this life ever end.*

Chapter 48
The Inquisition

Nothing but frosty blue silk and red curls commanded York's line of vision when he surveyed the ballroom. Abby would not be sixteen until February, but she out-dazzled everyone in the room at the Christmas Ball of Mlle. DuBonnet's School for Young Dames.

York changed Abby's dance card entries to bear his name only. While filling their buffet plates, he deliberately poured punch on the vest of handsome Thaddeus DuPree, III because he'd attempted to dance with her.

"Aunt Janine, he thinks I am wealthy, and he wants to see me again," Abby said when she stole away from York. "What should I do?"

"Ma chérie, by all means see him again. What harm can be done if he thinks you are as wealthy as he? We are not exactly poor."

When she is mistress of Vermillion Hall she will be wealthy.

Abby glided back to York's side and they exchanged a few words. He squeezed both her hands and left.

Camille Arceneaux's command performance invitation to tea at four o'clock on December 27, 1850 arrived by messenger. Mlle. Janine accepted.

After dressing, re-dressing, and undressing four times, Abby sat in a pile of clothes.

"Ma chérie, the white dress with the blue sash is lovely on you," Aunt Janine suggested.

With Aunt Janine's help, she at last dressed, rushed to the kitchen, slipped behind Perinne, and rummaged in a kitchen cabinet. She reached for and opened a bottle of vanilla flavoring. With a satisfied grin, she daubed some behind each ear, just as she had seen beautiful Mémère do.

Abby could still hear Price Hodgger's constant harassment of her mother.

"I didn't know I'd be gettin' damaged goods when I paid ya' way from France. An Irishman needs a woman what can dance. I'm 'shamed to take ya' out in public what with the way you wobble-walk and all."

Her mother cleaned and cooked for that sot but nothing pleased him. She was frail, just as Abby was. "Delicate of bone and fair of face," as the marriage broker in Paris had described her in his letter to Price Hodggers. His mental and physical cruelty hastened her death, as it had his first wife's. The only thing Price Hodggers ever gave his daughter was her halo of red hair.

"Abby, our carriage is waiting."

"I'll let him do most of the talking lest I slip up and say something wrong."

"Abby, your speech lessons were just to give you a bit more confidence," said her aunt. "There is nothing wrong with having an Irish brogue and your French is flawless. Your father was Irish, so you *should* have a touch of that. Remember, too, York speaks French."

Upon their arrival at Vermillion Hall, Luther helped Abby and Aunt Janine from their carriage and explained, "Mrs. Arceneaux is not ambulatory. She waits inside."

Abby did not know what ambulatory meant and dared not ask. Awed by the size and beauty of Vermillion Hall, she couldn't speak. Aunt Janine winked at her and some of their rehearsed small talk surfaced.

"Your home is lovely. Thank you for having us," she managed.

"You are everything our son said you were," Luther said, kissing her on the cheek.

Abby blushed and ducked her head.

"Where is York, Mr. Arceneaux?" she asked coyly.

"Oh, my wife must have sent him on an errand. He should be home soon."

In a cruel twist of fate, he would give her the same assurance seven months later.

At that moment, Camille entered from her lift.

"Ah, here's my wife," said Luther, looking perturbed. "This is Mademoiselle DuBonnet and her niece Abigail Hodggers. This is Mrs. Arceneaux."

It seemed forever before Camille spoke. *What a beastly name: Hodggers. Pity her father couldn't have been French instead of Irish...but she is pretty.*

"Welcome to Vermillion Hall. I can see why my son has been raving about you, my dear. Won't you please come into the parlor?"

"Where is our son, Camille?"

"I sent him into town so we ladies could get to know one another. York thinks our guests are coming tomorrow," said Camille in her little girl voice. "Don't you think we ladies will be more relaxed with no handsome men around to distract us?"

Luther blushed, explained he had paperwork to do and left the ladies to their tea party.

Eager servants strained to see the "young miss" Mr. York was smitten by. After initial peeks, Camille asked Aunt Besa to "shush them all away." They scattered and returned to their duties in the kitchen separated for safety reasons from the big house, but joined by a covered brick walkway.

What should have been social proved to be more of a courtroom cross-examination.

"...and her mother's name was Monique Boujalais? Why is your last name different?"

"We had different fathers."

That much was true. They had had different fathers, different mothers, too, for that matter.

"You're her guardian or is she just visiting you?"

Completely excluded from the conversation, Abby managed a slight smile.

"I'm her guardian as her only close relative."

"How did her parents die?"

"While returning from Switzerland, when Abigail was two, they were trapped in an avalanche. She lived in Paris with my mother until a year ago. Then she came to live with me."

"Why did she leave your mother? Was there trouble?" Camille asked, narrowing her eyes and turning to Abby.

Aunt Janine answered quickly.

"My mother died. Abigail is an only child but there may be some distant relatives somewhere in Ireland on the Hodggers' side."

Abby relaxed.

"They visited Ireland often as her father had holdings there."

"Are you aware that my son wants to marry her?"

Abby froze. Could they hear her heart pounding? She almost choked on a swallow of tea. *He wants to marry me. He wants to marry me.*

"Yes, Mrs. Arceneaux, her dowry is sizable, but a provision in my late sister's will prohibits any of Abigail's dowry or inheritance from going to her until she has been happily married for five years. She knew I would care for her until she wed."

Just then York burst into the room with packages in his arms.

"What's going on? I thought they weren't coming until tomorrow. Camille, you told me the wrong day."

Camille smiled smugly.

"Good afternoon, York," said Aunt Janine, breaking the tension.

"Good afternoon, Mademoiselle DuBonnet, Abby. I'm sorry I was not here to greet you."

"Your mother has been entertaining us, York, and we met your father," Janine DuBonnet answered.

"Come, Abby. I'll show you the grounds," York said, his brow knitted.

"Mademoiselle DuBonnet, my son has never cared for a young woman before. He is very serious about your niece."

"Mrs. Arceneaux, my niece has never been alone for one minute with anyone but your son."

"Is it agreed then, we have made a match?" Camille asked, concluding her transaction.

"Yes, it is agreed."

Chapter 49

Look at the River

York showed Abby the rose garden then started toward the stables. An exceptionally warm November and December welcomed a profusion of bright-pink camellias still blooming. When they stopped to pick a few, York put some in Abby's hair.

"Let's skip the stables and go to the third floor to look at the river."

They walked by the parlor, nodded to Aunt Janine and Camille, and pointed upstairs.

"We're going to watch the river, ladies," York called.

They raced up two flights of stairs and headed for the balcony.

"With those flowers in your hair you look like a Botticelli painting."

Having no idea what he was talking about other than it must mean something wonderful, she answered.

"I do?"

"Look at the river, Abby. See that sand bar? We'll row out there this summer and take a picnic. Would you like that?"

She nodded.

"We'll be married by then and our rooms will be on this third floor. Then we can look at the river anytime we want."

"I'd like that."

"I'll be right back," said York, stepping inside to retrieve something from beneath the bed. The tinkle of an open music box filled the room. He stood and beamed.

"This ring belonged to my grandmother Larissa Arceneaux. I want you to have it because it is only days before we will wed."

Abby's eyes softened as he placed the ring on her trembling hand.

"Oh, it's so pretty...thank you, York," she said, her voice quavering.

"I had to give it to you now. We will be married soon. I feel we are already," York said taking her hands and kissing her palms.

Sparkling sunlight bursts rendered the river a radiant ribbon of amber.

"I've never seen anything as beautiful," York said.

"Neither have I. It's so lovely."

"I meant *you, not* the river."

Guiding her from the balcony back to the bedroom, York patted the matelasse coverlet on the massive, lace-swathed, canopied bed and motioned Abby to sit beside him. Her blue sash and coppery wind-tousled curls highlighted against an otherwise pristine, snow-white setting. He traced the complete outline of her face with his knuckle of his thumb, then caught her cheeks with both hands and kissed her.

"You're hurting me York." *Why does he press his mouth so hard on mine?*

"I'm sorry, Abby," he said, baby-talking to her. "What is that smell? It's wonderful."

He continued to kiss her face and nuzzle closer to her neck. The vanilla flavor mesmerized him. Head now resting on her chest, he raised his face and kissed her again and again, nudging her to a reclining position. She stopped struggling. Her arms circled his head and drew him closer. The river below swished to a liquid fork dividing at the sandbar and hurtling toward the Gulf of Mexico depositing rich, fertile top-soil as it had done for thousands of years.

The jingling servant-bell near the bed vibrated the wall and brought them back to reality.

"Your Aunt Janine must be ready to go. I love you."

They kissed, the fading light playing through the lace swags cascading on the tester bed. She stretched her hand out, looked at the sparkling ring and replied, "I love you, too, York."

Straightening their clothing, she fumbled to retie her sash then they scrambled down two flights of stairs to the knowing eyes of Janine and Camille. Abby cupped the crushed camellias in her hands.

"Mademoiselle, Camille, I have given Abby Grandmother Arceneaux's ring. We want to be married within the week."

"There is no hurry. Her aunt and I have so many details to work out."

"The banns must be posted at the church," Janine added.

"You need to return to Yale and give us time to have a trousseau made. We don't need men around. I know your father will agree."

From the hall Luther asked, "What will York's father agree about?"

"Luther, York wants to be married this week."

"Your mother is right, everything takes time. You and Abby have the rest of your lives to be together."

"York, you and Abby can't be married that soon, but it's very romantic of you two to be so much in love. If both of you feel the same this summer, you'll have my blessing. I'm sure Mr. and Mrs. Arceneaux feel the same."

They both smiled at Aunt Janine.

"But I don't want to return to university. I don't want to leave Abby."

"Do you want me to give the ring back?" asked a tearful Abby.

"No!" York said, rushing to her side. "Don't ever take it off. Ever."

"We have to do as they ask, York. I'll be waiting for you," Abby said, rising and joining Mademoiselle DuBonnet.

"I think they best not see one another until summer," Janine suggested to Camille and Luther before leaving the parlor. They nodded.

York ran to his room on the third floor and Besa followed from where she stood listening.

"Mister York, six months is not a long time. It will pass before you know it."

This was the first time she had seen him cry since he was nine years old and it pained her.

"Aunt Janine, you don't know how I long for a house of my own," Abby said back in New Orleans. "It doesn't have to be grand like your house or Vermillion Hall. Just a small one with York."

She looked at her ring and smiled. *Mrs. York Arceneaux. He loves me. He wants to marry me.* Aunt Janine dried Abby's tears and sat with her until she fell asleep.

An early morning trip into the city and Aunt Janine returned all smiles.

"Abby, Jean-Joseph Vanderchamp, an artist from Rambervillers, France, is in residence here in New Orleans and will begin your portrait in two days from now."

"I've never known anyone who had a portrait painted."

"You know me. My portrait in the music room was painted by Monsieur Vanderchamp when I lived in Paris."

Two days later Abby was driven to the Vanderchamp Studio and he was thrilled to be painting the niece of a former patron,

A sullen York returned to Yale. He would not talk to Paul or Abraham most of the trip, but pretended to be engrossed in a book of Shakespeare. They pretended to not notice and ignored him.

Chapter 50
Solomon and Bridey

Late spring snows paralyzed most of the Eastern coast and flooding followed so that the promised June wedding could not be celebrated. York waited at Yale; not with patience.

He'd never cared for any human being as he cared for Abby: not for his mother, who always played military officer as she inspected him to see if he passed muster; nor his father, a man little more than his pawn. It was a game with him to see how much he could squeeze out of the peasant. York could not remember his mother embracing him or his father, but he wanted to hold Abby to him so that she would never get away, never leave him.

Always painfully thin, Abby suddenly began to bloom. Beautiful in love and heavy with York's baby. York did not know. Then Janine saw her changing clothes. Her shock turned to concern.

"Ma chérie, you're expecting a child, aren't you?"

Abby dissolved in a flood of tears in Aunt Janine's arms.

"Yes, yes. This ruins everything, doesn't it?"

"This ruins nothing. York loves you and you love York. Now dry those tears. Everything will work out. I promise."

"What about the wedding?" Abby sobbed.

"I'll post the banns at St. Louis Cathedral tomorrow."

"But my size. Aunt Janine, I'm getting big."

"Empress Josephine wore an Empire wedding gown when she married Napoleon. You'll just do the same," Mlle. DuBonnet said with a smile.

New Orleans near the river can be chilly even in late April, so it didn't appear odd that Abby had taken to wearing a cape when she went out. This evening she and her aunt were dining at Rodin's. She asked the waiter, who pretended not to recognize her, "Is Bridey Bohan working tonight?"

"No, Mademoiselle. She and our chef left without giving notice several weeks ago. I'm sorry. Did you need something?"

"Thank you, no. I see my aunt is ready to go."

Tired of shabby treatment from Rodin's owner, Bridey and the chef, Solomon, had quit. Although several years older than she was, he and Bridey married and opened a tavern on the other side of the Vieux Carré. They served generous portions of Irish fare in the small dining room Bridey decorated with red geraniums and red and white checkered tablecloths. They lived above their establishment.

"Bridey, we must never turn a hungry soul away who is without funds, for we both know the pain of want," Solomon told her when they opened. "But the want of liquor is a different matter. They pay."

Bridey smiled and agreed. A hungry soul never left their premises and any leftover food went to St. Agnes' Orphanage, delivered by Bridey herself.

"You've made me a happy man. Not only are you beautiful, but you work harder than any woman I've ever seen. I was young when I came from Europe. I just worked hard and saved my money, but I never even thought about marriage until I saw you."

He leaned his muscular arms on the counter of the bar and took a satisfied draw from an ornate pipe. His angular face would have made a beautiful bronze.

"You're a good woman."

Chapter 51

Flight to Vermillion Hall

Bridey completed her delivery to St. Agnes' Orphanage, where the Pauratore fish wagon blocked her exit. She reined in her carriage horse and saw Clive Hodggers coming toward her.

"Why didn't you come to see me and Abby when our pa died back in October?"

He said, his lip curling.

"You're tryin' to shame me and I won't listen to it. You know that old man was evil, but I would have come if Abby hadn't already run away and started living at Mademoiselle DuBonnet's School."

She realized too late that she'd said too much.

"Move your wagon, Clive Hodggers." *Why did I let him make me so mad?*

He complied and sat trying to remember where he'd heard the name DuBonnet. Finally, he recalled delivering fish to that big house several weeks ago.

Oblivious that classes might be in session, Clive knocked on the school's front door. Mlle. DuBonnet answered it herself. A disheveled young man stood before her.

"I'm Clive Hodggers and I want to see my sister Abby."

Mlle. DeBonnet blanched. *Not if I can help it.*

"There's no one here by that name. Good day."

She tried to close the door but Clive wedged his foot in it. Her butler hurried to her aid.

"Young man, you get right back in your wagon and leave here," he said in a firm voice, taking him by the arm.

Clive broke free, threw his hat on the brick walkway and began to cry, "I want my sister."

The muscular butler scooped the hat up, placed it on Clive's head, pushed him out the iron gate, and locked it.

"Don't come back," he shouted, his face reddening.

Janine motioned Abby out of history class and whispered to her. Then rushed her to her room.

"Get your cape, ma chérie. It's a beautiful day for a ride." They left in a closed carriage via the back entrance.

"Where are we going, Aunt Janine?"

"Vermillion Hall. The heat in New Orleans has been unbearable and you haven't been feeling too well. We must protect you for your upcoming wedding. It will be much cooler there near the river. The Arceneaux will understand."

It thrilled Camille and Luther to have their future daughter-in-law as their house guest. Abby's Richilene trunk arrived that same afternoon. The servants placed it in a suite of rooms on the third floor, a silent sentinel to the canopied bed and its secret.

Daddy Luther, as he wanted to be called, adored this bundle of red-haired sunshine and Camille, as she wanted to be called, took delight in being able to question Abby whenever she pleased.

"How did your parents meet, Abby?" she asked over tea on the verandah.

"In Paris."

"But how, my dear?"

"I think it was an arranged marriage; you can ask Aunt Janine. She'll know." *It was an arranged marriage, indeed. Mamere was a casket girl who packed her few belongings into a tiny trunk and came to New Orleans to be wife to a drunken Irish widower with a four-year-old son. Oh, Mamere...Mamere, with your twisted foot and beautiful face.*

"It's really not important. I just wondered," said Camille, a satisfied smile crossing her thin lips. "You enjoy the nice breeze."

She reached for her brass bell and the clanging din echoed against the Corinthian columns.

"Besa, I need you." *Arranged, what a wonderful word. Arranged means lots of money must have been involved.*

Besa rolled Camille's wheelchair to the lift.

Down the steps from the verandah, Abby drifted toward the still-blooming camellias that seemingly had forgotten the seasons. Her previous Irish Channel mud yard had boasted only swill, loose pigs and chickens.

She surveyed her surroundings, patted her stomach and relished the stirrings of the womb-safe infant she carried. Her hands were so swollen she could no longer wear her beautiful ring and she had tucked it away in the music box under the bed. *York will be coming home to stay and we have Daddy Luther. Dear God, don't let my life ever change.*

Camille admired her image in her boudoir mirror, congratulating herself on arranging such a suitable union for York. She was already aware of Abby's condition. In her mind, this proved a plus. *The bargain, and dowry, is now sealed.*

Chapter 52
The Wedding Banns

Two Sundays later, Clive decided. *I've never been in that St. Louis Church where all those uppity people go. I'm just as good as they are.*

He stared at the marriage banns posted on the front doors.

"*Mlle. Janine DuBonnet announces the betrothal of her niece Abbigail Anne Hodggers of Paris, France and New Orleans, Louisiana to York Crumpton Arceneaux, son of Mr. and Mrs. Luther Arceneaux of Vermillion Hall Plantation.*"

Clive paused at the church door. He heard, "*Benedictus qui venit in Domini,*" "blessed is he who comes in the name of the Lord," and turned to a policeman and asked, "Where is Vermillion Hall located?"

"At the end of Bayou Conét Road in Tachérie Parish. Do you and that Pauratore boy deliver that far out?"

"I soon will." *I sure will deliver me out there and I'll be blessed by the Lord.* He laughed at his own joke.

The wagons with the other servants went to Congo Square without Hatch. He'd ridden his horse into town alone to see Mary. Although married seven years now, they both continued to live at their places of employment. They'd not begun to furnish their house on Bayou Bequet.

Camille, Luther, Abby and Besa lounged at home this Sunday. They had finished late breakfast and Abby and Besa had started clearing the verandah table when a lone rider appeared on the horizon.

The rider nodded to Luther.

"I'm Clive Hodggers. I see my sister there; I need to talk to her." He dismounted, pointing.

"You can't be her brother," Camille said, her voice rising. "She doesn't have any relatives except her Aunt Janine."

"She ain't got no aunt. I'm her only kin. We usta live on Gautier Street - 'til she run off."

"Gauthier Street," Camille spat out the syllables. "Is he telling the truth, Abby? That's the Irish Channel."

Abby didn't answer. She first ran into Besa's arms, then headed inside the mansion with Luther following.

"Why you're nothing but an alley cat," Camille called after her. "And I'll never let you marry my son."

Luther ached at Abby's humiliation.

Camille commanded Clive to stay so she could question him further. While not eloquent, Clive's story proved succinct.

"Ma'am, I didn't want to cause no trouble. I just wanted to see my sister."

"You wait here. I'll be right back. Your sister needs to talk to you."

She wheeled herself inside and strained to hear the on-going conversation. She jerked her head in disgust at her inability to translate when Luther and Abby slipped with ease from English to French.

"My Mamere, a casket girl, went to a workhouse in place of her aged father who owed someone some money. My pa paid the debt and her passage to New Orleans. She died almost four years ago. I left her little chest of things when I ran away. What am I going to do? I have nothing."

"Abby, we know about your little one. It will grow up here at Vermillion Hall. Everything is going to change and be wonderful for you. York will be home from school soon. It's going to be alright; just wait and see."

"Speak English!" screamed Camille. They ignored her.

"But Daddy Luther, Camille hates me now."

"It's not *where* you come from, it's *who* you are, and you're special. I was just a Cajun farmer when I first saw Camille and I thought she was wonderful. She once was so gentle. She'll come around."

Abby stopped crying.

"Daddy Luther, let's go to the third floor where York said we'd have our rooms and look at the river."

"Let's take the lift," he suggested.

"No, I want to climb the stairs like York and I did."

With effort, they climbed to the first landing, Camille shrieking from below, "Get that strumpet out of my house!"

Startled, Abby turned too quickly, lost her footing, fell backward down the stairs, and felt the first violent pangs of labor. Besa and Clive heard Luther's distressed call and rushed to help.

"There's no time to take her to bed. Get her to the cot in the kitchen where there's water. The baby is almost here."

Clive, bewildered, wandered toward the kitchen.

"You say she's havin' a baby? She's just a little girl. She shouldn't be havin' no baby."

Neither Luther nor Besa answered. They got her to the kitchen and onto the cot.

"You men get out of here and let me do my work," Besa said, wiping Abby's brow.

"Besa, I'm so scared."

"It's alright, baby, you're doing fine. Give me one big push and we'll get through this."

Denis Luther Arceneaux entered this world at not quite seven months. He came into a hostile environment with a shocking head of red curls befitting one of St. Peter's own.

He would not have the icy-blue eyes of Camille, the green eyes of his father, or the deep blue eyes of his mother, but rather the almost black-brown eyes of his grandfather: Cajun, farmer and his protector.

"You can come back later, Mr. Clive. She needs to rest," Besa told the anxious young man. "The baby's a boy, Denis Luther."

"Can I see the baby?"

"Sure," She held him up and pulled back the blanket.

"He's awful red and wrinkly. Is he sick?"

Besa and Luther looked at one another and pretended not to hear. They knew. Clive left.

Chapter 53
What Did She Whelp?

Unable to contain her curiosity any longer, Camille unleashed her harpy voice and screeched from the great hall doorway, "What did she whelp, a male or a female?!"

Luther ignored her.

"It's a boy, Miss Camille," Besa answered without looking up.

Luther neared, holding little Denis close to his chest to keep him warm.

"I fear this little fellow is not going to make it, Besa. Hold him while I get a carriage hitched up to take him to Dr. Cornevise."

He returned and whispered something to Abby, easing the baby down for her to kiss, then carried him to the carriage in a grapevine basket heated with bricks wrapped in blankets.

Dr. Cornevise and his wife Anne still visited in front of St. Louis Cathedral after services. Luther arrived and motioned them toward the carriage. They went straight to the doctor's office.

"His little lungs don't sound good, Luther. Anne, could you find a wet-nurse till we can get him back to his mama?"

"There is a Mrs. Delacroix from Paris who has a six-week-old baby. I'll get her address from your office."

Soon she returned.

"This is Mignon Delacroix. She's offered to help, but she and her son return to Paris at high tide."

They handed her the baby.

Denis nudged the ample breast, gulping as he fought to breathe. Mignon raised her nipple. He rooted closer. His breathing relaxed somewhat when the milk began to flow.

"He's an eager eater, just like my son."

The kitchen provided the perfect place for Abby to regain her strength. Only three hours before she had given birth. Curled up on the cot, she resembled a sleepy, tawny kitten. Besa prepared a cup of café au lait in a China cup and placed two beignets, French doughnuts, left over from breakfast, on a tray.

Abby propped herself up on an enormous feather pillow.

"Um, coffee...thank you, Aunt Besa."

A voice sweet as powdered sugar suddenly came from the great hall.

"Besa, could you help me get down these steps. I've acted so badly and I need to spend some time with my grandson's mother to try to ask her forgiveness. Could you give us some time together so I might apologize? Those two big pots need to be sand polished. Maybe you could do that while we visit?"

Besa did not want to leave Abby, but she thought if anything could make Camille act kindly toward this child, she'd sure try to help it along.

"I have a task to do. You ring this bell if you need me, Miss Abby."

"Run along, Besa. I'll take care of her."

Camille's claw-like hand scratched along the wainscoting as she maneuvered her wheelchair to be closer to Abby. *I'll take care of her, yes I will.* She smiled.

Besa heard the bell just as the sand polishing had begun. Scrambling up, she knocked one pot into the well. The kitchen blazed. Camille's wheelchair blocked the door. She could hear Abby's screams, kicked the wheelchair aside, pitched a bucket of water on the engulfed cot and grabbed

Abby. She placed her on the walkway's cool bricks. Her own injuries she'd not notice until hours later.

"She set me on fire," Abby whimpered.

Camille lurked in another wheelchair, peering down from the great hall's elevation at the frenzy. In calculated calm, she watched Besa put lard on the burns.

Hatch rode up at that moment. Besa met him.

"Go get Dr. Cornevise, Miss Camille set fire to Miss Abby. We can't move her. Hurry."

He left on a fresh horse and she rushed back to Abby, who was writhing in a semi-fetal position on the herringbone walkway, her body a torsade of human flesh.

Hatch reached Dr. Cornevise's office and relayed the horrible news. At first almost catatonic, Luther regained his composure. Although his feet felt nailed to the floor, he began to formulate plans and alternate plans.

"Keep putting that salve on the baby's chest every two hours until I get back," Dr. Cornevise advised, hurrying to gather his black bag and bandages.

Luther asked Anne Cornevise to go for J. Leenard Ragland. She brought him back with her.

Shaken, after alerting the doctor, Hatch entered the side door of Solomon's Tavern to get a drink. When he told them what happened, Bridey fainted. When she revived, she prayed, *Please, dear Lord, don't let her die.*

"Did you know Miss Abby?" Hatch asked.

She nodded but couldn't stop crying enough to speak. Still sobbing, she went upstairs.

This proved to be one of the few times anyone ever got a free drink. Solomon had one with him, too.

Hatch returned to Vermillion Hall to be met by Dr. Cornevise leaving. The doctor stopped at the gate, his waistcoat off and his shirt perspiration-soaked.

"She didn't make it, Hatch. She's dead."

"Oh, sweet Jesus, no. Not the little miss," he moaned.

Distressed at not being able to talk to Abby, Clive returned to New Orleans, though still determined to see his sister. *She's all I have and that little baby looked so sick.* His usual best friend, alcohol, beckoned him to Solomon's Tavern. He wandered in and Bridey met him with the news. For the first time in his life, whiskey rose second in his thoughts. His return to Vermillion Hall was swift.

Clive went to the smoldering kitchen where he'd last seen Abby. Dazed, he staggered toward the most visible lights. The stench of burned flesh hung thick as Spanish moss. He entered the great hall, opening directly to a red, silk-paneled ballroom. He walked past pilastered two-foot-wide Corinthian piers, ten on each side and six at each end. The far end opened through five sets of French doors to a railed verandah overlooking a formal garden of infamous white roses.

Besa had placed Abby in the ballroom, where she should have reigned over many glittering affairs. Instead, cold and still with a pained expression, she held court from three planks on sawhorses draped in lace-trimmed bed-linen dressed in her ice-blue ball gown. Convulsed emotions powered Clive across the room.

"My sister can't be dead. She..." He recoiled at the seared, rippled flesh partially covered by Abby's pale blue evening wrap. "Where's Mrs. Arceneaux?"

"I haven't seen her since I pulled Miss Abby from the fire."

After searching all rooms, he found her on the third floor. Camille gazed transfixed at the river. Abby would have destroyed all the dreams she had for York, but she remembered her guide in India telling her and her friends how mothers-in-law often set fire to their son's young wives' saris to get their dowries.

Abby's dowry would have been her Irish Channel Heritage. Well, I took care of Abby...protected York from...

Clive startled her, his red-rimmed eyes menacing. She scurried from her standing position and returned to her wheelchair. He walked to the back of her chair and plunged it from the third floor. The chair fell on her and broke her neck.

Clive's horse passed York's carriage near the newly completed Kennington Shadows. At darkness neither noticed the other, but directed their attention toward the twinkling lights from the magnificent new mansion revealing a covered furniture-laden barge tied up at the pier.

Just outside the Vieux Carré, Clive dismounted and turned Joey Pauratore's horse loose knowing it would go home on its own. Then he disappeared into Bayou Conét.

Chapter 54
Exodus

Part of Besa died when her deft hands finished their dreaded task, as women had done since the beginning of time. They birthed, suckled, guided, and too often prepared their own children for burial. Although she had never birthed, suckled, nor tried to guide Abby, she felt she was her own, just as she felt York also belonged to her.

Gathering her soaps, oils and water to leave the big house, her home, she heard the wagons returning from Congo Square. *I must warn them.* She threw her supplies on the herringbone walk and dashed to meet them.

"Go, put your belongings in your wagons and leave. Miss Camille's gone crazy. She killed Miss Abby. Set her on fire. Hatch has all your horses hitched and saddled. Don't waste any time. He has barrels of food, too. Be sure to set the dogs loose.

"Where will we go?" asked Uncle Sib, stunned.

"Don't fret about anything. Hatch has land and everybody can find work. He and Mary even have a house on that property. You just sit here on the steps 'til he says to go. He already has your things packed."

The old man looked relieved, nodded and sat.

Vermillion Hall fell silent as Besa, the only human being stirring, went to extinguish the candles around Abby's body. A shout from the ballroom's entrance stopped her and York's words echoed around the cavernous room.

"Aunt Besa, where is everyone and what happened to the kitchen?"

He raced to her side, then stopped, retching over the verandah railing. York's fingers longed to caress the shriveled flesh of Abby's partially covered face. He stared at her red curls, made a gesture to touch them, but changed his mind. His hands raised and fell, zombie-like, to his sides.

"Don't blow out the candles yet, Aunt Besa."

"You'll have to take care of things yourself. I'm leaving."

"Oh, please don't go. What kind of accident was it?'

She dreaded having to tell him.

"It wasn't an accident. Miss Camille set fire to Miss Abby in the kitchen."

"What are you saying? It can't be true."

"It is Mr. York. I don't lie. You know that."

"Where is Camille?"

"I don't know. In her room, I guess. She disappeared when I tried to help Miss Abby."

"Help me find her."

"I can't. I don't want to see her. I'm leaving Vermillion Hall *now.*"

"This is your home. You can't leave me. Where will you go?"

"Probably walk to Echo Trading Post and stay until I can decide something."

"You can't *walk.* Take my horse, Big Boy. Will you ask Daddy to come in here?"

"Your daddy went to New Orleans."

He's lost Abby. I can't tell him about that little baby who'll probably die, too. He'll find out from Mr. Luther, not me.

York grabbed Besa and buried his head on her shoulder.

"I love you, Aunt Besa."

"I love you too, Baby."

This time he didn't object to a childish name.

Besa and Big Boy headed into the night, not stopping at Echo Trading Post, but continuing on to New Orleans.

Near the Pontalba Building, something moved in the shadows. Luther and J. Leenard jumped toward the movement. It was Besa.

"What are you doing here, Besa?"

"What are you doing here? Why aren't you with little Denis? Did he die?"

"No, he's alive. He's with a wet nurse at Dr. Cornevise's office. I'm taking him to doctors in Switzerland. The wet nurse said she would go with us. We sail tonight."

"I had to find out about the baby. Mr. York is home, Mr. Luther. I prepared Miss Abby, but I can't stay there anymore. I had to leave."

"What did he say about the baby?"

"I didn't tell him, but he needs you now."

"His little son needs me more. York has Camille."

His stern look softened.

"Besa, why don't you come with me? I'll sure need help, the kind you've always given York."

"Yes, Besa," J. Leenard added. "Please consider it. My wife can give you extra clothes."

Chapter 55
The Dogs Are Let Loose

York staggered toward the kitchen rubble, stumbled over the wheelchair and touched the doorframe's scorched surface. His driver followed. Unknown to both of them, the dog yard gate stood ajar. Circling animals greeted them with bared teeth, then recognized York and calmed.

"Should we try to pen them up, Mr. Arceneaux?"

"No, just let them stay out. You and I both need to get some rest. There's clean bedding on those shelves just inside the hall door there."

"I'll sleep in the first cabin, if that's all right."

"Anywhere you like. Thank you for bringing me home."

York dismissed thoughts of finding Camille after looking in her bedroom. *I don't care if I never see that woman again. I hate her. I hate her.* Still wearing his soot-covered boots, he sought the comfort of the memory-laden bed on the third floor.

About six the next morning, a piercing scream, then growls and baying roused him. Benumbed, he struggled to the balcony. Ground fog obscured his view. *Ummm, that old swamp panther does sound like a woman screaming and he's riled the dogs up.* He did not notice the broken banister. Silence. He left the gallery and fell back in bed.

His driver awakened him at 8:15, saying, "I went outside earlier...heard noises, but the fog covered everything. You need to come with me now, Mr. Arceneaux."

York rubbed his brow to clear his head, then followed his driver to the servant's quarters. Bits of bloody ecru lace, bones and other remains of Camille littered the shepherd's-crook path leading back to a spot beneath the third-floor balcony. Her blood-spattered mahogany chair lay mangled and condemned, as though cast down from Above.

"My God, was that your mother?"

"No, it was a woman named Camille," came his torpid reply.

"I'll get a shovel and gather everything into a bedsheet for you."

The driver started toward the mansion and the storage area. York pointed to the tool shed.

"Yes, please do that. Your pay will be on the front hall table. I'm sorry I can't offer anything to eat, but I know you need to get back to Natchez."

The driver left him on the ballroom floor next to Abby's body, where their overseer Chad Boulanger found him hours later.

"Mr. York, welcome home. Saw the kitchen...was anyone..." he stopped; horror stricken.

"Yes," York said, turning toward Abby's body.

"What can I do? She was so beautiful."

He moved closer.

"Go into town and get Sheriff Duchon. My father's wife is dead also."

"I sure will. I'm so sorry. Sorry I wasn't here, too. I've been in Baton Rouge on business. Your daddy sent me." *Father's wife? That's strange.*

"And Mr. Boulanger, take a wagon and bring back a pine coffin."

York stopped at Ruvasha en route to New Orleans.

"Abby's dead, Mrs. LeFleur. Camille set her on fire."

Too dumb-struck to reply, Tedelia covered her mouth and gave a muffled cry.

J.P. asked, "Where is your mother, son?"

"She fell from the third floor gallery and I don't know for sure what happened then...panthers, dogs...I don't want to talk about it."

He clenched his teeth and slowly moved his head from side to side.

"We're burying Abby tomorrow morning. The weather is too hot to wait any longer."

He shuddered.

"Have you seen my daddy? Aunt Besa said he left for New Orleans before Camille..." he said, shuddering again. "I sure need him."

"We haven't seen him," J.P. answered.

"I've got to go tell Father Prejean and her Aunt Janine, then select a casket."

"Do you want me to go with you?" J.P. asked.

"No, I have to do this myself. Thank you, though."

"I'll go with you," Paul offered.

"I really need to be by myself."

"We'll get dressed and go on over to the house. Who's there?" Tedelia asked.

"No one. Mr. Boulanger went into Deltran to get the sheriff. The servants deserted the plantation. They left last night."

York turned his team around and headed toward New Orleans.

Abraham, who had remained silent, suddenly hugged Tedelia.

"We sure are glad to be home, My Te. We're a lucky family."

Tedelia started crying.

Gilbert LeFleur crossed himself and said to no one in particular, "just when we get our boys home from Yale, this terrible thing happens..."

York had hoped the Arceneaux family cemetery would never resemble the New Orleans charnel cities of above-ground crypts, but the angels adorning the tombs, ordered by Camille from Italy, rose to four feet above the vaults and reached solemnly toward mammoth Carolina oaks like a celestial rooftop caucus.

Sheriff Duchon examined Camille's remains and the scene where she died, filled out papers and left. York and Boulanger unceremoniously dumped Camille's cereclothed remains in the pine box. It rested in the yawning earth of a grave without a headstone. It would never boast a marker in York's lifetime.

As carriages of mourners and the curious arrived for Abby's funeral, Luther rode the high seas headed for Switzerland. His small party consisted of Besa, Mignon Delacroix, her infant son and Luther's future, his precious grandson Denis Luther Arceneaux. Mignon agreed to delay her arrival in Paris to stay with them until they obtained medical attention.

Heat strangled the throngs attending the closed-casket funeral. Men loosened their collars and corseted ladies nearly swooned. Father Prejean eulogized Abby, ensconced in a gleaming, brass-trimmed coffin. They placed her in the vault next to Larissa's husband Marcel Arceneaux. Aunt Janine hugged York, but the trauma had left her speechless. Janine DuBonnet gave thanks, too, assuming Abby's pregnancy went with her to her grave. J. Leenard Ragland approached York at services's end.

"My condolences."

"Thank you, Mr. Ragland."

"I understand your father has disappeared. He executed legal documents several months ago," he lied, "and left them with me. We need to go over these papers together. Tomorrow morning when the bank opens?"

"Yes sir. And he has disappeared. I don't know much about legal matters, Mr. Ragland," he lied. "You'll have to explain them to me."

York waved to departing buggies.

Chapter 56
A University Man

Outside the Banque de la Nouvelle Orleans the next morning street vendors hawked their wares, the St. Louis Cathedral Choir practiced, and the heady scent of magnolia filled the air. Carriages hummed by, filled with laughing people. Everything seemed so normal. Yet York felt his life was over. Inside the bank, life became even more oppressive.

"First, you'll be glad to know, the police found Big Boy at the edge of town."

"But I gave him to Aunt Besa."

"Well, he was wandering loose. They have him over on Bateau Avenue at the city stables."

"I'll get him, thank you."

"Basically, your father has designated a monthly amount for you and your mother—your late mother," he corrected himself, "to be used exclusively for your personal needs. I will administer a separate fund for your schooling."

He showed him a figure on the papers spread out on his desk.

"You may draw on it as you wish. However, an account to operate Vermillion Hall, which I will administer, will be out of your hands."

York scowled, "But I've been to Yale. I'm a university man. I know how to manage money, especially my own money."

"This is your father's money until I hear otherwise. Your overseer, Chad Boulanger, may submit written requests for funds, which I will honor," J. Leenard said, rising. "I believe this concludes our business."

York wanted the wording:

Abigail Hodggers Arceneaux

1835-1851

cherished wife of

York Arceneaux

carved on her tomb. Instead, after talking with Father Prejean, he settled for:

Abby 1835-1851

cherished

York had all the angels chiseled off and smashed to pieces. He then tossed some of the marble fragments on Camille's grave. The white roses he ripped from the ground and replaced with red. A solemn ceremony launching each uprooted rosebush on a downstream river journey completed his familial cleansing. He never spoke Camille's name again.

Aunt Janine would not learn of Denis for many years. Besa was the lone person left when Abby gave birth. His existence was a carefully guarded secret. Clive had vanished, the Raglands and Cornevises were not talking, and Camille was dead.

York spent weeks searching for Luther. He finally gave up and almost became a recluse. One of the workers, named Oscar, who'd rebuilt the kitchen and repaired the banister, stayed on as cook and handyman. Other than that, the plantation was virtually closed. Oscar knew the way to Marie LaVeau's house, as he often delivered a message from Mr. Arceneaux to her. Chad Boulanger's parents lived in Baton Rouge and he lived there most of the time, as York did not want anyone around.

Chapter 57
Switzerland

Besa, safely aboard the *Ile de France* bound for Europe, watched Luther pace the deck. Mlle. Delacroix nursed Denis, whose eager sucking proved at cross-purposes with his erratic breathing. Small-gulp feedings sustained him for the remainder of the trip. His tiny body shrank by a full pound before they dropped anchor in Nice and started overland. Minty ointment applications continued.

Open air flower markets painted the picturesque city of Lausanne, where Mignon Delacroix turned Denis over with tears to the doctors and nurses of a large hospital.

"I feel as if I've given up a little baby of my own," she said, indignation replacing gratitude when Luther offered her an envelope of money. She refused the money but did thank him. "Just see that he grows strong."

Mignon rested one night before departing for Paris.

Six weeks passed before Luther learned of Camille's death and other news from Vermillion Hall: the kitchen had been rebuilt, the railing replaced, and the roses in the garden returned to red. Being a man above gossip, J. Leenard did not communicate references nowadays to the plantation as "Bloody Hall" nor of the mysterious lights, probably foxfire, dancing over Camille's grave.

Months passed quickly. Besa remained at little Denis's side in the hospital where they had a suite. On rare moments when she needed to be away, she always found him in the arms of a well-dressed woman when she returned and not his private nurse. The woman introduced herself as Martha-Louise.

"Do you work here?"

"No, I live here."

Assuming the woman to be a patient, she continued to be confused.

"I have a weakness for little red-headed boys. I didn't mean to intrude," said Martha-Louis, leaving.

"Inge, who is that woman?"

"Oh, I thought you knew. That's Mlle. Pontaine. She owns the hospital. She and her late husband, Dr. Pontaine, lived on the top floor. She still does. He had red hair."

Mlle. Pontaine's husband gave up a career in banking to become a physician when their toddler son, who also had red hair, died. She continued an affiliation with the bank as a board member and often saw Luther in passing. They would not actually meet for two years and she had no inkling the red-headed toddler belonged to him.

Chapter 58
Voodoo

A well-oiled drone replaced the creaking of Marie LaVeau's carriage wheels as her journey to Vermillion Hall progressed. Ebony veiling swathed the mocha tint of her exotic beauty. Shimmering moonlight seeped through the Spanish moss, creating dark curlicues on the sleek cabriolet's surface.

Their speeding intrusion along Bayou St. John disturbed a warren, scattering rabbits as droplets of an unexpected sneeze. The huge, dark driver commanding the reins wore an expressionless face.

"Just a few more miles," she said out loud.

Her rib cage rose and fell, breathing increased to little short gasps, then eased back into fluid rhythm. Diamonds of perspiration jeweled her entire body, almost unseen in her deep scarlet dress. Her tignon hid luxurious raven curls.

Seven trips to Vermillion Hall this month. Seven trips to the fine gentleman without a heart. This Creole's manhood could not be restored with her snakes and voodoo, but still he sent for her and she came. Marie LaVeau could work almost any magic, but she could look into this living man's eyes and tell that his soul had been dead for a long time.

She patted the satin finished, lidded straw basket in her lap and felt a lunge from something inside.

They arrived.

Plantation shutters opened to a side verandah where her driver waited, a man of patience, well paid and well fed. This, her entrance and exit route, provided complete privacy. York was mesmerized by the silken red dress clinging to her undulating, lithe body. The incantations and use of the lidded basket added to the sensuality of the total experience. The night held many secrets. Spent wax candles puddled around York's bed, where he lay in an exhausted sleep.

She left the great mansion just before dawn. Once inside the carriage, she rubbed a velvet sack of coins against her face and smiled. A smattering of ground fog hugged their path and mysterious bird songs broke the silence. Her carriage cut through the mist like a dagger parting flesh.

Arriving home on Bayou St. John depleted, she slipped into a red velvet bed with a mounted cheetah skin incorporated into an intricately carved mahogany headboard.

York gave up his search for Luther and returned to Yale. He replaced his former apathy with learning fervor. Paul and Abraham marveled at the transformation, but could not understand how eyes afire for knowledge could appear so vacant and unreceptive to human beings.

About the same time at summer's end, the Roussel sisters, Nadeleine "Leine" and Millicent "Mila," eleven months older, moved from Natchez to their parents' newly completed mansion, Kennington Shadows. They debuted together and suitors swarmed, hoping for favors. Blessed with graceful movements of proud racehorses, their manes of blonde curls framed alabaster complexions accented with cornflower-blue eyes.

Their father, General Alain Roussel, felt pride in four things: his wife Arianna, his daughters Leine and Mila, and his tenure as an instructor at West Point—in that order. His French and Natchez textile mills and wealth mattered little. To someone else, they would prove paramount in his plans.

Chapter 59
Reunions

"Rolfo, my wife saved your bread in the back. We were running out," the baker called over the din in the crowded Lyon bakery.

Blonde curls topped by a pink bonnet bounced and swirled to bring Rolfo face to face with enormous piercing blue eyes.

"Your name is Rolfo?" she asked, lifting her chin to see him better.

"Yes, why?"

"I've only heard that name once before in my entire life. Where are you from?"

"Lyon. Where did you hear the name?"

"Oh, it was a tiny place, not even a village...a vineyard in Italy."

"I lived in Italy," he said, becoming defensive.

"Where?"

"Somewhere near Rome and in Rome."

"Did you live at the Brazzio Vineyard?"

"I don't know,"

"Why do you not know?

"I was a small child then."

"Do you have a relative named Ludii?"

Rolfo stiffened.

"What is your name and why do you want to know?" He felt the muscles in his cheeks pulsate. Other patrons began to stare.

"I once lived at the Brazzio Vineyard and there I knew a small boy who was very dear to me. His name was Rolfo. I now live in Lyon. My name is Sofia Entremont.

"So-fi-a," he whispered, syllables rolling out slowly.

He looked down from his rangy height to an exquisite woman of not more than five feet and fumbled to pay for the bread the baker handed him.

"It *is* you, Rolfo," she squealed, startling several patrons.

He caught her arms and ushered her out to a sidewalk café.

"Two coffees, please."

He stared at her.

"Sofia, I've thought of the way you cooked fish so many times. It tasted wonderful. Are you still a good cook?"

"Heavens, I was not a good cook, but I've never forgotten the fish you would catch for our suppers. I've always said a prayer for you at mealtime—to this day."

"You're such a grand lady now. Was the transition difficult for you?"

She almost spit out the coffee laughing.

"Dear, sweet Rolfo," she said, patting her mouth with a lace-trimmed handkerchief. "I went to school first in Switzerland, then Rome. There the groundskeeper's son was my undoing, my Fedducio. I never had difficulty getting re-accustomed to being rich. I did have trouble, back then, learning how to be poor."

Rolfo flushed.

"I had no idea. You were always so kind to me. Those memories helped me through many dark times."

Their conversation switched back and forth from French to Italian.

"Do you have any family, Rolfo?"

"I don't know. I don't know where Ludii fits in. What about your family?"

"My husband Celestin and his family in Nice. I had a sister who died of smallpox when I was ten and both my parents died after I left Italy."

She cast her eyes down.

"They willed everything to the church with the stipulation their villa should go to me, if I could be found within five years. I had corresponded with my best friend and she told her father where I was. He was their attorney."

She took a long drink of coffee and her eyes filled with tears.

"Please tell me more, Sofia."

"We often go to Rome during the opera season."

"You have a good life, it seems. Are you happy?"

"I love my husband, but I am not as happy as I could have been. Seeing you and knowing you are well has added much to my well-being."

"I'm so glad to have found you, Sofia."

"You wore a tiny cross years ago," she said, suddenly remembering. "Did you lose it?"

Rolfo reached under his shirt for the remnant, now with a gold chain and frame. He proudly held it up for Sofia. "No, I didn't lose it, but it is a bit battered."

"Oh, it's broken. It was caked with grime back then, but you wouldn't let me touch it. I wanted to give it a bath," she said with a laugh.

"No, it just shrank a little," he said, tucking it back in his shirt.

They were both laughing when the waiter freshened their coffee.

"I've gone on and on. Tell me about you. Is there a young woman in your life?"

"No. My work keeps me busy in the shop of the jeweler, Yigal Levron. You know of him?"

"Yes, I've purchased from him."

"He's also instructing me in Hebrew and Greek. And I assist the Sisters of Charity at St. Solange Convent when I can. They saw that I learned Latin, much to my dismay."

"Heavens, Rolfo, how many languages do you know?"

"Italian, French...a little Spanish, German, English, Romani, some Greek...and I'm still working on Hebrew."

"Why so many?"

"When I was with the gypsies—yes, I lived with gypsies—it was important to speak the language where we were. I also lived in a convent. The sisters thought Latin necessary and Monsieur Levron says Hebrew and Greek are, too."

He became very serious.

"How did you come to be in Lyon?"

Sun drenched her blonde curls, changing them to radiant gold. They sought shade at another table beneath blue and white striped awnings and continued their intense question and answer session.

"I went to another harvest, this time here in France, in Nice. There I worked at a large chateau teaching the vineyard owner's children. The owner had one grown son, a beautiful man who liked my eyes... probably liked me, too. We have been married almost ten years."

"But why did you leave Italy?"

"I did not tell a skinny little boy my secrets then, so why should I tell you now?"

"Oh, I did not mean to pry. It's just..."

"I am joking with you, Rolfo, but I am not joking when I tell you that at seventeen I ran away from school and married a poor, handsome boy, my Fedducio. I loved him very much but my parents disowned me."

"I have no right to this information, Sofia."

"You do, Rolfo. You are an important part of my life."

"I fail to see how."

"The year I found you at Ludii's, my husband and the baby boy I was carrying died when our cart overturned in a nearby stream. Ludii's hut was where they took me. My Fedducio and our baby are buried in that little cemetery near there."

"I'm so sorry."

"You should not be sorry. You were the only bright spot in my life. I taught you to read, cooked for you. You were the curly-haired little boy I had lost."

"But you left."

"The grapes were gathered and Ludii told all of us to go. It was his house."

"I didn't know why you left. I left the same night that I found you gone."

"Was Ludii your uncle?"

"I don't know. I don't know anything except that I had to get away. He was evil."

"Where did you go then?"

"To Rome. You had told me about Rome."

"How did you get there and what did you do in that huge city?"

"I walked and caught rides, then made friends in Rome and...um...lived with them."

He could not bear to tell her the sad truth.

"Ah. Then how did you get here?"

"Gypsies brought me to France. Then Sisters at St. Solonge took me in. Monsieur Levron accepted me as an apprentice seven years ago and I have been here ever since."

"Well, bless the Lord for gypsies. Celestin lets a band of them camp on our land every spring."

"Who is their leader, Sofia?"

"I don't know. Celestin always talks with them. They are the same group that camps with my in-laws in Nice."

For a brief moment, Rolfo felt a twinge of sadness—not for the open road, but for the warm sense of belonging he'd shared with the Roms. He thought of LaLa and her crystal ball. What had she seen that she'd refused to reveal to him?"

"Rolfo, Rolfo."

He shook his head.

"Please excuse me. Guess I got caught up in gypsy magic."

"You and Monsieur Levron must come to dinner. I'll send a carriage for you on Sunday at six."

⚜ ⚜ ⚜

"Celestin, I found Rolfo today in Lyon. He's lived here for years."

"The child you told me about?"

"He's no longer a child. I've invited him and Yigal Levron to dinner on Sunday."

"Why Yigal Levron?"

"He works with him."

"You're not going to cry again, are you?"

"No, this is a time to be happy. I've found him. Celestin, what is the name of the gypsy leader whose caravan you allow to camp here every spring?"

"Prince Swar."

Spring never seemed happier to Rolfo than when Celestin notified him of the caravan's arrival. Immediately, he rode Naji II to the campsite and presented himself to a stunned Prince Swar, whose face bore evidence of much adversity.

"We thought you died. Never in these past years have we returned to the Convent St. Solonge. We couldn't bear to go near."

"I am well. You tell me the news of everyone and all your adventures."

"Very few are still at the convent. They talk of closing it and moving closer to the coastal area. Sister Albertine is still there. I work for a jeweler."

"I am being selfish. Come. All must greet you and know you are still alive."

LaLa hugged him with enthusiasm he never dreamed her reserved demeanor possessed. Yesef jokingly tried to hand him his violin. He pretended not to want to accept it, then took the instrument and thrilled the crowd with his playing. Music and merriment lasted well into the night.

This springtime reunion would continue for several years to be interrupted by an unusual happening, civil war. Smoldering events in America would precede and cause the first break and, by a twist of fate, cause the resumption of later reunions.

Eventually, the loss of reunions would be less painful than previous situations. Established, he had a home, a horse, a profession, and a life with meaning. He no longer bit his nails. He'd practically abandoned his Bohemian lifestyle, but his years with the gypsies gave his manner of dress a flair admired by all. Often, too—weather permitting—he left his massive mahogany bed to stargaze after crawling out on the roof with his gray-beard blanket.

Rolfo remembered winter rains in Rome paving the way for splendid fields of strutting red poppies, so proud, so intense in hue. He drank in the profusion of color and had gathered an armful when an old man on a twisted cane approached him.

"You're taking those to your mama?"

"No, to my...uh...my brothers. They probably have never seen anything this pretty."

The old man smiled, nodded, crunched his cane in the pebbles and shuffled into the Roman night, most likely with thoughts of his own mother.

Rolfo relished that memory, left his rooftop stargazing and returned to the warmth of his bedroom.

Chapter 60
The Deception

"But the Sisters had me study Latin, so why do I need Hebrew and Greek?"

"Because you have exercised your body on Naji II, your hands with your future profession and the violin, and now you must exercise your mind. You must be a complete person or I have failed you."

Levron stuck his unlighted pipe in his mouth.

Anger gave Rolfo courage.

"Your pipe isn't lighted."

"I know. It's a nasty habit, so I never light it anymore. Now come into the library. We have work to do."

Levron never told anyone Sister Albertine had shared information about Rolfo's bad lungs. He prayed the young man would remain healthy.

Weeks and months passed quickly. Levron bought a second violin and they played together. Rolfo's jewelry creations impressed and pleased. With his Latin studies background, he eased into Hebrew and Greek as a true scholar. He was becoming a complete person.

Rolfo returned from the convent, brushed Naji II down and went straight to the sewing room adjacent to Monsieur Levron's bedroom. *I must get in and out before he sees me. Tomorrow it will be all over.* He dropped something just as Levron entered the room.

"Why are you in my Hediah's sewing room? I never thought I'd give refuge to a thief. Did you take some of her jewelry hidden in there? What did your gypsy friends teach you?"

Levron brushed his unruly gray hair from his perspiring forehead and collapsed on the chaise longue.

"What did you do? You have no business in there," he said, weeping and moaning from deep sadness.

Rolfo tried to comfort him as he had comforted the little ones in his bridge family but Levron pushed him away.

"I put it back, Monsieur Levron, I..."

"Why have you betrayed me?" the man wailed.

Caleb arrived home and rushed upstairs. He did not see Levron before he blurted, "Rolfo, did you get it?" to the startled young man.

Rolfo wanted to run and hide. He backed into the hall with tears streaming and raced to the stable.

"Come back here, tell him!" Caleb yelled, following close behind. Naji II whinnied as Rolfo threw a saddle blanket over his sleek, lustrous back.

"You can't just leave, Rolfo."

"Yes, I can," said Rolfo, continuing to saddle the horse. "I can take Naji II. Monsieur Levron gave him to me. He'll never trust me again, anyway."

Evening shadows cast the long silhouette of a small man nearing the stable with something in his hand.

"I was wrong, Rolfo. I'm very sorry to have doubted you," Levron said, holding the mended sweater and yarn Rolfo had tried to return after Sister Theresa re-knitted the holes. "Can you forgive me?"

"Today is your birthday," said Caleb, turning to Levron. "It was to be a gift. We knew you didn't want to throw the sweater away, so we had it repaired."

Rolfo unsaddled Naji II.

Five years passed. Ivy proliferation kept its covenant with the deteriorating abbey stones it had held together, and time-ravaged walls decided to release those vines from their four-century promise.

The Sisters knew, but Rolfo refused to believe that the convent, which had given him sanctuary, would soon be deserted.

"We have to leave, for our buildings have not been safe," Sister Albertine reminded him. "You saw firsthand when you were a boy. They can no longer be repaired."

He watched the wagons loading in disbelief.

"Does it have to be so far away?"

"You may still come and visit, just as always. The new convent is not that much farther. It's near the town of Vienne. You pass that way taking your jewelry to Avignon and Marseilles."

Rolfo stared at the Bishop, who was directing the movers, and tried not to view him as an adversary. In two days, the last wagon-load had gone.

Three years later, Yigal Levron's stooped body trembled.

"I am an old man. My beloved Hediah died without giving me children. You are like a son, the son I never had. I want my work to be carried on. Take care of Caleb, he has been faithful."

He pulled his fleecy shawl closer around his thin shoulders and buttoned his brown sweater.

"I will, Monsieur Levron."

"It is important that you teach someone else everything I have taught you and you, my Rolfo, have taught these tired old eyes much. I am grateful."

His tremor worsened.

"I lie down for a while. I'm cold."

The menorah's shadow flickered on the chaise longue where Rolfo helped him settle near the fireplace.

"No, it is I who am grateful, Monsieur Levron. I will try to pass the knowledge on. It will be difficult, for you are the master."

He threw an oak log and cedar strips on the fire, stoked the remaining embers, and watched Levron breathe deeply to take in the cedar scent filling the air.

"When I awaken, we shall have a small celebration: two kinds of cake," said Levron as Rolfo drew the drapes and placed a spread over the old man, who caught his hand and patted it until sleep stopped his motion.

He did not awaken.

Rolfo inherited everything except a sum given to a synagogue where Levron's wife's limestone crypt nestled safely. He was entombed at her side under hundred-year-old yew trees standing sentry in the ancient adjacent cemetery.

Rolfo was alone again.

Chapter 61
Kennington Shadows' New Year's Eve Ball

At Kennington Shadows Plantation, all pink and white like proud delicate stems of gladioli, the Roussel sisters paused and each took an arm of their father. Regal, measured strides scarcely caused their golden curls to bob.

General Alain Roussel led Nadeleine "Leine" and her sister Millicent "Mila" around the ballroom for all to see. Their neighbor Gilbert LeFleur followed, escorting Alain's wife Arianna in the stately prerequisite promenade which the other guests then joined.

Even with their large age difference, Janine DuBonnet secretly adored Gilbert and felt a jealous twinge as he and Arianna marched by. She was not oblivious to her handsome escort, Colonel Mikey Thibodeaux, a friend of General Roussel's from West Point. While Gilbert seemed to be everywhere, his contacts with the opposite sex were fleeting. *He always looks preoccupied.*

Gilbert fulfilled his social obligations but stopped there. His memories of exuberant Katté, her formerly dark curls bleached white by adversity flying statically around her slumped shoulders, as she languished in a Swiss asylum haunted him.

Although of a different nature, Gilbert's inner conflict riddled him with guilt. Lovely Katté, trapped in a living death, and his beloved Larissa, four years in her grave; the only women who had or would ever occupy his thoughts.

The move from Natchez by the Roussels allowed greater flexibility for their growing textile involvement. The General already had two new factories in Lyon, France and had begun to scout New Orleans for personnel to operate them.

Paul LeFleur and Mila danced almost every dance. York had not been to a ball since falling in love with Abby. *Is it possible it has been only a little over a year?* He felt like an old man, staying on the fringe of the room and not dancing all evening.

The mammoth grandfather clock showed nearly midnight when someone tapped him on the shoulder.

"Mr. Arceneaux, I'm Leine Roussel and I believe this is our dance."

York managed a faint smile. At that moment, his eyes fell on Aunt Janine chatting with Arianna Roussel. *I must avoid her.* He quickly accepted.

As they danced, he thought of Abby and how he could not possibly talk to her aunt. What else could he say? He had no right to attempt an explanation of what Camille had done. He still did not know that except for Besa, everyone had gone to Congo Square. Secrets remained secrets. Still thinking Abby's pregnancy had been taken to the grave, Janine DuBonnet did not want to talk with York, either.

The clock chimed the first bell of midnight. York bolted from the room with Leine following closely behind. Tears fell and he sobbed with no control as she held him. He had not felt the warmth of a woman in a long time. He took her by her shoulders and kissed her, gently at first, then not so gently.

Chapter 62
A Second Proposal

"Mila has agreed to be my wife, York. We'll be married as soon as the banns are posted then move to Lyon after the wedding trip."

Paul noticed York's shocked expression, but continued.

"General Roussel wants me to manage one of his factories there."

"Congratulations, Paul, you've pulled off quite a coup. You're a lucky man."

He's done it to me again. He'll have even more money than he already has, all because he's marrying Millicent Roussel. If Paul can get such a deal, so can I.

"Thank you, York."

"Well, you've also carried out your romantic campaign twenty-four hours before I did."

"How so?"

"I plan to propose marriage to Leine tonight. Wish me luck."

"Certainly, just think, we'll be brothers-in-law. We've already been together all our lives."

"We certainly have, Paul."

Yes, all our lives, but life has been so easy for you...so easy...while I've been shackled with little money, an aristocratic witch for a mother, a father who's disappeared, and the horrible memory of seeing Abby dead.

They shook hands and parted.

Having more money than he could spend intrigued York.

Surely, General Roussel will offer me an important job, too. This prospect sounds very appealing. Leine is a beauty. I could do worse.

He would escape the stigma of Camille's deed by living in a different country. If he worked this just right, he, too, could manage the other Alain Roussel factory in France.

The Roussel library at Kennington Shadows proved even more impressive than Vermillion Hall's.

"General Roussel, I'd like to ask for Leine's hand in marriage. Our plantation brings in a handsome profit, my stocks have increased appreciably, my home is in good repair, and my social station guarantees your daughter will continue in a life similar to that she currently enjoys."

He did not mention that he could not get his hands on any plantation profits, that his stock gains would not be his until he was thirty, or that he didn't actually own his home.

"Young man, this sounds well and good, but you have neglected one important factor," Alain Roussel replied, resting his slender hands on a slight paunch that would never have been allowed to form if he'd still been teaching at West Point.

"What is that, sir?"

"You've mentioned social, economic, and creature comforts, but you've left something out. Do you *love* my daughter?"

"Well," he said, already lying. "I thought that was understood, sir. I...I...certainly do. The Natchez women are the most beautiful I've seen in the United States. She is truly a prize."

He meant that part. *She is a beauty and her dowry will be a prize. Sedate, compassionate, but nothing like Abby...kittenish, childlike, funny...oh, Abby. .*

Larissa's impressive engagement ring, clutched in his perspiring hand, fell with a soft clunk to the parquet floor. A subconscious act?

"York, you have dropped something."

"Oh! Yes, sir...thank you," he said, plucking it from the fringe of a plush oriental rug.

"You have my permission. Would you like to ask Leine and her mother to come in now? Congratulations, my boy. Welcome to the family."

Something about York's gaze held a hidden agenda...it was a look he knew well from his own son, Emil.

Chapter 63

Counterpoint

An unexpected guest interrupted York's breakfast at Vermillion Hall.

"Bring a plate of bacon and eggs for General Roussel, Minette."

"No, thank you. I've eaten. Just some coffee, please. York. I've come to discuss a little business."

"…Well, I don't know, General. I have so many responsibilities here. Paul doesn't have the burden of Ruvasha, but I have no one except myself and my overseer, Chad Boulanger, to take care of things."

Roussel cleared his throat.

"Will you talk to him and see if he wouldn't be able to run Vermillion Hall by himself? My girls have always been so close. It would break their hearts to be separated."

"I'll have to give it some thought. The idea never occurred to me of working with you, much less of you taking care of us financially."

"You would be working for me, but I'd not be taking care of you two financially," said the General, perspiring. "My other factory needs someone to run it. You are my first choice. You'd simply be paid for doing a job—and I might add, paid rather handsomely."

York nodded, saying nothing and continuing to eat.

"If you don't feel my first offer enough, we'll negotiate."

York's face is saying "no," but his eyes are saying "yes." I've got him interested.

York stood as if to dismiss his future father-in-law.

"Well, I'll get back to you as soon as Mr. Boulanger and I can talk. Of course, I'd have to pay him a lot more for his additional responsibilities."

"Ten thousand more to the salary I offered you and we'll put production quota raises on top of that with a yearly bonus."

York nodded.

"Sounds fair."

I have him squirming. He's playing right into my hands. York's smile congratulated himself.

"Arianna, I talked with York. I think the boy will come around, but don't say anything to the girls until I get a solid 'yes.'"

"It's just a few weeks before the double wedding. They'll be upset until we know something for sure," said his wife, thinking of her own loneliness with both her daughters' being an ocean away, but then imagining how devastated Mila would be if Leine were not in France with her. A frightened expression crossed her face. "Alain, do you think Emil will try to come to their wedding?"

"He'd better not show his face. I'll turn him into the authorities."

"It's hard to admit that our own firstborn, our own flesh and blood, is so disreputable. Life was always a game to him, something he had to win at, no matter the stakes—or consequences."

Her eyes filled with tears.

"There, there, Arianna. We haven't seen him in years. He's not likely to show up now. We did the best we could by him. There never seemed to be enough of anything to please him."

He cradled his wife in his arms, saying, "He always wanted more."

"I know. I'm borrowing worry, Alain, but it's just like him to try to ruin things for the girls."

"He was last seen in Australia. He's probably still a long way from New Orleans. Now smile for me, mother-of-the-brides."

She gave a half-hearted grin.

"What do you say we give our girls their wedding trip as a gift, Arianna?"

"That sounds generous. You know they plan to be gone six weeks. New York City is a long way off, and expensive."

Three days later, York Arceneaux entered the Banque de la Orleans and asked to see the president. "

Mr. Ragland, it has come to my attention that my late grandmother bought that strip of land where Echo Trading Post is before she moved to Paris, and, as everyone knows, the trading post enjoys a profitable business."

His eyes lowered for a moment, then flashed.

"That Indian has lived there rent free all these years. I think it's time I reclaimed the Arceneaux property. I'm expanding our sugarcane acreage."

"Is that all you want to say young man?"

"Well, just that I need our property returned to us. Why wasn't that Indian moved west when all the others were? Indians can't own property."

J. Leenard rose from his desk and began to pace.

"I'll try to answer one thing at a time. First, you are right that your grandmother bought that property and put it in trust for Quila. She purchased it with money he and his family had earned. Second, he wasn't moved west because the Bureau of Indian Affairs considered his commercial endeavor vital to our local economy. He provided an outlet for people in the bayous to become self-sufficient. Some of the people are half-breeds."

He stopped pacing and looked at York.

"Which half are you going to send west and which half are you going to allow to stay in Louisiana?"

York clenched his teeth and tapped his boot on the floor, not answering.

"Third, you're not moving him and his family off that land because fourth, I now own the land. Larissa sold it to me when she visited New Orleans over ten years ago. You're not moving anybody."

J. Leenard watched York's face redden.

"Let's see how these vital local economy helpers get their fur and produce-loaded pirogues over a muddy field when I have my men dig canals and divert the bayou from their back door," he sputtered.

"York, your plantation would perish if I chose to dam the river upstream from Vermillion Hall. You make one move to hurt the Chickasaw family's business and I'll build that dam, if I have to get out and carry the sandbags myself. Now get out of my office."

Crimson-faced York headed straight for Kennington Shadows, worried about finding money for a wedding trip.

"General Roussel, I've reviewed everything with Chad Boulanger and while I'm agreeable, well, he's made some demands I was not prepared for."

Of course, York had yet to talk with Boulanger.

"With the crops not in, Vermillion Hall doesn't have liquid assets to spare, so I'm in an awkward position."

"I understand, my boy. I'll advance you whatever sum you need for Boulanger and Mrs. Roussel and I would like to give you and Leine the trip to New York City as our wedding gift."

"Oh, we couldn't accept such an offer."

"Nonsense, my boy. Here are two checks. I insist."

I've got York right where I want him.

"Thank you, General. Please, thank Mrs. Roussel when she returns from shopping in New Orleans with Leine and Mila. We're lucky they won't have to miss shopping at the House of Richilene. My late grandmother helped to establish the one in Paris over twenty years ago."

"Might be unlucky. My girls sure like to spend money," said General Roussel with a chuckle.

"I need to make arrangements with Mr. Ragland for the time we're in New York, so I'm headed back to town," said York.

That was too easy.

"I look forward to working with you."

Alain watched his carriage pull away.

Paul had said working "for" you. York says "with." There's something about that boy...

York raced to Creole State Bank and swaggered into the office of Robard Christian "Rat Cheese" Zedohr, president and scoundrel extraordinaire.

"I think it is only fair that I do a little business with you, too," York said. "My future father-in-law needed Vermillion Hall's next cotton crop for his factories in Lyon, so I thought, why not? He's practically family."

Zedohr motioned for an assistant to take the checks and smiled broadly.

"Oh, I'll need about eleven thousand of this in cash. Big bills," he said, avoiding Zedohr's eyes. "I have to leave quite a bit of this with my overseer. Put the rest in an account for me."

"Yes, sir, York. A pleasure doing business with you."

"Well, Mr. Boulanger, money is tight, so there is no way I could increase your salary, however, when we've moved to Lyon, you'd be allowed to live on the second floor of Vermillion Hall as if the place were your own."

York's mouth stretched into a conceited smirk.

"I know you don't have a wife, but it would have a certain social advantage for a bachelor living here and all..."

"That sounds fair, Mr. Arceneaux. I appreciate the trust you've put in me."

"Oh, yes...and I still won't be paying you. Mr. Ragland will continue to honor all your expenses for the plantation and your salary. He asked me to take that responsibility, but I refused. Told him he's getting paid to do that. I don't have the time."

With a twinge of conscience and a sudden burst of generosity, he handed Boulanger five-hundred dollars.

"This is because you are doing a fine job and I appreciate you. Any clothes I leave here, please keep and wear. They'll probably be out of style when I tire of France."

"You're very kind, Mr. Arceneaux."

Kennington Shadows was a floral encrusted bower, the weather beautiful, as were the brides. The feared appearance of their brother Emil never happened.

Paul and Mila glowed as they waved to the last of the guests. York drank too much and Leine tried to hide her embarrassment by engaging her parents in conversation.

"The coach is here, Alain," said Arianna motioning to the servants to load the smaller pieces of luggage.

Alain Roussel glared at York, who was oblivious to everything.

"Miz Roussel, are you sure these girls' Richilene trunks gonna be on that boat already?"

"Yes, Winnie. We sent them this morning."

Alain caught Paul's arm.

"Be sure and contact my former student, Lt. Grant, when you get to New York. I've written to him. Goodbye, all."

On board ship that night, Paul and Mila finally drifted off to sweet dreams. In the next stateroom, York looked at Leine through bleary eyes.

"Your hair's not red."

"Who said it was?"

"I said it was," York slurred.

"Why would you say something that foolish?" she said, teasing him.

"Because I wanted it red."

"York, you're drunk."

"And you don't have red hair."

"Goodnight, York."

With no reply, thus a similar pattern of communication was set for the remainder of their married life.

Chapter 64
Rouge et Noir

At the Zedohr mansion on Esplanade Boulevard, where imposing oaks protected Creoles for decades in an area known as the Garden District, familial actions belied architectural grandeur.

Although now president of Creole State Bank, R.C. still harbored monumental resentment against his deceased father and his own lack of a male heir. Eighteen years had passed and he rarely even talked with his beautiful seventeen-year-old daughter Angelique.

R. C.'s always-locked business valise at his side, he left for work. No goodbye kiss for Mary Elizabeth, just a quick nod as he exited.

Angelique smiled at her mother.

"You'd think Daddy had the Vatican treasures in that case the way he guards it."

"It must contain very important business papers."

"Has he always acted like that, Mother? He's always busy; never has he come to even one of my piano performances."

"Pretty much. He's a businessman; thinks music is frivolous."

"I'm going into town at two, may I bring you anything?'

"Thank you, no. I have to go in tomorrow myself."

Golden-haired Angelique left in a slight swirl of perfume, her curls encircling dainty shoulders—a typical young woman strolling through Jackson Square, probably on her way to meet friends, with her frilly parasol shading her delicate complexion.

At the Creole State bank, R.C. placed a *DO NOT DISTURB* sign on his office door, unlocked his valise to remove a disguise complete with mustache, wig, hat, and gaudy vest. He exited through his private alley entrance, walked two blocks north, three blocks west, and four blocks south.

Two huge, turbaned black men guarded the door at Madame Crechelle's House of Entertainment, where a harp and two violins played from a cantilevered area. An enormous mirror behind a pewter bar reflected beautiful women dancing, smiling, and drinking.

"Mr. Lex, how are you?" Madame Crechelle's rich voice asked. She brushed an errant marabou feather from her forehead.

"Quite well, Little Chell."

"What can we do for you this afternoon?"

"Something really special," he said, placing several large bills on a silver tray.

"You need our new one. She's so sweet, we call her Sugar. Room twelve."

R.C. unlocked room twelve, removed his disguise and everything else, checked his bicep reflection in the gigantic mirror over the bed, and stood waiting with anticipation.

The door opened to an unbelievable vision. A gossamer pink negligee over a barely-there, even more sheer gown left him awestruck. Masses of golden curls floated around her narrow shoulders.

"Daddy?!"

"Angelique!"

Dressed, sans disguise, and bundled next door to a gaming house, his obituary read: *Prominent banker, R.C. Zedohr, of this city, died Tuesday of a heart attack while engaging with friends in a game of rouge et noir. His mass will be celebrated Friday at 2 p.m. at St Louis Cathedral. Survivors...*

Six months later, Mary Elizabeth met a young bachelor from the New Orleans Cotton Exchange named Jason Marchand. He was returning to Lloyd's of London, insisted they marry posthaste, and that Angelique's name be changed to Marchand.

Angelique renewed her interest in music and enjoyed a remarkable career in London as a concert pianist. Her new grandfather, a symphony orchestra conductor, relished her every accomplishment.

Chapter 65
York Sees Denis

Lieutenant Grant delighted in forays from Sackett's Harbor into New York City. His past association with General Roussel at West Point provided another treat. The General's daughters and husbands invited him into dinner at Sabbo's. They met at his hotel, Astor House.

"My, my! You girls were just tadpoles when I last saw you. Now you're swans."

"Are we too grown up to still call you Uncle Lyss?" Mila asked.

"Goodness, I hope not. Miss Julia sends her regrets. She would not have missed meeting you, but is very busy back at the fort as I'm being transferred to Ft. Vancouver in the Oregon Territory."

"When will your family be leaving, Uncle Lyss?" Leine asked.

"Soon, but Miss Julia and little Frederick Dent will be going to live with my parents in Ohio. I'll be going to Ft. Vancouver alone."

Paul sought to lighten the mood.

"All four of us will be going to France when we return from our wedding trip. Our plantations, Ruvasha and Vermillion Hall, will be open to you and your family anytime you are able to get away."

"Mother and Daddy extend an invitation to Kennington Shadows, also. We're all neighbors," Mila said.

Lieutenant Grant promised to visit, returned to Sackett's Harbor, and prepared to move to Oregon. The two couples continued to tour.

Illness plagued Mila when she returned to Louisiana. A difficult pregnancy followed, delaying travel to Europe until the birth of her son, Jean-Paul "Trey" LeFleur, III. Six weeks later they left to join Paul, already in Lyon with Leine and York.

Later that year, yellow fever raged, devastating New Orleans and surrounding areas. Fortunately, Mila and Trey had reached Lyon. Among the more than 5,000 stricken were General and Mrs. Roussel. The horror swept Kennington Shadows and killed seven. Officials limited visitors to lower Louisiana and immigration came to a standstill. When word reached Lyon of the Roussels' deaths, York's ironclad contract was his only concern. Leine and Mila were heartbroken.

Their time in Lyon flew. After four years, the sisters continued to enjoy shopping and dinner parties. Still childless, Leine spent a great deal of time with Trey as a doting aunt.

The couples vacationed together. On their way via train to a mountain resort, York left the dining car to check their tickets. A well-dressed, exotic woman entered the car at a Swiss station, preceded by a young boy of about six.

"Besa?"

"Mr. York!"

They stared at one another. Luther startled York, who'd been transfixed by the child's red curly hair. Besa bustled Denis to the next car.

"Daddy, where have you been? Who is that child?"

"York, everything was so sudden. I had no time to make plans except to get your tiny son to the best doctors in the world. He was born early and in hospitals for two years."

"But, Daddy, why didn't you let me know?"

"I didn't think he would live and then I feared you would take him away from me. Please, say that you won't. Besa cares for him just as she did for you."

"No, I won't take him. Every time I would look at him would be a reminder of Abby. What is his name?"

"Denis Luther Arceneaux, Abby's idea. He says he wants to be a doctor. He was born about four hours before she died."

"You mean before she was murdered."

"Yes, unfortunately you are right."

"Why didn't somebody protect Abby?"

"They were all gone, except Besa, who helped Abby give birth. We never thought Camille had that much hatred in her."

"Has he ever asked about me?"

"Yes, many times, and I tell him your work keeps you busy, but that you love him very much and that his mama died the day he was born."

"Thank you for that."

An awkward embrace followed. They exchanged addresses, but did not promise to write.

"The next town is our stop, York."

Besa came rushing from the car behind with Denis just in time to see York disappear into the car in front.

"Grandpère, you and Aunt Besa know everybody in the whole, wide world, don't you?"

"Not quite, son."

Chapter 66

Crossroads Mistake

The Lyon dinner party afforded interesting conversation, wonderful food, brandy for the men to savor with their smokes, and sherry for the ladies. It was a perfect evening when a noise at the door ruptured the contentedness of the moment.

"Mr. Paul LeFleur, I have an urgent message from your father. I saw your parents in New York."

"Is he ill? Is my mother ill?"

"They are both well, sir. The North and South are at war. South Carolina has seceded from the Union."

"Is New Orleans under siege?"

"It wasn't when I left New York. I am on my way back to New Orleans."

The guests crowded at the door to hear any further news the messenger had. York pushed the small group apart and shoved the man.

"Go back to New York. We don't associate with your kind."

Paul stared at York as did the other guests and stepped in to protect the man.

"Tell my parents that I will join them as soon as possible to fight to preserve the Union. Thank you for bringing the message," Paul said.

"Goodnight, Mila. My wife Leine will never come to this house again."

York summoned their carriage and Paul apologized to the other departing guests.

Eight days after York's wretched behavior, Mila and Paul hoped his irrational actions had subsided, but Paul found the impaled remains of Trey's dog at their front door with a note that read: *Dishonor equals Death.*

"He's loved dogs since we were children. York must be demented to allow something like this to happen. We're dealing with a madman."

It was decided that since Mila had not been well from the night of the ill-fated dinner party, she would go to the Convent Soeurs de Merci and Trey to America. The distraught family rushed to make travel arrangements.

In darkness and a light rain, the driver carefully parbuckled Mila's huge trunk and smiled to reassure his frightened passenger. As the rain grew heavier, he maneuvered the carriage toward the convent. Unsure of the exact route and filled with fear that he could not protect his lady, his thoughts raced quicker than his eyes, and he missed a badly positioned crossroads sign directing him to the right. His other fear was being detected by nearby tavern ruffians who would easily recognize the coach's distinctive LeFleur crest on the door.

At last he saw a cross outlined by a shy moon just chasing the rain away and thought he had reached his destination. He lowered his lady's trunk, instructed her to use the massive bell at the door. He disappeared from sight thinking he had delivered Millicent Roussel LeFleur to the Convent Soeurs de Merci, while in fact she had entered Our Lady of Adoration Convent.

The first fingers of dawn spread brightly as he began his return trip. In broad daylight the route took him by the very tavern he had tried to avoid, just as York and a gang of his drunken friends emerged. The driver, no longer a young man, proved easy prey.

The hooligans turned the horses loose, torched the coach, and left his remains hanging from a tree in a secluded section of forest. Circling vulture squawks provided his requiem and the charred coach was only discovered weeks later.

Martine, the new factory manager for Paul, notified him in Sadorus, Illinois, where he served as Senior Advisor in the U. S. Civilian Cartography Unit of the United States Army, of the discovery of the burned LeFleur coach.

Countless letters and inquiries to French police and attorneys yielded no information about Millicent LeFleur or the coachman.

Tedelia and J.P. returned immediately to New Orleans and decided to stay at Ruvasha for the duration of the war. J.P. would prove vital in attempting to quell the unrest later in the troubled city of New Orleans during the Union occupation, but with a sad ending.

Chapter 67

Occupation

On Sunday mornings, the First Baptist Church on Canal Street resounded with the beautiful voices of the faithful. Among those faithful were the three maiden sisters, Myrtle, Doris and Nell Chavannes, who shared a home on Poydras Street in a lovely, verandah-wrapped house. Their voices rang clear and strong from having attended the Music Conservatory in Baton Rouge, where they had earlier made their debuts. Papa's late marriage to a younger woman had moved them to New Orleans and they now had half-relatives all over.

A battalion of Union soldiers bivouacked in an open field about a block from the house with music wafting from its open windows.

"Hurrah for the Bonnie Blue Flag that bears a single star,

Hurrah, hurrah, hurrah for Southern Rights,

Hurrah, for the Bonnie Blue Flag that bears a single star."

The Southern song, outlawed by Major General Benjamin Butler with a fine of $25 dollars for even whistling it, sent young recruits running toward the source, bayonets drawn, only to find three maiden ladies who had carefully calculated the length of time it would take the fresh-faced Union soldiers to reach their front gate, where only the rhythmic clicking of knitting needles and the squeaking of three rocking chairs could be heard.

Lt. Col. Terrence Richardson, liaison to General Butler, was aware his troops had done their best as peacekeepers in New Orleans and wanted to boost his young soldiers' morale. He dressed with care and told his men to follow.

They marched to the unlawful songbirds' home, where he knocked, bowed at the waist when they answered, and introduced himself.

"Ladies, I've heard you three sisters have the most beautiful voices in all New Orleans. While I am a Union Army representative, my thoughts and heart will always be in Maryland, where my genteel mother is much like you ladies. The fact is, I'm homesick. All of my men are, and we would be honored if you would sing two requests for us."

"Why certainly, Colonel. What are your requests?"

Hearing the first request to be "Amazing Grace," with a polite nod, Myrtle excused herself, entered the parlor, seated herself at the piano, and called to her sisters, "Ready, girls? Key of C."

The girls' voices intertwined to stir floods of memories for the homesick men crowding the yard and front porch, spilling onto the street. One sixteen-year-old turned his head from his buddies to hide his tears. Muffled sniffs and throat-clearing became audible when they sang the last note.

The Chavannes seemed pleased with themselves.

"And what will be your next request?" Nell asked.

Curbing an urge to smile, Col. Richardson said, "The Battle Hymn of the Republic."

"I know it is a new song, but I bet you've heard it."

The sisters gasped slightly, looked sheepish, but sang the most beautiful rendition of the song any of the troops had heard. The men thanked them profusely and never heard strains of "The Bonnie Blue Flag" again.

Later, the Canal Street Baptist Church often had navy-blue military uniformed visitors and provided Lt. Col. Richardson the opportunity to meet JoVera Hough.

Unfortunately for New Orleans, all did not go as well elsewhere in the city. Rumor-mongers and the irrefutable press blew any minor clash between Northern and Southern, Negro or white, out of proportion.

Abraham Friedman, an invaluable link between factions, often viewed atrocities on both sides, helpless to intercede. His unbiased actions as mediator for the New Orleans Freedmen's Bureau gave him entry into many groups. His former classmate and neighbor, York Arceneaux, remained lord of the manor even after the Emancipation Proclamation.

With the disbanding of York's Louisiana battalion, an elegant cane for an affected limp helped him promulgate the illusion of a crippled soldier. His childhood dream of battle at last became a pseudo-reality, but his inner and real battles continued.

Since Luther still lived in Switzerland, little had changed in how York now ran Vermillion Hall; demanding and oppressive. Several former slaves had drifted off only to return to the sanctuary and cruelty of their previous situations, still indentured to a sadistic personality. Dissension continued between York and J. Leenard, who still controlled Vermillion Hall's purse strings per Luther's instructions of years ago.

Home now as a Confederate veteran, York seethed with thoughts of the Freedmen's Bureau occupying Kennington Shadows, yet had no power to change anything.

Marabella lived at Vermillion Hall, seventeen and naive, except when escaping the clutches of enamored male servants.

Dusk fast approached and field chants could be heard from neighboring Kennington Shadows as workers returned from freshly cut cane fields.

Satyr, as he had been nicknamed, was of Caribbean stock, and wielded a machete with such force, his daily harvesting yield surpassed his closest competition. He proved to be her most ardent pursuer, constantly chasing the petrified Marabella. His courtship methods resembled a caveman's: seizure equals ownership.

York sat cleaning his guns on the brick walkway near the kitchen when Satyr darted from behind a huge shrub and grabbed Marabella. She shrieked and ran toward the big house, cowering behind York and hiding just inside the great hall. He remembered Abby's trembling that afternoon years ago and felt compassion for this frightened girl for the first time in his life.

"You have other women. Leave her alone," York said as Satyr hung his head and walked away.

Marabella darted into the kitchen, out of harm's way, then screamed when Satyr climbed through a kitchen window to chase her again. York bounded for the kitchen only to see Satyr disappear through the canebrake with Marabella as another commotion broke out. Two female servants pelted Satyr with stove wood near the well. He held tighter to Marabella as the women continued their assault.

Then the cold steel of York's gun against Satyr brought a sudden, "No, buckra!" which was African for "master," and Satyr released his grip while York did not. Satyr retreated and quiet settled on the plantation.

Screams from the carriage house brought York from his reverie and running. He threw the wide doors open and found Marabella hysterical, crying in a corner as Satyr, naked from the waist down, stood over her. York raised his gun and fired. Satyr fell where he stood and did not move.

York wrapped a carriage lap blanket around Marabella and spoke to Lucallie in the gathering crowd, "Help this girl get to bed."

Two male servants dragged Satyr's body to the edge of Bayou Conét. When morning came, the gurgling waters hid all trace of the human being once lying crumpled at the bayou's edge.

Chapter 68

Changes

J. Leenard and Josephine Ragland thought this beautiful Sunday afternoon could not have been more grand. Hatch Washington surprised them by pulling his wagon into their long driveway at Starnes Lake, where the sun reflected rippling, jewel-like patterns disturbed occasionally by a fish lunge.

"What brings you over this way, Hatch?"

"I needs to talk to you, Mr. J. Leenard. In private."

Hatch hopped down and headed to the side lawn.

"Why come all the way out here to the lake instead of the bank?" asked J. Leenard.

"Mr. R.C.'s dead and we had this same talk almost ten years ago through his bank's side door."

"What talk? Do you need money?"

"No, sir, I just don't want to get in any trouble. Mr. R.C. helped me out, so I knew you would, too, 'cause you work at a bank and I knew I could trust you."

"What are we talking about?"

"Let me pull my wagon over here under this shed," Hatch said, maneuvering under the shed as far as possible and throwing feed sacks off two metal chests.

J. Leenard could not believe his eyes, seeing the seal of the king of France.

"Where did you get these?"

"Dug 'em up on my land. Mr. R.C. got rid of one for me. Said I could get in trouble for havin' it. He even gave me two hundred dollars just in case something bad happened. Said he wouldn't tell a soul. He was a fine man."

J. Leenard held his tongue.

"Get me that hammer and wedge off that bench."

His pounding broke the rusted locks with little effort and real amazement set in.

"Hatch, this is worth a fortune. Coins and jewels. You're a rich man."

Hatch just shook his head and looked embarrassed.

"I'll have an appraiser in my office tomorrow morning. Leave it in your wagon and I'll get someone to help you bring it in the front door. We don't have to sneak around. There's no telling how much more is buried out there."

The appraiser waited at the bank when Hatch arrived and gave them a figure. J. Leenard cabled Mary-Elizabeth Marchand in London, who gave them permission to search the Zedohr mansion and the location of a door key.

They found the hidden chest and, in a final act of defiance, Mary-Elizabeth gave the Zedohr mansion to Hatch Washington.

Today some of the items are part of a special collection on loan to the New Orleans Museum from the museum's curator, Dr. Hatcher Louis Washington, V. More chests did surface and one item inside, a necklace, is on display at the Louvre in Paris.

A message sent from a United States military camp in Sedorus, Illinois:
Dear General Grant:
This request is made with full knowledge that the circumstances of war will probably preclude any consideration which you might render in reference to the preservation in Tachérie Parish, Louisiana of the following plantations:

Ruvasha, home of the LeFleurs—my grandfather Gilbert and parents J.P. and Tedelia LeFleur; Kennington Shadows, *home of the late General Alain Roussel retired, United States Army, and his wife Arianna, my in-laws; Vermillion Hall, home of my wife's sister, Nadeleine Roussel Arceneaux. All are on Bayou Conét Road. If this request is possible, your speediest attention to this matter will be greatly appreciated. If not, I will know your lack of action means you had to concentrate your attention elsewhere to help end this terrible carnage. Sincerely,*

Jean-Paul Lefleur, Jr., Senior Advisor

A swift return communication soon followed.

U. S Civilian Cartography Unit Sadorus, Illinois

Attention: Generals Sherman and Butler, employ every means in Tachérie Parish, Louisiana to protect the lives and property of the residents of following plantations in that parish: Ruvasha, Kennington Shadows and Vermillion Hall. The owners are fighting to preserve the Union.

General U. S. Grant

Tedelia served afternoon refreshments at Ruvasha.

"Papa Gilbert, don't you think you'd be better off in Illinois with Paul and Trey?"

The LeFleur patriarch didn't answer for a long time.

"I was born on this land before it was a part of this dis-United States. I don't intend to leave it now. I do appreciate your concern, I truly do. Now please warm my coffee and give me another piece of that pie, young lady."

Tedelia smiled and served him another slice of pie.

That old charmer. Me, a grandmother, and he still calls me "young lady." She never mentioned his going north again.

How fortunate Gilbert LeFleur had not gone north, for the conquering North had already come to him and he would be safer at home than chancing involvement in an isolated skirmish en route to Sedorus.

Chapter 69
Solomon's Tavern, 1862

Bridey approached the handsome Union soldier with an eyepatch who was standing at the bar. She had not seen him before.

"And what will ya' be havin', sir?'

"I'd like a wee bit o' Irish whiskey."

Her face reddened.

"I'll not be havin' the likes of you makin' fun of a poor widder woman's speech," she said, her face red. "Now be gone with ya."

"Why, if some lout made fun of such a fair specimen of womanhood in me father's pub, I'd be obliged me-self to pitch him out on his ear,"

"Oh now, ya would, would ya? Did ya be saying where yer from, Yank?" she said, smoothing her hair.

"Woodlawn, New York, but I'm a County Limerick first generationer. The potato blight sent us to these shores. Davey O' Flannery at yer service, ma'am."

"So yer father has a pub, he does?"

"He did when I left home. I'm hopin' me mither and me older brother, Brian, are still helpin' him run it, what with me gone and all. Me brother's got a bum leg, but he's strong as a mule. I haven't heard from me mither in a long time."

"Here's yer Irish whiskey. I'm Bridey Solomon."

He gave a polite nod, put his money on the bar, gulped his drink, swung his lank frame over the bar, and put on a barkeep's apron.

"Bridey, being it's the first of the month, and payday, I tink ya need a little help. Where might I wash me hands?"

She motioned to a washstand near the back door.

"Ya might be takin' yer uniform jacket off first!" she yelled.

Later from the back of the room, Davey heard scuffling and, "you son of a swine!"

He straightened, glared at the offender, and silence ensued. With the O'Flannery hulk in the background, no one dared get rowdy. He and Bridey closed the tavern and feasted on corned beef and cabbage.

"Where did ya learn to cook like this, Bridey?"

"My mother was from Ireland, too," she said with a giggle.

He saluted her with his fork.

"How'd ya get that eye patch, Yank?"

"I'll tell ya if you'll quit callin' me 'Yank.'"

She nodded.

"At First Bull Run they gave us a poundin'. Many of our b'yes were captured and sent to Castle Pickney prison in Charlotte. I managed to get back to our lines with this little reminder," he said, touching his eyepatch. "But our regiment doctor of the New York Fightin' 69th said I'd be fit in no time. Some of our b'yes weren't so lucky."

New Orleans had just begun to fight when Commodore Farragut swooped into the city and brought its efforts to a standstill, and now, for the first time, Bridey realized the South was not alone in its pain. Her steel demeanor dissolved with tear-welled eyes.

"I'm sorry, Davey, I really am. I only knew work and hardship until my late husband Solomon came into my life. Then he died. I've been thinkin' too much of my own problems."

Davey patted her hand, a natural reaction fraught with sympathy, but then jerked his hand back.

"Excuse me, ma'am."

Bridey wiped her nose on the back of her hand.

"Where is Woodlawn, New York? And this tavern you were tellin' me about?"

"Woodlawn is a village outside of the city. The tavern is there and it's called McLinn's in honor of the son of Ireland who established it, rest his soul."

He crossed himself.

"He already had it goin' when the potato blight brought us to America. Me father invested every cent he had—eighty-five-dollars—to buy into it, never takin' any wages, just puttin' it back into the business. Me mither sewed and ironed to keep our bodies fed and clothed. Then McLinn was killed by a runaway horse. Right in front of church, he was. A saintly man with never any time to marry. Me father got the tavern and me mither could quit working for other people."

"I worked for other people too, until Solomon, me late husband," Bridey said, pausing and twisting her hands. "It was Ma, Auntie Lou and me for a long time before that. Me Pop was dead. They both died of malaria when I was thirteen. I went to work at Rodin's in the kitchen. That's where I met Solomon. He was the cook and a lot older than me, but a kind man."

When Davey's military day ended, he headed straight for Solomon's Tavern and stayed each night until closing.

"No, no money; just feed me."

This continued for three months until one day he said, "Bridey, this is no life for a single woman. I would be honored if you would be me wife."

Six weeks later Bridey Bohan Solomon became Mrs. David James O'Flannery, II. They bought a cottage nearby and moved Mrs. Wallace out of the Irish Channel and to the second floor of the tavern. Mr. Wallace had died, her son Hiram was now a police officer who could work nights and tend bar, her daughter Annie-Laurie helped cook and serve, and Mrs. Wallace proved capable of managing everything. Much of Bridey's drudgery was relieved.

"Bridey, a letter from home."

Dear Baby Davey,

"She still calls me 'Baby.'"

Your letter posted in Maryland, covered in muddy stains, arrived the same day as your wonderful letter telling us the news of your marriage. We are especially happy to learn your ceremony was conducted in St. Louis Cathedral by Father Prejean. He and your father were chums at St. Basil's when they were boys in Ireland before he was sent to France.

Father Prejean also writes us that your Bridey gives freely of her time and money to the orphans in his Parish. He says she is a fair colleen as well. We are happy for you. Know that the Lord will bless you and pray for an end to this terrible war.

Our wonderful news is that your brother has had the first of two operations to correct his twisted leg. We prayed about it and decided that if the Lord had not intended us to have it done, he wouldn't have given us such good doctors here in America.

Some men came in our pub who had met your Uncle Jimmy in California, but it had been five years, so the information was quite old. He still has not written to your father since their disagreement. I can only pray about it. The men asked about you. Said Uncle Jimmy talked about you all the time. I told them you were in New Orleans with the Army.

Your loving Mother,

Ellie Kate

P. S. Bridey, we welcome you into our family and will be sending you Grandmother Maureen O'Flannery's lace tablecloth. She gave it to Mr. O'Flannery and me when we married.

By now Brian had received his second successful surgery, but Davey and Bridey would not get the news or the tablecloth for quite some time as the war continued.

Chapter 70
The Letter Opener

Martha-Louise Pontaine opened her door and Denis ran into her waiting arms. She reached for a huge, gift-wrapped package and placed it in eager hands. It was his sixth birthday and he tore open the wrappings with a squeal, gleefully dumped the contents on the floor: thirty tin soldiers. He began playing with the toys immediately, then stopped abruptly and crawled into her lap.

"Madame Pontaine, will you be my grandmère? I don't have one." Luther stood behind Denis and mouthed the words, "*I love you*" as he touched his heart.

"*Will you marry me?*" He slipped an imaginary ring on his own left hand and pointed to her and then to himself.

"Yes, to both of you boys."

The wedding was simple, the bride beautiful, and the honeymoon was spent in Paris. The bride, the groom, Besa, and Denis took two suites of rooms at the Hotel LeGrande because the new grandmère could not bear to leave Denis in Switzerland for four weeks.

One sunny day, Martha-Louise announced the day belonged to the ladies and they went shopping. Steel-gray eyes followed them as they left the hotel. Martha-Louise felt a faint recognition of the gentleman, but in the excitement of the anticipated shopping trip she completely put him out of her mind, nor did she notice him tip his hat. He went immediately to the hotel owner's office.

"Mademoiselle LeGrande, who is the woman with Mademoiselle Pontaine? I must meet her."

"I don't know a Mademoiselle Pontaine."

"You must. I know her from a bank in Switzerland. She is a guest here. I've seen the other woman with a red-haired boy."

"Oh, you mean Madame Arceneaux. She's honeymooning here. I think the other lady is the boy's governess."

"What is her name?"

"Mademoiselle Besa Loque."

"Thank you."

He bowed in an almost too polite gesture and closed her door. Cilla LeGrande felt an inexplicable uneasiness as soon as she'd answered Dex Lord's last question. Everything about him made her uneasy from his heavy eyebrows to the manner in which he dressed; the tailoring was always perfect, but the diamonds seemed a bit much.

She tried to concentrate on her paperwork, but couldn't. The bell-pull alerted her house detective, but he, anxious to leave on holiday, dismissed notifying security.

The police are already in the hotel. They know what to watch for. I won't tell them how to conduct their business.

Cilla now felt confident.

The police have everything under control. Surely, he's not the wanted fugitive. I'm imagining things.

The next day, Luther answered a rapping at the double doors of their suite and was greeted by two burly men.

"Monsieur Arceneaux? A delivery for your wife."

Luther cleared his throat and appeared stunned. Martha-Louise rushed in. "Luther, is something wrong?"

She signed for the delivery and tipped the men.

"I didn't mean to concern you," he began. "I was simply shocked for a moment."

"At my buying something that large?" she asked with a giggle.

"No, but that's a Richilene trunk and the only other one I've ever seen belonged to Denis's mother. They're made in New Orleans. Did you know that?"

"No, and I didn't know my wonderful husband knew so much about ladies' clothing and doings. What other secrets are you keeping from me?"

The suite next door had a delivery also, an enormous bouquet of red roses with a card that read, *Mademoiselle Loque, you are ravishing. Devotedly, Dex Lord.*

Besa remembered forgetting a package in the carriage yesterday when they'd returned. Dex Lord had appeared from nowhere and introduced himself, saying, "I will see you again," as he handed her the package.

Over breakfast the next morning, Luther told Besa that Denis wanted to go to the park with him and his wife.

"You have the day to yourself," he said.

"He'll enjoy that. I think I'll just stay here and relax," she said, no sooner settling on a chaise when the chambermaid knocked to change the linens.

"Mademoiselle, I have forgotten your towels," she said upon finishing. "I will return."

"Just leave the door slightly open," said Besa, soon nodding off only to be awakened by a smiling man. "Did you like my flowers?"

Dex Lord's face was inches away from her.

"What are you doing here?"

"You left your door ajar. Was that not careless?"

"You shouldn't be here."

"I asked you if you liked my flowers?"

"They were beautiful. Now will you please go?"

"When I introduced myself yesterday, I told you I would see you again," he said, starting to sit.

Besa said, "I thought you were just being polite."

"I never say things I don't mean. You are beautiful. Do you not know you and your green eyes are amazing?" he said, catching her hand and starting to suck her fingers.

"Turn me loose or I'll scream."

"Do and you may never scream again."

In the hotel laundry room, the chambermaid had gathered towels for Besa when a frenzied young woman zoomed into the area.

"Quick, get lots of towels. The tub in room 306 has overflowed and the old man in there is frantic."

Twenty minutes later the maid knocked on Besa's door.

"Sorry I couldn't get back sooner, Mademoiselle. I hope I didn't inconvenience you."

"Don't come in. Just tell Mademoiselle LeGrande I must see her immediately," Besa requested in a monotone.

"Oh, Mademoiselle, you're not going to report me, are you? I really need this job."

"No, I've been attacked. It was not your fault. Please. Hurry and get Mademoiselle LeGrande."

Luther and Martha-Louise returned to a tension-filled situation. Mademoiselle LeGrande's assistant took Denis downstairs for milk and cookies.

Luther was first enraged, then calm.

"And what of this Dex Lord, Mademoiselle LeGrande? Why did you allow him to stay here if you knew he was a wanted criminal?"

"He was not a guest of the hotel, Monsieur Arceneaux. He merely took his meals here. The police have been watching him for days. They asked me not to alarm our guests, to act as if nothing was wrong. We did not know for sure he was a wanted criminal."

"Apparently, they weren't watching him today."

"Monsieur Arceneaux, he must have come up the back stairs because the lobby has police posing as guests around the clock waiting for him to make one false move."

The police-filled room waited for the chief.

"Everything is confirmed," he said on arrival. "He is wanted on four continents—North and South America, Australia and Europe. His real name, although he has many aliases, is Emil Roussel and the dead or alive reward for him is very large. He is from Natchez, Mississippi, and the son of a respected American general.

"Chief, might you save any additional questions for later? Our guests are exhausted."

"One other of Mademoiselle Arceneaux. How did you know him?"

"I barely knew him. He came to the Banque Internationale de Swiss in Lausanne. I'm an officer there, but he did not use the name Dex Lord."

"Thank you, Mademoiselle."

A sheet draped the lifeless body of Emil Roussel. The letter opener Besa had plunged into his back bulged beneath the fabric before the policemen eased him onto a gurney.

Besa struggled to think of happier thoughts from the day before. Visiting with Echo at the Paris House of Richilene had been more than she had hoped. She, too, had viewed the display trunk in the store and remembered Abby's trunk when she came to Vermillion Hall, but said nothing lest she cloud the moment of Martha-Louise's purchase.

His grandparents' honeymoon over, Denis resumed boarding school. He amazed the kitchen staff by visiting them often and sharing choice hints he'd learned at Besa's side.

"We must meet your Aunt Besa."

"Oh, I can arrange that," he replied to the headmaster. "She will be coming with my grandmère on Friday when we begin holiday."

Besa arrived as promised and Monsieur Henslier lost no time seeking her out.

"Where did you learn to cook?"

"At Vermillion Hall in New Orleans."

Monsieur Henslier nodded, not knowing what Vermillion Hall was, but thought intuitively it must be a famous American cooking school. Besa held herself proudly and offered no further information. By the time she rejoined Martha-Louise and Denis in the carriage, she had a signed contract to cater dinner parties for the trustees' next three meetings.

Johann Brandt and Verlis Henslier introduced Besa to their friends, all clamoring for her delectable cuisine. Soon she couldn't handle the demands and sent for Vedette, who joined her in Switzerland and would be part of a new venture in Paris.

Besa enjoyed all the benefits of family, a beautiful home, gorgeous clothes, and a sizable income, but the reward for Emil Roussel completely financed her Paris adventure. Martha-Louise saw that the sum accrued handsome interest.

Chapter 71

The New Orleans Wharf

The fractious crowd surged toward the docks. Struggling desperate hands flailed the air—black, brown, café au lait, griffe, and other degrees of mulatto belonging to hungry, frustrated, bewildered men. Although some were barefoot and some were shod in fine leather, the underlying theme was one, the need for change.

With their pitchforks, broomsticks, barkless tree limbs, knives, and a few decaying guns, they swarmed the wharf like agitated insects. Abraham scrambled atop a pile of barrels and tried to talk to the belligerent men.

"Don't listen to him. He's just a white man. He's a LeFleur," someone in the crowd yelled.

"He's *pass en blanc!*" cried another.

Barton Dewitt tried to steady the barrels as the molten throng inched closer.

"I know who I am," Abraham replied. "I've never turned my back on my race."

The jeers continued as Hatch Washington stepped forward and raised his hands to the crowd.

"Let the boy speak. He was my neighbor. I knows him."

Abraham began again.

"The LeFleurs are right here," he said, touching his left breast. "But the blood and struggles of my people rages through my very being. I want what is best for all of us, black and white."

Profuse perspiration forced him to remove his jacket.

"We're going through hard times—everybody is—but there's hope. Kennington Shadows Plantation, through the Freedmen's Bureau, has opened its doors to all of you, but you must work for what you get, whether it's seed, clothing, shelter—whatever. Go there and make your needs known."

"Why should we listen to you? We're tired of promises. We were all promised land."

A wildly thrown rock missed Abraham but found a target in Barton DeWitt and a wound to the temple felled him on the pier. Spraying blood in rhythmic spurts, each pump of his heart thrusted him closer to death. In the confusion following, many were injured, and three blacks and two whites died. J.P. lay in a pool of his own blood, dead.

At Hilon Hospital, Barton suffered for days. The wound would not heal.

"Mrs. DeWitt," Dr. Cornevis said, lowering his voice as he motioned for D'Eljoie to come from her husband's room. "Dr. Pitman and I would like to try a radical new approach, but we need your permission."

"What is this new method?'

"The late Dr. John Gorrie patented a mechanical cooling machine. Refrigeration, it's called. It artificially cools the patient and, in many cases, hastens the healing process."

"I don't understand. How does it work?"

"It seems to fight the infection. We don't understand the principle, either, but it works. We'll just go on faith, if we have your permission."

"When can you start?"

"Immediately."

Barton DeWitt healed enough to return to his mediating job in three weeks. Kennington Shadows first began to give assistance to the needy and displaced at a slow trickle. Gradually, they came. The plantation was awash with activity now and Barton, Abraham and the Freedmen's Bureau worked endless hours to fill continuing requests.

King Cotton's collapse brought relief from one oppression, but would thrust both black and white of the postbellum South into an economic situation envied by none.

May 14 1862

Dear Paul,

Your father never took up arms against either side, but he died bravely April 10 from a stray bullet as he tried to keep peace at the docks. Your sainted mother has held us all together.

He was a fine man and I miss him sorely. We buried him under the big oak at the back of the cemetery next to your great-grandparents, who died of the fever. We regret you were not here, although we know you are doing your part to end this terrible madness that grips our nation.

Union troops are still here and they treat us well. General Grant has honored your request. Ruvasha, Kennington Shadows and Vermillion Hall are untouched. Uncle Lamb's youngest boy, Uriah, died at Shiloh last month. His wife was expecting a child. We begged him not to go, but he said he had to help protect the South.

Barton DeWitt was hospitalized with a wound he got at the wharf the night your father died. He has almost recovered. Abraham's work with the Freedmen's Bureau is outstanding but he's often criticized by people we thought to be our friends.

Our love to you and Trey,
Your Devoted Grandfather

Chapter 72
The War is Over

Amid death, deprivation and losses too numerous to mention, the American Civil War has ended. Lives and dreams have been shattered; hope gone for some. On the brighter side, unions of young people from both sides have been forged, but New Orleans remains occupied.

Solomon's tavern has a new part owner and Bridey Bohan Solomon is now Mrs. James David O'Flannery, II. JoVera Hough, Sunday school teacher at Canal Street's First Baptist Church and daughter of a local attorney, wears a beautiful engagement ring from Lt. Col Terrence Richardson. The wedding date will be announced as soon as his mother can safely make the trip from Maryland and yes, the Chavannes sisters, Myrtle, Nell and Doris, will sing at the wedding. They like to think they are the thread that brought Terrence and JoVera together. He will leave the military and teach architecture at Tulane.

The nation mourns the death of Lincoln, his politics still questioned. Hatch and Mary Washington have moved into the Zedohr mansion and own a large part of New Orleans. Uncle Lamb has been made assistant to Jules Pascal at Echo Trading Post. Deenah Vermillion continues at the House of Richilene. Countess Aviva Bogoff had a Yankee general at her beck-and-call, but decided her work was still her husband.

Uncle Sib lives with the Washingtons, the Freedmen's Bureau continues to help displaced and needy individuals, York Arceneaux scowls at every sunrise, Leine volunteers at the Hilon Hospital, Quila has a fur export company, Mrs. Wallace cannot wait to finish buying the tavern, Bridey and Davey now work less, and Paul and Trey will soon return from Illinois.

With the war ending, education now proves to be one of the many areas lacking, especially in the South. Convents across Europe collaborate their efforts to help the war-torn states. Our Lady of Adoration has been notified its Sisters will be the first to go to America.

"Yes, Rolfo, the Bishop has informed us we are to establish a school in Louisiana. Their war is over, and they have great need for education. Our city is New Orleans."

"I can leave my jewelry business with Caleb. His skill is as good as mine, maybe better."

"This may be a hasty decision. Perhaps you should pray about it first."

"You and the Sisters have been my family since the gypsies left me in your care. You can't get away from me that easily. It is decided. I will go."

Our Lady of Adoration Convent closed and the cemetery caretaker, Claude, moved into the outside rooms. Sister Theresa wanted to bring one of the baby goats, but Claude convinced her he would take good care of the little fellow.

The entourage totaled seven and included Sisters Albertine, Mary Magdalen, Bernadette, and Theresa, two novices and Rolfo.

The voyage to America proved exciting, but not without sadness. The Irish nun Bernadette died aboard ship and they buried her at sea. She had brought cuttings from the convent vineyard, hoping they would flourish in New Orleans. Sister Albertine guarded them carefully and brought them to their new home in America.

Naji II, also on board, stayed calm during the voyage and Rolfo visited the ship's hold often. At night, for him the ship's creaking tweaked long-ago thoughts of someone walking on a wooden floor. While a good memory, not being able to give it a time and place was disturbing.

The hospital's Sisters of Mercy worked and scoured for weeks to make ready the Sisters of Charity Convent and School occupancy.

"It must be perfect when they arrive. Take plenty of fresh fruit, Sisters. They haven't had fruit in a long time," directed Sister Claire as they loaded baskets, bedding and cooking utensils into a huge wagon.

The usually somber, now giddy, sisters greeted the ship bringing the future occupants of the new convent with smiles and giggles. On hand to welcome the Sisters, the French Ambassador to America, Guilliame Sapir, and his wife Judilene, stopping en route to Washington, had pulled many strings to assure the new order of the Sisters of Charity could spend their first night in New Orleans in their own beds.

When they docked, Rolfo busied himself with Naji II and did not meet the hospital Sisters of Mercy for several weeks.

Chapter 73
On the Count of Three

York and Leine did not attend the theatre often, but one ordinary evening turned into an extraordinary happening.

The gaslights glowed to a packed crowd, the acting was exceptional, the candle-powered footlights enhanced the talented performers, and the rich burgundy curtain rang down for the final standing ovation. It should have been the perfect night, but it was not to be so.

Leine excused herself to the powder room but rushed instead to Paul LeFleur's carriage at the head of the line.

"Paul, I must get away from Vermillion Hall and the first place York would look is Kennington Shadows. I can't go there. May I hide at Ruvasha?"

York exited the theatre just in time to see the carriage leave. His own carriage, far back in the line, delayed his pursuit.

Tedelia greeted Leine with open arms and hastened her upstairs.

Incessant pounding brought Paul to Ruvasha's front door, where York began a tirade against Paul and everything LeFleur.

"I want my wife. I saw her leave in your carriage."

"She doesn't want to see you."

"First, you LeFleurs are scalawags, fighting for the North, then carpetbaggers, coming back South for the spoils. Now add adulterer to your name."

Paul's glove answered with a stinging blow to York's face.

"Sir, you have defamed the LeFleurs. You will not continue to defame your wife's name. Choose your weapon, time, and place."

"Derringers, at sunrise on the sandbar near my home."

The next morning, Paul locked Leine's bedroom door and placed the key on the small table outside. Abraham had already arrived to serve as his second. Paul's servant had left in the middle of the night to get Abraham and excitedly leaked word of the duel and a parade of carriages had been streaming by Ruvasha since about four-thirty in the morning.

The sound of Leine beating on the door followed them as they left the house. Gilbert sat outside her door with the key in his pocket, refusing to budge, but finally, at Tedelia's pleading, he relented. Leine jumped in a carriage alone and raced to Vermillion Hall.

This expert horsewoman had difficulty controlling her team as tears blinded her.

Dear God in Heaven, please make everything right.

The carriage almost overturned as she passed the bend at Kennington Shadows still inhabited by Freedmen Bureau refugees.

He was so handsome when I first saw him at our New Year's Ball...tall and strong, but like a little child who'd been hurt...deeply hurt. I thought I could make the hurt go away.

"On the count of three, raise your weapons and fire. The first to inflict injury is the victor and the matter is settled," said J. Leenard, voice booming, while he wondered why York, an accomplished swordsman, had chosen pistols. *A death wish?*

Leine reined her horses underneath the bluff on the count of "one." She stood helpless in her carriage; the sandbar where the duelers faced off and the pier a blur, and she dared not call out lest she startle either of them.

On the count of "two," York raised his gun and fired. Even his second, a friend from Lyon, stood shocked. The bullet entered York's own forehead, spilled blood on his ruffled white shirt, and he fell on the sandbar of his and Abby's dreams. Dried, rotted, buried driftwood beneath York's foot made steadying himself impossible.

In the middle of the river, the sandbar sat squarely between Tachérie and Drapeau Parishes. Illegal dueling caused authorities on both sides to pretend the jurisdiction belonged to the other.

Young Trey had slept late and enjoyed a leisurely breakfast with Gilbert and Tedelia, never knowing why both appeared so relieved to see their grandson and son walk through the door.

"Josephine, that scoundrel would have killed Paul in cold blood," said J. Leenard, exhausted. "I wondered why he chose pistols. He fired on the count of 'two,' but something under the sand shifted and he shot himself in the head. What a troubled life."

Leine placed York in the crypt next to Abby, took a maisonette in the Pontalba building, and continued her work at Hilon Hospital.

Chapter 74
"Where is My Hat?"

His tenure with gypsies had given his manner of dress great flair, even for colorful New Orleans. From his flowing-sleeved, white poet shirts to the multi-hued soutache vests, cummerbunds and rakish hats, everything was a study in symmetry.

Rolfo had time for his jewelry, the Sisters and his wardrobe. Local literati relished time spent in his courtyard. Appreciative glances from the ladies went unnoticed until the night he decided to attend a performance of local chanteuse Lisa Chavannes.

Near a minute stage, at a small table, he positioned his lanky body into one of the mercifully larger chairs. A rich, clear voice emanated from a chestnut-haired young woman.

She has perfect teeth.

Then he focused again on her singing, "New Orleans Has You."

New Orleans has its late, late hours,
Lovely women and yesterday's flowers,
Smoky taverns, lights so pretty,
River winding 'neath the city,
River singing a haunting song,
This is where you belong.
New Orleans has its late, late hours,
Lovely women are not few,
River has such strange, sweet powers,

'Cause New Orleans, chérie,
Forever has you,
New Orleans, chérie, Forever has you.

Many songs later, it was one o'clock in the morning. He was not a drinker, evidenced by the ungracious return to the banquette outside that of which he had partaken. He not only failed to maintain the jaunty cadence with which he'd arrived, but he was also too sick to make it home unassisted, so he sat on the curb.

Is that lady talking to me?

He wasn't sure due to his mackled vision.

"Where do you live?"

She is talking to me.

He gave her an address.

She smells good. Where is my hat?

They arrived at her house after much effort to get him there. She drew him a bath, removed his boots, helped him undress to his underwear, and gave his soiled clothing to her maid.

Lisa began to wash his back and then his hair. She noticed the unusual cross he wore on a gold chain.

"Sing to me," he pleaded.

"No, it's too late," she said, hushing him.

"Please," Rolfo begged. "No one's sung to me in a long time."

"I sang tonight."

"No, I mean just to me," he said, remembering Sofia.

She relented and sang softly as she towel-dried his hair. He took the enormous Turkish towel she offered, wrapped himself and dropped his wet underclothes to the floor, curling up on a huge bed and falling asleep. She tiptoed out.

He's a brooding man even in slumber. I've seen him many times, but he always seemed so preoccupied. We've never even been introduced.

At eight, Lisa's maid awakened him with a polite knock.

"Here are your clothes, sir, all pressed and clean. Miss Chavannes is waiting for you in the courtyard. Here is hot water, a stack of towels and a razor."

She left before he could thank her.

A sheepish Rolfo entered the courtyard and shaded his eyes.

"Do you know where my hat is?" he managed to ask.

"Oh, it met a tragic end. You'll have to find another."

He'd outgrown his "tank you" of years ago, but at this vulnerable moment, he reverted to old ways.

"Tank you for everything... for taking care of someone who doesn't know how to drink. I never learned."

"You're welcome."

She did not say "velcome."

He smiled at his private joke, but said nothing, just wishing the sun had stayed hidden. He squinted.

"We're going to Café Du Monde. You like beignets?"

He nodded.

The many cups of café au lait, although delicious, could not compare to the splendid conversation. They strolled, bought fruit from vendors, bought a hat, and watched an assortment of ocean-bound vessels populating the harbor.

Rolfo thanked her again.

"Anything for my adoring public."

"I do adore you, you know."

"You're being absurd. We just met."

"Lisa, we may have just met, but I've watched you come and go at the House of Richilene for months. My shop is next door. I always saw you with a man. I assumed you were spoken for."

"The man you saw me with is my brother Luc, my manager. You slept in his room last night, used his razor. He's in Baton Rouge arranging appearances for me."

"Your music is wonderful."

"It's my life. Someday I hope to sing opera," she said, noting a dream that would later haunt them.

Chapter 75

Our Lady of Adoration Cemetery

Rolfo's former convent family often visited his shop and one day he mentioned something he'd observed at the House of Richilene.

"Sister Albertine, the trunk you brought from France is similar to others I have seen in the window next door. I know it has always been a bit of a mystery, so you might want to take a look."

They went together.

"Rolfo, the crest is the same as the crest on the two keys I have," she said. Inside, they explained the situation to Countess Bogoff and she agreed to go to the convent to see the trunk.

Aviva saw the trunk and remembered.

"We don't have records. Harris Lloyd and Son's records were destroyed during the war, but I certainly remember this green one because two identical trunks were made for the Roussel sisters before they married and moved to Lyon."

She pointed to the "M. R." clearly for Millicent Roussel, then pausing and reassuring them, saying, "only recently has production resumed on the trunks. I could tell this was an older model by the different hinges."

"Does this second key belong to her sister's trunk?"

"No," the Countess answered. "The second key unlocks a secret storage area, but the Harris Lloyd and Son plaque must be removed to gain access to it. The entire velvet panel comes off."

"Has anyone contacted her husband, Paul Roussel?" Sister Albertine asked.

"She married Paul LeFleur. Roussel was her maiden name. We must notify Mr. LeFleur at Ruvasha Plantation immediately. His wife has been missing for five years. Is she alive?" Aviva asked.

"No," Sister Albertine replied.

"I'll go for him," Rolfo volunteered.

The two men returned to the convent. Upon seeing the trunk, Paul blanched.

"How? How? How?" he repeated before they could explain. "Where is my wife? How did you get her trunk?"

"Your wife is deceased. She came to us after a terrible storm. She only told us your first name and that you were helping Mr. Lincoln to end the war. She told us only that to protect us, and nothing more."

"How did she die? My son and I had planned to return to France this Monday and continue our search."

"From giving birth."

"That's why she was so ill. I never knew. What of the child?"

"A beautiful baby girl died, also. She seemed healthy at first, then took a turn for the worse. A young unmarried woman from Paris had given birth just hours before, but she insisted on caring for your wife and the tiny infant."

"What of the young woman?" Paul asked.

"She left with her own infant shortly after. The babies looked like twins. Both had masses of black hair."

She handed him the keys.

Paul held the keys in his hand, staring, then he opened the trunk, took out his pocketknife and unscrewed the inside plaque. The second key opened the secreted niche, where he discovered the packet of money he'd prepared for Mila, a bundle of un-mailed letters written to him, the emerald and diamond *parure* her father had commissioned for her, and the few pieces of other jewelry she'd taken with her that fateful night.

"We tried repeatedly to find you, even wrote Mr. Lincoln. Sadly, we had the wrong name," Sister Albertine said. "When the difficult birth was over, she tried to tell us her name. We thought she was naming the baby. She was only able to say part of her name, 'Millicent Roussel,' before she became delirious."

"Did you ever hear from the young woman? I'd like to thank her."

"We never asked questions. I think she did tell Sister Bernadette, rest her soul. Her name was Estella and she worked for a hospital in Paris. She was very kind to your wife and they became friends. The loss hurt her deeply. She cried constantly. She had hair as dark as your hair...she was a tiny woman."

Rolfo helped load the trunk onto a wagon while Paul struggled with how to tell Trey his mother was dead. Neither had lost hope during the war years when they lived in Illinois.

This was the second time Tedelia Chavannes LeFleur had placed black crepe on the doors at Ruvasha—first for her husband, J.P., and now for the daughter-in-law she had not seen since Trey was an infant. She tried to think of happier times, which was difficult, even with Abraham's and Micalea's impending wedding to fill her thoughts.

"Tedelia, I can run things if you'd like to go to France with Paul and Trey. I sure can," Gilbert said.

"No, Papa Gilbert. That's kind of you to offer, but after the mourning period, I'll be busy with wedding plans for my other child."

Gilbert did not dare to think of going to France himself. The last time he had visited, although Larissa had not returned from Russia the entire time he was there, she had been alive and well. By not returning to France, he could continue the illusion that she still lived.

Sunlight shone through the crumbling walls of Our Lady of Adoration Convent as Paul and Trey walked into the adjacent cemetery. The only unifying thread for Mila, the infant and other souls resting here, was the happenstance of proximity when the angel of death called.

They found the graves with wooden crosses.

A bewildered Trey said, "Dad, the names are wrong, and Mother's doesn't have the date she was born on it."

Paul apologized for not warning him.

"Stonemasons are already working on a single marble monument with information added and corrected," he said, producing a piece of paper and handing it to the thirteen-year-old. Aside from the obvious corrections, he had left the infant as "Millicent."

Paris hospital records produced only one nurse named Estella. She was sixty years old. Documentation from five years ago provided nothing. They searched small hospitals in all the surrounding villages, coming up with nothing.

Paul and Trey returned to our Lady of Adoration Cemetery to inspect the monument. Trey ran his fingers over the polished surface with etched flowers and angels on both sides.

"It's beautiful, Dad, like she was, but it's sad we never got to see my baby sister."

"Yes, it is, son. The nuns said she was a perfect little baby with jet-black hair like all the LeFleurs have."

Just as Paul and Trey disappeared from sight, another carriage pulled into the cemetery gate carrying a young brunette woman who appeared to be searching for something. She stopped at the new marble monument and began to cry. The bouquet she carried dropped from her hands and her child scurried to pick up the flowers and place them in the monument's urn.

"Don't cry, Mama. Did you know the people buried here?"

"Yes, ma chérie. I knew them," she said, continuing to cry.

"Did I play with the little baby?"

"No, she was too little. She didn't live very long. We'd better go now."

Just then a ragged figure appeared and startled them.

"Didn't mean to frighten you, Mademoiselle. My name is Claude," said the man with a smile, removing his beret and approaching the pair.

The woman eyed his shabby clothes.

"I live in a shack I built next to the abbey and those outside rooms. I take care of the cemetery since the convent moved months ago. Bishop told me I could be buried here among my friends, as I have no family. They pay me to look after things. Saw you stop at that grave."

"Could you tell me why it has a new headstone?"

"A Monsieur Paul LeFleur from New Orleans, Louisiana, and his son came last week and had the old one removed. Said it was wrong. Workmen replaced it yesterday. They just left before you drove in."

"Thank you, Claude. She was my friend."

"Thought she must be, or family. I've seen you here several times. Never seen your little girl before. She sure is pretty."

"I appreciate the information," she said, pressing folded francs into his hand. "Come, Millicent."

Chapter 76
I Haven't Always Been a Nun

Glistening religious items in the shop's small windows caught the undivided attention of Sister Claire. A bell's tinkle as she opened the door triggered a broad smile from the handsome young man seated at a workbench. It had been years since she had seen work this beautiful.

"Good morning, Sister. I am Rolfo Roma. Welcome to my shop."

She wore an intricately carved, large wooden cross suspended on a golden chain. The crispness of her starched bib formed a stark backdrop for the rich, dark jewelry.

"Good morning. I am Sister Claire of the Sisters of Charity. I need a gift for another Sister."

"Please feel free to look around. It is obvious you admire handsome jewelry, such as the lovely cross you are wearing. Where did you get it?"

He gave a faint touch to his own, hidden beneath his shirt.

"It is the only one like it in the world. I'm glad you like it. My husband made it for me."

She acknowledged his puzzled look, saying, "Oh, I have not always been a nun. My husband was a jeweler and created a smaller version for our infant son. My beloved was murdered in a robbery many years ago and shortly after..." she tried to select the correct words to ease the pain still there. "My two-year-old son was taken from me, not through death, just stolen. So I decided to build a new life doing God's work."

Anyone could see she was happy in her calling. Rolfo nodded and smiled.

"You are new to our city, are you not, sir?"

"Yes, I came from France when the Sisters of Mercy established their school here."

"Yes, yes, you are the young man who adopted *them*, to hear Sister Albertine tell it. She says the Lord sent you to them. I just failed to make the connection. I don't come into New Orleans' Jackson Square very often."

She selected a simple chain and gold cross. A mass of flowers circled its arms' juncture. He placed it in a black velvet bag and would take no money.

"The Lord has blessed me and my work. Please allow me to help with His."

Rolfo's eyes followed the rustle of flowing, black garments as she left the shop.

Is it possible? No, no, forget it.

He brushed his chest again, tracing the outline of the wooden cross which had become his touchstone, hope, and mystery.

"Please come again, Sister," he called after her, feeling oddly perspiring.

He unbuttoned his shirt and removed his broken cross, mentally comparing it to the one worn by Sister Claire. Squinting in a mirror, he examined his eyes, his nose, the shape of his face, and compared them to her features, which he'd committed to memory. Why had he not talked to her more, questioned, pried? Perhaps because he feared a negative answer.

Chapter 77
Little Mountain Goat

Sister Claire's fluttering habit caught Rolfo's attention when he spotted her coming from St. Louis Cathedral. He flipped the "Open" sign to "Closed," locked the shop and sprinted to her side.

"Sister, I'd like to talk with you, if you have time."

"Certainly, Rolfo. I had intended to stop by after dropping reports off to Father Prejean. He has been so helpful. Sister Margaret was very pleased with your gift."

He gestured to a bench in Jackson Square and smiled.

She looks like a face on a cameo.

"Tell me about your life in Rome, when you were a girl, about your family—everything," he said.

She pulled a cloth holding breadcrumbs from a pocket and began to feed the pigeons.

"I used to do this in Rome with my son. You can't possibly be interested in my life, young man."

"But I am," he said, stretching as if to relax for infinite time, his eyes glued to her cross.

"I was born in England. I have a brother. My father came from Rome to attend Eton, met Mother and never returned to Italy. I came to Rome to study, met my husband, and never returned to England. Our parents lived in Penner, a beautiful village that had many celebrations," she said, embarrassed. "I know I'm boring you."

"No, please. I'd really like to know more."

"My brother came to Rome to visit and fell in love with the city. Then our parents died of influenza."

"I'm sorry. Where is your brother now?"

"He is still in Rome, Cardinal Andrew Fioriti. My husband's mother Catarina Rolfolini, still lives in a lovely villa there."

"Tell me about your life right after your marriage."

"We were married for a year and a half and our son was born on February 19, 1830. He was a perfect child, so full of life. We lived happily, watching him grow. My husband was a jeweler and was killed in a terrible robbery," she said, faltering then regaining her composure. "My son's father called him his 'little mountain goat' because he was such a climber. Once he almost lost the little toe on his left foot in a sharp crevice. We rushed him to a surgeon, and he was able to sew it back as good as new."

"Please, return to my shop with me," said Rolfo, alerted.

They startled pigeons in their rush across the square. Once inside, he was a man with a single purpose.

"Sister, may I see your cross?"

"Of course," she said, holding it for him to see.

"Could you please remove it?"

She complied and he carefully placed it on a red velvet pad. He then unfastened his top shirt button, removed the gold chain holding his own broken cross and placed it next to the wide-eyed nun's. Except for size and wear, they were identical.

"Where...did you get that?" she asked, stunned.

"I've always had this cross."

"You lived with gypsies. They stole it and gave it to you, didn't they?"

"No," said Rolfo. "I've had that cross from my earliest memory."

She reached for and clutched it in her hands. He feared she would crush it. She fell to her knees and was silent, old hurts rendering her mute. She covered her face as she held his cross, then asked, "Is my son dead? Did you know him? He had one just like this."

Rolfo quickly removed his left boot and sock.

"I've often wondered about this long scar," he said and pushed his left foot toward the distraught woman.

She took her hands from her face and blinked, her mouth remaining a tight line. Her vision finally cleared of tears, eyes bright, and kissed her fingertips to caress his scar.

"You really are my son, Vittorio. I cursed God when you were taken from me...tried to atone by doing His work...and He gave you back to me. He protected you. I often feared he would strike me dead," she said, crossing herself.

"Your Grandmother Rolfolini reminded me that she, too, had lost a son, your father. Only her loss was through murder, so I began to rearrange my life, even though I feared you were dead, too."

They fell together, crying and hugging and talking, trying to take in this amazing reunion. Rolfo's thoughts roiled. His life had been too horrible to reveal to this gentle woman who had borne so much loss. He could never share everything, but he must convey to her that he, too, had been struggling with forgiveness for the lost years.

There had to be a solution, but what and how? He called her "Mother" at least a dozen times before they went to St. Louis Cathedral to give thanks and light candles.

Sister Claire was anguished by the information of the agony Vittorio had experienced. He never discussed the depths of despair he had endured, or accused her for the degradation subsequently thrust on an innocent child.

Although he appeared in control, her mother's instinct told her his innermost emotions were not calm.

As she had been led to the church for answers, she hoped he, too, might find some degree of peace there. Rolfo, loving his new-found mother and trying to understand and be at peace, decided to return to Rome.

Lisa Chavannes rushed into Rolfo's shop with a breathless eruption of words.

"Rolfo! I have the most wonderful news. Liesel-Maria Numna is taking me to Rome to study opera with her. Remember how much we enjoyed her performance here last Saturday?"

He stared a long time before speaking.

"Lisa, I'm going to Rome, too."

"That's wonderful. We'll be together in the most famous city in the world."

"I'm going to become... a priest."

She mouthed the word "priest" but no sound came.

I must get out of here.

She left the shop unable to focus from the stream of tears, an earthquake victim awaiting the aftershock. No sobs, no gasps, silent grief.

Her carriage whisked her home, where she began to fill her Richilene trunk mechanically and without feeling.

Liesel-Maria Numna soon arrived with all the travel plans and enough tasks to keep Luc Chavannes busy in New Orleans aboard ship and for the next six months in Rome.

It turned out to be excellent training, as he later enjoyed a five-decade career as house manager of the Teatro Apollo. Mercifully, the couple and Rolfo did not sail at the same time, but fate would cross their paths many times in coming years.

Chapter 78
Millicent

A messenger brought Paul LeFleur word requesting he meet at the Hotel St. Louis with a Dr. Corchene.

He entered the elegant suite to be greeted by a petite woman.

"I must be in the wrong suite, Miss."

"Are you Monsieur Paul LeFleur?"

"Yes."

"I'm Dr. E'toile Corchene."

Dark hair framed her beautiful face.

"What is our business, doctor?"

"I cared for your wife in the convent."

"I was told a nurse named Estella cared for her, a young, unmarried woman from Paris. I've always wanted to thank her. I've never been able to find her."

"Monsieur, Sister Bernadette from Ireland could never pronounce my name, so I asked to just be called Estella. I told her I worked at a hospital in Paris. I did not tell her I was a doctor."

"Why were you there?"

"Mihiel and I were raised in a Catholic orphanage. Neither of us had family. We managed to go to medical school, then married. Our futures looked promising."

"Why are you telling me all this?"

"He was healthy one day and dead the next. He must have contracted something from a patient. I entered Our Lady of Adoration to become a nun not knowing I was expecting his child. When it became obvious, they thought I was unwed. I would have left, but I knew Millicent needed me."

"So you and Millicent really were friends?"

"Yes. She told us only her first name until she was dying, and then only Millicent Roussel. We thought she was naming her baby."

"Did she suffer?"

"She was sick almost the entire pregnancy, gave birth and shortly after, she died."

"Thank you for being there."

"Monsieur, our babies were born hours apart. Sister Bernadette assisted me and I had an easy delivery, unlike Millicent. She and my baby died at almost the same moment."

"I'm so sorry for your loss."

"I switched the babies," she said, starting to weep. "I could not bear to think of this child being raised in an orphanage as my husband and I were."

"Where is she now?"

"She's with her governess in the park near here. Until I saw the new headstone, I had no idea as to how to reach you. Claude told me you and your son had just left the cemetery when I arrived."

"When can I see her?" he asked, standing.

"We'll go now. I had to find you and try to make this right. The babies looked like twins with jet-black hair."

As they entered the park gate, a tiny, raven-haired child of five rushed into her mother's arms. She turned with a shy smile to face Paul.

"Monsieur LeFleur, this is Millicent."

Tears brimming, he stooped.

"Could I have a hug, Millicent?" he said in French.

Paul had prayed that someday he would be able to properly thank the elusive Estella. He and Trey had visited every hospital in and around Paris but learned nothing. This outcome exceeded his dreams.

Dr. E'toile Corchene eventually taught at Tulane Medical School. She insisted Millicent's name be hyphenated. Little Miss LeFleur-Corchene enjoyed a fortunate life of being loved by many people.

Chapter 79
His Eminence

Both Signora Rofolini and Cardinal Fioriti received letters from Sister Claire stating the day Rolfo would arrive, but Cardinal Fioriti's letter requested Rolfo first be allowed time with his grandmother.

The Cardinal's carriage deposited a prideful man of about fifty at the docks, umbrellaed by an underling. Scarlet clerical robes commanded distance as he strode through the crowd of bowing unwashed. He headed straight for the gangplank; his lackey two paces behind.

He will probably be the tallest man to disembark. You will have no trouble recognizing him. Sister Claire had written to her mother-in-law and brother.

A fluttering white handkerchief from an open carriage caught Rolfo's eye, but he was visually assaulted by a rushing mass of crimson.

"You are Vittorio Rolfolini?" he asked without pausing for an answer, "I'm Cardinal Fioriti."

How warm, how friendly...he can't be my mother's brother.

Without breaking gait, Rolfo nodded but headed toward the handkerchief.

He took both the owner's fragile, black-lace gauntleted hands in his and surveyed his smiling, newly-discovered treasure of a grandmother.

"Welcome to Rome, my handsome grandson."

The befuddled cleric shadowed him.

"Young man, we need to talk. You have to report to me. We have much work to do."

His grandmother smiled and nodded to the Cardinal, who had not recognized her. Taken aback, he saw that it was his primary benefactor. He adjusted the red and gold cords on his cappello and stammered.

"Good afternoon, Signora Rolfolini. How nice to see you. My sister wrote that you would be spending time with my nephew. I did not realize you would be meeting him."

"Uncle, I have not been with my grandmother since I was a tiny child. I believe the Lord's work can wait a little longer. I have your address," Rolfo said, setting the tone for their relationship.

Andrew Fioriti executed a hasty face-saving retreat. The little umbrella man scurried, black robe taking flight, to match the Cardinal's departing stride and saw His Eminence safely returned to his enclosed carriage.

"Grandmother, they've begun to unload the livestock. My horse, Naji II, should be out soon. We won't have long to wait...oh, look...there, that beautiful high-spirited one. He's coming down the gangplank now."

Rolfo took sugar cubes from his pocket and Naji II eagerly gobbled them.

"The deck hands gave him water before bringing him ashore. I'll tie him to your carriage and we'll be ready to go."

"In my excitement, I forgot to order bread," said his grandmother. "We shall have to stop for some on our way home. It won't take long, Vittorio. Now tell me how your mother is doing as we go."

"I love the smells in a bakery," he said, smiling.

Vittorio...I was Rolfo when I went to bakeries in Europe and New Orleans. This "Vittorio" will take some getting used to. Even when his mother called him that, it sounded strange. I don't want anyone who knew me then calling me Rolfo. I don't want to know what terrible things might have happened to my bridge family. I'll have to get used to Vittorio. This is my new life. Now I belong.

He thought of Lisa Chavannes and how she smelled. *I must learn to forgive.* Pangs of loneliness overwhelmed him just as when he had been a child in the vineyard.

The now twenty-three-year-old Panifio Prudore e Figli sign had begun to droop a bit. The painted letters peeled, but the quality of the bakery's products had not diminished. Little Prudore feet traipsing in and out—and untold scores of clients had crossed the marble threshold.

"Signore Prudore, this is my grandson from America, Vittorio Rolfolini. Vittorio, this is Signore Lorenzo Prudore."

"I am happy to meet you, Vittorio. I can understand your grandmother's pride."

They shook hands.

Prudore, Prudore.

What of your family? Do you have a brother?"

"Sadly, no, but my life is blessed. I have five sons: a banker, a professor, an architect, a doctor and a baker...and six grandchildren...and a wonderful wife, Dorcena."

Rolfo nodded and smiled, but his hopes died. *I guess Prudore is a common name.* He'd only remembered Gian's father by "my Papa" where he'd been imprisoned and his last name. All remained but a dim memory with Rolfo. He'd tried to forget so much.

Lorenzo knew the whole story of the fortunate meeting between Sister Claire and Vittorio from Signora Rolfolini, even his time with the Zingari, but never a mention had been made that he'd been called by the familiar name, *Rolfo.* Prudore filled their basket and they were on their way.

Of the many magnificent villas they passed, only one caught Rolfo's eye. The villa with the Janus gate next door to his grandmother. The last job he had before joining Prince Swar's tribe would remain an irony too sweet and too sad to reveal to anyone.

Signora Rolfolini's staff greeted Rolfo, stabled Naji II, and served him a sumptuous feast, sans wine.

"I'm not much of a drinker," he said before he and Catarina sat by the huge fireplace and asked one another scores of questions.

The candles burned low and Catarina rose.

"Vittorio, come see the rooms where you, your mother and father lived," she said, leading him to a part of the house sealed off with a massive, decorated folding screen. "I rarely go in there. Everything seemed to be taken from me at one time."

Double doors squeaked slightly and opened to five spacious rooms. Upon entering, the hardwood floors squeaked—the long-ago memory he'd tried to place. He savored this added revelation but did not share it.

"Was this rocking horse mine or my father's?"

"Both. You fell off once. You said it 'threw you,' so you never rode it again."

Rolfo brushed the horse's mane with his fingers and his grandmother struggled to hold back tears.

"All of your tiny clothes are still in these wardrobes," she said, pointing to massive furniture not opened for many years. Slivers of candlelight pried into a carved Italian cypress chiffonier revealing long-ago laundered and folded toddler and infant clothing. It was a bittersweet moment for Rolfo, whose thoughts drifted back to the dreaded vineyard, scavenging for food in Rome, his bridge family, and the kindnesses of gypsies and nuns...and Yigal Levron. *I could have been safe in the arms of my mother and grandmother.*

"Vittorio?" Signora Rolfolini's gentle voice disturbed his reverie. "We'll go through everything tomorrow. You must be tired from your voyage."

Rolfo tried to sleep, but the memory of Cardinal Fioriti's glare gave him chills. *Have I made the right choice? Am I going into a mare's nest?"*

When they met again, Cardinal Fioriti gave Rolfo enough guidelines to last a lifetime and then sent him to another series of instruction from Father Bocchetti. He had not anticipated this— the priest who had sent his bridge family to a "home." *I can't do this. I can't face him.*

He bit one nail and stopped. *What if he doesn't remember where he sent them, or won't tell me. I won't tell him who I am...and I remembered him being so kind.*

"My son, I've been expecting you. Your grandmother and the Rolfolinis before her have been a mainstay of the church for generations. Welcome."

He introduced himself as Vittorio Rolfolini. *It's obvious he doesn't know me from before.*

"I'm told you've placed many orphans here in homes," Rolfo said.

"Yes, the Lord has helped me. I could not have done it alone."

"Probably found some of them in deplorable situations, too."

"Yes, many of them were ill, hungry, and badly clothed."

"Do you remember a situation where boys lived under a bridge and one of their fathers had been sent to prison?"

"Yes, yes. A sad outcome. He was a baker by trade and had been falsely accused and sent to prison."

"Did he die there?"

"No, he gained his freedom and opened a bakery."

"What of the boys?"

"That's the sad part..."

"Why is it sad... what happened?" Rolfo asked.

"Signore Prudore and I moved the boys to their new home above his bakery, but one of the boys could not be found. We returned to the bridge many times, but he had vanished. We searched all of Rome. He must be dead," Father Bocchetti said, putting his hands over his eyes and trembling.

"Father, do you not know who I am?" asked Rolfo, his heart melting.

"Yes, you are Vittorio. You just told me."

"I am the boy who could not be found. I'm Rolfo," he said, realizing he could be called Rolfo again.

Father Bocchetti sat with tears streaming onto his cassock. *Thank you Lord.*

Chapter 80
Hotel St. David

"Bridey, me Uncle Jimmy who went to California to pan for gold has died and left me a hotel," Davey said, hanging his head. "I wouldn't be wantin' ya to sell out here, but we ought to go there to see just what it is I'm inheritin'."

He spread papers on the kitchen table.

"This letter from San Francisco lawyers doesn't tell me a whole lot, but this check for five thousand dollars...I'm gonna take it to the bank right now and see if it's real. It's from B. J. Forsyth and Michael V. Cowan, attorneys at law. They're askin' me to come out there."

J. Leenard Ragland wired the Nob Hill Bank in San Francisco immediately and received a reply by mid-afternoon.

"It's as good as gold, Davey. How do you want it?"

"I'll be puttin' one thousand of it in mine and Bridey's savin' account, the rest I'd like in cash."

Davey's eyes fell on a lilac dress and hat in the window of the House of Richilene as he left the bank. He'd never been in a ladies' emporium.

I'd" be likin' to know how much this is, ma'am."

"Oh, it's not for sale. It's just a sample. Every item is created expressly for our patrons."

"Ma'am," he said. "I'll be needin' one in a hurry."

The lady in the salon smiled behind her fingertips and his face reddened.

"Oh, ma'am, not for me be needin' one, but me wife will."

Aviva Bogoff came out after hearing the conversation. Her seriousness lent credibility to his request, though she, too, had giggled while behind the drape.

"We'll see what can be done, sir. What is the emergency?"

"Well, me wife and me'll be goin' to California soon and she'll be needin' a nice outfit to travel in."

"When could she come in for a fitting, sir?"

"Oh, that one looks like her size."

"I'm sure it is, but we'll need to personalize it for her. Say tomorrow at nine?"

"Oh, that would be fine, but I don't want to be puttin' ya to trouble."

"It's no trouble. We'll just replace it with another sample. And what name, sir?"

"Davey O'Flannery, er...Mrs. Davey O'Flannery."

"Fine. We'll look forward to seeing Mrs. O'Flannery at nine o'clock tomorrow morning."

"Yes ma'am, thank ya."

Davey walked on air as he left the salon, sprinted to his horse and flew to the tavern. Bridey bustled about the tavern, which was not open yet. Mrs. Wallace and Annie-Laurie had already left for the market. He burst in with the confidence of a conquering hero, smiling broadly.

"Mrs. O' Flannery, you're expected at that dress shop on the south side of Jackson Square at nine sharp tomorrow morning. They'll be fittin' you for clothes for our trip to California on Saturday by stagecoach and then by train. The check is good."

He bent with an exaggerated motion as if to bow slightly.

The tavern was now under the care of Mrs. Wallace's watchful eyes, Davey's tenure with the U. S. military as paymaster had ended, they had money in hand, and now he and Bridey were free to travel.

The lilac ensemble created a lot of positive attention on their trip to California. With the House of Richilene furnishing everything else, Bridey arrived at the hotel looking like royalty. San Francisco Bay teemed with energetic Chinese, freed blacks, fishermen of all nationalities, European expatriates, Southerners hoping for a fresh start, and bustling commerce infused with the sweat and blood of railroaders and forty-niners.

Bachelor James David O'Flannery, Uncle Jimmy, had left New York after a family spat during the gold rush and none of the back-east relatives thought he would still be alive. Now, he wasn't and his nephew and namesake, James David "Davey" O'Flannery, II, inherited almost everything of his uncle's labors.

The Hotel St. David held court like a marble sphinx from its lofty peak on Nob Hill. The rich and near-rich paid homage to this shrine that gleamed like sunlight on a snow-capped mountain.

The hotel's interior was gray with splashes of burgundy, white and gold. The paintings were European. Bridey had never seen so many plants indoors in her life. Their mouths were still agape when a courtly gentleman approached them wearing gray trousers, a striped cutaway jacket, ascot with diamond stick-pin and spats. Davey thought the spats looked silly.

"Do you have a reservation, sir?"

"Uh, no..."

"Well, I'm sorry. We have no vacancies. We are the finest hotel in San Francisco, and we stay booked. I could recommend another establishment two blocks down the street from here."

"Since we're already here, could we just look at Mr. O'Flannery's office?"

"Sir, I don't understand. Were you a friend of the late Mr. O'Flannery?"

"Uncle Jimmy was me godfather. I'm Davey O'Flannery and this is me wife, Bridey."

"Oh, Mr. O'Flannery, Mrs. O'Flannery, please accept my apology. Our solicitors did not inform us you would be coming so soon. Boys, here," he said, snapping his fingers.

Three bellmen in white uniforms embellished in gold bolted to attention. "Take Mr. and Mrs. O'Flannery to Mr. Jimmy's suite."

"Sir, I'm the one who should be apologizin'. We got so excited I forgot to let anyone know we were even on our way."

The distinguished gentleman with the graying temples whispered something to a fourth bellman, hastened up burgundy carpeted curving stairs to the mezzanine floor, and stood as a host welcoming Bridey and Davey to the magnificent suite.

An entourage of twelve assorted hotel staff members followed soon after with vases of red roses, trays of food, and smiling faces. They waited like tin soldiers as Bridey and Davey drank in the beauty of the inherited suite. The new owners gawked, but didn't move, so the staff didn't budge.

Finally, Bridey said in all her Irish brogue glory, "Oh, it's a grand place with a grand view and we're thankin' ya all."

The spell broken, everyone smiled again. Staff members rushed to place flowers, leave towels, and spread food for the happy couple and left.

The man with spats, yet to identify himself, motioned to an ornate bell-pull.

"If there is anything I might do for you, please ring, We will tour the hotel as soon as you are rested. Oh, excuse me; I'm General Manager Cyrus W. Byrd," he said, closing the door with a flourish.

Not everyone in the hotel was delighted. In the executive offices, two doors down, a petite woman's voice shattered the quiet.

"You know it's mine, Uncle Cy," she whined.

"This hotel is not yours. He was not your father. Your mother owned the Velvet Lady Saloon and grubstaked him. Mr. Jimmy found his lucky vein and repaid her. You were already a toddler when they first met."

"Why did he raise me when she died? I always thought 'Jimbo' was really my daddy."

"Because he felt an obligation to your mother. I never thought I'd have to tell you this, but your father was a married man."

Cyrus took his jacket off, perspiration on his brow, and removed his tie.

"Who is my daddy?"

"I can't tell you that."

"Can't or won't?"

"Mr. Jimmy left you a fortune. You need to leave well enough alone."

"You owe it to me. Who is my daddy?"

Cyrus sat and burst into tears.

"I am. I was the camp assayer. My wife was friends with your mother and we loaned her the money to buy the Velvet Lady. She turned it into a gold mine at the gold mine. My wife couldn't have children, so we talked with your mother and she agreed to have my child and allow my wife and me to raise it as our own."

"Why didn't you?"

"My wife died before you were born and I would not disgrace her memory by having a scandal that I had cheated on her."

Now his daughter was crying.

"Mr. Jimmy knew everything and, as a single man, he thought it best if everyone assumed you were his." "

"I'm sorry I've acted so badly. Why did you never remarry?"

"You were too precious for me to start another family. As Mr. Jimmy's right-hand man, I knew I'd always be near you. You have my long-deceased mother's name, Belinda and you look just like her. Your inheritance is my part of the hotel: I own half of it. Mr. Jimmy and I set it up that way to protect you in case something happened to me."

"Daddy," she began, haltingly. "I...I... need a new nameplate for my door."

He didn't have to wait long for her embrace.

Chapter 81

The Opera Season

This was the opera season in Rome and Lisa Chavannes' performances excited patrons and filled the sonorous house to overflowing. Her vitality attracted money and theatre-goers not seen in years. Sofia and Celestin became ardent fans and often hosted parties in her honor. Rolfo arrived with Father Bocchetti. It seemed destined to happen...at one such gathering.

"My dear, you have given music a new voice," Father Bocchetti said, greeting Lisa, who was attempting to make small talk when a surge of admirers rushed in. She had not seen Rolfo standing less than three feet away and turned pale when she did.

"This is my first performance to attend," he bumbled, using all his breath to get those words out. "I didn't know you knew the Entremonts...I..."

"My dear, you must give equal time to the laity and the clergy," said a tall blond man who led her to another part of the room.

Rolfo felt as empty as a discarded eggshell.

"My son, are you all right?"

He nodded, wanting to bite his nails but refraining. His eyes trailed after Lisa and the man who'd whisked her away. He did not have thoughts of a priest. He crossed himself.

"Who is that man, Father?"

"That is Prince Umberto, second in line to the throne. He has always been a patron of the arts. It's only natural he should want his fiancée to visit with other aficionados."

Father Bocchetti watched Rolfo's reaction with amusement.

"Rolfo, what is wrong? It's obvious you know Lisa Chavannes."

"Yes, I knew her in New Orleans."

I have to get my life in order.

"You stay, but I must go," he told the priest.

"No, I'll go with you. Just let me speak to the Entremonts."

Rolfo waited near the door and relived dozens of New Orleans nights and endless sidewalk café trysts. He seethed, crossed himself again, and continued to stare at the blond man with the sash and ribboned medals. He imagined he could smell her perfume.

"We need to talk, Rolfo," Father Bocchetti said in a gentle voice, motioning toward the carriage. "You're right, but not now."

They returned to the monastery in silence.

Chapter 82
I Am Rolfo

Rolfo awakened to swirls of golden autumn leaves fluttering outside his sparsely furnished room. It held a bed, a washstand, a desk and chair, and clothing pegs that reminded him of the convent. Whistling wind at the window also triggered memories of damp stones and frigid nights beneath the bridge.

I have warm clothes, a warm bed, food, a mother and a grandmother... unfortunately, also an uncle, but I still feel my life is not right. Will this restlessness never cease?

He fell to his knees, crossed himself, and raised his eyes to the crucifix above his bed for encouragement. Father Bocchetti's voice called from the door as if in answer to a prayer.

"Rolfo, I need some help. My legs are not as strong as they once were. Could you take care of the church's banking for me today?"

"When, Father?"

"Now, today; I have everything written on this paper."

Upon entering, Rolfo caught the attention of the most imposing man in the bank.

"Welcome, Father. I am Giovanni Prudore, president of Blanca Italia. How might I help you?"

Rolfo's spirits lifted by a mile when he heard the man speak his name.

"Could we sit?" he asked.

"Certainly. Here, in my office. Please, have a seat."

"Might I have a piece of paper?"

He took the paper and wrote three words: *I am Rolfo* and pushed it across the desk to the executive. Gian said nothing, too overcome with emotion. He shook his head and smiled, then they embraced, both crying unabashedly. They talked for a long time, recalling childhood memories and laughing, their visit constantly interrupted by bank business.

"I've been with our bank in Milano for a long time. I just came back last week," Gian said. "And you?"

"I've been to many countries. I returned here from New Orleans some time ago. I'm supposed to be taking care of Father Bocchetti's banking..."

"Father Bocchetti! I haven't seen him in years. He married us. We lost touch. How is he?"

"He's getting older, but he's the same kind man."

"He won't remain kind if we fail to get his banking done. Let's take care of that now. We've talked for hours; it's almost closing time."

They stood outside the bank.

"I'd like you to meet my family," said Gian, as a carriage arrived. "This is my wife Brianna and my son Rolfo. Say hello to the man you were named for."

The boy of seven waved shyly, both Rolfos grinning.

"My father told me you were very brave. I am glad to have your name, Father Rolfo. I did not know you were a priest."

"And I did not know of your birth, young man. I'm honored you have my name."

They shook hands.

Father Rolfo. It sounds right now. I don't mind it any longer. Back in his own carriage, the buildings whizzed by as quickly as his racing thoughts. *Life has passed me by while I've tried to piece the links together. Have I chosen the correct path?*

His driver opened the carriage door.

Vespers, the evening meal, then more prayers and back to his solitary room. He thought of Prince Umberto. He did not want to think of Prince Umberto. He thought of the blond man touching Lisa's creamy-white arm. *He has no right to touch her arm. Yes he does. He has every right in the world. He is to be her husband.*

He collapsed on his bed. *I should be her husband.* Praying for emotional release through sleep, he crossed himself. Low-burning candles whiffed themselves out in wax puddles.

Fitful sleep ensued as Ludii appeared riding a black stallion and wearing a red sash with medals gleaming and snatched Lisa away. Riding toward a cliff, Rolfo lunged after him only to plunge into icy water below. Rolfo awoke drenched in perspiration.

He arose, changed garments, then rummaged to find another candle, prayed, and suddenly realized something. *I now know where my other bridge brothers are and they are doing well.* Feeling somewhat better, he closed his book and, mercifully, sleep came.

When morning arrived, Rolfo made a concentrated effort to think of work and give it his best effort, but thoughts of Lisa clouded his very being. It would be many months before he gained the courage to attend the opera again. *I'll be strong this time. I have much work to accomplish.*

Chapter 83

The King is Dead

"A Zingaro to see you, Father. He claims to be a friend. Shall I send him away?" the novice, Caracallo, asked in a hushed tone.

"My door is open to all, especially Zingari. What is his name?"

"Count Yesef," he replied.

Rolfo rose from his desk.

"I'll greet him myself," he said, striding toward the door with the anxious novice following. *He'll make a great candidate for Cardinal some day.*

A quick right turn and the men faced Yesef sitting on a massive bench. Age had not been kind to the Rom and his sad face added years.

"King Swar is dead," he said, rising. "Riders spread word as we speak."

"When did he die?" asked Rolfo, feeling his knees weaken.

"An hour ago, here in Roma."

"How?"

He waved Caracallo away and sat.

"His heart. Our tribe will bring ice from the mountains as we wait for everyone to arrive. The body will stay perfect for many days."

The vaulted hall seemed an enormous prison to Yesef and he wanted to run. Rolfo encircled his shoulders as they sat on the covered bench weeping.

"What can I do to help?"

"King Swar often talked of you and your commitment to your God," he paused. "He'd even started going to church. Could you say a few words over him like the Christians do when someone dies?"

Rolfo knew the obstacle that lay ahead, but reassured him, saying, "I'll be there."

He sped to the gypsy camp to comfort LaLa at almost the exact spot where they had accepted him as one of their own. Grief was now a terrible emotion compared to the usual light-hearted experience when he had neared the bridge area.

Malik, wracked with sobs, appeared inconsolable. LaLa and her black-draped wagon, Yesef, Kalahn, their wives and grown children now with their own grown children, four newcomer families who'd joined three years ago, and the regal carriage which would bear King Swar's body to a tiny cemetery outside of Rome comprised the assemblage. Roms from throughout Europe would gather in and around the city.

The flower-bedecked bier shaded under a white canopy festooned with wind-rippling silks of red, green, yellow, purple, and blue seemed garish for the occasion. Six white horses pawed the grass where they were tied, practicing for their part in the cortege.

No one asked Malik where he acquired the horses or the carriage.

Chapter 84
Marriages

Lavender wisteria clusters and magnolia provided a fantasy setting for the wedding of Abraham Valois LeFleur Friedmen and his enchanting bride, Micalea Tassin.

The couple moved into Kennington Shadows, where Abraham continued his work with the Freedmen's Bureau and Micalea left the Hilon Hospital to extend her nursing skills for the benefit of those being helped by her husband.

Tedelia hardly had time to recover from one wedding before she had to plan another. Paul proposed to Leine Roussel Arceneaux and she accepted. Trey served as his father's best man and Millicent LeFleur-Corchene, their flower girl.

At thirty-six, the bride was still beautiful and the ceremony perfect, but Leine had an unbelievable secret.

"Is something wrong? Are you having second thoughts about marrying me? You've been so quiet." asked Paul, watching her unpack her Richilene trunk and looking anxious. "Did you not want to come to the Natchez Azalea for our wedding trip?"

"It's none of those things, and I'm thrilled to be your wife. There's something I haven't told you."

"Well, what is it? Nothing could be that bad."

"I don't know how to start, I'm so embarrassed. I don't want you looking at me when I tell you."

"We can fix that," he said, turning the gaslights off and holding her in the dark. "Now what does my beautiful bride have to tell me?"

"My marriage to York was never consummated," she said, shivering and laying her head on his shoulder.

Room service delivered their evening meal.

Nine months and two days later at Ruvasha Plantation, Tedelia had assisted the servants many times and probably could have tended the birth by herself, but since this was Leine's first child, they erred to caution.

Her labor was mercifully brief; after two huge pushes, "It's a boy!" was followed by a loud squeal. Dr. Cornevise turned to Tedelia, cut the cord, cleaned up, and patted Leine's hand.

"You did fine, Mrs. LeFleur," he said, turning to leave.

"Wait!" called Tedelia. "There's another one!"

Before he could get his coat off, she caught the healthy baby girl in a fire-warmed blanket.

Tedelia motioned for Paul, hovering at the door, as soon as the cord was severed.

"Leine is fine. You have a son *and* a daughter."

After Dr. Cornevise left, an anxious Paul entered the room, Gilbert following.

"Grandfather, would you like to name our son?" Leine asked, uncovering one tiny face from the squirming bundles.

"Could I name the girl, instead?" They caught their breaths, fearing it would be Matilda, Zerphinia, Prudencia...or something worse.

He continued. "I always thought Larissa was a nice name."

"What a beautiful name," Paul and Leine replied almost at once, smiling and relaxing.

"Larissa it is, Grandfather. We'll give her Leine's middle name, Marie," Paul said.

"Now you get to name our son, Leine."

"How does Edmund Alain sound?"

"Edmund Alain LeFleur sounds perfect."

Gilbert hummed as he walked to his room, sat at this rosewood-inlaid desk, and began to write in a flowing calligraphic hand, *Larissa LeFleur,* in as many different styles as the memories he had locked in his heart of the Larissa who was never a LeFleur.

Chapter 85
The Cardinal

Rolfo anguished before gaining enough courage to go to St. John Lateran, the Cathedral Church of the Bishop of Rome. The building loomed as a travertine marble stumbling block, but he had to see his uncle.

"Good evening, my nephew. Which downtrodden are you saving today?"

He extended his ring hand, awaiting the perfunctory kiss. Rolfo knelt and complied.

"Eminenza, I come with a special request."

"Good, we have anticipated our only nephew aspiring to something greater than his present station. We remember when we were Cardinal designate...the pageantry, the excitement...our reception in the Borgia Apartments. But all of that is of little interest to you, we imagine..."

"Eminenza, I wish to attend the funeral of the man who saved me when I was a little child. King Swar. It will be outdoors, not in a church."

"Oh, we know of this man. All of Rome is overrun with those thieves since he chose to die here. Thankfulness is one thing, but jeopardizing one's career is quite another," Cardinal Fioriti said, drawing himself up. "He is an infidel."

His smile vanished and he turned to face a floor-to-ceiling Rococo mirror behind his desk. The remainder of the conversation was conducted with Rolfo talking to his preening uncle's reflection. Rolfo had come to expect part of his uncle's ritual, but not the mirror routine. Perhaps to the Cardinal's thinking, his caressing an elaborate, foot-tall, solid-gold cross on his desk enhanced his holiness to visitors.

"No, we forbid it," the Cardinal said, pursing his lips.

"What do you mean, 'no'?"

"Simply and plainly: no. Are you a Paladian to gypsies?"

"Uncle, I challenge you to show me any Divine-inspired writings stating one man is better in God's eyes than another."

The Cardinal adjusted his biretta and cleared his throat.

"We have heard of your many so-called missions and we are displeased," he said, tenting his long, slender fingers.

"Displeased? You sit here in your ecclesiastical tower and ignore the hypocrisy and injustice in today's world."

"That's enough, Father Rolfolini. Do you forget to whom you are speaking?"

The mirror reflected more superiority than even a Cardinal should be allowed. "You are dismissed."

"Not only will I attend his funeral, but I will deliver the eulogy," Rolfo said, leaving the massive mahogany door open and striding down the hallway.

Chapter 86
Six White Horses

Days later an endless procession ribboned its way into the hills of Rome. Mountain ice preserved the body as scores of people made their sad journeys to pay last respects. Gone were the colorful scarves. Now black plumes graced the strutting horses' heads and quivered in the wind. The ebony hearse-carriage where King Swar rested held a single white wreath atop his black coffin. Never had a royal Rom procession been more dignified.

Behind King Swar's wagon, Rolfo tied his carriage. He and LaLa rode in the wagon; the gloom unbearable until they came to the burial site, where nature had washed the slope in a sea of red poppies.

Exhilaration replaced despair and Rolfo knew his message would be about rebirth. He delivered it in perfect Romani to an appreciative hillside congregation.

"King Swar was a gift from the Almighty. Nature is a gift from the Almighty. We are all part of a Master plan and just as this magnificent field of poppies has bloomed again, Prince Swar will be reborn. *Bater*." (Romani for *Be it so.*)

While mourners still threw coins into the grave and the body was being lowered, a rumbling from the back of the crowd distracted Rolfo. An agitated Malik and his band wanted everyone to know they were displeased.

"What is wrong, LaLa?"

"Malik has been passed over. Since he is now a Duke, he thought he would be the new King of Gypsies. He is not fit to rule. You know that, I know that and the *Krisatora*— the judges from different tribes—know that."

"Who will they choose?"

"They wanted Count Yesef, but he says he is too old. The new king was to be announced before Pamona, the feast for the dead."

Lookout whistles warned of approaching outsiders. Two dozen mounted policemen, called *shangle*, fanned out in the crowd. Their *shanglo*, or captain, called in a booming voice, "We seek the Zingaro Malik. He is wanted for grand theft. No one else will be detained."

Three of the *Krisatora* judges gave him up, his closest friend smirking as they led him away.

"No prison can hold Duke Malik," he said. The shangles also confiscated the stolen white horses and hearse-carriage.

Six weeks later, his friend's prophecy proved right: Malik had escaped.

For now, Kalahn's son Vedass accepted the royal title. Before the sun rendered the crimson poppies golden, Rolfo stopped and filled his carriage with them as the tribes and kaleidoscope of vurdon wagons scattered in all directions.

A soft rain patterd on Rolfo's carriage as he returned to Rome. For a few moments, he longed to rejoin the gypsies and be Rom again - free. Thoughts of his grandmother, his now retired mother, his bridge family brothers and his two unresolved issues, strong feelings for Lisa and his deep-seated need to forgive, refocused his priorities.

Rolfo remembered the old man's words of so many years ago.

"Are you taking those poppies to your mama?"

This time, he was thankful to be able to do so.

He swung by the Rolfolini villa, gave the poppies to his mother, and returned to the abbey, still troubled. He had disobeyed. What would his next step be?

Chapter 87
Ludii

A month had passed since King Swar's funeral and Rolfo, continuing about his duties, had received no communication from Cardinal Fioriti.

An unmerciful deluge of rain scattered pilgrims and pigeons from the de San Marco Piazza, sending street vendors to drier ground. Inside the church, Father Rolfo entered the lancet door of the confessional to find a reeking body on the other side emitting an acrid odor.

"Father, I have sinned, and I am sick. I fear I will be condemned to eternal hell. Forgive me."

The familiar voice paralyzed Rolfo: Ludii. He again became a frightened child hiding behind tattered curtains, perspiration beading his brow and trickling down his spine. He winced. His heart raced. He put his nails to his lips and struggled to regain composure.

"What is your sin, my son?"

"I have been unkind to children and young boys," said the old man amid fits of coughing.

He clawed at the wooden cross beneath his clothing to drive away the awful, too painful to remember, thoughts. He could tell this old man he would never be forgiven. For years he had thought of what he would do or say to Ludii if he ever met him, but never had he thought it would be in a confessional. After several deep breaths, he asked, "When was your last confession?"

"I do not remember, Father."

"It is not a sin to discipline one's children," Rolfo said, digging to make him admit everything, although sickened to hear it.

"They were not my children. I mistreated their bodies in unnatural ways," Ludii said, laboring to speak.

"Say forty Hail Marys and a novena to the Patron Saint of Children, St. Nicholas. Go and sin no more. You are forgiven, my son."

"Thank you, Father. Thank you."

With unsteady hands, the old man clutched his tattered, rain-soaked hat, pushed it on his graying head, and trudged from the cathedral. Twelve Hail Marys later, he collapsed in an alley a few blocks away. He lay motionless on the cobblestones, blood oozing from his ears.

Rolfo left the confessional light-hearted by forgiveness, that cathartic purge. Elated, he wanted to shout to the world that he no longer hated. Undaunted by driving rain, he made his way to another church to confront a second problem of equal weight.

Since Father Bocchetti neared retirement, this would be the last time he could visit him at the church of his youth, the church where he had received answers to many childish questions. Now, three decades later, he hoped for answers to an adult dilemma. He knelt briefly, remembered the fright he shared with Gian of the Christ-figure above the altar, crossed himself, and went directly to Father Bocchetti's study.

"My heart is troubled, Father. I have forgiven my only enemy, but now I know I can no longer continue to serve the Lord in my present capacity. I am consumed with love for a woman."

The old priest began slowly.

"Do not talk with me and do not talk with God," said the elder priest, his withered fingers clutching the cushioned arms of his velvet chair. "Talk to your heart. This is neither a fraternal nor spiritual matter. I turned my back on my heart many years ago and she married my best friend."

Rolfo could never have imagined Father Bocchetti, his friend since childhood, making such a declaration, but this proved to be exactly what he had hoped to hear.

"I have christened her children and grandchildren. As I hold them in my arms, the hurt is still there," he said, cupping his hands as if holding precious memories, then clenching his fists and softly pounding his chair. "Go, Rolfo. Go with my blessing."

The younger priest genuflected and whispered, "Thank you, Lord. Thank you, St. Jude."

Dust particles danced wildly in sunlit streaks as he opened massive carved doors. Rain still dripped from the overhang. Whistling as he went, he walked from the dark cathedral into the piazza and sprinted over sun-warmed puddles.

Rolfo attended the opera with his grandmother, his resolve clear. He remembered nothing after Lisa Chavannes' lyric soprano rendition of "Love, Fly on Rosy Pinions." The words, *"in this dark hour of midnight, I hover round thee, my love,"* seemed to be sung to him only. *Was it fate that Verdi's opera "Il Travatore," the Troubadour, had many of the elements of his convoluted life? It included gypsies, evil, mistaken/hidden identities and the church. His senses reeled.*

The Teatro Apollo house lights raised and he almost sleep-walked until Lisa touched his arm at the elbow. His stomach muscles tightened. He knew everyone around must have heard his sudden intake of breath.

Regaining his composure, he praised her performance. *Her red dress is dazzling.* Cardinal Fioriti lifted one eyebrow and stared at the scenario, curling his lip.

Signora Rolfolini assessed the situation, melted into the crowd of well-wishers, and positioned herself directly in front of the snarling cleric.

"How nice to see you, Cardinal, and how opportune."

His quick smile hid obvious contempt, but she commanded his undivided attention.

"Good evening, Signora Rolfolini."

"I've decided to provide the necessary funds to complete your building project. Can you meet with me and my advisors on Monday morning at ten o'clock to decide on an amount? You know the address."

Indeed, he did know their address, for he often drank from their monetary well.

Cardinals do not like dictated itineraries, but for this he would make a large exception. He wondered how much of her will would be devoted to the needs of the church and how much longer before she went to her Great Reward.

He smiled again, saying, "Ten it is."

A dimly-lighted hall with window seat alcove provided the perfect cozy spot for Lisa and Rolfo to talk.

A year had passed when an elated Father Bocchetti, retired to the Monastery of Galloro, welcomed the news of the birth of Lisa and Rolfo's son and the bottle of brandy that Artur, Signora Catarina Rolfolini's right-hand man, brought him. She rarely carried anything heavier than a small purse or fan herself nowadays, but she did still host glorious dinner parties.

The three sat, talking little, sipping tea from a small cart wheeled in by a Brother. Father Bocchetti recalled that afternoon over a year ago.

"Rolfo had come for advice," he said, a contented smile extending to his twinkly eyes. In an unconscious movement, he hugged empty air—the imaginary child he would never sire—slipped into another of his many naps and they quietly left.

That same night, Rolfo traced his hand over his cross. He, too, remembering that afternoon he had sought advice from Father Bocchetti. He thanked God for giving his life new direction and watched his wife sleeping with their day-old-son nestling at her breast.

Chapter 88

We Had Different Fathers

At Mademoiselle DuBonnet's School for Young Dames, Dr. Denis Arceneaux sat, relaxing with his mother's Aunt Janine. His practice in New Orleans had been established and the school's French teacher, Gia Pauratore, had accepted his proposal.

"Aunt Janine, tell me about my mother."

"She was beautiful, as you can see from her portrait," she said, motioning to the painting dominating the room. "She was gentle, kind, funny. She would have been the perfect mother...and how she loved your father. He was her first and only love."

"I've been thinking about her a lot lately."

"It's only natural, with your wedding so near."

"Tell me about my grandmother, Monique Hodggers."

Mlle. DuBonnet looked sad and fumbled with her cane.

"My sister did not marry into a good situation, but if her life had been any different, I would not have had you," she said, struggling for words. "Your grandmother was a beautiful woman, just as your mother was and just as you are a handsome man."

"Thank you, Aunt Janine. You've helped me a lot over the years. Grandmère Martha-Louise and Grandpère Luther could not tell me all the things I wanted to know...and thank you for the red hair," he said with a grin.

"We had different fathers."

That *was* true.

"So our lives took different paths."

Even in her dotage, Aunt Janine refused to give up her designation as a relative. She and Luther had discussed the situation when he returned with Denis to set up his practice and both had agreed that some secrets should remain so.

"Gia and I could live here on weekdays and spend weekends at Vermillion Hall until she can train the DuPreé girl to take over as headmistress, if that is satisfactory with you."

"Having both of you would be wonderful. Speaking of Gia, did you know her father was your Uncle Clive's best friend?"

"Yes, now that you mention it, I believe Mr. Pauratore did say something about it once. Wasn't he my half-uncle and didn't he disappear about the same time I was born?"

"That's right. He worked for your future father-in-law's dad before the Pauratore's business grew into a big wholesale company. He was a fisherman. Some thought he might have drowned, but there never was a body, so we don't know."

"Grandpère Luther said my Grandpa Hodggers was a fisherman, too—a shrimper—and that he drowned. They never met, but he read it in the newspaper. What was he like?"

"I never really got to know him, but he loved the ocean," she said, making it up as she went. "I was still living in Paris when he and my sister married. Then I moved to New Orleans to be near her, but the school kept me busy. He died shortly after I got here."

"That gives me a little insight."

"He must have been a nice person. Look at you. Denis, this is changing the subject, but I still have your mother's wedding dress. Do you think Gia might like to wear it?"

"She's shopping right now, but I can ask her. Could I see it?"

"No, you foolish boy! If she decides to wear it, it would be bad luck for you to see it before your wedding day," she said, smiling and thinking of Abby's wedding gown, laying undisturbed for twenty-seven years, shrouded in white cambric linen to protect it from dust, in a Richilene box atop an armoire.

A week later, Aunt Janine looked with pleasure at the brunette beauty modeling the wedding dress.

"It will need to be taken up a little in the rib-cage area, Gia."

"Mademoiselle, I love the empire style; I love the dress. I love the beading, the lace. To think, Denis's mother and I were almost the exact same size!" she said, whirling.

Aunt Janine sighed.

"Almost ma chérie, almost."

Chapter 89
The Hero

Travel into remote bayous proved difficult for the uninitiated, but campaigning for governor and lieutenant governor in the swamplands showed it was not their first foray there.

Having spent their youth in those Spanish moss caverns, on intimate terms with the bayou landscape, Trey and Abraham knew the inhabitants, mystical sounds, smells, and dangers and they were accepted with enthusiasm by the warm Cajun-Creole denizens ensconced in their stilt-raised homes and dependent on the gurgling, laughing waters for their existence.

Jambalaya, etoufée, or bisque welcomed their boat each time it moored, and a long, low whistle brought a pirogue armada when danger threatened.

Kurt Sweigleman and Thaddeus DuPree, IV, governor and lieutenant governor hopefuls also, appeared to be dependent on the limited vote of all those city folk, born and bred as they had been. The majority did not appear to be in their camp.

In Jackson Square, gubernatorial candidate Trey LeFleur spoke to wild applause.

"...and in conclusion, I'd like to thank my constituents and my esteemed opponent Kurt Sweigleman, whose prudence will probably cause him to concede defeat early in the evening Tuesday night."

"My worthy opponent's constituents would probably fill the same amount of space as the afore-mentioned's brain area," responded Kurt Swiegleman,

The attempt at humor failed and a crowd chant of "LeFleur-Friedman" grew to a roar as they booed Kurt off stage. Trey and Abraham shook hands and waved to the crowd with their campaign manager, Dr. Denis Arceneaux.

Late Tuesday evening, results were in and Governor-elect Jean-Paul "Trey" LeFleur, III and Lieutenant Governor-elect Abraham Valois LeFleur Friedman stepped before an exhilarated throng of forty thousand in Jackson Square.

Some clung to lampposts, some stood in carriages. All jostled to better view the handsome, soon-to-be state officials, their campaign manager, and their families. Tedelia was not the only elated relative in the crowd. With secret pride, Santé and Antoine Faine watched their son and nephew as he climbed the first rung of his political ladder.

Suddenly, the bunting-festooned platform teemed with police and bodies were pushed aside. People panicked. Shots rang out. A derelict threw himself at Denis Arceneaux and caught a would-be assassin's bullet in the back. Police swarmed the tramp before they realized he had been killed. The gunman, atop a four-foot vantage point, proved an easy target and police shattered any future plans with a rain of bullets.

Police searched the poorly dressed man's body on the stage for identification but found none. Placing him on a waiting gurney, Tony Pauratore touched Police Chief Hiram Wallace's shoulder.

"Hiram, that's Clive Hodggers. Dr. Arceneaux's uncle."

"Are you sure, Tony? I was just a child back then."

"Sure am. We worked together as young men."

Clive's misspent youth had been redefined. Avenging his sister's murder by killing Camille Arceneaux and now he had made the ultimate sacrifice to protect Abby's son. From the bowels of the Irish Channel to the sanctuary of the bayou, his journey ended near its beginning, in the shadows of New Orleans, his last moment on earth a shooting star.

This event brought a multitude of questions for Joey from Denis. He disclosed part of the Hodggers background, but never told him—nor would he ever—about the horrible confession Clive Hodggers had made when he sneaked into the city right after Camille's death.

"Joey, when I went to Solomon's Tavern, he told me what Mrs. Arceneaux done to Abby. I went back to Vermillion Hall, tied your horse up and sneaked to the back. The whole kitchen was gone and the smell was awful. I went into a big, red room and saw Abby laying there dead. I looked till I found that woman walking around on the top porch of that big house."

Clive's shoulders heaved and he breathed loud gusts through clenched teeth.

"She weren't no cripple. She jumped back in her chair and I pushed her and that wheelchair over the railing to eternal damnation."

"What did you do then, Clive?"

"I think the fall broke her neck. I just left her there, brought your horse back to town, turned him loose and run off into Bahkonay," Clive said, rubbing his hands together as if he were washing them.

"Why don't you come back to New Orleans and help me at work? I could use some good help. They can't prove you killed her. She deserved to be dead after what she did to Abby. York thought she fell and the dogs or that swamp panther got to her."

"Naw, Joey. I got everything I want in the bayou. I don't need to come back here. I do miss goin' to church."

"Why did you come back if you're not gonna stay?"

"I got to go see Father Prejean. I done wrong. I got to ask forgiveness. Maybe I'll see you someday."

That was the last Joey had seen Clive until election night when he saved Denis's life by stopping a deranged gunman's bullet.

The gunman was no stranger to police on two continents. Tolly L'Heureaux was jokingly called "The Hero," from a mispronunciation of his name. He had had no plan, no target; he just craved attention. Notes found on his body said he "hated to see happy people."

Around midnight, Gilbert LeFleur, too infirm to attend the festivities, was told of the landslide victory. He smiled and nodded.

"I think I'll have a glass of wine to celebrate."

Chapter 90

It Must Have Been a Great Love

A somber mood engulfed Ruvasha. Gilbert LeFleur struggled to breathe as he remembered the first time he had seen Luther Arceneaux. Even then, he knew the child to be his biological son. Now the irony was that Luther's grandson had become his physician.

Many times, he had wanted to proclaim to the world his and Larissa's brief union had produced this fine man, but he could never have sullied her name. *I'll just share a little of my secret with my own great-grandson.*

"Young man, I'm going to tell you a secret not another soul in this world will know but you and me."

"What is that, Mr. LeFleur?"

"I loved your great-grandmother Larissa, and she loved me. She loved me."

"Really, Mr. LeFleur?" Denis said, placing his stethoscope to the old man's chest. He listened and drew a resigned breath.

"It must have been a great love," he said, pausing to commit Gilbert's features to his arsenal of memories, knowing it to be a fleeting moment that would not be repeated.

Ah, at last he had been able to declare his undying love for Larissa to someone. Denis watched fading light play on the hundred-and-eight-year-old smiling face.

Denis had, in fact, known of his great-grandmother's love affair with Gilbert LeFleur. His Grandpère Luther had been entrusted with this information by Larissa Arceneaux, but York had never known. Luther had saved this little family secret for his beloved grandson who had held the trust sacred and managed to appear as astonished today as when he had first heard it, twenty years ago. He wanted to say, *Yes, sir; I know she loved you and I've known you were my great-grandfather almost half of my life.*

"I'm leaving this medicine...if the pain gets worse," he said, hugging the old man's frail body and snapping his medical bag shut. "I'll see you tomorrow, Great-grandfather. I love you."

Gilbert trembled and the biggest smile he had owned since the Yankees ended their occupation of New Orleans crossed his face. Denis stopped with the private nurse outside Gilbert's door.

"Here; keep him comfortable."

She took the bottle, muffled a sniff, wiped her nose, and returned to her bedside vigil with red-rimmed eyes. Gilbert's tears and smile were from happiness.

Now almost eighty, Tedelia waited at the foot of the stairs with several of her grandchildren and great-grandchildren.

"He's very weak. Probably won't make it through the night. Do you want me to stay, Miss Tedelia?"

"No, Denis. My boys are due in any minute. Paul's gone to the railroad station to pick up Abraham. He's coming all the way from Washington, D.C. *Her boys...Paul, retired from the Cotton Exchange; Abraham, a third-term U. S. senator having given up the office of Lieutenant Governor to run for national office; and her grandson, Governor Jean-Paul "Trey" LeFleur, III, on his way from Baton Rouge.*

"You go home to Gia and Alexandra and take this jar of fig preserves to them. I put them up myself. Thank you so much."

At Vermillion Hall the following morning, Denis walked downstairs holding the *Picayune*.

"Gia, it is official. We already knew, but Trey is running for another term as governor."

"You don't have time for breakfast," she said, rushing to meet him. "Miss Tedelia just sent for you. You'd better hurry."

He raced out, tossing the newspaper onto the old, weathered with age Richilene trunk that Gia had restored as a table in the entry; the trunk that had brought generations of families to love, loss, misunderstanding and mending, together over so many years.

Epilogue

Rolfo and Lisa add a daughter, Catarina, before his grandmother dies. His jewelry becomes known all over Europe. Lisa's career continues to flourish and Claire Rolfolini, now retired, lives years missed with Rolfo through her two grandchildren, Sabino and Catarina.

The novice Caracallo, Rolfo's former assistant, mortally wounds Cardinal Fioriti with the gold cross His Eminence had on his desk. His defense? "God made me do it."

Besa and Vedette's joint-venture restaurant in Paris proves highly successful. Vedette marries a dashing chef with his own restaurant. Although happily wed, she jokes, "That man only married me for my cooking." Besa adopted two bi-racial brothers. One has green eyes. They now manage Chez Loque. She volunteers at the orphanage where she found them.

Out of respect for Tedelia, Antoine and Santé/Suzette Faine wait until her death to contact Abraham. They go to Washington during his third term as U. S. Senator Friedman from Louisiana. He learns the entire story. "Thank you for giving me the sweetest mother in the world if I couldn't have had you. I know it must have been a difficult decision."

Luther and Martha-Louise visit Denis and his family in New Orleans often. Both die in Switzerland of natural causes. Half of Luther's estate goes to Besa Loque and the remainder to Denis. Martha-Louise leaves the hospital to Denis and her banking interests to red-haired Alexandra.

Countess Bogoff buys the New Orleans Bosolét Hotel and maintains a boutique in the lobby. Deenah and Quila purchase the New Orleans House of Richilene where they incorporate his extensive fur processing company into the existing business.

Echo buys the Paris House of Richilene and changes the name to House of Vermillion. She marries a top designer from another house, but keeps the Vermillion name.

Aunt Janine bequeaths her school to her niece-by-marriage, Gia Pauratore Arceneaux. When Alexandra begins school, Gia resumes teaching at the school.

Bachelor Governor Jean-Paul "Trey" LeFleur, III marries the lovely debutante Marilene Stringer in a beautiful Governor's mansion wedding, the bride's father, Alphonse Stringer, could not have been happier, as he had previously served as Governor of Louisiana.

The Pascal children and grandchildren operate Echo Trading Post now. Puppies abound. Uncle Lamb dies in his sleep.

Kurt Sweigleman comes in third against Barton DeWitt in New Orleans' mayoral race. Kurt retires from politics.

After almost two hundred years, descendants of Ilana and Erik continue to operate the House of Richilene in New York City.